THE SILVER PRISON

THE SILVER PRISON

By Peter Shokeir

First paperback edition March 2023

Book design by CoverKitchen

ISBN 978-1-7386765-0-7

www.petershokeir.com

CHAPTER 1

The sun would soon be no more.

But for now, it beat down upon Henry. Sweat gleamed on his forehead. He wiped it off with a dirty work glove. He just needed to dig for another hour. Then he could head back to the Bunker, where there was air-conditioning and water that wasn't lukewarm.

He stabbed the ground with a shovel again and barely got a handful of dirt for his efforts. He had dug the square hole six feet deep and eight feet wide over the course of several days. Now he needed a stepladder just to climb out.

Henry had always been a little spacey, but ever since he'd joined cadets it had only gotten worse, resulting in numerous punishments for incidents not quite his fault. It sometimes got so bad that he had to go see the nurse. But he only needed to remember three things today.

Dig. Throw. Repeat.

He jammed the shovel into the ground, expecting tough soil, but the shovel hit a solid object instead. Henry looked down at his handiwork and saw that he had struck gold.

Or, rather, silver.

Henry sighed. "Sure hope that isn't the septic tank ..."

The silver glinted in the sun. He put his shovel down and began to push the soil off the shiny surface with his hands. The object was somewhat spherical in nature. It felt smooth and polished despite being in the ground for who knows how long. He started to pull it out. As he tugged, he realized that the base of the object was attached to something, a heavy something, a fleshy something.

A human body.

The cadet jumped back and stared at the object with fascination and dread. It was some kind of silver helmet. His scattered mind also focused upon the inanimate figure wearing it. He spent half a minute hyperventilating before forcing himself to take a deep breath. He leaned forward a little to examine the body, keeping his distance.

The body convulsed.

"Waa!" Henry yelped. The body convulsed again. And again.

Then it went still.

Any composure Henry had left vanished. He screamed, ran for the stepladder, and began to unfold it. He had just set it up when he felt a hand on his shoulder.

"Hey there, scrawny boy!"

Henry shrieked. The hand spun him around, forcing him to face its re-animated owner. The figure standing before him was about six feet tall. It wore tattered clothes, old combat boots, and gloves covered with holes.

The body then grabbed Henry's throat with one hand. Henry gagged. He clawed at the limb, but the body didn't react even when his nails drew blood.

"Please ..." Henry croaked. "Let go ..."

The body complied. Henry fell on his backside and gasped for breath, feeling the dry air fill his lungs.

"I ... Who are you ... ?" he asked.

The body scratched its silver helmet. The helmet was smooth and wrapped completely around its owner's head. It also had no eyeholes or any distinguishing marks. Henry didn't know how its wearer could breathe, let alone see. The helmet seemed to go underneath the jaw, all the way to the neck. It looked impossible to take off. The silver surface gleamed. It reflected back Henry's petrified face.

"Are you scared?" the body asked, sounding constipated. "Is it because I'm bald? Don't worry. Bald people creep me out too."

Henry got on his feet, gingerly touching his neck. "My throat ..."

"Whoa, no need to whine. You were the one poking me with a shovel. How was I supposed to react?"

Henry snatched up his shovel. He pointed it at the Helmet Man. "By the–the authority of the Western Union … you're under ar–arrest …"

The Helmet Man put his hands on his hips and laughed. "Oh, please. Don't hurt me. I'm no match for a dehydrated teenager with a shovel."

Almost on pure instinct, Henry hit the Helmet Man in the leg with the shovel.

"Ow! You actually did it!" The Helmet Man collapsed and tried to crawl away.

"You're not getting away from me!" Henry yelled, not stuttering this time. He raised the shovel and hit the Helmet Man's torso repeatedly.

"Ah! What kind of parents raised you?" the Helmet Man cried.

Henry was on autopilot. He didn't know he had it in him. A small smile materialized on his boyish face. He couldn't wait until Gilda heard about this.

But the Helmet Man grabbed the end of the shovel just as it was coming down for another hit. He tore the shovel out of Henry's hands and smacked him right in the jaw with it. Henry fell to the ground. His eyes rolled back.

"Ha, the tables have turned!" the Helmet Man yelled. He got up and walked over to Henry, holding the shovel above him. "Prepare to die, piggy!"

A gunshot interrupted his attempted murder. A soldier in a dark green uniform appeared on the edge of the hole with his rifle aimed at the Helmet Man.

"Uh … I mean prepare to live a long and prosperous life."

The soldier cocked his weapon.

"What? What did I do?"

Henry's head was filled with visions of silver. There was also sand. And a moon. It was a terrible moon. The iron grip around his throat grew tighter and tighter until he couldn't breathe.

Henry awoke.

"Relax," a voice told him. "You're okay."

Henry blinked. It took a moment to realize where he was. It took even longer for him to recognize whom the voice belonged to. It was the nurse. He was in the Bunker's infirmary.

"You must be thirsty," the nurse said. "Want some water?"

Henry nodded. The dryness in his throat was painful.

The nurse brought a glass to his mouth. He sipped greedily.

"Whoa, take it easy," the nurse said. "The water isn't going anywhere."

Henry finished his cup and asked for another. The nurse went to fetch some more. Examining himself, Henry saw he was out of his dirty green cadet clothes and in a hospital gown. He also noticed the bed he lay on was ridiculously comfy, much better than the mattress in his room. The infirmary was filled with a dozen white beds. All of them were currently unoccupied except for his. Everything was plain and sterile, lacking any exciting colors, although the last thing he wanted right now was excitement.

The nurse came back and gave him a full cup. She was a pretty blonde in her early thirties and the only nurse the Bunker had, though a doctor was also on staff.

Henry sipped his water. "Thanks ... I ... uh ... Can I ask what happened? I can only remember digging a hole."

The nurse raised her eyebrows. "You were attacked by a crazed man."

Henry remembered the Helmet Man. He touched his throat and winced.

"You have some nasty bruises," the nurse said. "Dr. Taylor thinks you don't have a concussion, but to be safe, we're going to keep you here overnight."

Henry looked at a mirror hanging beside his bed. He saw a bruised and battered version of himself. He had dark hair, brown eyes, and a pudgy face that made him look fourteen instead of sixteen. The bruises on his neck stood out. They looked better than they felt. The real nasty-looking bruise was on his jaw, but it didn't feel particularly bad for some reason.

The nurse handed him an ice pack. Henry gratefully put it on his neck.

"What happened to my attacker?" he asked.

"They have him in custody," the nurse said. "But they didn't tell me—"

Three men entered the infirmary, taking both Henry and the nurse by surprise. The cadet tensed up as their shadows drew closer. Was he about to get in trouble again? The last thing he wanted right now was for his sentence to be extended.

The men reached his bedside. They stared at him for a few seconds, evaluating him, judging him. Henry was just about to wither away when the silence was finally shattered.

"Well, you seem to be okay," one man said. Henry recognized him as Dr. Taylor. "But I need to do a quick examination, if that's okay."

Dr. Samuel Taylor was a black British man with a shaved head and a smile that reassured Henry some. He was tall enough that his lab coat barely reached his thighs.

The doctor took a penlight out of his pocket. He knelt beside the bed and shined it into Henry's eyes. "Can you remember your name?"

Henry followed the light, his pupils dilating. "Henry Marker."

"Can you tell me where you are?"

The other two men moved closer to the bed. Henry also recognized them. One of them was General Eisenhorn, the man in charge of the Bunker. He wore a green uniform with a peaked cap. At age sixty, his hair had already become steel gray. He also had a turkey neck and dull gray eyes that were hard but confused. Henry had never gotten along with the general, mainly because Eisenhorn was hopelessly unbalanced.

"Boy, answer the doctor!" Eisenhorn yelled, his voice rough and unpleasant.

Henry stiffened. "Ah ... we're in the Sahara Desert at the Bunker."

Taylor nodded, putting his penlight away. "Yes, you seem well enough, but I'm going to keep you overnight just in case."

Henry relaxed a little. "Oh, I'm not in trouble, then?"

General Eisenhorn scoffed. "Your cowardice sickens me ... Get out of my office!"

"Sir, we're not in your office," the third man said.

"Quiet, Johnson! It's just a figure of speech."

Henry also knew the third man. Johnson had a wiry build and neatly combed hair. He wore a civilian suit with a striped tie, not a uniform, since he was technically not military personnel. Henry tried to recall if Johnson used to be in the military but gave up after feeling a mild headache coming on. Maybe he would ask Gilda later.

Johnson gestured toward Henry. "Sir, I don't think we should question the cadet yet."

Eisenhorn scoffed. "Nonsense. The boy has had three hours to take his toddler nap."

Johnson sighed. "Okay, but please go easy on him, sir."

The general ignored the advice and glared at Henry. "What happened, boy? Speak true and I'll go easy on you. But lie to me and prepare to be digging holes for the rest of your natural life. I might even book you for a pruning session ..."

Henry, wishing for more water, was quick to spout out what he remembered. The digging, the resurrection, the strangling, beating a man with a shovel, everything. He finished with a sigh and waited a moment for a response from his audience.

"Well, that's an interesting load of crap," Eisenhorn said.

"That's what I saw, sir ..."

The general nodded knowingly but seemed lost.

Johnson came to the rescue. "Sir, I think we should question the prisoner now."

Eisenhorn snapped back to reality. "All right, boy. You may think you're off the hook, but you're still gonna be digging holes. I haven't forgotten about Betsy. Poor dog ..."

Eisenhorn turned and walked out of the infirmary, followed by the other two men.

The nurse scowled. "That Eisenhorn ... Johnson isn't doing his job properly. Sorry you had to go through that, dear. Why don't you go back to sleep?"

"Okay ... thanks."

After the nurse helped him get settled in, she switched off the lights and left the room. Henry sighed. His head sank into the pillow. He was out within a few minutes.

He dreamed of the moon.

***

The corridor was tight. Johnson and Taylor had to walk single file behind General Eisenhorn as they went to the cell. The Bunker had been a closed-down military base before reopening as a cadet training facility, so there were plenty of prison cells on the bottom level, all adequate to hold a prisoner.

The general turned down another hall. He stopped at a metal door with a keypad. After a moment of forgetfulness, he typed in a code and the door opened inward, revealing a large cell containing a gurney. Strapped to the gurney was the Helmet Man, wearing only his silver helmet, which looked clean and gleaming, and a new pair of boxer shorts. His body was pale and muscular. Numerous scars crisscrossed his torso and limbs.

General Eisenhorn turned to Taylor. "You couldn't get that doohickey off him?"

Taylor shook his head. "No, sir. No cracks or openings could be found on the helmet. The only opening is the neck hole. I tried welders, drills, saws, even chemicals. However, no marks could be made. I don't know what that helmet is made of, but from what little research I've done, this kind of material shouldn't even exist."

"Is there any way to identify him?" Johnson asked. "I made an emergency call to our superiors, and they want to know exactly who this man is. Did you try using an imaging device to see through the helmet?"

"I'm afraid all imaging devices have failed."

The general continued to stare at the Helmet Man. "What about that DNA test? Don't tell me you screwed that up too?"

Taylor ignored the insult. "Well, sir, we can't find a match in the database or any results with fingerprints, but when I examined his blood, I found very little oxygen in it."

Johnson raised an eyebrow. "How much is a little?"

"Not enough to be alive. This man's helmet completely prevents him from breathing, seeing, hearing, eating, or speaking."

Johnson's face turned ashen. General Eisenhorn said nothing.

"Then how is he alive?" Johnson asked.

"The human body takes energy from its environment in order to survive," Taylor said. "This man, however, is not only maintaining and healing his body without fuel but also seems to be doing it at an accelerated rate."

"So, how does he do it?" Johnson asked, his voice cracking. "How does he heal and run his body without food?"

Taylor pointed at the helmet. "Maybe that helmet holds the answers. I believe it acts as an insulator of some sort. For what purpose, I don't know."

"I want to know who this jackal is," the general said. "My curiosity is piqued."

"I can tell you," a grating voice said.

All three men jumped. Taylor backed up into the wall. The general buried his head in Johnson's suit, whimpering.

"Uh, sir ..." Johnson said.

The general, suddenly aware again, pushed Johnson away. "Johnson, what were you thinking?" he yelled.

"Sir, I didn't mean to—"

"Are you some kind of pussy? I expected better from a soldier!"

"Technically, I'm not a soldier …"

"Now we have insubordination!"

The voice laughed. The three men now realized it was the Helmet Man who had spoken. He was still restrained to the gurney with leather straps.

Taylor wiped his forehead with a sleeve. "How … how the hell are you talking? We shouldn't be able to hear you. Your helmet is a perfect insulator."

"Oh, let me tell you!" the Helmet Man yelled. "I vibrate the air with electricity, which makes sound. I can only do it close to me, sadly, so I can't throw my voice like some kind of ventriloquist. If I was a ventriloquist, I'd have a dummy with an afro!"

Johnson cleared his throat. "Well, we got that answer pretty fast."

"But that doesn't explain how you can hear me," Taylor said.

The Helmet Man laughed. "I generate this kind of field thingy. If an object is close to me, this field is distorted. It's a weird way to see."

"I asked how you were able to hear, not see."

"Pal, be grateful for what you get."

The general frowned. "Listen, chrome dome. I want to know who you are and why you attacked one of my cadets, so quit the monkey business."

"First of all, chrome dome is a terrible insult. Secondly, eat a turd."

"Watch it, punk! You best start talking or else."

The Helmet Man shrugged. "Okay, I'll tell you stuff."

"You most certainly will! Start with your name."

"They call me Slate."

Eisenhorn scoffed. "What kind of idiot name is that?"

"Well, I did plan on calling myself Lord Evil, but that sounded too tacky."

The general crossed his arms. "Slate isn't a real name. It's some kind of alias. What's your real name? Don't make me take off my belt!"

"I'm gonna choose not to take that the wrong way."

"You piece of shit! I oughta—"

Johnson was about to stop General Eisenhorn when he heard a phone ring.

"Great, that's only supposed to be used in emergencies," Johnson said.

"I'll handle Eisenhorn," Taylor said. "Go and answer it."

Johnson nodded and ran out of the cell. He got to a phone on a wall and picked it up, ignoring the not-so-faint sound of Eisenhorn's ranting.

"Hello, Johnson speaking."

"Sir, we got a call from a unicopter en route to the Bunker."

"That's not right … Nobody's expected to come all month. Who are they?"

"They said they're carrying a representative of Zaidi Industries. They'll be here in about fifteen minutes. What should I do, sir?"

"It's okay. I'm on my way up."

The top of the Bunker was nothing more than a large metal shed with a reinforced door. Only two other buildings were on the surface. One was a garage that housed vehicles, equipment, and fuel. The other was a communications tower next to a landing pad.

Johnson and two soldiers stood in front of the pad. He had convinced Eisenhorn not to come up with him. Zaidi Industries had numerous contracts with the Western Union. It was by far the most powerful private organization in Africa and Western Asia, producing weapons, walkers, aircraft, and various other technologies. Understandably, Johnson didn't want to incur the wrath of this organization or his superiors by letting Eisenhorn antagonize these guests.

The unicopter was now in view. The aircraft slowed until it hovered above the landing pad. The unicopter's design was standard, oval in shape, with a single rotor on top and repulsion pads on its sides. Unicopters did not require a tail rotor, unlike obsolete helicopters, thanks to the repulsion pads that kept the fuselage from spinning.

The aircraft descended. Four landing legs folded out of its bottom like a giant insect settling down. While the single rotor was slowing, it still raised up enough sand to obscure Johnson's vision. He covered his eyes, coughing and cursing.

The sand cleared. The unicopter had landed safely, and its single rotor began to retract inside its fuselage. Johnson finished coughing and dusted his suit off. He loathed the outdoors.

The unicopter's door slid open, and the stairs automatically unfolded. An elegant young woman walked out of the aircraft. She wore a casual blue blouse, accompanied by white pants and red high-heeled sandals. Her hair was black with streaks of blue and tied in a ponytail. It was also clear to Johnson that she was filthy rich.

"Welcome to the Bunker," he said. "I'm Jeffery Johnson, the civilian coordinator."

The young woman walked off the landing pad. With a polite smile, she held out her hand, which Johnson shook firmly yet delicately.

"Lovely to meet you, Jeffery," the girl said. "But I had the impression that Eisenhorn would greet me himself."

Johnson let go of her hand. "General Eisenhorn has a lot on his plate. He hopes that you can forgive him, Miss ... ?"

"Oh, excuse me. I almost forgot to introduce myself. I'm Victoria Zaidi. My father is ... I mean *was* the CEO of Zaidi Industries."

Johnson kept his expression neutral, but he had no idea this girl was the daughter of the world-famous Ammar Zaidi. "I'm so sorry."

Victoria nodded. "Thank you for your kindness." She headed toward the entrance of the Bunker. "First, I need to take a shower. Then I can begin my business here."

"Of course ..." Johnson said, following after her. "Do you need help with your luggage?"

"Don't worry. My bodyguard will take care of it."

Johnson looked toward the landing pad. A very large man in a white suit came out of the unicopter. He had a short black beard and thick eyebrows that nearly covered up his small but attentive eyes. With perfect ease, the man carried two large suitcases, one under each arm, and a small duffle bag over his shoulder.

"Zubair looks scary, but he's a sweetheart," Victoria said, arriving at the closed shed door. "Do you mind?"

Johnson typed in a key code and swiped his card. His actions rewarded him with a door that swung open on its own.

"After you," he said.

Victoria walked in, followed closely by Johnson. Her bodyguard marched in after them with the luggage. The two soldiers that had accompanied Johnson stayed behind to refuel the unicopter and clear the landing pad.

The inside of the shed was plain, having a simple concrete floor and metal walls. There was a large elevator door and a small stairwell entrance next to it.

The elevator opened with a groan. The group entered it and began to descend.

"Seeing as I've never been here before, I would appreciate a tour," Victoria said.

Johnson glanced over to her. "Yes ... well, the Bunker was originally a military base built twenty years ago, but it was never active due to financial problems."

"What kind of financial problems?"

"It costs a lot to run a facility out here, and there's not much enemy activity in this region. Not even the vultures like to fly out this far. It raises the question of why they built this place in the middle of the desert to begin with. Anyway, the Bunker was reopened seven years ago and turned into a cadet training facility. It has ten floors buried underground with the main entrance on the surface. We have about a hundred cadets, a dozen civilian staff members, and twenty military personnel. This facility can house up to two hundred people, however, so we have plenty of space for guests."

"I heard this place is famous for training cadets with particularly important parents."

"Well, you must understand, Ms. Zaidi, that everyone is eligible for conscription in the Western Union due to the impartial lottery. Cadet training facilities are typically put near active combat areas so recruits can be deployed immediately upon turning eighteen. It's also to give them a feel for where they'll be fighting. However, the Bunker is the farthest cadet camp from a combat area, so the most influential individuals naturally want to send their young ones here. Even so, we don't give these cadets special treatment. Training is still rigorous."

The elevator stopped on the eighth floor. The doors groaned open.

Johnson led them out. "Did you two eat?"

"Yes, Zubair and I had dinner at the airport," Victoria said.

"Okay, this way." He led them down a corridor with many doors. They stopped at the third one they came across. Johnson turned the knob. The door opened with ease, revealing a compact bedroom containing a captain's bed and a small desk with a plastic chair.

Victoria glanced around the room. "Oh, it's … quaint."

"Standard cadet quarters," Johnson said. "Very economical."

She walked into her room and sat on the bed. "Where's the bathroom?"

"It's across the hall. And you don't have to worry about sharing it with cadets. You have the entire floor to yourself and your bodyguard. His room is next to yours."

Zubair walked into the room and put the two suitcases down on the floor, keeping the duffle bag for himself. "Is there anything else you need, ma'am?"

"No," Victoria said. "You can unpack. I'll see you in the morning."

Zubair turned on his heels and marched out the door.

"So, Jeffery, do you know why I'm here?" Victoria asked as she kicked her high-heeled sandals off. She lay down on her bed, relaxed.

Johnson shook his head. "No, but I'm eager to hear."

"It sounds like you want me gone," Victoria said, checking her nails.

"No, of course not," Johnson lied. "It's just that we're molding these cadets into soldiers. We don't want them to be distracted."

"Jeffery, a soldier should learn to expect the unexpected. My presence here can only further enhance their training."

Johnson gave her a false smile. "I'll keep that in mind. Now, about your visit …"

"I'm looking into the death of my father."

"Was his death unexpected?"

"I wish to keep the exact details to myself, if it's all the same. I'm just following up on a possible lead. Nothing to concern yourself over."

"Well, I'm afraid your search might be in vain."

"I'll find that out for myself, but I trust that you will assist me until I am satisfied, won't you, Jeffery?"

Johnson sighed. He was starting to regret telling her his first name.

***

The bell rang, warning the cadets that first period was about to begin. Henry had spent the night in the infirmary. He had trouble sleeping, tossing and turning for three hours straight. Dreams of silver and the moon haunted him. His whole body ached, but General Eisenhorn was still making him go to classes.

Eyes followed Henry as he went down the hall. Most of the cadets at the Bunker were Americans, though a few were from Europe. A pair of female cadets whispered to one another as he went by. Other cadets gave him strange looks. A few even snickered. Henry walked fast, hoping his cheeks weren't red.

Henry reached the classroom. He decided to sit in the back row to avoid being noticed. After sitting down, he felt the back of his head get slapped and he yelped. He turned around to see a girl standing behind him. She had purple hair and a playful smile plastered on her face.

"Relax, Hen," she said. "Don't want you laying an egg."

Henry found himself smiling too. "Hey, Gilda. You might be getting a little weak in the arms. I barely felt that slap."

Gilda hit him on the head again, this time a lot harder.

"Okay, that one hurt…" Henry moaned, rubbing his noggin. "You know I got hit on the head with a shovel yesterday, right? I might actually have a concussion."

Gilda pulled out a chair and planted herself at the desk beside him. "Aww, does the baby need some milk as well? Get over yourself. Now tell me how you got into the infirmary."

"I can't. I was told not to talk."

"I can always hit you till I get the scoop."

Another ache went through his skull. "Fine, I'll tell you. But later. Class is about to start, and I don't want anyone overhearing."

Gilda glanced at the whispering cadets in front of her. "Are they bothering you? Come on. Don't waste a thought on these gossiping roaches."

"Thanks." Henry sighed. "This all had to happen right when everyone was forgetting how I accidently ran over Betsy with that Jeep."

Gilda scoffed. "Yeah, I bet that was unintentional."

"I keep telling you, it was an accident. There was so much sand in the air. Maybe if the general's dog had been barking, I could have—"

Gilda punched his arm.

"Ouch! Why did I deserve that?"

"Just be grateful it wasn't your head this time," she said, snickering. Her parents had chosen to genetically alter her during her embryo stage, giving her dark purple hair that she cut short. Such alterations had become a fad of sorts. She also had fair skin that somehow didn't burn, even though they were in the middle of the Sahara and she had ripped the sleeves off her cadet uniform. She also wore black eyeliner and purple lipstick, not usually allowed for cadets. She only managed to get away with these numerous infractions because her dad was a vital military scientist and more important than most Western Union politicians.

The teacher, a sickly civilian with a pencil-thin mustache named Mr. Mendez, came in. The class only went quiet when Mr. Mendez turned on the projector.

"Okay, class," Mr. Mendez droned. "We're starting our history unit today, so we're going to watch a short video to get us started."

A couple of cadets cheered and whooped. Mr. Mendez waited for the room to quiet down before turning on the projector.

The room went dark. A holographic screen appeared, floating midair. Then the movie began. A waving American flag faded in.

"America," the deep-voiced narrator said. "Once the bringer of liberty and justice, it had led the world into a state of peace and prosperity."

The screen switched to a clip of someone arguing with a man behind a desk. Then it changed to a picture of a massive lineup coming out of a government building.

"However, as technology progressed, people began to believe that governments were incapable of running this new and advanced world."

It cut to protesters in front of the White House.

"The people wished to remove the governments they believed hindered the progress of humanity. Their wish soon came true. Private corporations took over government duties, including infrastructure and military defense. Corporations soon became more powerful than most world governments. It was exactly what the population wanted, but this overconfidence in the system would be the major factor that would lead to catastrophe."

The screen now presented a South American village burning to the ground, a skyscraper covered by a giant plastic sheet, and a pile of dead bodies coated in lye.

"The Great Choke was the most devastating event in history. One billion people lost their lives in a short span of ten years. Indonesia was wiped out, and massive casualties occurred in South America and Eastern Asia. The corporations meant to serve the people scrambled to find a solution, but their competitive nature made it difficult for them to pool their resources."

A short clip of arguing businessmen stressed this last point.

"But there was hope on the horizon. In response to this threat, the nearly dissolved governments of North America and Europe banded together to wipe the virus from the face of the Earth, saving countless lives."

People were being injected with vials of clear fluid. The screen then showed several politicians shake hands as a crowd cheered in the background.

"After the Choke, it was clear these private enterprises were not dependable. America, France, Germany, the United Kingdom, Australia, Canada, and other Western nations seized power from these corporations, reestablishing their dominance. These governments then decided to join and form one autonomous international organization, which would not only govern but protect its member nations from harm."

A waving flag appeared again, but not Old Glory. This time it showed a blue flag with a white "W" and "U" overlapping each other.

"This government was and is the Western Union. It is run by a council of appointed representatives and headed by the United States president. Truly, it is a fair and just rule, giving a voice to the people while protecting the people."

The screen showed men in burettes shooting villagers, a marketplace being bombed, and shrapnel ripping through an old vendor.

"But there is a threat to this benevolent power. The Middle East and Africa had been in turmoil ever since the Great Choke. Rebels, terrorists, and warlords taint these lands, most notably the United Third. The Choke itself hadn't claimed many lives in these areas due to the virus's poor transmission rate in arid regions, but the countless deaths around the world had sparked an apocalyptic mentality, reigniting extremist ideals."

Planes were shown bombing cities, followed by images of marines rescuing children from rubble and crowds of people cheering the arrival of Western troops.

"Now the Western Union must liberate and rebuild Africa and the Middle East. Our only response to this horror is to stabilize the region. We must respond to this madness. We must prevent a disaster that could surpass even the Great Choke."

Young men and women appeared on-screen. They wore green cadet uniforms and stood in rank. They saluted the flag of the Western Union as trumpets blared.

"The Union needs its cadets now more than ever. Your class on history will help you not only to know your enemy but also yourselves. Fight tyranny! Embrace the West!"

The screen cut to black, ending the video.

Gilda raised an eyebrow. "That was cheery."

Henry's stomach bubbled when the lunch bell rang, but not because he was hungry. Throughout the entire class, the other cadets had discreetly kept trying to weasel the story out of him. They weren't about to pass up an opportunity to get some juicy gossip.

Of course, his refusal to tell the others anything would only make them more determined to find out what happened. The only deterrent he had against these foes was Gilda, but even she couldn't hold off a horde of teenagers with nothing better to do. At least in the mess hall he could put some distance between himself and everyone else.

Henry arrived at his destination and got in line for lunch. He didn't have to wait long before reaching the serving station. An old woman called Sally the Cook handed him a tray. She was the cook, obviously.

"Well, don't stand there collecting mold," she told him. "Get moving."

Henry realized he had been spacing out. He shuffled off to the table where Gilda had already made camp and sat across from her. He poked at his lunch, which was some sort of yellow-brown slop.

"Hey, don't play with your food," Gilda said.

Henry stuck his fork into the goo. "Sorry, I'm just trying to figure out what this is."

Gilda took a forkful from her own tray and put it in her mouth. "Hamburger Helper," she declared.

Henry took a bite and managed to choke down the slimy concoction. "Well, it isn't poisonous. I just wish we had food that didn't come out of a dispenser."

"And I want to be a walker pilot," Gilda said, slurping back another mouthful of lunch. "But we don't always get what we want."

"You just need to work at it."

Gilda smiled. "I already clocked in a hundred hours on the simulator. If I don't get to pilot one of those babies soon, I might as well get pruned. Better than becoming a peacekeeper. Literally the most boring job you can have, and you get no respect."

A tray clattered next to Henry, making him jump in his seat.

"Relax, Marker. It's just a tray. Take it easy, brah."

Next to Henry was Kevin Straper, a fellow cadet with oily blond hair and a bad case of acne. Straper was somewhat of a bully, although he mostly just bothered Henry.

"Why don't you go pop those zits and leave us to our lunch?" Gilda snarled. "Or do you have nothing better to do than be a pest?"

Straper raised his hands. "Excuse me! I just want to ask my brah here about his accident yesterday. I mean, the people have the right to know."

Henry took a breath in. "Straper, please leave me alone."

Straper turned his attention back to Henry and put a greasy hand on his shoulder. "Sorry, buddy. Afraid I can't do that."

Gilda stood up. "Get walking. You want to get stabbed with a fork?"

Straper let go of Henry and shook his head. "Well, Marker, your big sis fought your battle again. Just know that I'm not satisfied." He chuckled. "I'm seriously wondering how you managed to top running over Eisenhorn's dog this time."

Henry watched Straper walk back to his table where a group of cadets was waiting for him, already laughing.

"Forget that creep," Gilda said. "He's just trying to impress his friends over there. I can't believe it. It's like you and I are the only decent people around here."

Henry took another bite of the barely edible slop. "I can't really be mad at them. This place is boring. Anything that's even remotely entertaining is a valuable commodity."

"That doesn't give anybody the right to mess with you."

"Thanks, I—hey, I think Mr. Johnson is making an announcement."

Gilda turned to the front of the room where Johnson and two soldiers stood. He held a tiny microphone.

"May I have your attention?" he asked.

The room went quiet unusually fast. All these rumors had made them hungry for news. Now Johnson was about to fill the trough for them.

"We have special visitors who arrived last night," Johnson said.

The cadets started talking, the dam of silence broken.

One soldier slammed his foot on the floor. "Attention!"

The cadets snapped their arms to their sides and sat up straight. Quiet also accompanied their improved posture.

"These people are representatives of Zaidi Industries," Johnson continued. "I expect that you cadets will treat our visitors with respect. Any harassment of our guests will be met with serious repercussions." Johnson nodded to the entrance of the cafeteria. "Please welcome Victoria Zaidi."

Victoria walked out to the front of the room. She wore a loose-fitting green dress, blue high-heeled shoes, and a polite smile. A few of the boys would have been tempted to whistle had they not been sitting at attention.

Victoria took the mic from Johnson. "Thank you, cadets. I have nothing but respect for the Western Union and its military personnel, so much that Zaidi Industries is considering testing new training equipment here at the Bunker. I have come to see if you're the cadets we've been looking for. I hope to get to know some of you personally, so I might ask some questions while I stay here. And thank you again for being so cooperative with Zaidi Industries and me. Let us work toward a long-lasting partnership."

She gave the mic back to Johnson and left the room with a smirk.

Johnson cleared his throat. "I cannot stress how mischief of any kind will not be tolerated. Your afternoon training will begin soon, so finish your lunches. That is all."

Johnson handed the mic to a soldier and walked out of the cafeteria too.

"At ease," the soldier said.

The cadets eagerly resumed their conversations.

Gilda's eyes twinkled. "Henry, do you know what this means?"

"No ... what?"

"If Ms. Moneybags thinks us Bunker cadets are good test subjects, they might give us more advanced training equipment. This is the best news I've heard all month. I could become a walker pilot twice as fast with a better simulator."

Henry was glad for Gilda, but he was not so thrilled himself. He felt a heavy foreboding, as if the moon was about to fall.

***

The least favorite time of the day for Henry was afternoon lessons. All the cadets were brought to the surface of the Bunker to do basic training. Some days the cadets would go through an obstacle course the instructors had set up earlier. Other days they would practice shooting at targets. But almost every day, they had plenty of marching.

Henry was terrible at all outdoor activities. He stumbled while he marched, earning him push-ups. He always missed his targets, one time almost shooting an instructor in the foot. He couldn't even drive straight, a fault perfectly demonstrated during the Betsy incident. If there was a way to screw something up, you could count on Henry to find it.

But the worst part for Henry was that Gilda didn't attend afternoon lessons. She mostly worked with the mechanic, Ernie, in the Bunker somewhere during this time. If she had been with him, Henry knew his training would have been a lot more bearable.

The cadets marched two miles out to a shooting range. The sun was especially merciless today, radiating down upon their heads. At least they carried canteens and wore hats while outside. That much Henry was grateful for.

The range was set up differently than in the past. Instead of the usual rifles that were laid down by mats, there were longer rifles and no mats. There were also no targets in sight, just desert as far as the eye could see.

The instructor today was Sergeant Barnes, a mean-looking man with a shaven head and a bulldog's face. Civilians were in charge of the morning classes, but the military had the afternoon. And boy, was it an afternoon.

"I see you all look nice and toasty today," Barnes said. "But don't worry, because it's going to get a lot hotter, so enjoy this nice cool weather while it lasts."

It already felt like a hundred degrees to Henry. If it got any hotter, he might just faint.

"Anyway, it's time for our exercise," Barnes said. "We only have twenty of these rifles, so Alpha Squad will stay here and shoot. The rest of you will march until it's your turn. Frankly, you cadets could use a little practice. Now fall out!"

The cadets turned right and broke out of rank. Henry and the other cadets in Alpha Squad then gathered around Barnes.

"I guess it's time to show you the ropes," Barnes spat. He gave them a brief overview of how to operate the gun. "Do you cadets have any questions?"

"I—I have one, Sergeant," Henry said. "What are our targets?"

Barnes pointed downrange. "Those cans."

Henry squinted. He could barely make out the line of small objects he assumed were the cans. How could he possibly hit one of those?

"All right, hop to it," Barnes ordered.

The cadets went for their rifles. Each one settled down on the ground after performing a rifle check. The ground had many little sharp rocks, so Henry had trouble finding a comfortable position. They loaded their guns and looked through their scopes.

"Take aim!" Barnes yelled. "Fire!"

Henry pulled his trigger. Right when the bullet left his rifle, he knew he had missed. The cadets continued to shoot for fifteen minutes. Each cadet had been given ten bullets, and Henry was sure he had wasted every one. But judging by the groans of his squad, they were firing about as well as him. This only slightly dulled his shame.

After the range was cleared, Barnes went to inspect the cans. He walked back to the cadets with only one can. It had multiple bullet holes through it.

"I'm disappointed," Barnes said. "Some of you took too long to shoot, while the rest of you fired without even looking. Only one of you managed to hit a can."

Barnes walked over to Straper and patted him on the shoulder. "Good job, Straper. You have a natural talent for shooting. Perhaps there's some hope for you yet. You can go back to the Bunker and have the rest of the day off. The rest of you, march!"

Straper gave a smug grin as he left. The rest of the cadets began to disperse.

"Marker, stay here for a minute," Barnes said.

Henry froze mid-step. A lump grew in his throat.

"Marker, you doing okay?" Barnes asked.

Henry gawked. "Uh ..."

"I thought you would have gotten a few days off after what happened to you. That General Eisenhorn is unreasonable even at the best of times."

"I ... I'm doing okay, Sergeant Barnes. Just confused is all ..."

"That's understandable. I was a little confused myself when I came across that scene."

A light went off in Henry's head. "You were the one who saved my life."

"No need to thank me. Just glad I got there in time. I had to keep the freak at gunpoint while I called for backup."

"Sergeant, do you know what happened yesterday? I wasn't told anything."

Barnes gave a hoarse laugh. "Same goes for me. Nobody told me squat. You didn't tell anybody about that helmet weirdo, did you?"

Henry shook his head.

"Best keep it that way. We both need to keep quiet. You get me?"

"Yeah, I promise."

***

"Okay, we're alone. Now tell me what happened."

Gilda had dragged Henry into an empty classroom. He had just gotten back from marching outside for over an hour straight. Most of the other cadets were using this free time either to catch up on homework or hang out in the rec rooms. All Henry wanted to do was drink an ice-cold cola and have a nap, but he was too tired to resist Gilda's persistence.

"Gilda, I promised I wouldn't. Twice."

Her steel fist jabbed into his arm.

"Ouch! Okay, if you insist …"

Both of them sat down in chairs, and Henry told his story. He found himself more talkative than expected and was only encouraged to continue each time he got a reaction from Gilda, whether it was a smirk or a sharp intake of breath.

After about seven minutes, he finished his recap with a sigh.

"Wow," Gilda muttered. "You definitely had an interesting time."

"Yeah, it almost seems like a dream."

Gilda laughed. "I can't believe you tried to arrest that crazy guy. Not only that, but you actually beat him with a shovel. That took some guts."

Henry gave a happy shrug. "I acted mostly on adrenaline … It's nothing special …"

Gilda punched his arm again.

"Ow! Come on!" Henry tenderly poked his abused limb.

"Nobody talks bad about you. Not even you. Quit selling yourself short. Be proud."

"You believe me? It doesn't sound too weird to be true?"

"Hen, you couldn't lie properly if your life depended on it."

"Well, that's good to hear," a new voice said.

Henry and Gilda jumped in their seats. They saw that the door was open and a figure stood in the hall.

"Who the hell are you?" Gilda demanded, locking her eyes on the figure.

"Oh, weren't you in the cafeteria?" Victoria asked. She walked into the room, followed by her lackey, Zubair. Her friendly demeanor was gone, replaced by a cold smile. Zubair, however, was the most frightening. His eyes were empty and focused.

In his hand was a gun.

"I'm glad this young man lies poorly," Victoria said, circling the room. "It's time for him to answer the questions that have haunted me for weeks."

Henry gulped. His heart was beating so fast that it felt like it was about to fly out of his chest. Gilda, on the other hand, was calm. Her eyes were trained on Zubair's gun.

Victoria stopped pacing. "First, tell me all you know about the Helmet Man."

CHAPTER 5

enry's and Gilda's hands were bound tightly with cords. They had trouble breathing through the dirty rags in their mouths, almost choking on the taste. The whole floor was deserted since everyone was eating dinner now. Nobody would hear their muffled cries through the thick concrete ceiling.

"Sorry for the rough treatment," Victoria said, smirking at the two captives shoved into a storage closet. "It's better than being knocked out, am I correct? You two just stay here and enjoy each other's company. You'll get out eventually."

She slammed the closet door shut, leaving the two cadets in darkness.

"Let's go, Zubair."

Victoria's phone rang. Most phones weren't able to get reception down in the Bunker, but hers was state-of-the-art. Victoria looked at her phone, smiled, and answered it.

"Hello, Lawrence."

"Sorry I didn't call last night," a young man said on the other end. "I was busy at a meeting with the board of directors."

"I'm just glad to hear from you," Victoria said. "Is something wrong?"

"No. Well ... kind of ..."

Victoria sighed. "What happened?"

"The board wants me to give a speech at the opening ceremony for the Helios Tower."

"You'll do fine. Just ask Goldberg to help you."

"But he's not here."

"Wait, Goldberg isn't in Dubai?"

"No, he left for Cairo. He said he'd be back in time for the ceremony."

"Look, just write out your speech and practice it. That should help."

"Oh, thanks. But Goldberg …"

"You're almost twenty years old. You don't need a babysitter."

Lawrence gave a nervous chuckle. "I think I do. Everyone keeps asking me all these questions, and I can barely keep up with them. The catering company wants to know if we want Champagne, the band asks what kind of music they should play, and an executive is wondering if he can bring his family to the ceremony."

Victoria thought for a moment. "Yes, we want Champagne. The Middle East is a bit dry, but we have investors from the Western Union who want to wet their lips. The band should play classical music. No new-age stuff, and especially nothing from the twenty-first century. And tell this executive he can only bring one guest. Father never liked playing favorites."

A sigh echoed over the phone. "Thanks, you always know what to do. Just like Father …"

"Anything else you need? I have somewhere to be."

"When are you coming back? The board wants you at the ceremony."

"I won't be back in time. I'm at the Bunker."

"You're at the Bunker? What exactly are you doing in a hole full of conscripted rich kids? I thought the Bunker's location was kept secret from the general public."

"Well, I'm not the general public. Look, I got to go. I have a meeting to catch."

"Oh, with whom?"

"Just some brute."

Lawrence chuckled. "You better not slander the military like that. They're our best customer, after all."

***

Zubair pushed the door open with one hand, his other hand holding a gun. Victoria flipped a light switch, revealing a pale muscular man in boxer shorts strapped to a gurney. He wore a smooth silver helmet that looked impossible to take off.

"I didn't think that cadet was lying," Victoria said. "But I'm still surprised to see he was accurate in his description of you. What is your name, exactly?"

"They call me Slate," the Helmet Man said in a constipated voice. "How old are you?"

Victoria couldn't help but blink at the ridiculous voice but quickly regained her cool. "My name is Victoria Zaidi."

"Did I ask you that? I asked how old your sweet little heinie is."

"I'm seventeen," she seethed.

"Oh, you're much too young for me. Please come back in a year."

"Zubair ..."

Her bodyguard slammed his pistol into Slate's gut.

Slate chuckled. "You seem upset. Did you already call dibs on her?"

Zubair slammed his pistol into Slate's arm this time.

"Whoa, I expected to be tortured, not massaged by Fabio. Hey, do you think you can get my lower back? Being strapped to this table is killer on my glutes."

The ferocity almost steamed off Zubair. He slammed the pistol into Slate's crotch.

"Ah! Oh! That was not pleasant!"

Victoria smiled. "So, the fool feels pain. Don't worry. We're not finished yet. Zubair, hand me the needle."

The manservant reached into his pocket and produced a brutal-looking syringe. He handed it to his employer plunger first.

"We'll teach you respect later," Victoria said, grabbing the syringe. "For now, I'll just put you to sleep so you won't cause us any trouble. Then we're going to fly out of here to a more proper setting, where we can discuss—"

The door slammed shut behind them, trapping them all in the cell. Victoria jumped at the sound, while Zubair emitted a low growl. Slate raised his gleaming head.

"I don't think you'll be leaving anytime soon," a voice said over an intercom.

"Jeffery ..." Victoria hissed. "How did you know we were here?"

"I had a hidden camera placed near the base of the stairs a long time ago to make sure no cadets were sneaking around," Johnson said. In truth, it was to make sure the general didn't get drunk in the prison cells. "I had decided to check the feed regularly, since I had Slate down here, but I was shocked to find you trying to kidnap my prisoner."

"Jeffery, I don't think you understand what you've done …"

Slate laughed. "Ha! That guy's name is Jeffery? Priceless!"

"Shut up! You're in no position to act foolish."

Johnson chuckled over the intercom. "He does have an effect on people. You better get used to him, though, because he's your new cellmate."

"You can't do that! I'm the CEO of Zaidi Industries. I don't answer to worms like you."

"Understand this, Ms. Zaidi. You're not going anywhere unless I open that door. Understand also that when the Western Union comes to pick up Slate, they'll arrest you and your lackey. I wouldn't even be surprised if you both got pruned."

The intercom cut off, leaving the three prisoners alone in their cell.

"Okay, we got to establish some ground rules if we're gonna be bunking together," Slate said. "First, quiet time is from ten to six."

"Shut up!" Victoria exploded. She threw her syringe at Slate. It shattered as it hit him, but it didn't stop his rambling.

"Secondly, let's keep the banter interesting," Slate continued. "Since you two are not exactly what I consider good conversation starters, I will be in charge of that. Good, now that we got that outta the way, let's enjoy our slumber party!"

"Shut up! Shut up! Shut up!"

Johnson snickered as he overheard the screams coming from within the cell, but his amusement didn't last for long. Dark thoughts dampened his mood, as did unnerving questions.

Slate, a man who wore a virtually indestructible helmet, was found buried near the Bunker. Then the daughter of a dead corporate tycoon tried to kidnap him. Johnson had a suspicion before that Victoria Zaidi was here for Slate, but now it was confirmed. Just what motive did she have for trying to kidnap the Helmet Man? More importantly, who was Slate, really? Where did he come from? What trouble would his reveal bring?

Whatever the case, Johnson didn't think he would get the answers.

His thoughts were interrupted by the phone ringing. He jogged over to the hardline phone on the wall and picked it up, doing his best to ignore Victoria's wailing.

"This is Johnson."

"Sir, we have another arrival."

"What arrival?"

"They contacted us. They're the escort party for the prisoner."

"What? That can't be. They shouldn't be here until tomorrow morning."

"Sir, they gave us proper clearance codes. They're going to arrive in an hour."

"Okay, fine. I'll have to get General Eisenhorn ready."

"Sir, they've also requested that all staff and cadets go up to the surface."

"That's highly unusual."

"Apparently they want to disguise this as an official inspection, sir."

Johnson wrinkled his brow. "Fine, get the cadets in their dress uniforms, and form them in ranks near the landing pad. I'll be up soon."

"Yes, sir. I'm on it."

***

The heat was unbearable. In fact, it was so hot that Victoria was tempted to take off her shirt. But she wouldn't do it. She had her pride. Sweat coated her skin. It was like a sauna in the cell, the air humid and sticky. Zubair had stripped down to his pants. He sat in the corner of the room, resembling a wilted flower.

The only permanent fixtures in this cell were a toilet and a small sink. Victoria kept shuffling off to the sink every couple of minutes to get a drink or wash her face. She also had to pee, but she didn't dare do it in front of the other two. The pressure in her bladder was quickly reaching critical levels.

The thirst and heat only added to her discomfort. But even these burdens couldn't compare to the biggest annoyance in the room.

Slate snickered. "Hot in here, ain't it? I bet you want to take off those clothes. Don't worry. I can't see squat. You can show off your glistening skin. Or maybe you're just shy around your butler. But he's more naked than you are right now, so who's more embarrassed?"

"Be quiet ..."

"Heat doesn't really affect me, since I don't sweat or need water. But you, on the other hand, need your precious fluids to live."

Victoria took out her phone.

"Too bad Jeffery didn't take that phone away. Of course, if he tried to come into this cell, that hairy bodyguard of yours would have shot at him. Now we both have to wait for our new captors to take us away. They'll probably gas the cell when they get here. I don't breathe, so I guess I'll just lie back and laugh as they drag you away to be tortured."

She managed to open the back of the device.

"Hey, you're wrecking your phone. Rich people are so wasteful!"

Victoria hadn't planned on using this, but after all the effort, she couldn't possibly let this opportunity slide. The Western Union would soon take Slate away.

She had to get information, at any cost.

"Wait, I know what you're gonna do," Slate said. "You got something hidden in your phone to help you escape. Now that's spy stuff."

Victoria took out two electrodes attached to her phone and placed them on his chest.

"Oh, what's this? Are you giving me a physical? Well, I've been pistol-whipped recently. I also got this rash—"

Slate convulsed on the table. The belts held his gyrating body down.

"This is what you get," Victoria told him. "I might have felt bad about doing this if you weren't so obnoxious."

The phone stopped automatically. Slate ceased convulsing.

Victoria smiled. "Great, now tell me what your real name is. I think the truth would be less shocking than what you just experienced." She giggled at her terrible joke.

Slate didn't move.

"Lost for words? Well, that's an improvement, but I still want answers."

There was no response. He remained still.

"What, do you want another taste? Answer me!"

Zubair jumped up and ran over to the Helmet Man. "Something is wrong."

"What?" Victoria cried. "Absurd! The electrodes were at minimum power. Even an old man could take a hit like that."

Zubair touched Slate's neck right below where the helmet met.

"No pulse," he said.

Victoria covered her mouth. It couldn't be …

Slate's heart had stopped.

CHAPTER 6

Gilda kept slamming into the door and letting out muffled screams. After ten minutes of this, she stopped her mindless labor and sulked. The closet was cramped and getting stuffy. Henry wished for all it was worth that neither of them would fart. How long were they going to stay in this closet? The level they were on was only used during the mornings since it was all classrooms. Nobody would notice they were missing until tonight's roll call, and that was in an hour. And even if people did start searching for them, it could be yet another hour before anybody found them.

Gilda eventually managed to spit out the rag. As soon as the filthy cloth fell from her mouth, she howled as loud as she could. "Help! Get us out of here!"

There was no reply. Gilda gave up screaming after five continuous minutes. She slammed her head against the wall, her teeth bared.

"That rich brat is going to pay!" Gilda yelled. "I hate this!"

Henry tried to speak, but he still had a rag in his mouth.

"Crap, I forgot about you," Gilda said, a little calmer than before. "Sorry, Hen. Let me try to get that out for you."

Gilda tilted her head, trying to position her mouth so she could bite his rag. It was awkward, but she succeeded, getting hold of the rag with her teeth and tugging it out of his mouth in a sudden jerking motion. The rag fell to the floor.

Henry coughed. "Thanks ... That thing has a nasty taste to it."

"Don't mention it. Mine tasted like oil."

"Great, now we need to get untied."

"You turn around. I'll try undoing your knot."

Henry gracelessly shuffled around to show where Zubair had tied his hands. Gilda had little success untying the cord, her hands still bound behind her back and the knot too tight. She then tried gnawing on it like a rodent.

All she succeeded in doing was making her teeth sore and covering the cord with slobber. She gave up.

"That didn't work like we hoped," Henry said.

Gilda raised her head. She spat the taste out of her mouth. "Let's not try that again."

"Hey, don't spit in here."

"Then you taste it. See how you like it."

"Okay, sorry ..."

Gilda rolled her eyes. "You see. That's your problem."

"Um, what problem?"

"You're too soft. It's so easy to walk all over you. Forget about that bad memory of yours. That isn't the problem. You need to be more assertive, more in command. Why do you think Straper always picks on you?"

"Because I'm weak ..."

"That's not it. It's because you *act* weak. Do you think I'm as tough as I behave? Do you think I never felt weak before?"

Henry lowered his eyes.

"You're too nice. Nobody likes nice, despite what some people say. The military is no place for the kind. It is only for the cold and hard. They respect endurance. They respect taking charge. They respect—"

She was interrupted by a kiss.

When Henry's lips touched hers, it was a clumsy effort on his part. It was his first time kissing a girl, and despite his lack of grace, he enjoyed every second of it.

The same could not be said of Gilda.

After a few seconds of initial surprise, Gilda jerked her mouth away from Henry. She then tilted her head back and head-butted him. A wave of pain went through his skull, but the wave didn't seem to stop, rolling back and forth instead. He gritted his teeth, moaning.

"What was that?" Gilda demanded.

"Ow ... I ... You said to ..."

"You can't just do that! I'm not something to prove your worth on."

Henry tightened his lips together. His cheeks glowed such a bright red that it almost lit up the dark closet. "I'm sorry ... I just ... You're always so nice to me ... I thought ..."

"Nice? Nice doesn't mean I love you! Are you an idiot?"

"But ... you were so ... I really ..."

Gilda wasn't paying attention to him anymore. She shifted around so she wouldn't have to face him. Henry squeezed his eyes shut, stifling a whimper.

But then they heard footsteps outside.

Both cadets raised their heads. Briefly putting their unpleasant encounter aside, they slammed their bodies on the door and screamed. Neither of them could hear the approaching footsteps over the noise they made, so when the door opened, they were taken by surprise.

Henry flew out of the closet and crashed in a heap outside the door. Pain flared in his shoulder from the rough landing. Gilda fell right next to him, gasping and cursing. It took the two of them a moment to gather their wits and see who had freed them.

Henry looked up at a pimple-covered face.

Straper grinned. "Well, what's this? Damsels in distress?"

****

Zubair pumped Slate's chest but with no success. The manservant was still sweaty and shirtless, panting as he tried to revive his cellmate. He had been at it for a minute since the failed attempt to restart Slate's heart with the phone. Victoria screamed and banged on the door, trying to get the attention of Johnson or anyone else out there. Slate couldn't die. Without him, her entire quest would have been for naught.

Eventually, the intercom turned on.

"What is it?" Dr. Taylor asked through it.

"We need a doctor now!" Victoria yelled. "This idiot's heart stopped."

"Slate?"

"No, I mean the Chinese emperor. Get in here now!"

There was a brief pause before Taylor responded. "The gun needs to go on the floor. Both of you will put your hands on the wall opposite the door. I'll look through the window to see if you've done this. Then I'll come in with a gun and cuff you both to the sink."

Victoria wore a sour look, but she would comply. Zubair put his gun on the floor. The two prisoners then turned around and put their hands on the concrete wall. Taylor peeked through the door's small window. Johnson had asked Taylor to watch the prisoners while he got the general ready for the faux inspection, but it looked to Taylor like he would be doing a lot more than just watching.

Satisfied with the prisoners' compliance, Taylor opened the door and entered. He seemed less cheerful than usual, especially with a pistol in his hand. He spotted the gun on the floor that belonged to Zubair and snatched it up, as though it might sprout legs and crawl away. Careful to make sure the safety was on, he shoved it into his waistband and walked toward the prisoners. The only reason Johnson hadn't come in here already was Zubair had a gun. It had been risky for Taylor to enter a cell alone with an armed prisoner, but he was a doctor. Saving Slate was all that mattered to him right now. It may have been an elaborate trap, but he couldn't wait for help, and the situation seemed too real to be a charade.

"Move slowly to the sink," Taylor told them, taking handcuffs out of his pocket.

"Just save Slate," Victoria said.

"Move to the sink," Taylor repeated.

The two captives complied, careful not to provoke the gun-wielding doctor. As soon as they reached the sink, Taylor attached one end of the handcuff to Zubair's right hand.

"Kneel next to the sink," Taylor told Zubair.

Zubair followed his orders, kneeling.

"You too," Taylor told Victoria.

She did but with a dirty glance.

With the gun pointed at Zubair's head, Taylor knelt down as well. He fed the free end of the handcuffs around the back of the pipe coming out of the sink's bottom. He then attached it to Victoria's left hand. Now both of them were restrained, and Taylor could treat his patient without worrying about getting stabbed in the back. He was finally satisfied after giving them a quick pat-down. Victoria scrunched up her nose as this happened, but again, she didn't complain.

"Did you do compressions yet?" Taylor asked.

"Yes," Zubair said.

Taylor went over to the gurney. "What happened?"

But he didn't need an answer, for he saw the phone and the electrodes coming out of it.

Taylor sighed. "You're desperate, aren't you?"

Victoria kept silent.

"What level was it at?" he asked.

"One, but we used level four to try restarting his heart," Victoria said.

"That can't be right," Taylor said, putting a hand on Slate's neck to check his pulse. "That level couldn't possibly—"

Then a bulb flickered on in his brain.

But it was too late.

An electric current went through Taylor, freezing his muscles. He collapsed in a heap but didn't feel any pain when he hit the floor. The last thing he remembered before passing out was Slate convulsing on the gurney.

****

Sergeant Barnes examined the scene with a critical eye. He stood in front of the cadet formation, which had assembled near the landing pad. All the cadets were in their proper ranks, wore dress uniforms, and had arrived in a timely fashion.

The cadets had circles under their eyes. Many of them had just been getting ready for bed when the announcement was made. Barnes had been supervising one of the common rooms at the time. Of course, he knew this inspection was an essential cover so the fake inspectors could pick up the prisoner under the radar, but it still irked him that he had to drag all the cadets, dressed and ready, to the surface right before lights-out. Some cover up. At least the sun was setting, so the desert was getting cooler, and as far as he knew, all the cadets were present and looking their best. Not a single parade shoe had gone unpolished.

Barnes then remembered he had to do head count. Sally the Cook, Mr. Mendez, Mr. Harper, Mrs. Liebert, Nurse Elena, Ernie, and all the other staff were standing to the side, except Dr. Taylor. He must be working on something. Barnes didn't have time to get Taylor, so he just decided to forget about him. Johnson and Eisenhorn were supposed to be here too. The general must be making things difficult. Whatever. Barnes was about to count the cadets when he saw five unicopters approaching from the horizon.

Sergeant Barnes instantly forgot about the head count. He usually didn't forget about his responsibilities, but a feeling of deep unease came over him. It felt as if a shiver was trying to escape his body but kept hitting his stomach instead. The unicopters flew in an arrow formation, aiming right at the Bunker.

Now all the cadets and staff were watching the approaching aircraft. The sound of multiple propellers filled the air. The lead unicopter stopped right above the landing pad and hovered there for a minute before beginning its descent. Barnes felt the sandy air slap his face as the unicopter stirred it up. It landed on the pad and powered down.

A sliding door opened. Three men stepped out. Their leader was a tall African, a colonel according to his uniform. Barnes knew the Western Union sometimes recruited natives from war regions, but he had never seen an African with such a high rank. Natives usually didn't get promoted past sergeant. The other two soldiers were American men ranked privates. They had thin builds and dead expressions.

Barnes called the cadets to attention. The colonel marched up to Barnes as if he had a metal pole for a spine. Barnes gave him a salute. The colonel returned one.

"Sergeant, how is the Bunker doing?" the colonel asked in a thick accent.

"Sir, the Bunker is doing just fine. How was your flight?"

"Very good, but I'd like to get down to business."

Now that Barnes was closer, he could see the man's features properly. The colonel had a hard face that looked stiff yet amused in some way. Even under the uniform, the man was very muscular and towered over Barnes. He had no hair, his head smoother than a cue ball. But the colonel's most notable feature was his blue eyes. They were very strange for an African. Even a European would not look completely right with them.

"The inspection is starting now," the colonel said. "Is anyone missing?"

"Just General Eisenhorn, our civilian coordinator, and our doctor," Barnes said. "There's also our soldiers in the control tower, but they could come down if you find it necessary."

"Where are the civilians from Zaidi Industries?"

"They're locked up with the Helmet Man. We caught them breaking into his cell."

"Good. That's all I need to know."

The colonel took out a handgun.

Barnes's eyes widened.

A bullet ripped through him. A trail of blood was left behind as it exited his torso. The cadets gasped and screamed. The adults were simply dumbstruck.

"Kill them all!" the colonel bellowed.

The hovering unicopters aimed their mounted guns at the cadets.

They opened fire.

Straper chuckled. "What were you two doing in there? Probably making out."

It had taken Straper three minutes to untie Gilda and Henry, since he was in no hurry. He was naturally surprised to see them but still maintained a smug attitude, as though he were superior for not getting tied up himself.

"Hey, I want to know what happened!"

Henry and Gilda ignored him, which was not easy. They were both running down the hall with Straper trailing behind.

"And where are you two going?" Straper questioned.

"To see Mr. Johnson," Gilda growled. "Where is he?" She wasn't even close to out of breath. Neither were the other two cadets. Their physical training had paid off handsomely.

"How should I know where Johnson is? He's probably babysitting the old fart. Seriously, how'd you end up tied in a closet? Come on. Spill it."

"Shut up!" Gilda yelled.

"What a harpy you are." He turned to Henry. "Brah, talk to me!"

Henry didn't pay him any attention, his mind distant and thinking of his screw-up.

But Straper was not the kind of guy to have any amount of patience. He grabbed Henry by the shoulder and slammed him into the wall.

"Hey, brah! I'm sick of being out of the loop. Why don't you be polite and enlighten me? I—hey, where's the Amazonian warrior?"

Gilda ran into a stairwell. She slammed the door shut behind her.

"Whoa, had a little falling-out, huh? Looks like you're in the doghouse for a while." Straper leaned in close to Henry, who gulped in response. "Now that your gal pal isn't here to fight your battles, I guess we can talk about—"

Henry heard a thump. Straper's grasp loosened as he collapsed.

Henry squeaked. He turned his head to see an African man with blue eyes. The man held a pistol. Blood dripped from the butt of his gun.

"Glad I found you," the colonel said with a grin. "I needed directions ..."

***

What had happened was beyond Victoria's belief. After Taylor fell to the floor, Slate continued to convulse for a few seconds and then stopped abruptly. Both Victoria and Zubair, still handcuffed to the sink, tried to scurry away but failed. They were trapped.

The straps that held Slate down broke. The two prisoners jumped. Slate sat up and stretched his arms, like he just had a cat nap.

"Ah, he's alive!" Slate shouted. "In case you confused folks are wondering, I'm talking about myself in the third person."

"Did you fake having a heart attack so you could escape?" Victoria screamed.

"Yep! So, where were we? Ah, now I remember. A cell. And it seems men are coming to kill us. Or maybe just to kill you. I'm not sure yet."

"What are you blathering on about?"

Slate pointed up. "Using my super sensing abilities, I just 'saw' that a couple dozen men with machine guns are coming to kill us. They're working their way down, level by level."

"What? There's no way you could know that."

Slate chuckled. "Then you don't know me, missy."

Now that he'd had his fun, Slate hopped down from the gurney and landed spryly on his feet. "That was a nice snooze, but I'm tired of waiting for my dad to show up. I'm gonna have to find him myself." Slate kicked open the ajar door.

"How did you stop your heart like that?" Victoria asked. "Who are you?"

"Here's what's gonna happen," Slate said, ignoring her question. "Not only will I save you, but I'll tell you everything you want to know. I'm doing this because I need help finding my dad, and you seem like a handy girl."

"What makes you think I'll ever team up with you? My father's dead because of you."

"Hey, I don't know who your dad is, but I want to find my father, and you want to know who killed yours. Our goals aren't that different."

Victoria snorted. "I tortured and tried to kidnap you. You, on the other hand, have been acting insufferably. We both have nothing in common. I hate you. You hate me. Why should I help you with anything?"

"Relax, your lame attempts at torture didn't bother me in the least."

Victoria only stared at him with calculating eyes.

"I'm asking you to help me," Slate said. "And right now, there are men coming to kill you. So, are you gonna help yourself by helping me, or are you gonna be stubborn and die?"

The cell was silent. Zubair glanced at Victoria, waiting to hear her thoughts. His life also hung in the balance as his employer pondered the trustworthiness of Slate.

Finally, Victoria decided.

"How about we get some clothes on your back first?" she asked with a small but noticeable smile. "I think black would suit you nicely, don't you think?"

Slate chuckled. "Missy, you read me like a book."

"Excellent, so could you get the keys to the cuffs now?" Victoria asked as if she was talking to a toddler. "They should be on that doctor."

Slate nodded and knelt beside Taylor. He spent about a minute patting him down and searching pockets before stopping abruptly.

"Uh ... I can't find them."

"Look again," Victoria hissed.

"I already did a double check," Slate whined.

Snarling, she turned to her faithful manservant. "What about you, Zubair? Are there any bright ideas from my employee who should have gotten me out of here already?"

The bodyguard rubbed his chin. "He could try breaking the pipe."

"Good idea. Do it, Slate."

"Okey dokey!" Slate yelled. Victoria winced. It would take some time for her to get used to that irritating voice, but she didn't think she would ever come to enjoy it.

The Helmet Man walked over and grabbed the pipe. He gave it one good yank and tore it right out of the wall. However, the entire sink also got pulled free. Water sprayed everywhere.

"What is wrong with you?" Victoria shrieked, immediately soaked.

Slate dropped the sink on the floor. It made a loud clatter and splashed even more water on Victoria. She now had a visible vein throbbing on her forehead.

"Oh, my bad," Slate said.

"Shut up," Victoria spat. "Let's just get out of here."

Zubair got up and almost dragged Victoria along, both of them still cuffed together.

"Hey, easy there," she told Zubair. "I still want to keep this arm. Stop in front of that man. I want to see if he has the keys on him."

They knelt down beside Taylor, who was still alive but out cold.

"You folks don't have time to search the doc," Slate said. "Get moving already."

"Wait!" Victoria yelled. "We can't leave him here."

"Why? He'll just weigh us down."

"We take him. I'm okay with tying up cadets and breaking into military facilities. I'm even okay with torturing imbeciles. But not this."

"Fine, if it'll get you to shut your trap." With little effort, Slate picked up Taylor and casually threw the unconscious doctor over his shoulder. Victoria reeled back. She couldn't hide her amazement at how strong he was.

"You folks need to hide while I clean house," Slate told his companions as he walked out of the cell. "And I need to get some clothes. I'm not going on a killing spree in my underwear. Been there, done that."

***

Straper woke, groggy and bleeding from the head. Turning his head, he found himself tied up next to Henry. They were in the classroom where Mr. Mendez had taught them history just this morning. That lecture seemed like an eternity away.

Two men in ragged clothing stood before them. They seemed relaxed, in no hurry to commit their crimes. Straper was still disoriented and struggling to keep his eyes open, while Henry shivered in fear with his eyes squeezed shut.

"Hey, English boy," a deep voice said.

The colonel walked into the classroom. Of course, he wasn't a real colonel. He had given up acting like an officer and now moved like a common thug, relaxed and informal.

"Uh ... me?" Straper asked. His scattered brain thought it best to cooperate. The gaze of those blue eyes burned right into him. They were full of hate and playful cruelty.

The colonel walked right in front of Straper, towering over the boy. He knelt down and put his lips right next to the cadet's ear.

"Do you have respect for me, English boy?" the colonel asked.

"Ah ... yes ..." Straper said.

"Yes, what?"

"I—what do you ... ?"

The colonel pulled away from Straper and kicked him right in the gut. The young cadet coughed and wheezed, leaning forward to protect himself.

"No, stupid dog," the colonel hissed. "You should have said 'sir.' But instead, you disrespect me."

More coughs escaped Straper. Tears threatened to come out of his eyes. "I'm ..." He coughed again. "I'm sorry ... sir."

"The time for calling me 'sir' is long past. Now you must call me 'Master,' English boy."

Straper couldn't hold back the tears anymore. Thankfully, there were only a few.

"Yes ... Master ..."

The colonel and the two other mercenaries began to hoot, although one of them didn't even know English. They just liked to see others suffer.

The colonel snickered. "That's a good dog."

"Leave him alone."

Henry didn't know why he spoke those words, but he couldn't take them back now. He immediately regretted his actions.

The colonel's good humor vanished. He turned his attention toward Henry. "I thought this one would have behaved better. What is that name? You know, the small dog ..."

"A Chihuahua!" one mercenary yelled.

"Yeah, that's it. He's a Chihuahua. At least the other one looks strong, but this little mutt hardly has any skin on his bones."

The colonel slammed his fist into Straper's head, knocking him out for the second time today. Straper fell to the floor in an untidy heap. Henry let out a small yelp.

"The only reason you English mutts are still alive is we need to weed out some other dogs," the colonel said, flexing the hand with which he had knocked out Straper.

Henry couldn't breathe. "But ... we'll be shot anyway ... right?"

A small chuckle escaped the colonel's lips. "You're right, little puppy ... We're not through with putting mutts down today."

"Stop it, you dolt! That's too tight. What are you trying to do, strangle me?"

"Sorry, sir. We just need to get to the surface and greet our guests."

The general scoffed. "Relax, I'm a general. Our 'guest' is a mere colonel."

"Sir, you are retired from active duty," Johnson said as he adjusted the general's tie to properly fit around his turkey neck. "Plus, it's a sign of respect."

"I know that. I ain't a recruit."

"Of course not, sir ..." Johnson had spent the last fifteen minutes getting General Eisenhorn ready for the arrival of Slate's soon-to-be captors. The general wore a new uniform, since his regular one was covered in stains and something foul-smelling. His medals gleamed, his boots shined, the creases in his pant legs were sharp, and, miraculously, no stains could be seen. He almost looked like a proper leader again.

Johnson finished with the tie and dusted Eisenhorn's suit off. "There, looks good."

"Of course it does!" Eisenhorn yelled. "After all, I'm the one wearing it."

The door to the general's quarters flew open and hit the wall with a loud thump. Gilda sprinted into the room and grabbed Johnson by the arm.

"Plato!" Johnson yelled. "Why aren't you on the surface?"

"Mr. Johnson, listen!" she almost shrieked, but it came out like thunder instead. "That Zaidi girl and her thug trapped me and Henry in a closet for hours. If she's still around, you need to grab her. I think she's after the guy who attacked Henry."

"What! Are you all right? What about Marker? Is he hurt? Are you hurt?"

"I'm fine. But what about—?"

"Johnson!" Eisenhorn barked. "You didn't notice that two of your cadets were missing? Are you deaf, blind, or just plain idiotic?"

"Sir, please," Johnson said. "Plato, how long were you trapped?"

"A few hours, but forget that. Arrest the tramp who put me there."

"Calm down, Plato. Ms. Zaidi and her associate are in—"

A muffled sound interrupted him. Neither Gilda nor Johnson could place what it was.

But Eisenhorn figured it out immediately.

"Gunshot ..." the general whispered.

A deathly silence hung in the air. Everyone stood still.

Breaking the spell, Eisenhorn rushed to his desk, which was the only furniture in his filthy little den besides his captain's bed. He reached under it and started fiddling around.

Johnson went pale. "Sir, please. It could have been an air-conditioner on the fritz."

"I'm no idiot!" Eisenhorn yelled. "I can tell a gunshot from a donkey's fart any day. I wouldn't be worth my weight in manure if I couldn't figure that out at least."

The desk made a squeak. A hidden drawer slid out, revealing a shotgun resting on a folded tablecloth.

Gilda's jaw dropped.

"Sir, what are you doing?" Johnson cried. "A cadet might just be fooling around with a practice rifle, or maybe it's a war movie playing loudly! You can't just—"

"Shut your hole, Johnson," the general said. He reached for his shotgun and picked it up reverently. It had taken a lot of effort to sneak this baby onto the base. He reached into the side of the secret drawer and took out a small black bag of ammo. He plopped the bag onto the table, unzipped it, and loaded the shotgun with shells.

"Sir, put the gun down," Johnson told him in a firm yet calm voice.

"Johnson, don't give me orders!" the general spat. He slammed the butt of the shotgun onto the desk, establishing his dominance. "I can tell what a gunshot sounds like when it's being used for practice. I can tell when it's being used just for fun. But that shot sounded like murder. A weapon has emotions, Johnson. That gun is crying out! Can't you hear it?"

The general pointed his weapon at the entrance to his domain. Johnson backed up into the wall, grabbing Gilda by the shoulder and dragging her with him as he did. She seemed to be in shock. Johnson couldn't blame her. The general was having some kind of breakdown. He might have to try to wrestle the shotgun away from Eisenhorn before anyone gets hurt. Johnson swore to himself. When did this place turn into a madhouse?

"How can anyone stand that sound?" Eisenhorn asked with agitated eyes. "Oh, it haunts me! It haunts me every day!"

General Eisenhorn saw Johnson move toward him from the corner of his eye.

"Idiot!" he bellowed. "Can't you tell we're under siege?"

"Sir," Johnson said, stopping and raising his hands. "Put the gun down."

"You must think I'm crazy!" the general smiled maniacally.

"Well ... sir ..."

"Look at the surveillance video! You told me earlier that you set a camera up to make sure nobody was snooping around the cells downstairs."

"Sir, don't do this. You need to put the gun down."

"I'll put my gun down when you check the video."

"Mr. Johnson, just let him look at the stupid recording!" Gilda yelled. "He'll calm down if he sees nothing there."

In truth, Johnson could not even fathom what Eisenhorn might do next. The general was unpredictable and dangerous. The first thing Johnson had to do was get Gilda safely away. Then he could take down Eisenhorn when the opportunity presented itself.

But for now, he needed to play nice.

"Fine, sir. I'll indulge you."

"All right, then," Eisenhorn said, sounding somewhat pleased. "Your insubordination will be forgiven. I can't blame you for losing your war face. After all, you've been babysitting these little brats for a while now." Eisenhorn chuckled. Gilda frowned.

Johnson went to the general's desk and turned on the holographic screen. He then clicked an icon. The screen was replaced with a live feed of a hallway.

"Here it is, sir."

"Good, let me show you the error of your ways, Johnson." Eisenhorn stepped forward to view the video, lowering his shotgun. Johnson tensed up. If he could keep the general distracted, he might be able to sneak up and wrestle the gun away from him. Or maybe Gilda's prediction would come true and Eisenhorn would surrender on his own, but Johnson was doubtful about that. Remembering Gilda, Johnson waved her away discreetly.

However, a triumphant cry interrupted his plotting.

"Ha! Told you, Johnson!" the general yelled.

Johnson glanced at the screen. All thoughts of trying to overpower the general vanished. His eyes were now glued to the images in front of him.

Mercenaries poured down the hallway on-screen. There were a dozen, maybe more. They held machine guns and an energetic demeanor, eager for the kill.

Gilda also watched the screen. She felt her knees go weak but managed to stand straight.

She could not, however, keep the cracking from her voice.

"Oh, shit ..."

After a moment of shock, Johnson began to move again. He turned off the camera feed. Next, he opened the safe hidden behind a portrait of the president and took a pistol out of it. He then grabbed Gilda and shoved her into Eisenhorn's bathroom. It contained a toilet, a sink, and a small shower, all in desperate need of cleaning.

"What are you doing?" Gilda demanded.

Johnson loaded his firearm. "I'm keeping you here for your safety. Keep quiet and stay inside. This is not negotiable."

"I know how to use a gun."

"You're still a cadet. Besides, I don't have another one. Stay here."

He slammed the door before she could protest. The next step was to call for help. Johnson ran to the computer and tried to send a message, but an icon in the corner of the holographic screen told him no connection was available. This was bad. The communications tower must have been disabled somehow. He would have to get a satellite phone, but they were several floors below in storage.

And that floor was crawling with enemies.

"Johnson!" The general was holding his shotgun, his face stern yet filled with a renewed sense of purpose. Johnson was taken aback. Was the general actually enjoying this?

"Johnson!" Eisenhorn barked again. "We need to get our keisters out of here. Getting to the surface is our best shot at survival."

Johnson shook his head clear. "Sir, we need a phone."

"Cell phones are contraband material. The Bunker's location is supposed to be a secret. Can't have teens texting about the place."

"Maybe we can negotiate. They must be—"

"No! Those animals don't want us alive. They'll tear down this place until nothing is left. Staying here is a mistake. Some satellite phones are on the surface. They're in the vehicles we keep in the shed."

"What ... sir ... ?" How was the general thinking this clearly? Eisenhorn could barely tie his shoes on the best of days, yet here he was, leading the way. For a moment, Johnson saw the man he respected, the man he had given his life to. Even so ...

"No, we'll barricade ourselves here until reinforcements arrive," Johnson said.

"And how long do you think that'll take? The cavalry ain't a thirty-minute pizza."

"Sir, I—"

"We're just waiting to get shot. Those terrorists managed to get into the Bunker. What makes you think a couch in front of the door will stop them?"

"But they're definitely on the surface."

"There's an emergency exit, ain't there?"

"Well ... yes, the one only authorized personnel know about, the hatch that opens up in the middle of the desert. It's two hundred yards from the main entrance. Almost nobody knows about it, so our attackers likely won't know either ..."

"Then let's escape through there."

"It's—it's too dangerous."

"If we stay, we're dead."

"You ... you may be right."

"Of course I'm right. Now hurry up and grab the cadet. We need to move."

Whether Johnson liked it or not, a decision had been made. Johnson let out a breath, nodded, went to the bathroom door, and let out a scowling Gilda.

"Sorry about that," Johnson told her. "Plato, we're going to head to the surface. Follow the general and me. Stay between us and keep your head low. Understand?"

Gilda's scowl gave way to a hint of fear. "I understand, sir."

"This isn't a drill. You could get shot if you act foolish."

"I ... I understand."

"Stay close. I'll get you out of here alive. I promise."

"Don't flatter yourself, Johnson," Eisenhorn said. He opened the door leading out of his quarters and waved over Gilda and Johnson.

They obeyed.

The horde of mercenaries easily kicked down the stairwell door. Some were African, others European, a few American, whoever was willing to accept a bloody check. They poured out of the stairwell with their guns at the ready. Gilda, Johnson, and Eisenhorn watched this live, courtesy of the hidden camera.

What they didn't see was the massacre.

Jogging down the hall, the raggedy mercenaries noticed the flooded floor but ignored it. The first mercenary stopped at a cell. It was wide open. A gush of water spewed out of a wall within it. The mercenaries gathered around the door, exchanging looks as they stood in the water.

None of them saw the Helmet Man stepping into the hallway from an adjacent closet until it was too late.

A bolt of lightning came out of his fingertip.

It struck the wet floor. Half a dozen men convulsed and smoked. They all took a moment to do a little jig before falling down and dying.

Slate now wore a black long-sleeved shirt, the collar going up to the base of his helmet, as well as a black vest over it for added cover and style. He also had on black pants, black gloves, and black combat boots. He really liked black, despite not being able to see.

The Helmet Man skipped down the hall, stepping on dead mercenaries like a frog hopping on lily pads. "Thanks for keeping my feet dry, ding-dongs!"

One mercenary managed to avoid the initial attack by standing in a dry spot. He appeared at the end of the hall and sprayed bullets down the corridor. The projectiles struck the walls.

But none hit Slate.

Instead of getting shot, Slate jumped in the air and began to run on the wall like a sprinting spider, having to crouch in order to do it effectively in the tight corridor. It was an elaborate way to avoid getting wet and psych out the enemy. It worked. The mercenary dropped his weapon, crying a bunch of unintelligible prayers.

Slate reached the end of the hall and dropped down on the floor. He then kicked the mercenary right in the head. For good measure, he made sure to electrify his limb. Sparks flew. The smell of ozone filled the air. The mercenary flew back and crashed dead into the wall.

Six mercenaries were left on this level. They appeared in front of Slate from a dry, adjoining hallway. Two killers stood ahead of the other four and fired their machine guns. Slate ducked, evading the bullets, and pointed his index fingers at the two closest men. Electric bolts came out. They hit the men dead-on, stopping their hearts.

Before their bodies had time to hit the floor, Slate crouched down and sprang forward. He flew through the air as if being shot from a cannon and plowed his fists into the two falling bodies when he flew between them. The other mercenaries fired, but Slate used the corpses as shields. Bullets pelted the dead flesh. Slate continued to fly forward and slammed into the four other mercenaries, knocking them backward onto the floor.

Slate let go of the corpses and landed on his feet. He had flown over the four remaining men. Now he turned around to finish the job.

One merc got back on his feet and squeezed his trigger in a blind rage, but his efforts proved to be in vain as Slate simply swatted the firing gun out of his hands. Slate punched the merc's face, his fist charged with energy. The mercenary collapsed in a lifeless heap. Two other men got up and tried to shoot the Helmet Man as well. Slate gave both men uppercuts to the jaw simultaneously. Both convulsed, firing their guns into the walls. Their bodies fell, and they died in a charred heap. All that remained was one man, who decided to drop his gun and back up against the wall.

"Please, sir ..." the man sniveled with a thick French accent. "I ... I didn't kill nobody. I don't want to die. I won't hurt nobody ... I promise. Please, let me go!"

"Then why are you holding a grenade behind your back?" Slate asked politely.

Before the man had a chance to take the pin out, Slate fired a bolt. The mercenary was struck. He convulsed on the floor, threw up a little, and died.

"A full minute to kill thirteen people," Slate said. "I must be getting sloppy. It should have been half a minute max!"

***

As the general led the way, Johnson wondered if the whiff of violence had reawakened Eisenhorn's inner soldier. He didn't know how long this clarity would last. He hoped it wouldn't go away anytime soon but knew this was all wishful thinking. Eisenhorn could revert back to being a nutcase at any time, maybe in a few hours, minutes, or even seconds. But until that time arrived, Johnson would follow him.

They climbed the stairs, which was tough going. So far, they hadn't encountered any mercenaries. Johnson was under no illusion they could win a firefight. Their only chance was to slip out undetected and call for help. He just hoped the other cadets and staff were okay, though this was also wishful thinking on his part.

The trio heard a scream. Johnson couldn't place the voice.

But Gilda did.

"Henry ..."

Gilda ran ahead.

"Plato!" Johnson whispered, but it was futile. Gilda had already gone through a door to the third floor where the scream had come from.

"Stupid girl ..." the general muttered. "Grab her before she gets her head blown off!"

The two men followed Gilda. Johnson opened the door and used a piece of tinfoil he found as a mirror to see around the corner. The coast was clear. Both men exited the stairwell and tiptoed down the hall. Johnson held his pistol. The general clutched his shotgun. They scanned their surroundings and went to the end of the hall. They used the tinfoil to see around the corner again. This time they saw Gilda in the reflection, frozen in place.

"What's her malfunction?" Eisenhorn asked.

Johnson shrugged. They went around the corner to find out.

And then they saw why.

In front of Gilda lay Henry.

Blood dribbled out of the hole in his chest.

Johnson found himself unable to breathe. This couldn't be. The full realization of what was happening at the Bunker had not really hit home for him. Sure, he was concerned about the other cadets, but in truth, he had been preoccupied with his own predicament.

But now Johnson found himself staring at Henry's body. The boy wasn't even out of his teens, not even in the actual army. He was just a cadet, but he had been shot and left to bleed out all over the floor. Johnson couldn't take his eyes off the body. He was transfixed by the gaping wound, almost mesmerized.

A sickening cackle brought Johnson back to reality. A man dressed as a colonel stood down the hall past Henry's body. The man held a cadet in his arms who struggled very little. The colonel also held a gun to the cadet's head.

"Hello there, Westerners," the colonel said, grinning with lots of teeth. "I want the Zaidi girl. Give her to me, and I will let the English boy go."

Eisenhorn pointed his shotgun right at the colonel's head. "Did you shoot that boy? Tell me!"

The colonel cackled again, his eyes glinting with amusement. "He talked back to me, and I only need one English boy to get the Zaidi girl."

"Why hurt the cadets?" Johnson asked with no emotion.

"Westerners have so many enemies. Kidnapping all of you would take too long. Killing is easier. Not as much money, but more fun."

"Two birds with one stone, huh?" the general spat. "You sick puppy! No way are we going to let you—wait! Girl, stop!"

Gilda didn't stop. She walked forward as if on a stroll. Her eyes were vacant.

"Stay back, English girl!" the colonel yelled. "Don't make me shoot the boy."

Johnson finally recognized the hostage. It was Kevin Straper. He could see the cadet was becoming more anxious with each step Gilda took.

"Hey, listen to the man!" Straper yelled. "He isn't messing around. He'll shoot me!"

But Gilda just kept on walking.

"Gilda, stop it! I'm sorry about Henry. I didn't want him to die either. Please, just stop walking!"

"Listen to your friend, girl," the colonel told her, but his voice became strained as well. "I'll shoot. Turn around!"

Gilda kept walking. The air seemed to grow colder the closer she approached. The colonel seethed. He moved backward, almost as if backing away from a blazing inferno. He ended up tripping, briefly letting his grip loosen on Straper.

At that moment, everything happened at once. Gilda ran toward Henry. Tears poured out of her eyes, emotions bursting. The general lowered his gun and ran after her as he yelled at Johnson to shoot. While the colonel's grip was loose, Straper elbowed him in the gut. Grunting, he let go. Straper was out of the way. Johnson shot the colonel in the shoulder. The colonel fell on the floor, moaning. Two mercenaries came out of hiding. Johnson and Straper ducked. Eisenhorn tackled Gilda, who had just reached Henry. Both of them landed on the floor. The two mercenaries started shooting.

"Idiots!" the colonel yelled. "Don't shoot at me!"

The men stopped firing. Johnson used this opportunity to fire back, hitting one mercenary in the head and grazing the other.

"Let's go, girl!" Eisenhorn yelled, restraining Gilda as she crawled toward Henry, trying to touch him, trying to be near him.

"No, please!" she sobbed. "You aren't dead, Hen. Get up! I'm sorry! You can kiss me again. Please, get up!"

Straper ran to them and helped Eisenhorn restrain Gilda. The two of them pulled her to her feet and managed to drag her down the hall. She wasn't resisting them any longer, even going so far as to walk with them, but they held her anyway as she yelled for Henry and cried.

"We'll see each other again! Don't die! You can't die!"

A bullet whizzed past them. The grazed mercenary was shooting at them again. Johnson held open the door as Gilda and others ran into the stairwell. Eisenhorn and Straper let go of Gilda. She followed them willingly, though she couldn't help but cry.

They were worried the last mercenary would follow them, but their fears were unfounded. The group ascended the stairs. They climbed the next few floors in silence before reaching a door with a keypad. Johnson entered his code and opened the door to reveal a small concrete room with a metal ladder on the wall. The ladder led up to a hatch on the ceiling. Johnson scurried up the ladder but did not immediately open the hatch. He tried to hear if anything unpleasant was behind it. After a moment, he gave the handle a twist and raised the hatch a crack. Sand and smoke drifted into the room. Eisenhorn and Straper coughed. Johnson could smell the remains of a fire but couldn't see much else through the crack. It was almost pitch-black outside. The desert night was just beginning.

"I'm going to sneak outside," Johnson said. "We need a satellite phone from the garage. Sir, please stay here with the cadets. I'll bring a truck around to—"

The hatch was thrown open. A beam of light shined in, blinding them. Two mercenaries stood above, wielding machine guns. Straper yelped. Johnson sighed. Eisenhorn growled.

Gilda, meanwhile, was too numb to react. The gunman yelled and gestured at them to come out. The group, taken by surprise, had no choice but to comply. Johnson was the first to raise himself through the hatch and onto solid ground. Gilda and Straper followed, with Eisenhorn climbing out last. They stepped into the cool sand, which swirled around their feet and got into their shoes. The light still shined down on them. It was coming from a hovering unicopter, which was accompanied by another four in the air.

Over twenty men waited for them outside. Most of the mercs were in a cluster two hundred yards away near the main entrance, but five were close enough to accurately aim their weapons at Johnson, who dropped his pistol and raised his hands.

"Insane ..." Johnson told the general. "I thought I'd die getting shot by you."

Eisenhorn snorted as he dropped his shotgun. "Guess they knew about this exit."

"They knew everything. How did they—?"

"Shut up!" one mercenary warned. "Where is the Zaidi girl? Tell us!"

Straper stood with his hands in the air as he searched for some means of escape. He could find none. Gilda only gave a light huff and closed her eyes, tearing up again.

"I'll be with you soon, Henry ..."

***

Only a minuscule amount of ambient light leaked into the closet. Victoria shifted, cursing as she banged an elbow on a box. Zubair squatted next to her. He was trying to listen to the gunshots outside, as if they would tell him a story. To Victoria, it was just mindless noise that would soon come to end her if events turned for the worse. All they could do was hide in this closet and wait for Slate to come back. At least she had found bolt cutters to break the handcuff chain and free herself from Zubair. Now they had some degree of independence.

A mysterious moan sounded. Victoria jumped but realized it was only Taylor. She had almost forgotten about him.

"Hmm ... where am I ... ?" Taylor asked, rubbing his head.

Another series of gunshots went off.

"What's happening?" Taylor almost yelled.

"Calm down," Victoria said. "We're being attacked."

"Hold on! What do you mean attacked? Who's attacking?"

"Calm down. I won't tell you again. I saved your life. You owe me compliance."

"What about the cadets? Are they okay? Where's Johnson?"

"I don't know. Shut up already!"

Taylor tried standing up. "I got to help those kids. I can't leave them alone! I—"

A ray of light hit Taylor's face. The door had opened. The brightness blinded Victoria. She went into a panic. Had the attackers heard Taylor? Were they really going to kill her?

"Look! It's a bird, it's a plane, it's super Slate!" an annoying voice yelled.

Victoria sighed. Relief and irritation flooded over her like a tide. She was almost glad the Helmet Man had returned. Almost. The three of them exited the closet, squinting as they emerged from the dark. It took a moment for their vision to come back.

They soon regretted it.

"I'll take the elevator up," Slate said. "You guys can take the stairs."

Nobody objected. They were too focused on the carnage. Bodies littered the floor. The smell of burnt flesh and ozone lingered in the air. The Helmet Man himself stood facing the elevator doors with his hands on his hips. Victoria had seen dead bodies before, but this was unlike anything she had ever encountered. Some of the corpses' eyes were still open. They almost seemed to be watching her, even following her. She quickly dismissed such idiotic ideas. Zubair also examined the area. He showed no fear, only caution.

"Crap, where's the elevator?" Slate asked. "I tried pressing the buttons and everything. Those jackass mercenaries must be behind this."

Taylor touched several bodies to see if they were alive. They weren't. He turned to Slate. He didn't bother hiding his disgust.

Slate shrugged. "What? What did I do?"

"You did this ..."

"No, the magic murder fairy did it. Of course it was me!"

Taylor walked up to him. He stared right into Slate's perfect helmet, only to look back at his own reflection.

"It's one thing to kill in self-defense. It's another to gloat about it."

Slate scratched his armpit. "Whatever, I gotta fly up the elevator shaft to deal with those buttholes. You folks just stay outta the way."

"Wait," Victoria said. "What do you mean by 'fly up'?"

Slate ripped the elevator doors open with relative ease. The elevator was not on their floor, so the shaft was empty. His chuckling echoed up it.

"The most literal of meanings, kid ..."

The Helmet Man jumped in feetfirst.

The Helmet Man flew up the elevator shaft, going seventy miles per hour, nowhere near his maximum. Electricity trailed behind him. He slammed into the elevator, which was parked on the seventh floor, and pushed the box up with him. It went so fast, the tracks sparked. Slate sensed he was approaching the top of the shaft.

But instead of slowing, he went even faster.

Gilda and the others turned to see the roof of the shed explode. An elevator box flew through the air, the Helmet Man carrying it.

"Holy hell!" the general screamed, his eyes popping out.

Johnson's mouth fell open. Straper shrieked like a dying goat. The mercenaries also cried out. A few even soiled themselves.

But for some reason, Gilda found herself smiling.

Bolts of energy came off Slate as he threw the elevator box. It crashed into an enemy unicopter. With the metal screeching, the elevator box and the remains of the unicopter, now a flaming ball of wreckage, fell to the earth.

All that noise woke up the mercenaries from their dazed state. They fired at Slate. He flew away from their line of fire. Bright blue electric bolts trailed behind him. Even with this bright indicator, the mercenaries still couldn't nail him.

Slate flew headfirst at another unicopter. He collided into the fuselage, wrapped his arms around the bulk, and sent a thousand volts into the metal beast. The pilot screamed. The rotor exploded in a blue burst, lighting up the sky for an instant. Sparks and electric arcs covered the surface of the aircraft as it went down. Slate let go of the doomed war machine and flew at another unicopter. Two down, three to go.

Slate snickered. "I'd say go pick on someone your own size, but that'd be pretty hypocritical. After all, I'm a lot bigger than you."

Johnson broke his awestruck gaze from the Helmet Man and grabbed Gilda by the wrist. He had to reach the trucks in the garage. Their unicopters were not immediately flightworthy, but the trucks were well supplied and full of fuel. They needed to get some distance from this warzone. He then thought of the other cadets and staff, over a hundred people, most of them not even old enough to grow a beard. What about them? Johnson realized they were most likely dead. A few might have gotten away, but that was doubtful. A sorrowful ache began to fill his chest, but he fought it off. Now was not the time.

"Come on!" he yelled, dragging Gilda along. "We need to find a truck."

Gilda tore her hand away. "Then let's head to the garage. You're going the wrong way."

Johnson turned around. She was right. The trucks were stored in the other direction. He needed to get his head on straight. It was a good thing Gilda was pulling through. If she had still been in her slump, they would likely be running the wrong way right now.

As the two of them ran for the garage, General Eisenhorn picked up his shotgun and ran to the smoking shed. Straper followed, cowering and cursing. The mercenaries had been so preoccupied with Slate that they hadn't noticed their prisoners had run away. Eisenhorn and Straper reached the shed and ran inside. After catching his breath, Eisenhorn poked his weapon outside and fired. Most of the mercenaries kept trying to nail Slate, but six of them started shooting at Eisenhorn. One merc got his head blown off. Another got hit in the chest.

After taking another two mercenaries down, the general ran out of ammo. He swore to himself. The last two mercenaries moved in closer. The shed itself was bulletproof, but the door was open. The general would have to cross the doorway to close it, getting in the line of fire. Great, what was he supposed to do?

Shadows then emerged from the stairwell. Eisenhorn's heart almost burst. He didn't recognize the man leading the way and had nearly taken him for an enemy, but when the man took out his pistol and started firing at the mercenaries, Eisenhorn relaxed. One mercenary got shot in the hand, crying out and dropping his gun, but his misery didn't last long. The other merc was soon killed too, barely having time to see a shirtless Zubair fire his bullet.

Victoria came out of the stairwell and ran in a crouch. Taylor followed behind her, scanning the battlefield. Neither Taylor nor Victoria were armed, which made them somewhat useless in this fight. Straper just crouched next to them, jittering about.

"You must be that Zaidi girl!" Eisenhorn shouted over some distant gunfire. The remaining mercenaries were still focused on Slate.

"And you must be Jeffery's psychotic boss!" she shouted back.

"Jeffery!" Eisenhorn laughed. "What a stupid name."

"Sir, we need to leave!" Taylor yelled. "Where's Johnson? How about the cadets?"

"Calm down! Give them a sec. They'll be here."

Two trucks pulled out of the garage, but the unicopters were far too preoccupied to deal with them. Slate made sure of that.

All the unicopters were gunning for the flying menace. The largest unicopter even fired three missiles. The unicopter's weapons system could be set to predict the movements of an ordinary target, but Slate was not ordinary. He moved in such an agile fashion that the bullets didn't even come within a foot of him.

The missiles, however, trailed him with annoying persistence. Slate stopped midair and dropped. The missiles followed. He plummeted like a brick a hundred feet. Just as Slate was about to hit the ground, he slowed his descent and landed. He then sprinted forward, hoping the missiles would strike the ground and not him, but they pulled up at the last second and continued their pursuit.

It was time for a new tactic. The Helmet Man stopped running and turned around. He stood Mexican standoff style. Raising both arms, he aimed his index fingers at the incoming missiles and fired a bolt from each. The missiles exploded only twenty feet away from him, creating a fireball that almost consumed him, but he flew up in the air, avoiding the blast.

"Time to do what I do best!" Slate yelled. "The offensive!"

The biggest unicopter hovered above him. It fired yet another missile. Instead of dodging, Slate had another idea. He flew at the missile but veered out of the way at the last moment. He reached out and grabbed the projectile with unnatural strength as he passed. In a quick spinning motion, Slate twirled midair, dragging the missile along with him. The missile tried to tug itself free, but his grip was iron. Slate threw the missile at the large unicopter. It hit the unicopter's blade. An explosion ripped apart the rotor and lit the entire aircraft on fire. The unicopter fell to the ground and crumpled in a heap of twisted metal and orange flame.

It was time to finish the job. Slate spun around to confront the last two remaining unicopters. But instead of fighting, they flew away. Slate would have gone after them if he didn't have to deal with the ground troops.

"Bunch of wimps. Seriously, how could child-murdering mercenaries be so cowardly?"

Meanwhile, the oddball group holding out in the shed wasn't doing so hot. The remaining mercenaries on the surface had begun to focus their efforts on the shed. Zubair was almost out of bullets as he tried to hold off the attackers. Victoria, Straper, and Taylor hid in the stairwell, while the general squatted next to Zubair, squeezing his empty shotgun.

"This can't be good for my ticker ..." Eisenhorn mumbled.

"I am out of bullets," Zubair said, lowering his gun and crouching next to Eisenhorn. "Those men will start advancing soon. Hurry, I shall try to lock the shed door, but that will only hold them off for so long."

"Don't be a jackass," the general told him. "Come with us."

"You have to protect Ms. Zaidi. Try to find a room to hold out in. Make a stand."

"Boy, I'm not—!"

Gasoline coated the mercenaries from above. A few of them coughed on the fumes and looked up. Slate had found a jerry can of the stuff and dumped it on them.

Just as they figured out what Slate intended, he zapped the ground.

All the mercenaries caught fire. They screamed as they tried to put themselves out. Slate then swooped down from above and shocked the burning men.

The fight was over within a few seconds. Slate landed before the charred bodies. He dusted off himself and surveyed the area.

Zubair and the general walked out of the shed. They stared at the corpses.

"Holy mother of ..." Eisenhorn whispered.

Slate wagged a finger. "Just remember, kids, don't piss me off."

Zubair heard a honk. He turned to see the two trucks from the garage approaching. Gilda and Johnson had done their share.

"At last, we can leave this place," the bodyguard said.

Slate knelt beside one of the charred bodies. His silver helmet reflected a smoldering face. He seemed to deflate a little.

"Yeah, well ... it won't leave you."

***

Two hours later, the fires had died down and the corpses began to smell. All was still. Only an eerie wind could be heard.

A single unicopter landed, breaking the peace.

"About time," a weak voice grunted.

Even after being shot, the colonel lived on. Now reinforcements were here to take him away. Hopefully, they had some growth patches with them. One of his men helped him along. Five other mercs were also alive and with him. They had been searching the Bunker for survivors when their comrades were slaughtered. Neither the colonel nor his remaining men saw the battle, but he would find out how those Westerners got the better of him.

The unicopter opened up. The mercenaries gathered around the aircraft. Out stepped one of the two passengers with a look of cool curiosity on her face.

"I see you boys had some trouble wrangling up a young girl," she said. "I can't say I blame you. A purse would be quite deadly if thrown right."

"Quit wagging that tongue and get us out of here!" the colonel spat.

"That's no way to treat a lady," she scolded, her smile never fading. She raised her smooth hands and twisted them.

The mercenaries' heads jerked sideways and snapped. Their bodies crumpled, littering the ground. The colonel, his helper now dead, fell on his hands and knees.

"What was that, you witch?" he yelled.

"They were failures, and they knew too much. The only reason you're still alive is that Houdini would like to know what went wrong."

A gunshot sounded. The colonel jerked his head in the direction of the sound. He found himself facing a bullet. It floated midair, only a foot from his face.

"I almost didn't catch that," the woman said. "Then again, I wasn't really motivated."

"Shut up!" the colonel yelled. "Who fired that?"

"Frost, cool off. Oh my, how tasteless."

Sergeant Barnes had clung to life, despite his gunshot wound. He had woken up with little time left and crawled to a discarded gun. Shooting that blue-eyed murderer had been the only thought on his mind, but now it looked like he couldn't even do that. He barely had enough energy to stay alive, let alone shoot again.

"You maggot!" the colonel yelled, spotting Barnes. "I thought I shot you!"

"His aim was pretty good," the woman said.

Barnes could barely see anymore, but the woman who just spoke caught his attention nevertheless. In her late twenties or early thirties, she had an oval face with fox-like eyes. A white gown flowed over her form. Her raven-black hair was smooth and straight with long bangs covering her forehead. Barnes had always loved his wife. Even so, the woman before him still made his weak heart beat fast.

Then something else caught his eye, a giant on the edge of his vision, the monstrous companion of the woman. It emerged from the unicopter.

The colonel smirked. "Oh, it's you … How about you kill the rat who tried to shoot me? Your way of murder is far crueler than anything I could perform."

The woman sighed. "If he must. This man won't live much longer anyway."

Gasping, Sergeant Barnes tried to crawl away. He wasn't afraid of death, but he was afraid of the giant. A brown trench coat fluttered. The face was dead. No, that was a mask …

Barnes barely made it a foot before the thing stepped in front of him. The colonel chuckled. The woman turned away, looking ill. The figure knelt in front of Barnes, taking a glove off his hand, which was shiny and shifting. Then the hand melted away in a cascade of silver, revealing a pointed blade. Fear ate at Barnes's innards. That thing was not human. It was melting. Heavy breathing sounds came out of the mask, like a big bad wolf. The blade sank into Barnes's neck. His fear left him, as did his life. The blade came out.

Cloak was cleaning up.

And the moon was full.

They drove, and they drove hard.

They spent all night and most of the next morning in full throttle, the two trucks going over eighty miles per hour, burning rubber faster than daylight.

No plan was conceived. No thought was taken as to what they should do next. In truth, when Johnson reflected on their actions, he knew they had left so fast not because they feared more mercenaries would come. They had only wanted to blind themselves, to stay ignorant, to keep their innocence. But that didn't happen. What they saw made sure of that.

Johnson had hustled everyone into the trucks with no discussion, everyone happy to oblige. Gilda, Taylor, Straper, and the general went in the first vehicle with Johnson driving. Johnson wanted to keep the Bunker's residents together. He also wished to leave Slate and the Zaidi crew behind. They could fend for themselves.

As they drove away from the Bunker, they came across a surreal scene. A large fire was still burning, illuminating the desert night. Smoke filled the air. The truck bounced, shaking everyone in their seats. Gilda gritted her teeth, Straper gave a small scream, and both Taylor and Eisenhorn swore as their heads hit the ceiling.

The violent bumping eventually forced Johnson to stop the truck. He exited the vehicle and waved some smoke out of his face as he tried to determine where he was. It then dawned on him this was the landing pad. But what had caused the fire? He began to make out a smoking heap of rubble, which was the source of the fire and light. This was where the communications tower used to be. That explained why he couldn't call for help. Those mercenaries weren't as dumb as they looked. It was a smart and destructive move.

A horrible sensation overcame Johnson. It wasn't physical but served as some kind of warning. What was it?

Then he remembered.

This was where the inspection was supposed to take place.

Johnson didn't stop to think. All he did was run back into the truck and slam the door.

The cadets in the back seat were silent. Dr. Taylor sat between them and dared to ask.

"What—what is it?"

General Eisenhorn, sitting in shotgun, turned to Johnson. His eyes became hard. "Drive."

The truck lurched forward. Everyone was thrown back into their seats. Hyperventilating, Johnson had floored the gas. His grip was so tight on the steering wheel that he may have broken it if he had squeezed any harder. Everyone kept getting their heads banged as they went over more bumps, but Johnson kept going. The bouncing got so bad that at one point the truck almost flipped over. Straper gave a guttural cry, Gilda bit her tongue, and all three men said a particularly bad curse in unison.

The smoke started to clear. They entered open desert.

Curiosity overcame Straper. He glanced out the rear window.

"No!" Johnson yelled. "Don't look back!"

But Straper did look back. After doing so, he opened his door, poked his head out, and proceeded to vomit.

Gilda could see the pimple-faced cadet lose his dinner as tears streamed out of his eyes. She found herself transfixed by the display. After there was no more to be hurled out, Straper let loose a howl that filled the ears of everyone in the truck.

"What was that about?" Gilda demanded. She turned her head to see what Straper saw, perhaps the greatest mistake she had ever made.

Over a hundred human bodies lay behind them. Blood and ash were everywhere.

***

Watching the desert go by, Gilda saw nothing of interest. It was a dusty waste-land with a thin layer of sand covering everything. Only rocks and the occasional shrubbery blemished the endless expanse of the terrain. Her mind was easily lost as the scenery flew past her.

The second truck had caught up with them a few hours ago. It contained Slate, Zubair, and Victoria. They followed Johnson's truck at close proximity. Johnson tried to lose them, making sharp turns, honking the horn, and even yelling out the window, but it was all for naught. They stuck to him like a piece of chewing gum in his hair.

At least Straper was no longer throwing up or yelling. He held his knees and shivered. Yellow vomit dried around his mouth. Gilda was glad he had stopped, or she might have been tempted to push him out of the truck. The bodies haunted her memory. She couldn't make them out, but they were ob-viously the rest of the Bunker's staff and cadets. Sally the Cook, Mr. Mendez, Ernie, that tramp Angie, pretty-boy Ryan, Nurse Elena ...

But Henry haunted her the most.

Why had she been angry with him? Because of one little kiss? She would kiss him a thousand times if it meant she could have him back. It wasn't fair. Maybe if she had enjoyed the kiss, the fight wouldn't have happened. Then they would have been together. He could have made it out with them. He could still be alive.

Why didn't that happen?

No more tears came out. She grabbed the upholstery of the seat and nearly ripped it off. Her blues gave way to inner red. Revenge would be hers. That man with icy eyes would die. The people who sent him, whoever they were, would also feel her wrath. The pain in her was now rage, directed toward one goal: to hurt those who had hurt Henry.

Gilda glanced around the truck to see how the others were doing. She had decided to be realistic about her revenge. She would need to get out of the desert first. Shaking, Straper still seemed to be out of it. Oh, how she envied him. Taylor was quiet, having sat silently the entire night. Eisenhorn was asleep and muttering about Koreans and Chinamen. Johnson was the only one she was impressed with. He had been driving for almost ten hours straight, and not once had he dozed off. Her admiration for him deepened with each passing minute. If they were going to live, it would be by his hands.

Well, his and Slate's.

Gilda didn't know what to make of the Helmet Man. He wasn't normal, possessing abilities no one should have. But what she did know was that he was an ally. Johnson may want nothing to do with him, but she knew that if Slate were on her side, nothing would stop her.

The truck stopped with a jolt. Johnson relaxed.

"We're taking a break," he said.

General Eisenhorn woke up. "Johnson! Where's breakfast?"

Johnson sighed. It seemed the general was back to his old self.

The truck following them stopped as well. Victoria Zaidi bounded out of the vehicle, along with Zubair from the driver's side.

And from the back seat came the man of the hour.

"Good morning, Sahara!" Slate yelled, stretching his limbs. "Boy, what a dump!"

Victoria and Zubair, on the other hand, appeared just as tired as those in the other truck. Zubair had found a green combat shirt to wear, while Victoria had put on a cadet's uniform and some reasonable shoes, presumably finding all this in the closet they had hidden in. Neither one was shaken up by the bodies as much as the others, but they would not sleep well for some time.

Without invitation, Victoria walked to the other truck and knocked on the side window. Taylor and Gilda snapped their heads toward her.

"What do you want?" Taylor spat.

Victoria pointed to her wrist, which still had a broken handcuff on it.

Taylor shook his head. He reached over Straper, who was still a mess, rolled down the windows, and tossed a key at the girl. Victoria caught it.

"Finally, my wrist was starting to chafe," she said.

"Good, now get lost," Taylor said.

"Our truck doesn't have a phone, or any maps or food."

"Then starve."

Victoria frowned. "All right, listen here. I don't—"

A gunshot sounded. Everyone but Slate jumped in their shoes.

"You!" the general screamed, holding a smoking pistol. "I want you gone!"

Slate chuckled, raising his hands. "What? What did I do?"

"You know what you did! Get the hell out of here!"

Slate walked up to General Eisenhorn, hands behind his back. "Nah, don't think so. You'll just have to shoot me."

The general jabbed his gun into Slate's chest. "Works for me!"

Johnson got out of the truck. "Sir, please!"

"This man killed my cadets!" Eisenhorn yelled.

Johnson reached the general and grabbed him by the shoulders. "Sir, it's not his fault. He saved our lives!"

"No! He must have lured those killers there. I know it!"

In a calmer voice, Johnson explained himself. "Slate saved us, General. I dislike his antics and childish attitude as much as you do, but he doesn't want to kill us."

"You know I can hear everything you're saying," Slate said.

Johnson ignored him. "It wasn't his fault, but I do know who's responsible."

He turned to Victoria.

"It's her," Johnson said. "They were after her."

Victoria stiffened. "What, are you accusing me of mass murder?"

"Those mercenaries were after you, and you led them right to the Bunker," Johnson told her. "We were only attacked because they followed you."

"I was only after Slate! He just happened to be there."

Eisenhorn pointed his gun at Slate. "Ha! So it *was* his fault!"

"Man, you guys are on a witch hunt," Slate said.

Johnson walked up to Victoria, nearly face-to-face with her. "You got them all killed because you wanted Slate. Why?"

Victoria didn't flinch. "To find my father's killer."

"I don't believe that for a second."

"Believe it, Jeffery." She turned away from him. "Now, if you excuse me, I have to figure out how Zubair and I are going to get out of here alive."

***

Frost slammed the door open and stormed out of the office. His bullet wound had been tended to, and he was now good as new. He no longer wore his colonel's outfit, now in combat boots, black pants, and a sleeveless white shirt. Snarling, he focused his cold blue eyes on the woman in white, who had been waiting outside while he was getting chewed out.

"Your turn," he sneered.

The woman smiled. "I hope you didn't enjoy that spanking too much."

"Shut your filthy mouth."

"Did that firm hand remind you of home?"

Frost decided to slap her, but just as his hand flew forward, a large, gloved hand caught it.

"Who grabs me? I—!"

Frost froze, realizing who he was talking to.

The masked man squeezed his hand, huffing and puffing.

Frost's face went slack. "I ... I didn't ... I wouldn't—"

"Scoundrel ..." the masked man wheezed.

Frost yanked his hand free and scurried away down the hall.

"What a coward," the woman said. "Thank you for saving me, Sandtrap, but I didn't need the help. Poor fool. He just doesn't realize how weak he is."

Sandtrap just stood there, breathing even more deeply, the urge to kill rising. The figure was almost a giant, towering over even Frost. He wore a heavy sand-colored trench coat with thick boots, grungy pants, and black gloves that all served well to cover his horrid form. His head was pale, covered in angry scars that crisscrossed in strange patterns. His face was concealed by a mask that was also sand-colored. The mask itself had two eyeholes with tinted black glass over them and a grill-like opening over his mouth.

The man continued to stand there. His huffs were now screams.

The woman placed a hand on his chest. He began to take his breaths easier. The tension in his body lessened.

"Stay here for a few minutes," the woman said. "I'll be back."

The woman left her friend in the hallway, the masked man now breathing somewhat normally. She entered the room and closed the door. A wooden desk took up the center of the office. A holographic screen floated behind it. Shelves lined the room, filled with books never read and awards never earned. She knew Houdini didn't have the patience to read a book or earn a worthwhile award. He lived in the present, the now.

"Enter," a voice commanded. Houdini sat in a leather chair behind the desk. It was turned toward the screen and away from the door, concealing him.

The woman smirked. "I'm already in the room."

Houdini growled. "I hate your sense of humor, Repulsa."

"You know I don't like that name. It sounds so ... repulsive."

"Like I haven't heard that one before. What are your thoughts?"

"Electric impulses being sent through brain tissue."

Houdini slammed his hand on the desk. "About the Bunker!"

Repulsa sighed. It was going to be a long day. "Most everyone is dead. The survivors were long gone by then. We could have searched for hours and still found no sign of them. The wind covered their tracks well."

Houdini leaned back in his chair. "I already found them. Our special friend is taking care of them as we speak. Soon, the last of the Bunker's rats will be drowned."

"Was the Bunker really where they were planning to send us?"

"We never got the chance to live there. It got turned into a playpen for spoiled snots after the Gifted rebelled, but now it's come back to haunt us ..."

"The hands of the Keymasters are still fiddling with our lives," Repulsa said, no longer in a good mood. "We were mere playthings, tools of suffering made to suffer."

"And now we shall play with them. The Keymasters may all be dead, but the Western Union still lives, as does our dream of revenge."

The holographic screen came to life, showing an image of the Sahara Desert from a bird's-eye view. Two vehicles could be seen sitting in the middle of the waste.

"Are we about to see a show?" Repulsa whispered.

"Yes," Houdini said with a smile. "It's practically pay-per-view ..."

Without the air-conditioning on, the truck was starting to become an oven. Gilda got out of the vehicle, thankful for the fresh air. She glanced back at Straper. He was no longer in the fetal position but still wore a blank expression.

"Hey!" she yelled.

"Leave me alone ..."

"Get out of the car. They're talking about what we're going to do next."

Slowly, Straper managed to slither out of the truck.

"Good, over here," Gilda said, pointing at the group of men. Johnson had brought Eisenhorn and Dr. Taylor together to discuss their plan of action. It had been a mere courtesy for Gilda to invite Straper. She wanted to voice her opinion or at least overhear what they said. Johnson and the others didn't even notice when the two cadets joined them.

"Calling for help is a bad idea," Eisenhorn said. "We don't need it."

"The only reason we haven't done it yet was because I couldn't get a signal before," Johnson said. "But we got one now."

"How do you think those terrorists found out where we were?" Eisenhorn asked. "The sneaks are probably monitoring the airwaves."

"That may be a possibility," Taylor told Johnson. "We need to be careful about this. Whoever attacked the Bunker has resources."

"I suppose," Johnson said. "But we need help, and we need it now. I don't want to keep driving around the desert aimlessly. Let's try the phone."

Taylor nodded. Eisenhorn grumbled but didn't disagree.

Gilda didn't know what to think. She wanted to get out of the desert, but she might never find out who was responsible for the attack if the military decided to prune them. For now, she decided to let fate take its course.

Johnson took out a bulky satellite phone. During all the confusion, Victoria had forgotten her phone at the Bunker. The satellite phone was now their only means of communication.

"Now let's leave this place and never come back," Johnson said.

The phone then sparked in his hand and died.

"What the—?" Johnson began, but the trucks sparked as well, their insides now fried.

The group stared at the ruined vehicles for a moment before blame was assigned.

"You!" the general spat, pointing at Slate, who leaned against the second truck. "You did this! I'll kill—"

That was when the missile struck.

Everyone covered their eyes. Debris flew everywhere. Johnson waved the smoke out of his face. He gasped. A smoldering crater had appeared.

Right where Eisenhorn had been.

"Sir!" Johnson screamed.

"Don't draw conclusions too fast," Slate said, lying on top of Eisenhorn a few yards away from the crater. He had flown at the general and knocked him clear of the blast zone.

Eisenhorn pushed the Helmet Man away. "Get off me, weirdo!"

"No need to thank me," Slate grumbled. "I just do this for fun."

Taylor pointed up. "You're about to have more fun."

Five missiles were coming right for them, leaving vapor trails in their wake. Everyone ducked down except Slate. The Helmet Man got up off the ground, pointed a finger at one of the missiles, and let loose a bolt of lightning. The missile exploded in a fiery flower. Gilda could feel the sharp heat on her face.

"Get under the trucks!" Johnson shouted.

The general was the first to crawl under a vehicle. Taylor stumbled right after him, squeezing beside Eisenhorn. Gilda dragged Straper with her as he kept shouting, "Why me?" Victoria and Zubair got under the other truck, followed by Johnson.

"Slate, quit messing around!" Victoria shrieked. "Don't let a single missile land near me!"

"Your wish is my screw-up!" Slate told her. He sent more bolts at the remaining missiles. All the projectiles exploded into bright orange balls. Flaming debris rained on the trucks.

The Helmet Man stopped firing. "All right, just wait here, folks. I'll go punch the kangaroo turd who's responsible for this right in the wombats."

With that crude statement, Slate flew upward.

***

The drone was about the size and shape of a human-piloted fighter jet. It was sleek, black, and made to kill. It was equipped with sixty missiles and five hundred tracker bullets. The Western Union flag was painted on its side. Its cameras saw everything. It had spotted the two trucks and inquired with its handler what to do. The handler said to kill them all.

As per usual, the drone had sent an electromagnetic pulse to disable all electronic equipment on the ground. Then it fired several missiles to wipe the pests from the Earth. Somewhere, Houdini was laughing as he watched all this from his holographic screen.

But a strange turn of events occurred. The missiles didn't hit the targets, and now an enemy was approaching. The drone could not feel surprise, but it was confused, having no idea what it was up against as the Helmet Man came at it.

And somewhere, Houdini was gaping.

***

Slate flew right at the drone.

He was going over a hundred miles an hour, arms to his side and electric bolts trailing behind him. The drone easily spotted his approach and turned toward the Helmet Man. It launched a missile, observing what Slate would do.

The Helmet Man threw several bolts of lightning. One bolt hit the missile, destroying it, while the others continued toward the drone. The machine weaved out of the way, the bolts passing it. Slate threw more bolts as he approached his enemy, but the drone dropped down, moved left, and did a smooth spiral, not getting hit even once.

It was time to take the big guns out. The drone fired all its tracker bullets at Slate. He made a sharp right turn and flew out of the bullets' path.

"Missed me, you worthless butterfly!" Slate jeered.

But they don't call them tracker bullets for nothing. The bullets had small fins on the side that allowed them to change direction on their own and follow their target. They could also propel themselves for a full minute.

After coming around in a large arc, the bullets were back on Slate's trail.

Slate groaned. "When did bullets stop going straight?"

The Helmet Man flew to the side. One bullet grazed him, making his arm bleed. The drone circled around Slate and released three more missiles. This situation was getting hopeless. Where could he go now? Then he remembered how the drone shorted out the electronic devices. Maybe it was time to fight fire with fire.

The tracker bullets were almost on him. The missiles came from the other side. Slate stopped in midair, hovering in place. He then raised his palms toward the swarm of bullets. Arcs of energy sparked out of his fingers. The energy fried the tracker bullets. They could no longer follow him. Slate flew down. The bullets passed right over him. Only one struck him, but it bounced harmlessly off his silver helmet.

Slate flew forward again, avoiding the three missiles still in hot pursuit. He pulled up and now flew toward the heavens. The missiles followed. Now he'd had enough. Spinning around, he shot a bolt of lightning from each hand. Two missiles blew up in a blazing eruption, but the third was almost on him. He kicked the air beneath his feet, producing an electric arc that hit the third missile. The explosion almost consumed Slate, but he accelerated up and avoided the explosion's destructive radius, though his legs did get burnt.

Observing this impressive routine, the drone decided to take drastic actions. It flew toward Slate and unleashed all fifty of its missiles.

"Now that's the definition of overkill," he said.

The missiles went in all directions. Slate realized he would only be able to short out some of them before getting struck. His only realistic option was to flee.

Slate flew through a gap between three incoming missiles. It was close, but he made it, almost brushing past a projectile. All fifty missiles changed course to pursue him. Each one could fly for half an hour before running out of fuel. Slate knew he couldn't outlast them. He saw only one other option. He flew up higher. The swarm of missiles rocketed after him. If he could get high enough, their engines would freeze. Slate didn't know if he could fly that high, but it was the least stupid idea he had.

But he wouldn't have a chance to implement it. The drone, taking him by surprise, rammed into him. Slate felt a few of his ribs crack from the impact.

The drone flew toward the missiles, the Helmet Man on the tip of its nose.

"Ugh! Screw you, airplane!"

The autonomous jet would act like a kamikaze pilot, flying at its own missiles in order to kill itself along with Slate. They were only ten seconds away from oblivion.

Not wanting to go down without a fight, Slate punched his fist into the drone. He sent ten thousand volts into it. The drone's circuits were fried. Its engines died.

The aircraft was now free-falling to the ground, the missiles almost upon it. Slate planted his feet on the body of the drone and launched himself off.

And then the world became an inferno.

***

Bright light bathed the area. A shockwave stirred up the sand. Hiding under the trucks proved to be a valuable idea, for if anyone had been standing up in the open, they would have been blown off their feet and pelted with debris. The trucks shook and even tilted, but they weathered the storm. Gilda felt sand hit her face. Straper screamed. Everyone else covered their heads, letting out muffled cries of their own. The ground continued to shake. Flames streaked the sky. Gilda feared the explosion would consume them all, that they would burn alive.

Instead, they survived. The sand soon stopped swirling. The fire above began to dim. Gilda opened her eyes. She and the others got out from under their vehicles. They looked up and saw a sight that made Taylor whistle.

A miniature sun had appeared in the sky. Its flames gave off a lively orange light. Half a hundred vapor trails led up to the sight of the explosion, all of them following a similar path. It almost looked like a stem attached to the bottom of a fiery blossom.

"That's something ..." Johnson said.

"Geez, won't this nightmare ever end?" Straper asked.

"Enjoy the view!" the general barked.

"Hey, I almost got turned into Kentucky Fried Cadet!"

"Great, now I'm hungry!"

"Look!" Taylor yelled.

A silver flash smashed into the ground. The group briefly covered their faces. Dirt sprinkled down on them. Gilda peered through her fingers. A smoking trail of dug-up ground led to a steaming crater. Bolts of electricity spat out of it.

"That must be him!" she yelled.

"Stay back!" Johnson yelled. "Electricity's flying everywhere!"

A hand reached out of the crater and clawed its way up, pulling along the Helmet Man.

"Ugh ... seriously, who'd you people piss off?" he asked.

***

The screen turned to static, the last blurred images showing a man in a silver helmet.

Houdini shut the screen off. "This can't be! What is the meaning of this?"

"Clearly, the drone didn't work," Repulsa said.

"Shut up! Are you glad we failed?"

"No, but I'm glad we found him."

Houdini got out of his chair and faced her. "Why?"

She gave a small smirk. "No reason."

"This is outrageous! I'm calling that buffoon." Houdini snatched the phone from its charger and pounded some numbers in. The call was answered almost immediately.

"I ... I don't know what happened," the voice said.

"Your drone failed!" Houdini yelled. "How could you let this occur?"

"That man in the helmet. It must be the prisoner Victoria went to visit. I didn't—"

"What! You didn't think to find out who she was meeting?"

"But didn't you know already?"

"Whatever, just get another drone!"

"I don't know if I can. The Western Union might—"

"Fine, you are clearly no help. I'll have to clean up your mess myself."

Houdini slammed the phone into the receiver, seething.

"Was that our contact?" Repulsa asked with childish innocence.

"He forgets his place ... After he gives us the prototype, I'll kill him myself."

"What about the survivors? What about *him*?"

Houdini let out a breath. He tapped his fingers on his desk. "Take Sandtrap with you and kill them all. I will share what we saw with the Gifted. They need to know Slate is alive."

Taylor put some gel on Slate's arm where the tracker bullet had grazed him. The gel was dark crimson and had little white dots suspended in it. As soon as the goo touched his flesh, the dots began to break apart and settle in his wound.

"What is this slime anyway?" Slate asked, lying on a mat with his chest bare.

"It's a growth patch," Taylor said. "The white dots are nanobots. The red gel itself is a cross between a bandage and artificial stem cells, a true technological feat."

"Can you put any of that fancy stuff on my broken ribs?"

"No, this particular type of growth patch is made for flesh wounds only. Besides, we don't want your bones to heal improperly. There, this wound will be fixed in a jiffy."

Slate cocked his head. "What's a jiffy?"

Taylor sighed. "The gel should harden, but don't pick at it."

Slate hopped on his feet and put on his clothes. "All right, thanks for the advice."

"Get back on the mat," Taylor ordered. "You need to heal."

"I'm fine, you quack. Stop babying me."

Taylor waved him away. "Fine, do as you will."

"Great, then let's get going."

"What are you talking about?" Johnson asked, walking up to him. Everyone except Slate had eaten, though no one was especially hungry besides Eisenhorn, who chowed down three rations' worth of food. Now everyone was asleep, their weariness finally getting to them.

"Time to go," Slate said. "Come on! Get those legs pumping."

"These people need rest," Johnson said.

"You know, I still haven't gotten that 'thank you' for saving all your lives."

Johnson exhaled. "I am grateful. We all are. But we're not like you. We can't shake off fatigue like you can. These people need rest. Taylor needs rest. I need rest."

"You regular people always need food or water. What are you, plants? You're all like, 'I need water!' or, 'Please don't electrocute me!' Bah!"

"We're staying."

"Fine, but I bet another drone's gonna be here any minute."

"Look, even if we wanted to go, we can't. The trucks are fried."

"Then just walk. It's only a couple hundred miles."

"I can't tell if you're joking or just crazy."

"Both! He, he, he!"

"He has a point, Johnson," Taylor said. "We can't stay here any longer."

Johnson sighed. "All right, have it your way."

Slate chuckled. "Thank you, I will."

"But give these people five more minutes of rest. They deserve that much."

"Okay, but you unload the trucks and make sure to grab plenty of water. You know, those lubricants you so desperately need. It's gross how much normal people drink."

Johnson sighed yet again. He went with Taylor to unload all the food, water, weapons, and other provisions for the trip. After they were done, Johnson woke up everyone. They weren't happy about it.

"Why don't we just take the trucks?" Victoria asked.

"Because their wiring and computers are fried, and the batteries are dead," Johnson said. "Or have you forgotten already?"

"I just thought you might have fixed it by now."

Johnson ignored her. He went over to Straper, who was still sleeping on the ground, and shook him awake.

Straper smacked his dry lips. "Hope this is a dream ..."

"So do I," Johnson said.

***

They walked until dusk, which was even harder than it sounded. Heat roasted them all, burning their skin. Taylor passed around sunscreen to everyone and advised them to wear hats.

Slate laughed. "Ha, even the sun hates you!"

Everyone kept pace, stopping only to drink from their canteens.

"How much water is left?" Taylor asked.

Johnson shook his head. "Not enough."

Everyone also carried their fair share, except for Slate, who carried nothing.

"You have super strength and won't give us a hand?" Victoria snapped.

Slate shrugged. "Hey, I'm not the one that needs constant watering."

Their destination was a distant village. Johnson saw on his map that it was the closest civilized area. It would be at least three days before they reached it, but they only had enough water for two more days, so Johnson asked Slate a serious question.

"Can you fly us out of here?"

"No, I'd be constantly electrocuting anybody holding on to me," Slate said. "Learned that the hard way when I tried rescuing a cat from a tree."

"Why not get us help?"

"I don't really inspire love in people. Someone might try to shoot me down from the sky or kill me. Not many people around here would want to help you guys anyway. I mean, the Western Union isn't exactly well liked by the African people. A military base is also out of the question. They'd only tie me up in a basement like you guys did. Just walk. We'll be fine."

"Okay, how about you get a truck and drive it out here?"

"Never learned to drive. Driving's for losers who can't fly. Besides, what if another drone came to kill you? I can't leave my weakling friends alone."

"Nice of you to say …"

So, they kept walking. Gilda watched Straper trudge along. She decided to walk next to him. Straper didn't seem to notice her until she began to send a number of questions his way.

"Why were you in the Bunker when everyone was supposed to go to the surface?"

"Oh ..." Straper mumbled. "I was ditching. Didn't want to go to that stupid inspection. Lucky me, I guess ..."

"You were with Henry, right?"

"Yeah ... when he bit the big one ..."

"How did he behave before he died?"

"Brave, I guess ..."

"That's good to know."

"Yeah, that icy-eyed thug used me as a punching bag. Henry stood up for me, actually. Told the creep to stop. I don't know why he did it, but he saved me, even though I was mean to him all those times. He died because of me ..."

Gilda glared at him. "Why did you torture him? Why did you bully him, hurt him, make him feel weak? Why?"

"I don't know. I suppose I just wanted to fit in. He seemed like a good target, so I picked on him for a while. Got popular real fast."

"It was all just to get popular? Despicable ..."

Straper sighed. He kicked at the sandy soil as they marched on.

***

The group stopped as the sun began to set. Nobody except Slate was spared from exhaustion. Straper fell to the ground. Eisenhorn passed out right then and there. Gilda slumped down with a little more dignity and fell asleep.

Taylor sat on the ground and rubbed his brow. "Johnson, I don't know how much longer we can take this."

"It'll be at least another two days," Johnson said. "Try to hang on."

Zubair helped Victoria along. She hadn't been able to walk on her own for over an hour. The loyal bodyguard panted and sweated. He placed Victoria on the ground and plopped down next to her. She wasn't built like the rest of the group. Living a privileged life, she rarely exercised her legs, let alone trekked across the Sahara.

Slate just stood there, looming over them.

"You're the sorriest bunch of wimps I've ever seen!" he yelled in his trademark constipated voice. "I could be in Vegas right now getting babes. Instead, I'm stuck here with you sad sacks."

"Watch over the camp ..." Taylor moaned. "Need ... sleep ..."

"Seriously? Fine, go ahead and rest! May I massage your filthy feet?"

Taylor didn't respond. He was already fast asleep.

Everyone else had also lost consciousness, their stores of energy tapped from the journey. Only Johnson stayed awake long enough to tell Slate something.

"We need to talk ... later ..."

Johnson then curled up and fell into a deep slumber.

As the Helmet Man watched his sleeping companions, he considered leaving them. Getting help was no option, and he didn't know anything about Africa. Anyway, they would be dead soon if they stayed out here much longer.

Then again, if it wasn't for that kid who died, he might still be buried under six feet of dirt, and with the kid dead, the only ones he could repay that debt to were these desperate people. He also needed to find his father. His dad wasn't with the Western Union anymore. He would already have come if that had been the case. But the Zaidi girl could help him find his dad. She was rich and had smarts. And until he found his father, these people were all Slate had, so he sat down and waited for the others to wake.

He had things to tell them.

***

It was night when Gilda woke up, but it wasn't dark. The stars shined down on them. The air had gone from blazing hot to deathly cold in only a few hours.

Taylor, meanwhile, went to shake Straper awake.

"Can't a guy get some rest?" Straper grumbled.

"Soon, but now it's story time," Taylor said.

From the corner of her eye, Gilda saw Zubair wake up Victoria. The beauty queen wouldn't be getting much sleep, Gilda thought. Johnson did the same with Eisenhorn. The general swore up a storm before rubbing his eyes awake.

Taylor now walked over to her, but she was already standing before he reached her.

"What's up?" Gilda asked.

"Slate wants to explain what's going on," Taylor said.

The group gathered around Slate, who sat cross-legged like some kind of monk. He waited until all of them settled down before beginning.

"The princess here wanted me to give her answers," Slate said.

Victoria let the nickname slide, for the moment had come.

"I don't have all of them," the Helmet Man said. "But I can give you my tale."

"How complicated is this story?" Straper asked. "My head already hurts from all the stuff that's been going on."

"It's simple. I'm a supersoldier created by the Western Union."

General Eisenhorn scoffed. "Sure, why would the military need you when they got soldiers like me? Right, Johnson?"

Johnson remained quiet.

"I was born in a lab," Slate said. "I was born to fight. Because of genetic engineering, drugs, and weird science stuff, I got special powers. I don't breathe, eat, sleep, or drink. And yes, I don't poop. Get your minds outta the gutter. I shoot electricity, conduct it, fly, move super fast, regenerate, and sense my environment with vibrations and an electric-field thingy. Not that you can tell, but I'm Asian too. They thought I could've infiltrated the Chinese Empire, but that plan had to be scrapped after I got my helmet. I can also go into hibernation if I'm hurt badly enough. All this in one package."

"Were you in hibernation when Marker found you?" Taylor asked.

Gilda felt a sudden burst of emotion but suppressed it.

"You got it," Slate said. "But you're getting ahead of me. Where was I?"

Johnson leaned in. "You're saying the Western Union made you?"

"Yep, they wanted superhuman freaks to fight their wars. I guess you regular folks weren't working out. Scientists were gathered from around the globe and given the world's most advanced labs to make us. These scientists called themselves the Keymasters. They wanted to 'unlock' human potential or some nonsense. I was the second soldier they made. They cobbled some DNA together from scratch and impregnated a bunch of women with it. These women then gave birth to us supersoldiers. Most of the dames died in childbirth. So did my mom. Never knew her. Can't say I care."

Slate clenched his fist. "Those scientists ... They poked and prodded us to make sure we fit their image. I hated every moment of it, but I managed to ignore them and even learned to fight back by irritating them. Only my father gave a damn about me. He's not my real dad, just a scientist who took pity on me. He always talked to me like I was a person and not some kind of dog in training. That made me happy ..."

He sighed. "But when I reached my preteens, my powers began to fully develop. I couldn't control them. I killed so many. They put this helmet on me. I know ... I know why they had to do it ... but how? How did they do that? How could they take my sight away? How could they leave me in the dark? How come they hated me!"

"Slate, calm down," Johnson said with a raised hand. Everyone around Slate stared at him as though he were about to turn on them.

The Helmet Man flexed his fingers. "I think I'll skip that part of the story."

His audience relaxed some.

Slate went on. "After I learned to 'see' and control my powers, I began to get missions. I mostly worked in South America. At first, the missions were simple. Destroy the truck. Kill those men. Take that plane down. I couldn't read, still can't, so I was pretty useless at gathering info. But my sensing abilities allowed me to dabble in some spy work. I was probably the Western Union's most lethal killer. Well, until ..."

"What happened?" Gilda asked.

"Another supersoldier, the first one, went berserk, killed a lot of civilians. I was told to stop him. I managed to kill the freak, but I got a huge chunk of meat taken out of me, so I went into hibernation like a fricking grizzly bear. Problem is I can't wake up until I'm fully healed, which could take forever. When I finally did, I was being poked at by some little snot with a shovel. Got a little irked, grabbed him, and ... that's how I ended up here. Questions?"

Silence hung over them like a bad odor. No one dared to break this peace for a while. It was Victoria who finally spoke up.

"Just how many supersoldiers are there?"

"There were eight others besides me and the guy I killed, but the military might have made more since then. Why do you ask, Princess?"

"Because one of them murdered my father."

"Time to start explaining, girly!" Eisenhorn yelled.

"Yeah, start talking!" Straper joined in.

Victoria stiffened and scooted backward slightly.

"Settle down," Johnson told everyone. He turned to Victoria. "It's time to fess up. Why are you after Slate? He told his story. Now you tell yours."

"Slate may be willing to talk, but I have a right to privacy," she said. "If any of you try to force me, you'll have to deal with Slate and Zubair."

"Why do I have to help you?" Slate asked.

"You're my subordinate. We had a deal."

"Quit being a spoiled brat. I only agreed to talk."

"Zubair, do something!"

"Ms. Zaidi, maybe it is time you told them," the bodyguard said. "We need these people's full cooperation if we are to survive."

"Yeah, spill the beans," Slate told her. "I gave you information. Now you do the same. Quidditch prong bono!"

"I think you mean *quid pro quo*, if I'm not mistaken," Taylor said.

"Shut up! I don't know French."

Taylor pinched the bridge of his nose. "It's Latin ..."

"Fine!" Victoria yelled. "Have it your way. I'll tell you my secrets so you can all judge me." She breathed deeply, cooling off. "I don't like telling stories, so bear with me."

"Can't be any worse than Slate's," Straper said.

"Shut your hole!" Slate whined.

Victoria sighed. "I got to start by talking about my father, Ammar Zaidi." She looked at the sky and sighed again. "My father wasn't a very ... open person. He rarely showed affection to me or my brother, but I knew he cared.

Lawrence, my brother, couldn't keep up with me at much. I was just better than him at most things. At first, my father tried to teach him about running the company. He wanted Zaidi Industries to be run by one of his children. But it wasn't Lawrence. My father chose me instead to take his place. Lawrence just wasn't suited for the job. He ended up staying at home with my mother.

"So, my father trained me, teaching me management skills and investment strategies. He even let me sit in at some of the meetings. When I was fifteen, I ran my first board meeting. I wooed them all. I soon began to take my father's place when he became sick. By the age of sixteen, I was running the entire corporation half the time.

"My older brother ... I realized he had nothing. Our mother died after falling down a flight of stairs, so he had nobody left to spend time with. Lawrence was struggling at school and didn't have any friends. He even got bullied on occasion. That's why I started to teach him the ways of the business, long after my father gave up. He learned, but much slower than me. He's still learning." She let out a laugh, but it dried up quickly.

"A few months ago, my father disappeared. I didn't know where he went. Nobody did. He just vanished into thin air. I had to pick up his duties and do everything on my own. Thankfully, I had Zubair and Lawrence to help me."

She gave her bodyguard a smile. He returned a smaller one.

Victoria continued. "I tried to find him, but he had disappeared from the face of the Earth. I contacted the police, private detectives, friends, family, business associates, but nothing materialized. Nothing was revealed."

"I never heard of this," Taylor said.

"It was all kept very hushed. Then, just a few weeks ago, I got a call. It was from a bodyguard who worked for my father. My father had been hiding out on his boat somewhere in the Black Sea. When the bodyguard did his routine check, he ..."

Victoria lowered her head, trying to hide a trickle of tears, but it did no good. They leaked out and hit the ground, the sand absorbing them.

"He found my father dead," she said. "After that, I flew out to see the body. The coroner said my father died of a heart attack. I couldn't believe it. Father's health was impeccable, and why had he gone into hiding without telling Lawrence or me? It was so confusing. I decided to search through his room on the boat and ... I found something ... a hidden camera behind a mirror. The camera, as it turns out, was recording when I found it." Victoria gulped. "I don't know why I looked through the recordings, but I believe it was because I knew, deep down, that my father's death was no accident."

A white moon hung overhead. It seemed so round and watchful that someone might have mistaken it for an eye. Despite the warm glow it emitted, the moon seemed to have a certain malice, filling the air with a foreboding atmosphere.

"So, I looked through it," Victoria said. "But I couldn't ... Never in my ..."

"You saw someone kill your dad," Slate said. "Someone like me."

"The man wore a balaclava. He sprayed a canister filled with an unknown substance in my father's face. Then he ... vanished ..."

"Vanished?" Johnson asked.

"Into thin air ... He just appeared out of nowhere and vanished ... I had the recording secretly analyzed, but it showed no signs of being doctored."

"So, someone ... teleported onto your dad's boat and killed him?" Gilda asked.

"Yes ..." Victoria took a breath in and continued. "Also, I found my father's journal. My father wrote about how he thought soldiers with ... abilities were coming after him, soldiers made by the Western Union. Of course, I've heard rumors about the military doing such experiments, but I thought it was just mindless gossip. I thankfully didn't show anyone else the journal except Zubair. Most people would have assumed Father had gone insane, but I remembered the video. I saw that man vanish. That murderer ... I had to bring him to justice. I started searching for anything unusual, doing research, checking databases. It got to the point where I used corporate resources to tap into classified military communication channels."

"You did *what*?" Johnson questioned.

"What!" the general bellowed. "How dare you? You're gonna be pruned for that! Just you wait!"

"Sorry, but I couldn't go to the Western Union with my suspicions. I carried a very dirty secret about a government that controls two-thirds of the world. Being arrested and pruned would have been a best-case scenario, even with my connections."

"So, you've been investigating this all on your own," Taylor said.

"Not even my brother knows. I only told Zubair so he could protect me."

"Ammar Zaidi was a great man," Zubair said. "He gave me a job when my family was on the verge of homelessness. When the Saudi Arabian Army was disbanded, I had no way to feed my children. But then Mr. Zaidi gave me the job of protecting his only daughter. Bless Mr. Zaidi. Bless his soul."

Victoria nodded. "Yes, bless him."

"How'd you find out about Slate?" Straper asked.

"I heard about Slate's discovery over one of the military communication channels I tapped. Using my superior status, I simply waltzed into the Bunker, expecting a grand welcome. I was not disappointed, thanks to Jeffery."

"So, we've come full circle," Johnson said, brushing off Victoria's last comment. "But who killed Ammar Zaidi? Where did the Keymasters and these other supersoldiers go? And who exactly attacked the Bunker? We're caught in a web of conspiracy. How these people found the Bunker, got clearance codes to land there, and managed to command a military drone is also a mystery. But I have a theory about that."

"Which is … ?" Taylor dared ask.

"The location of the Bunker, the codes, the drone, and the supersoldiers all fall under the umbrella of the Western Union …"

"Johnson!" the general cried. "You're talking treason! Are you saying our superiors are trying to kill us? I oughta throttle you! This nonsense about supersoldiers is nothing more than the deranged thinking of a psychotic human battery and a bored rich girl!"

"Sir, I'm only suggesting there may be a mole in the military working with whoever is trying to cover up Ammar Zaidi's death."

"That's impossible! What mole are you blabbering about? There is no conspiracy. Slate's a monster made by the Chinese Empire to discredit our fine leaders. This Zaidi girl is also a conspirator. Where is your loyalty, Johnson? You're lucky the president isn't here to see this nonsense. I'm sick of all this talk of supermen and vanishing assassins. Why are you taking this girl on her word? Do you believe the helmet freak too? I bet these cadets here have a better sense of patriotism than you do!"

Eisenhorn turned to Straper, almost foaming at the mouth. "What do you think, cadet? I hope you aren't falling for this elaborate ruse!"

"No—no, sir ..."

General Eisenhorn turned to Gilda next and grabbed her under the chin, making her look at him. "Come on, girl! You can't believe this. It's too crazy! It's too—"

Eisenhorn felt a fist slam into his face. He tumbled onto his back. He then looked up to see Johnson standing over him. His fist was still red from delivering the blow.

"Go back to sleep," Johnson managed to say in a level voice. "The only one speaking nonsense is you. And if you ever touch one of these cadets again ..."

The general snarled. He rubbed his cheek and crawled away from the scene, muttering obscenities to himself. Gilda's face darkened. Straper and Taylor stared at their feet.

Slate clapped his hands. "Well, this has been an awkward bonding experience."

***

It was morning when Johnson passed everyone their rations for the day. He gave some to Eisenhorn. The general took it without looking Johnson in the eye. He was about to sulk away when Johnson held his palm out.

"Give me your gun," he said.

Eisenhorn snorted. "Or what? You'll hit me again?"

"Perhaps."

Eisenhorn growled. He handed Johnson his piece and stormed off to eat his food alone. Johnson shook his head. Taylor, observing this, decided to walk over and talk with Johnson.

"Rough times, aren't they?" Taylor asked.

"You got it." Johnson gave a weary moan. "What did I do last night?"

"The only thing you could do. Eisenhorn needs to know his boundaries. He'll get over it."

"It's always bothered me that I treat him like a mental patient when he expects to be treated like an officer. But when I saw him fighting at the Bunker, he seemed like his old self, like a real soldier. I wonder if I treat him like a real general ..."

"I'd advise against that. Why he isn't getting psychiatric help, I will never know."

"It has something to do with the president. He and Eisenhorn were good friends at one time. The military also probably doesn't want the public to know one of the Western Union's greatest generals has become a raving loon."

"So, you punched a friend of the most powerful man in the world?"

"I said they were friends at one time. Past tense." Johnson frowned.

"What's the matter?" Taylor asked.

"A thought just occurred to me. Just how long was Slate buried underground?"

"A long time. It's hard to say. Do you think we should mention it? Does Slate even have any idea how long he was buried?"

"Let's keep this to ourselves. Who knows what kind of reaction Slate would have? We're going to need him at his best in order to survive."

***

The Sahara was even hotter than the day before. Gilda's vision was going blurry. She had trouble keeping balance and stumbled. Regardless, she kept moving forward.

The only way they could navigate in the desert was by the sun's position, since they had no electronic equipment, no compass, and no noticeable landmarks. This meant they had to trudge in daylight, risking heatstroke and being spotted, though the darkness would offer little concealment anyway, since the Western Union's drones could see in infrared.

The group was five hours into their journey before Victoria fell. Without being told, Zubair snatched his employer up, cradling her in his massive arms.

The next one to pass out was General Eisenhorn, who grumbled about pruning and betrayal before falling on his face.

"Slate, please carry him," Johnson said.

"In your dreams!" Slate scoffed. "Let the old fart die!"

"Do it. I'm in no mood to be trifled with."

"I have to do everything..." Slate walked over to where Eisenhorn had fallen and threw him over his shoulder like a sack of potatoes. The general grumbled but did not protest.

"Pretty soon, I'm gonna have to carry you all," the Helmet Man complained. "Just because I'm super strong doesn't mean you can use me as a pack mule."

"Actually, it does," Johnson said. "Keep moving!"

The group slithered forward. The temperature continued to rise.

An hour later, Straper fell as well, tumbling onto his side.

"Slate, grab him," Johnson said.

"Oh, come on!" Slate yelled, but he complied, throwing the cadet over his free shoulder. Now he was carrying two, but he showed little if any sign of fatigue.

Gilda kept on going, now swerving. The sun was getting lower, signaling late afternoon. Had it already been two days since the Bunker was attacked? Time flew fast, but her vow of vengeance was not forgotten. She would move forward.

They came upon a group of rocky hills. Half-dead bushes dotted these humps.

"I'm going to climb one of those," Johnson said. "I might spot some help."

Without complaint, the group moved forward, reaching the hills in about fifteen minutes. Johnson trudged up the first one they came upon. Once he reached the peak, he didn't seem to do much at first except stand on tiptoes. Then, urgently, he began to wave everyone up to join him. Excited but tired, the group ran up the hill. When they reached the top, Zubair and Slate put down their passengers, waking them up.

"Water ..." Straper croaked.

Taylor gave him a canteen. "Don't drink too much. There's only a little."

Straper took a greedy sip. "Ah ... thanks. What's up?"

"I spotted something in the distance," Johnson said.

Eisenhorn and Victoria, both groggy and irritable, also had sips of water.

"What exactly do you see?" Victoria asked.

Johnson leaned forward. "A convoy, I believe."

"We're getting out of here!" Straper cheered.

"Idiot, they could be terrorists for all we know," Gilda told him.

"Oh ..."

"That may be true," Johnson said. "But they could also be our salvation."

"Why don't we find out for sure?" Taylor asked. "Slate, what do you sense?"

The Helmet Man put his hands on his hips. "They're pretty far away, but there seems to be ten trucks. Can't tell if they're armed or not."

"Yeah, they have guns," Straper said. "Man, I thought we had a ride."

"How can you tell they have weapons?" Taylor asked.

"It's hard to make out, but I can see an armed guy hanging off the side of one truck."

Zubair squinted. "Yes, I can see. You have very good eyes."

"What do you expect from a stud like me?"

"They're not Western Union soldiers," Zubair said. "I'm sure of that."

"Great," Victoria said. "Why can't we catch a break?"

"Okay, here's the plan," Slate said. "I'll just go over there and kill them all. Then you guys can steal their trucks. Pretty smart of me, huh?"

"No!" Johnson yelled. "For all we know, they're friendly."

"Oh, so friendly they have guns?" Victoria asked.

"They could just be protecting themselves," Johnson said.

"A lot of good that's gonna do them," Slate said.

Eisenhorn said nothing. His eyes were fixed on the shape wriggling in the sand.

"The answer is no," Johnson told Slate. "We can think of another way."

The sandy soil started moving in more than one spot around Eisenhorn. Soon, most of the ground began to shift and turn.

"Johnson!" the general yelled.

The Helmet Man snapped to attention and made a fist. "Shit, they snuck up on us ... Must have been here the whole time."

"What are you—?" Johnson asked, but then he looked at the shifting sand.

"No ..." he whispered. "Pinocchios."

Taylor and Zubair went on high alert.

Straper gave a false laugh. "Uh ... you guys talking about the puppet?"

"No ..." Gilda said with a blank face. "They're not."

Mechanical spider limbs began to sprout from the soil, feeling for human flesh.

Victoria screamed. Everyone else just stared.

The Helmet Man chuckled. "We really can't catch a break, can we?"

Countless insectoid limbs poked out of the sand, squirming.

As revolting as the sight was, it didn't distract the team for long.

"Get back!" Johnson yelled. "Go behind Slate!"

"What am I, a human shield?" the Helmet Man cried.

"Yes! Everyone, get behind him. Hurry!"

They all did so, gathering in a small group behind Slate. Zubair and Taylor both took their pistols out and aimed them at the robotic spider legs.

"No worries," Slate said. "We're standing on solid rock. From what I remember, Pinocchios can't dig through that."

"They won't have to," Zubair said.

It was soon clear the legs had bodies. Eight limbs were clumped together for each Pinocchio that lurked beneath the surface. One Pinocchio's limbs bent down, their tips touching the ground. The creature then pushed itself out of the soil to reveal its hideous form.

"Okay, that thing freaks me out," Straper said.

Victoria shivered. "Join the club."

The mechanical menace had a disk-shaped body that was sand-colored and almost a foot long. The head had two glass eyes and a very long nose, much like the proboscis of a mosquito. This appendage was how the machine got its odd name.

The Pinocchio lowered its body to the ground, ready to pounce.

Slate just pointed his finger at the Pinocchio and zapped it. The machine shuddered and collapsed, no longer animated.

"They weren't able to jump before," he said. "Must be an upgrade. Whatever, those little pukes don't scare me. Bring them on!"

Half a dozen Pinocchios began to rise from the sand with twitching noses.

"You spoke too soon," Taylor said.

The Helmet Man lifted his foot. "Guess it's time for you guys to vamoose!"

He slammed his foot into the soil. The smell of ozone filled the air. A shock-wave resonated. Half the hillside became unstable, specifically the side that everyone except Slate stood on. They lost their footing as the ground crumbled beneath them. The Pinocchios buried in that area managed to scurry to safety before the avalanche picked up speed. Victoria screamed again, and Eisenhorn uttered several foul curses as they went down. Straper grabbed Gilda's arm, hoping to gain some balance, but they both fell down the hillside anyway. Johnson did a log roll, managing to protect his neck while doing so. Taylor could only claw at the loose soil. They all came to a halt at the foot of the hill. All of them were lying in a pile of human limbs and sandy dirt. Zubair was the first to get up and helped pull everyone else to their feet.

"Is anyone hurt?" Johnson asked.

Everyone looked dirty and scraped up, but they didn't voice any complaints.

Zubair pointed at the hill. "There they are!"

The Pinocchios were crawling down the hillside, spreading out.

Johnson, Taylor, and Zubair all took out their guns. The general tried to get his own out but remembered that Johnson had confiscated it earlier that morning.

"Johnson, give me my piece!" Eisenhorn yelled.

"Sorry, sir, but I might need the extra ammo," Johnson said, taking his safety off. "Don't worry. I'll be sure to use it wisely."

Slate, meanwhile, was busy being an electric fly swatter. At first, it was an easy job. All he had to do was kill the things before they could pounce at him. But pretty soon, he needed to use his other hand as well to shock the little buggers. More spiders poured out of the ground. A few even managed to jump at him, but he was quick to zap them as they sailed through the air.

It was time to fly. Slate launched himself and zapped the Pinocchios from above. The whole endeavor had become something like shooting fish in a barrel. He noticed that some of the Pinocchios had begun to go down the hill and after the others. Slate was just about to help them when a bullet hit his head. It bounced off his indestructible helmet, not even leaving a scratch. The Helmet Man spun around to figure out who had shot at him.

From a nearby hill, two long barrels poked out of its slopes.

More drones.

Slate groaned. "I fricking hate this desert."

These new drones began firing at him. Slate flew to the left, dodging the bullets. To his relief, they weren't tracker bullets. He wanted to go over there and fight those snipers, but he couldn't leave the Pinocchios alone with the others. He would have to go after the sniper drones later while they shot at him in the meantime. And to make matters worse, the convoy of trucks Johnson had spotted earlier was now driving toward them, probably coming to investigate the noise.

"Just pile it all on, why don't you?" Slate snapped.

Zubair fired a bullet. It nailed a pouncing Pinocchio right in the abdomen. The horror landed dead at his feet.

"How many more rounds do you have?" Johnson asked Taylor as he shot another Pinocchio crawling down the hill.

"Not enough!" Taylor yelled.

The Pinocchios had surrounded them. Retreat was impossible. All the unarmed members of the group huddled together while Zubair, Taylor, and Johnson shot at the spiders. The Pinocchios kept coming in swarms. There were at least fifty of them.

"What do those things do exactly?" Straper asked Gilda.

"You should know!" she yelled. "We got taught this."

"You know I always ditch class! Don't expect me to—"

Appearing out of nowhere, the trucks they saw earlier pulled up. About thirty armed men unloaded, all wearing a variety of shabby clothing. They also wore scarves over their faces to protect themselves from the sand.

"Not good!" Johnson yelled as he shot another Pinocchio.

The men started yelling in Arabic and ran toward them.

"Why us?" Straper asked. "Seriously, why us?"

"This is madness!" Victoria exclaimed.

"Wait, look!" Gilda yelled.

The men fired their guns, but not at them.

Hundreds of Pinocchios had emerged from all of the surrounding hills and came down like a flood. The newcomers shot at the approaching swarm. They didn't even have to aim. The mechanical spiders were everywhere. Many Pinocchios got taken down, but the others merely crawled over their fallen comrades. Pretty soon, the first of the new swarm was only several yards away from the men. One man, who was closer to the Pinocchios than everyone else, shot wildly at the sea of spiders. A few of the machines scurried toward him. Straper soon realized what was happening.

"That guy's being a diversion. No! Get out of there!"

The newcomer kept shooting. A Pinocchio launched itself at him. He shot it out of the air. Another spider, however, managed to sneak up behind him and pounce on his leg. The man tried shaking it off as he kept shooting.

"What's gonna happen?" Straper cried over the gunshots.

"Don't look!" Gilda yelled. "We can't help him."

Barbs came out of Pinocchio's legs, impaling the man. He let out a sob but kept firing, trying to kill as many of the vermin as he could.

The Pinocchio then exploded, taking off his leg.

"What the hell?" Straper screamed.

Now choking on the pain, the newcomer fell on his back as his smoking stump oozed blood. Straper gagged and stared. A dozen more Pinocchios crawled over the man. Some wrapped their limbs around his arms. Others grabbed onto his torso or one remaining leg. But a particularly cruel machine planted itself on his face.

The man's screams turned high-pitched as the barbs went into him. One last pleading gasp escaped his lips before the Pinocchios exploded.

"Monsters!" Straper cried. "No!"

Victoria let out a small sob. Gilda shuddered. Eisenhorn offered no comment. The other newcomers were too busy shooting the Pinocchios to look at the carnage that had occurred, though some of them cried out in rage as they kept shooting the spiders.

More Pinocchios came forward. One pounced at another man, attaching itself to his chest. He screamed as it exploded. A third man died in a similar fashion. Two more lost a leg each, sobbing as they tried to stop the bleeding.

But now Pinocchios had begun to march not toward the newcomers but toward the trucks. The newcomers kept firing at them, but it did no good. One spider bomb pounced onto the tire of the nearest truck and set itself off. The truck tilted to its side. More Pinocchios surged forward. Although these devices were mainly designed to be suicide bombers, grabbing onto any moving target for dear life and exploding, the Pinocchios were now going after the trucks, the only means of escape.

One newcomer, much larger than the others, ran into one of the trucks. A few seconds later, he came back out with a rocket launcher.

"Yeah, kill those bugs!" Straper cheered.

Johnson, Taylor, and Zubair kept firing at the spiders. They were almost out of bullets, but the creatures were more focused on the trucks than the people for now.

The newcomer with the rocket launcher got on the truck and aimed his weapon at the center of the Pinocchio swarm. But before he could fire it, someone yanked the rocket launcher from his hands.

"I'll take this!" Slate yelled, standing next to the man on the truck rooftop. The man froze, too shocked to protest.

Slate chuckled and fired.

The rocket shot out, flying right at the hillside the sniper drones were hidden in. It hit the hill dead-on. Sand flew everywhere. A ball of fire consumed one of the drones, destroying it. The other drone crawled away from the smoking hole in the hill to seek another hiding spot. The sniper drone looked like a massive rifle with spindly spider legs attached to it. A few newcomers spotted the drone and shot at it. The sniper drone fired back, killing one newcomer and injuring another. However, the men sent a barrage of bullets at the thing, tearing its legs away and wrecking its gun. The robot soon toppled to the ground and spat sparks.

Slate gave the fallen drone a rude hand gesture. "Super! Now I can focus my efforts on killing those buggers down there."

The Helmet Man dropped the rocket launcher and flew away. The large man on the truck gawked. The other newcomers had a similar reaction but soon went back to shooting.

Slate pointed his fingers at the ground. The energy built up in his hands. "I call this one the bug zapper!"

Bolts of lightning thirty feet long hit the ground, killing dozens of Pinocchios as he flew overhead. The swarm of mechanical spiders stopped going after the trucks. They went after Slate instead while he continued to shoot electricity down at them.

"That's right, you cockroaches ... Follow big daddy ..."

Slate landed on top of a hill, far away from the trucks. He picked up a pinch of sand and rubbed it between his fingers.

"That ought to be enough metal."

The remaining Pinocchios swarmed around the hill from every direction. "Wait a little ..."

The spiders crawled uphill, closing in. They were only a few feet away. "Now die!"

He slammed his fist into the ground. Electricity coursed through the sand. His energy was able to flow through with only mild resistance. The metallic arachnids began to convulse. The hill shook. Dust flew up. The newcomers simply stared as debris and lightning filled the air.

Slate took his fist off the ground. All the Pinocchios had shorted out, no longer able to blow themselves up. They were so dead that their limbs didn't even twitch.

A minute later, Slate flew over and joined his friends and the newcomers. He gave a loud and obnoxious laugh that echoed over the hills. "Well, I just saved your lives for … oh, right … the third time!"

"Good job," Victoria scoffed. "What took you so long?"

"A simple 'thank you' is all I ask."

"I shall thank you," one of the newcomers said. The man took off his scarf, revealing short hair and a scruffy beard.

Slate threw up his hands. "Finally, someone with manners!"

"My name is Barir," the man said. "I am the leader of this group of weary travelers. I thank you. We are in your debt."

"I know … I know … I won't make you grovel too hard."

Barir laughed. "You are a funny man. I like that, for we have few funny men." He waved over the large man who had stood on the roof of the truck. "Africa, come over here."

The large man walked over and took off his scarf as well. He was even bigger than Zubair, but the grin on his face made it impossible not to warm up to him.

"You took off before I could say hello," Africa said.

"Sorry about that rocket launcher," Slate said. "It really does have a kick."

"Not many men can handle that weapon."

"I bet. What the hell kind of name is Africa anyway?"

"You're one to talk," Gilda said.

"Hey, Slate is a handsome name!"

"Who are you?" Africa asked her. "You look fierce."

"Gilda's my name. Say, think we can get a ride out of here?"

"Hey, you can't make those decisions on your own!" Eisenhorn yelled.

"He's right, Gilda," Taylor said. "Don't overstep your bounds."

"That being said, I was just about to make the same request," Johnson said. He turned to Barir. "You wouldn't mind, would you?"

Barir chuckled. "Of course not. Anything for our savior."

Slate and the others sat in the back of the last truck in the convoy. They were now heading to their new friends' campsite. Johnson passed around water, courtesy of their hosts.

"What were those things?" Straper asked.

"You mean the Pinocchios?" Taylor asked. "They're autonomous anti-personnel mines the Western Union scatters around the desert. They're meant to discourage travel and reduce terrorist activity within certain regions."

"They're terrible weapons," Johnson said. "I never cared for them. I just wish that area had been marked off as dangerous on the map."

"If it weren't for us, those men might have fallen into the same trap," Victoria said.

"Who are these guys anyway?" Gilda asked. "I like Africa. He has style. Barir also seems nice, but those other men didn't look too happy to see us."

"I could feel their beady little eyes on me," Eisenhorn said. "They're obviously terrorists. Why else were they in a Pinocchio zone?"

"Sir …" Johnson warned.

The general crossed his arms, pouting.

"It is suspicious they were traveling through an area the Western Union had mined," Zubair said. "Maybe they *are* terrorists."

"Or arms dealers," Victoria said.

"Or drug dealers!" Straper yelled.

Eisenhorn snapped to attention. "Drugs, where?"

"That's enough!" Johnson shouted. "We are guests of these people. There's no need to accuse them of being terrorists just because of their skin color."

"Yeah, these guys speak English," Slate said. "That's a blessing right there. I could never learn Spanish."

Taylor sighed. "They're speaking Arabic."

"Look, I know terrorists," Slate said. "They're a bunch of bigots, the hill-billies of the desert, but the guys that saved us were a mix of races, right? No way they're baddies."

Johnson turned to stone. "No ..."

"What?" Slate asked. "You know something I don't?"

Everyone else became just as serious as Johnson.

"Okay, now you're freaking me out," Slate said.

"Geez, Slate ..." Straper said. "Even I know about *them*."

"It can't be ... *them*, could it?" Victoria asked.

"The United Third," Eisenhorn growled. "Damn it."

"All right, who are you guys talking about?" Slate asked.

Johnson covered his face. "It's the United Third."

"You ... You don't think Barir and Africa are members, do you?" Gilda asked. "They seemed so nice. No way could they work for *him*."

"We were blind, too desperate for help," Zubair said.

Taylor covered his mouth. "If it is the United Third, then this is very bad indeed."

***

Africa tried overhearing the strangers in the back as he drove, but the roar of the engine made it impossible to listen, so he gave up.

He knew what Barir was doing. They could never have fought a man like Slate, so Barir figured they could lure him and his friends into the trucks and take them away to a United Third camp where Barir could contact Incognito.

"Who knew we would find them so fast?" Africa asked himself. "This is all too—"

Something zapped his shoulder. Africa gasped. His muscles tightened.

"Talking to yourself is a very bad habit," Slate said. "I should know."

Africa gurgled as Johnson pushed him to the passenger seat and took the wheel. Both he and Slate had climbed onto the sides of the truck to get to the front. Slate had then zapped Africa through an open window with a non-lethal amount of energy.

The Helmet Man opened the passenger door, still hanging off the side of the truck. "Nothing personal, though I don't usually let people live, if that makes you feel special."

With that, he grabbed Africa and threw him out of the truck.

The trucks ahead began to slow down when they saw in their mirrors that Africa had hit the ground, but Johnson swerved out of their way and went to the left. Slate, meanwhile, climbed in through the passenger side and pointed his finger out the window.

"I like a nice drive!" Slate yelled. "Ah, the wind through my hair."

Johnson smiled. "You don't have hair."

Ignoring him, Slate shot several bolts at the other trucks. Their engines died. The terrorists would be unable to pursue them. All they could do was yell curses and shake their fists.

"I'm glad we didn't have to kill anyone," Johnson said. "After all, they did treat us well. So, where are we headed next?"

With his super strength, Slate punched a hole right to the back of the truck. Johnson and everyone in the back almost had a heart attack.

"What are you doing?" Johnson screamed.

"Hey, guys!" Slate yelled, now able to talk with them.

"You idiot!" Victoria snapped. "Have you no self-control?"

"Naturally, so what's our destination?"

"We're going to Cairo, nitwit!"

"That's at least a day's drive," Johnson said, forcing himself to relax.

"I have a friend there," Victoria said. "We can hide out at his place until we plan our next course of action."

Johnson thought this out. Cairo was a bit far away, but if there was a mole in the Western Union, the mole would likely be keeping a close eye on all nearby military bases and towns. At least in Cairo they would have more options, not to mention be safer.

But just how far did the conspiracy go up? Who could they trust?

"Sir, can I have a word with you?" Johnson asked.

"What is it, Johnson?" Eisenhorn sneered. "What more can I do for master?"

Johnson brushed off the sarcasm. "Could you contact the president?"

The general gave a false laugh. "Why are you asking?"

"Listen, I don't know who's trying to cover up Ammar Zaidi's death and the supersoldiers, but we're going to need friends in high places, and I honestly can't think of anyone higher than the head of the Western Union. So, can you?"

"Yeah, but it'll have to be through the military mainframe."

"Good, because if we can't trust the president ..."

"While you guys do that, the rest of us can hide out at Goldberg's place," Victoria said.

"Good," Johnson said. "We're finally getting somewhere."

***

The meeting with the other Gifted had not gone well. Houdini had sat down and told them how survivors had escaped the massacre at the Bunker. When he mentioned Slate, all of the Gifted were surprised, all except Sebastian, snide as ever. They demanded to know where Slate had been hiding all this time and why he had decided to reappear. Houdini couldn't answer. How foolish he had looked.

Rage fermented inside him. It had been almost a day since he sent out Repulsa and Sandtrap. They better get results. He pounded the number into his phone and waited for Repulsa to answer. Not in any rush, she picked up on the sixth ring.

"You never call as often as you should," she said. "Work has consumed our lives."

"Shut your hole. Did you find them yet?"

"We found the trucks, but they seemed to have pulled a Houdini on us."

"Time is running out," Houdini growled. "Where are they?"

"The desert wind covered their trail. Don't worry. Sandtrap and I have this covered. They're on foot, so they couldn't have gotten far."

"So the trail was wiped clean due to the desert wind? That's the same excuse you gave me last time. Fool me once, shame on you. Fool me twice, shame on me."

"Yes, shame on you," Repulsa teased. "I'm glad we both see who's really at fault here. Now, if you'll excuse me, I have to clean up your mess."

She hung up. Houdini ground his teeth. He smashed the phone on the desk, spitting out a whole list of obscenities. The phone was soon reduced to a crumpled mess.

"I see we still haven't managed that anger," a voice spoke up.

A pale man in his thirties appeared behind Houdini. He wore a blue suit and round sunglasses that concealed his eyes. His black hair was also combed to the side. It was almost as oily as the smile that never left his face.

"Sebastian, I am in no mood for lectures," Houdini spat.

"There's always time to learn new things," Sebastian said.

Houdini spun around to face him. Houdini also wore a suit, except it was gray. He had a short haircut and a well-trimmed beard. But Houdini's most defining feature was the gigantic glass ball that was substituted for his right eye. It was black, hideous, and bulged out of his head like a boil ready to burst whenever he got angry.

And right now, the dark jewel looked ready to shoot out of his skull. Houdini threw his broken phone, but Sebastian didn't even flinch as it flew right through him, his image shivering.

"Conversing via hologram really does have its advantages," Sebastian said, still wearing his oily smile. "I don't have to worry about getting hit by flying objects. Speaking of flying objects, how's the hunt for Slate proceeding?"

"You were at the meeting. I shouldn't have to repeat myself."

"Fine, forget it. I want to ask you about the prototype. Is it ready yet?"

"Our contact says it will take a few more days. That little coward ... He keeps whining to me, criticizing me. He was the one who neglected to tell me Slate was the prisoner the Zaidi girl was visiting. How dare he talk back?"

"How could he have known Slate was important? It's not like he knew Slate was one of the Gifted. You, on the other hand, should have had the foresight to ask him about the prisoner."

"You expect too much from me. I'm no magician."

"Then why are you called Houdini?"

"Shut up!"

"You see, there's that anger again," Sebastian said. He paced around the room as if he were there in person, but in reality, the second-in-command of Cloak was halfway around the world, attending to other matters. "I really wish you would respect your superiors, but I clearly can't expect anything resembling manners from you."

"Did you come here just to taunt me?"

Sebastian stopped pacing, his everlasting smile growing. "The Mentor would like you not to kill Slate. He must be captured alive."

"What! This is outrageous! I already have to transfer the prototype to you, blow up a tower, murder those survivors, and run this laundering business. Now you want me to spare a traitor who killed one of our own."

"If you wish, I can bring up any objections you may have with the Mentor."

Houdini froze. "No ... I ... That's not necessary ..."

"Good, then I'll send you a little gift to make transporting Slate easier."

"What about the others? Do I need to keep them alive as well?"

"Perhaps Gilda Plato. She's the daughter of George Plato, the reclusive yet brilliant military scientist. The Mentor may have need of him."

"I see ... Use his daughter as bait to lure him out into the open. Very clever. Do I need to spare anyone else?"

"That won't be necessary. Make sure they die."

Their truck arrived at a mile-long line of vehicles. The traffic stretched all the way to the electric fence circling Cairo. Some vehicles were waved through. Many others were diverted around to another stretch of road beside the entry line that led back to the desert.

But most people didn't go back. Instead, they drove off the road and camped out near the fence. Gilda and Straper peered out the back of their truck. Thousands of refugees were living outside the city in tents and small huts. Vendors tried to sell their wares to passing vehicles. Children nearby played with a ratty soccer ball. Straper even saw camels walk by and a street performer eating fire. He couldn't help but be impressed at these exotic oddities.

Gilda, meanwhile, was only disgusted. Holes in the ground were used as bathrooms, attracting flies and other pests. Women and children picked through piles of garbage. Nobody looked like they had bathed in weeks. Some people even had boils covering their bodies.

She sniffed the air and gagged. "Gah ... what is this place?"

"A slum," Zubair said coldly.

Victoria put a hand on his shoulder and gave him a weak smile. She turned to the others. "This place is for people who have been displaced from their homes. The Western Union believes putting civilians in one area makes it easier to monitor them, reducing the risk of terrorism and uprisings. Of course, many of these refugees come here willingly to seek employment or flee from an ongoing conflict."

"Why are they all staying out here?" Straper asked.

"They can't get in. Most of these people are simply unable to contribute much in the city. In order to keep the population density down, they must stay out here until a place or job can be found for them. This is what most cities in the Occupied Territories look like. Alexandria, Baghdad, Istanbul, Johannesburg, the list goes on."

"Do any of these people ever make it into the city?" Gilda flared.

"A few, but it takes months."

"Wow, we work for some pretty evil people!" Slate yelled. "They have killer robots, put people in slums, and are taking over the world. Whoa, maybe I *am* the bad guy!"

"This is war," Johnson snapped as he drove. "It's no game. None of you should be looking outside anyway. What if you were spotted?"

"Most people get in," Taylor assured. "It just … takes time."

"If anything, we're being too nice to these maggots," Eisenhorn said. "We should be weeding out every terrorist with a bat and some attitude."

"Hush up," Johnson told him.

"So, how are we gonna get into Cairo?" Straper asked. "If these guys can't get in, what makes our chances any better?"

"Don't worry," Victoria said. "I have my tricks."

As the line of cars crawled forward, Gilda continued staring outside. She watched a young woman bathing a toddler in dirty water. Next, she saw an old man behead a chicken with his bare hands. But what really caught her eye was a thin African wearing colorful robes standing on a plastic box. A few dozen people of various origins gathered around him.

"Brothers and sisters!" he proclaimed. "You live in a pit of sorrow and despair. These Westerners have degraded you, torn down your spirit. They litter our desert with their war machines and force us to live in poverty."

More people gathered around. The crowd began to grow restless.

"This occupation has taken so much from us. But what is this all really about? Is it to fight terrorists and rebels? No! Is it to steal from us? No! Is it simply to oppress us? No, no, no! All this fighting is about ego. The Western Union is arrogant in the belief that their way is the best way, the right way. They think they are civilized, that they know best, that we are weak. They are wrong! They are base creatures that devour fast food and objectify the female form. They live in a kingdom of sin built upon a legacy of imperialism."

The preacher raised his hands and looked to the sky. "But we have a savior. The United Third wants all of us—Africans, Muslims, Arabs, all non-Westerners—to rise against this power. Incognito, the leader of this grand movement, shall smite down the Westerners that poison the world. He will take the people's land back. He will take back our freedom. But most of all, he will give us back our way of life, our culture, our ideas!"

Everyone in the crowd went nuts. People cheered and threw their fists in the air.

"He got them riled up," Gilda said.

Taylor shook his head. "That's not good for them …"

"What do you mean?"

A unicopter appeared over the crowd. Sand was stirred up. The crowd shielded their faces as they coughed and yelled.

"CEASE THIS RALLY AT ONCE," a voice boomed from above.

The crowd only seemed to get angrier, throwing rocks at the unicopter. They bounced off its hull without doing any harm, but the pilot had lost his patience.

"YOU HAVE BEEN WARNED."

A cannon poked out of the unicopter. The crowd screamed. Some grabbed their skulls in pain while others vomited. A net landed on top of the preacher. He kept yelling his sermon as he got tangled up and fell off his box. The crowd was already dispersed when the unicopter landed. Two soldiers came out of the aircraft, scooped up the tangled preacher, threw him in the unicopter, and jumped back in themselves. The aircraft then took off and disappeared into the sky. All this happened in a minute flat.

"Geez …" Straper said. "What just happened over there?"

"The peacekeepers shot the crowd with an ultrasonic cannon," Taylor said. "It's a riot control weapon that fires soundwaves at people. No long-term effects come of it, but the experience is very unpleasant."

"Are they gonna kill that preacher guy?" he asked.

"No," Johnson said. "The Western Union doesn't need any more martyrs."

Gilda decided not to stare out the window any longer.

The traffic continued forward, slowly but noticeably. After about an hour, they got to the front of the line. Eleven peacekeepers in sky-blue uniforms guarded the entrance to the city.

"Peacekeepers …" Eisenhorn growled. "Bunch of pansies …"

"Stay down," Victoria told everyone. "I'll do the talking. Johnson, give me a scarf to cover my hair. I don't want to be recognized."

After concealing her hair, Victoria walked out of the truck and got into the front passenger seat. Slate and the others remained hidden in the back. Then Johnson drove up to the check-in point. A concrete barrier and the peacekeepers blocked the road ahead. One peacekeeper walked up to their window and poked his head in.

"We don't see a lot of Westerners driving through here," he said, sounding German. "This way is mostly used by natives. Did you get lost?"

"Yeah, we got lost," Johnson said. "That's exactly it."

The soldier frowned. "May I see some ID, please?"

"Just look at mine," Victoria said, a card in her hand.

The soldier took the card and examined it. His eyes went wide. "Ma'am, I didn't know you had a special permit."

"Well, we do, so please hurry before I call your superior."

"Ma'am, I'm so sorry. Men, let them through!"

The concrete barrier lowered. Victoria looked pleased.

***

"That was a pretty sweet move," Gilda said.

"Yeah, you're the ma—woman, Victoria!" Straper yelled.

"Thank you both," Victoria said. "Slate may be able to shoot lightning, but I have the power of bureaucracy on my side."

"Please …" Slate scoffed. "All she did was show a card. I fought a band of mercenaries, a drone jet, and a swarm of spider robots."

"Yeah, but she did it in style!" the general yelled.

"Quiet, you old fart!"

"I'm stopping here," Johnson said, hoping to defuse the argument.

The truck pulled over to the side of the road. Cairo was a beautiful city once you got inside. White and silver skyscrapers towered everywhere, with small sand-colored buildings and palm trees filling in the spare areas. Many Egyptians were walking around, but most of them did menial work such as picking up garbage or sweeping sidewalks. The Westerners dotting the streets, meanwhile, mainly lounged about or shopped. Armed peacekeepers stood on street corners, and the occasional military Jeep drove by. Beyond that, the city was almost a paradise, a paradise surrounded by a slum.

"Man, I just wanna grab something to eat," Straper said.

"A shower wouldn't hurt either," Gilda said.

"You're preaching to the choir," Victoria groaned.

"All right," Johnson said. "General Eisenhorn and I are going to try contacting the president. The rest of you are heading to Victoria's hideout."

"So, I'm babysitting?" Taylor asked. "Do you really trust this girl?"

"We're in the same boat. I can't drag everyone around with me, especially Slate. You alone will meet us back here in six hours. Make sure to stay out of sight."

Eisenhorn got out of the truck and dusted himself off. Everyone was dirty, but Johnson hoped he and the general wouldn't attract too much attention in their grimy clothes.

"Remember, six hours," Johnson told Taylor before stepping onto the sidewalk.

Zubair got behind the wheel. After a few final farewells, the truck drove away, leaving Johnson and Eisenhorn behind to fend for themselves in this foreign paradise.

***

"What's this Goldberg like?" Gilda asked Victoria as Zubair drove.

Victoria laughed. "He's ... eccentric."

"Can't be any worse than this guy," Straper said, gesturing to Slate.

"I ain't worried," Slate said. "Just wondering what we'll say."

"Yes, how are we going to explain this?" Taylor asked. "Telling him about Slate seems like it would be a very arduous task, not to mention risky."

"Marty was one of my father's closest friends, as well as his accountant," Victoria said. "I trust him with my life."

"We're here," Zubair said.

They parked in front of a building that towered over the others. It looked like a giant pillar made of yellow glass.

"Marty lives on the top floor," Victoria said as she got out of the truck. "We'll take the elevator. Follow me."

Everyone else also got out, except for Slate, who was wrapping a scarf around his helmet.

"Better keep hidden. I might attract a crowd of women if I was to reveal myself!"

Slate jumped out of the truck, and they all walked in together. The lobby of the building was filled with lush plants and ornamental sculptures. Nobody else was there. The far side of the room sported an elevator door. Next to the elevator was an intercom.

Victoria walked up to it and said, "Goldberg." The speaker made a few telephone noises. A deep voice answered.

"Who is it?" he boomed. "I'm trying to watch the soccer match!"

"Recognize my voice?" Victoria cooed. "You better."

"Vi–Victoria?" the voice cried. "You're alive!"

She frowned. "Of course I am. Let us in."

"Right, I'm on it!"

The elevator door opened. The group shuffled inside. The doors closed and the box went upward, making little if any noise.

"What was that about?" Gilda asked Victoria. "He thought you were dead."

"The world must have found out what happened at the Bunker," Taylor said. "Everyone must believe we've perished."

"Great, my parents think I'm worm food," Straper said.

Gilda had known the massacre would be discovered eventually. Such a development didn't surprise her. She only wondered how worried her father was.

The elevator reached the penthouse. They exited it and entered one of the most luxurious rooms any of them had ever stepped in. The carpets were white, the walls a bright amber. A red couch sat in the middle of the room and faced a window that took up the entire wall. The view was breathtaking, overlooking most of Cairo and the Nile.

"Victoria!" a huge voice shouted.

The group turned to see a massive man with a huge belly standing near the kitchen. He was bald, with a short white beard. His bulbous features reminded Gilda of Santa or the Budai statue her dad once got as an ironic Christmas present. He wore a white dress shirt with the sleeves rolled up, sporting a number of food and sweat stains. He looked as if he were about to cry, which he did. He ran over to Victoria, gave her a bear hug, spun her around, and sobbed all over her blouse, his massive belly nearly absorbing her.

"Marty, let me down this instant!" Victoria squeaked.

He complied, leaving Victoria completely disheveled. Zubair watched this with a mild smirk. The others held back laughter.

"I'm just so happy ..." Goldberg said, the tears finally stopping.

"We need a place to stay," Victoria said. "Can you be of help?"

"Of course! My home is your home."

"Some new clothing would also be nice."

"I have some spare clothes for the men, but I don't have any girls. I'm sure the young lady over there won't mind, though. She looks like a tomboy."

Gilda treated him to a deadly glare.

Goldberg gulped. "Uh ... I'll have some clothes delivered with haste."

Victoria walked over to the couch and sat down. "Good, but I need to fill you in on some developments first. These people—"

"Wait, haven't you seen the news?" Goldberg asked.

"No, why? What's on it besides the usual slop?"

"TV, news!" Goldberg yelled.

A holographic screen appeared in front of the couch. They were about to become privy to what the world knew of their plight.

A middle-aged woman appeared on-screen with tightly folded hands.

"This is Union Network," she said. "Our top story is the attack on the Bunker, where over a hundred bodies have been found. Most of the victims are teenage children of influential figures who thought they could keep their children safe at the remote facility, but now we see only death, destruction, and tragedy. We now take you to Jeff Springer."

The screen changed to show Springer, a thin American who looked like a used car salesman. He was sitting across from a scowling government official.

"Thank you, Amanda," Springer said. He turned to his guest. "Welcome to the show."

"Good to be here," the official said. His title appeared briefly beneath his image, but no one watching bothered to read the name. Only his revelations mattered.

"Please, tell us about this awful tragedy."

"Thank you, Jeff. This atrocity will haunt our collective memory for years to come."

"What exactly happened?"

"Approximately three days ago, terrorists attacked the Bunker."

"How exactly did the terrorists carry out this crime?"

"We believe the victims were lured out by some means and gunned down by unicopters. The perpetrators then stormed the Bunker and swept the place clean."

"Why didn't they take any prisoners?"

"Because they were killers. This was an act of barbarism and cowardice."

"Which terrorist group is behind the attack?"

"We're still investigating."

"Could the United Third be responsible?"

"Don't overestimate Incognito's power. He's merely an insane revolutionary with dreams of grandeur, a deluded peasant."

"Do you have any leads on the mystery man?"

"I believe we're getting off topic."

"Apologies. These terrorists are just so frightening."

"Don't be afraid of them. Pity them for not realizing what we're doing is for their own good. Stability must be reached before we can even consider withdrawing forces. The Bunker is a prime example of why we can't leave these violent people alone."

"Have you identified the victims yet?"

"Only half of them. A fire had broken out at the scene, burning the bodies and making identification difficult. We are using DNA testing and dental records to confirm—"

"TV, off!" Goldberg yelled. The screen vanished.

Gilda shook her head. "It's only been three days?"

"All of them are dead," Straper said. "Man ... I was supposed to get a date with Angie. Those guys didn't deserve any of that."

As much as Gilda had disliked her fellow cadets, she had to agree. Then she remembered Henry. She closed her eyes, picturing his face.

"They kept a lot of information out of the news, such as the involvement of Slate and Victoria, as well as the dead mercenaries," Taylor said. "Classic Western Union ..."

"Lawrence called me two days ago," Goldberg said. "He saw on the news that a passing drone had spotted the massacre at the Bunker. The boy was hysterical. He claimed you were there, Victoria, and you might have been one of the victims."

Victoria sighed. "Slate, take off that rag."

"All right," Slate said. "Just don't be blinded by my dazzling good looks!"

He tore off the scarf covering his silver helmet and let it fall on the floor.

Marty Goldberg could only gape at the Helmet Man.

"You keep strange company, Victoria ..." he said.

***

It took half an hour for Victoria to explain their unique situation to Goldberg, during which everyone else helped themselves to the fridge. Gilda and Straper chowed down sandwiches, Zubair sipped on soda, and Taylor ate leftover halibut.

At last, Victoria finished her story.

Goldberg rubbed his eyes. "That was very stupid of you."

"I didn't want to get anyone else involved."

"Well, now over a hundred people are dead."

"It's not like I murdered them myself!"

"You led those mercenaries there. Ridiculous, I should have—"

"What could you have done?"

"Do you think you were the only one distraught by the death of Ammar? I've also been doing some investigating."

"Is that why you're in Cairo? You came here instead of helping my brother run the company. He needs you."

"You're his sister. He thinks you're dead."

"I ... I will call him later."

"All you've done is get people killed. You should have left this to me."

"All right, enough!" Slate yelled. "Quit acting all superior, you beached whale. I bet you didn't know squat until we showed up."

"What did you just call me ... ?" Goldberg growled.

"Oh, sorry. I didn't know the blubber was insulating your ear canals."

"You just stay out of this!"

"Eat me, fat boy. Ah, who am I kidding? You were probably gonna do that anyway."

"You son of a—!"

"If you're so hot, tell us what you know about Victoria's dead dad, Quasimodo!"

"What are you talking about?"

"He means *quid pro quo*," Taylor said, still eating. "Please, ignore Slate. That's just how he likes to blow off steam. We would really appreciate it if you could tell us what you know. Perhaps if we pool our knowledge, we can get to the bottom of this mystery."

Goldberg let out a breath. "Fine, I'll talk, but you have to hear my proposal afterward."

"That's more like it," Slate said. Everyone else nodded.

"Okay," Goldberg said. "Well ... shortly after Ammar died, I received something he had left me in his will."

"What was it?" Victoria asked.

"He left me a file containing documents and financial reports. Ammar had hired private detectives to investigate some very dangerous people. The detectives all had very limited success, but they did make a few discoveries."

"Were the guys he was investigating the same ones who killed him?" Gilda asked.

"Yes, I believe so," Goldberg said. "They call themselves Cloak."

Zubair grew stiff. He dropped his empty soda can on the floor. Taylor almost choked on his halibut. The rest of the group exchanged glances.

"Who are these guys?" Straper asked. "Are they that bad?"

"It's the most dangerous criminal organization in the world," Goldberg said. "Cloak specializes in espionage, theft, kidnapping, assassination, and mass murder."

"Geez ... those are some bad guys."

"Mass murder ..." Gilda seethed. "Are you saying ... ?"

"Yes," Goldberg said. "They must be the same people responsible for the attack on the Bunker. I believe Cloak's top members are these supersoldiers you talked about. Ammar mentioned them in his file, but I never thought ..."

"So, my fellow soldiers have become world-famous criminals," Slate said.

Victoria turned to him. "Slate, I ..."

"Without me!"

Victoria rolled her eyes.

"I can't believe Cloak exists," Taylor said. "It's not just a conspiracy theory."

"I have heard only rumors," Zubair said, looking down. "They are supposed to be a band of merciless killers. Warlords, terrorists, revolutionaries, criminals, they all turn to Cloak as a last resort. I thought the rumors about Cloak were false or at least exaggerated. Seems I was wrong. Can they all shoot electricity like Slate?"

"Their powers are different," Slate said. "I'm one of a kind."

"It's time you told us about them," Victoria said.

"Hey, I don't even know their names!"

"And why is that?"

"The Keymasters didn't want us getting too chummy with one another. I only met four of the other supersoldiers. One guy I killed. Another was a short fellow. Then there was a prissy snot who acted like she owned the place. Reminds me of you, actually. The final guy was some angry one-eyed tool. Ha! I remember my dad complaining to the other Keymasters about how they were always finding him naked in the halls! Oh, man ... good times."

"None of that was useful," Victoria snapped.

"Why isn't the Western Union trying to find these rogue supersoldiers?" Taylor asked.

"It's not as if the Western Union can admit they illegally created supersoldiers who started the world's most infamous criminal organization," Goldberg said. "Besides, I think they are searching for them, just in secret."

"Tell us why you're in Cairo," Gilda said.

"You kids have no manners. Look, Cloak obviously makes a lot of dirty money committing crimes, correct?"

Straper shrugged. "Why else kill people? Gotta make bank, brah."

"Why else?" Slate gasped. "Because murder is a cool crime!"

"Not everyone is as pointlessly violent as you," Taylor said.

"Anyway ..." Goldberg said. "The Western Union taxes the territories they occupy to make the war effort sustainable. Of course, because this region is such a chaotic place, Cloak operates extensively here. Before I go on, do any of you know what money laundering is?"

Everyone but Straper raised their hands.

"Hey, come on!" he shouted. "I bet Slate doesn't know what it is."

"Yes, I do!" Slate yelled. "It's when you wash coins, stupid!"

Goldberg groaned. "Look, when you're taxed, you have to declare a source of income. If you don't, you could get investigated for evasion. Cloak's members obviously can't say they killed a bunch of people for money when they declare income, so they make it look like their money came from a legal source."

"How does Cloak manage this?" Taylor asked.

"In Ammar's file, he alleged Cloak ran a casino near Cairo to launder their money. When he died, I sought to uncover the truth and reveal it to the world. I knew I couldn't trust the Western Union or anyone else, so I took on this task all on my own. I went to this casino several times, but I've wanted to go back there and do riskier investigating."

"You mean break in?" Gilda asked.

Goldberg grinned. "Yeah, it's a real adrenaline rush."

Victoria lowered her eyes. "You accomplished so much ... You're right ... All I did was get people hurt."

Goldberg sighed. "It's time for you to give this up. I can hide you away until this blows over. Let me handle Cloak."

"Hold on," Gilda said. "What's this proposal you had for us?"

"Not for you, but for that moron in the helmet," Goldberg said.

Slate giggled. "Are you asking for my hand in marriage?"

"No! I want you to protect me from Cloak. Victoria told her story well. I don't think she's exaggerating your talents, and if I'm going to go up against Cloak, I'll definitely need protection, someone who can fight these freaks. No offense."

"Some taken, but do you really expect me to fight my own comrades?"

"Well ... I hope it doesn't come down to—"

"Nah, don't worry! I'm cool with it. They're a bunch of wussies anyway."

"Hey, Goldberg," Gilda said. "I want to ask you something."

Goldberg turned to her. "What might that be?"

"You need help?"

***

The streets were alive with activity. Three businessmen sat in front of a café, drinking coffee and reading holographic newspapers. Two young women laughed as they dragged oversized shopping bags out of a clothing store. A group of children ran down the street with a lady yelling at them to slow down. Cairo was not much different from everywhere else, Johnson thought, although the Egyptians didn't look too happy. Washing windows and emptying trash bags wasn't exactly a pleasant way to spend the weekend.

Johnson and General Eisenhorn had cleaned themselves up as best as they could, but their clothes were still ripped and dirty. All Johnson could do was splash some water on his face and walk with dignity.

The Western Union had set up its embassy near the center of the city. It acted as the enforcer of the law, but most decisions involving the economy, infrastructure, and other such matters were made by a city council. Of course, all the councillors had to be approved by the Western Union. The setup wasn't very democratic, but it was stable and prosperous.

The embassy itself consisted of several buildings clustered together where Tahrir Square used to be. It was surrounded by a high fence and guarded by patrols of peacekeepers. Johnson and Eisenhorn hid behind street-side plants as two peacekeepers marched past.

"Sir, we may not have a lot of time," Johnson said. "Make the call count."

"Not a problem," Eisenhorn said. He seemed a little more lucid than usual, a much-needed blessing. Johnson knew for a fact that the president was once Eisenhorn's friend, so he thought this plan had at least some chance of success.

A truck stopped nearby. A peacekeeper got out of it and walked away as he checked his phone. Johnson shook his head. That driver shouldn't be leaving his vehicle unattended. At least his sloppiness made their job easier. They went over and climbed into the front of the truck. Johnson pressed a button on the dashboard. A holographic screen popped up.

"Time to do your work, sir."

Eisenhorn climbed into the passenger seat next to Johnson. He did nothing but stare at the screen for a moment. At first, Johnson thought that Eisenhorn had clocked out again, but then the general began to touch the hologram and soon started typing in some codes.

"This is the secret way to contact the president," Eisenhorn said. "You put a special code into any military terminal, which sends a signal that lets him know your location. You can even send a short text message along with it. Extra secure. No one can tap it, and it won't pop up on anyone's radar. If we got a mole, he's screwed."

"Have you used it before?" Johnson asked.

"Never had to. For emergencies only."

"Do you think the president will get it, then?"

"I trust that magnificent man with my life. I know it's been a while since we've spoken, but I haven't forgotten. I'm sure he hasn't either."

Johnson glanced at his feet but did not argue.

Eisenhorn put in the last numbers. "Finished. What do you wanna write?"

"We need to request an emergency evac. The president can set us and the others up in a safe house until they catch the monsters responsible for—"

Bags went over their heads. Johnson found himself in darkness. They both struggled until hard pistols jammed into their backs.

"Listen here, Western fools," a voice whispered. "Move and you die ..."

"Absolutely not!" Taylor yelled. "I can't stop Slate from doing what he wants, but I'm in charge of you, Gilda. You're still a child."

"I need to help …"

"No! You don't need to help anyone but yourself." Taylor walked over so he could stare right into her eyes. "You have proven yourself in this crisis, but you've been through enough. Let the adults handle this."

"That's the problem!" Gilda yelled. "I *haven't* proven myself! I feel useless. My best friend died, and all I can do is tag along. What have I done to help us out? What have I done to avenge those who've been hurt?"

"You don't need to do anything!" Taylor barked. Never before had the cadets seen him this angry. "A teenager can't do anything. Look at Victoria. She thought that she could save the day and be a hero. Instead, she got a hundred people killed. Goldberg can play detective and Slate can play hero if they want, but as long as I—"

Slate grabbed Taylor's shoulder and sent a burst of electricity into him. Taylor collapsed. Straper and Gilda jumped. Victoria shrieked. Zubair nearly drew his gun.

"What the—!" Goldberg began, but Slate ran up to him. He grabbed Goldberg by the shirt and pulled him close. The silver helmet reflected Goldberg's terrified face.

"Listen to me …" Slate growled. "Taylor's just got knocked out. That tightwad's gonna be fine. But I can't say the same for you. The girl wants to fight. Let her."

"She …" Goldberg said, but the rest of the words got stuck in his throat.

"My gut tells me she'll be of great help," Slate said. "I've been watching these kids. They're full of endurance. Without them, we might not even be here.

Victoria got us into the city, Straper saw that a convoy of trucks had guns long before even I sensed it, and Gilda … well … she has a bluntness I really like."

Goldberg weighed Slate's words, but his bulbous lower lip continued to tremble.

"Here's the deal," Slate said. "Either you let these kids help, or else I won't join you. And I'll beat the shit outta you. All these kids have the right to avenge the ones they care about. Are you gonna stop them just because they're a little shy of eighteen? Those two cadets were about to shoot people in a year or two anyway. As for Victoria, you couldn't keep her here even if you wanted to. You might as well take her along."

Slate let go of Goldberg. He then walked to where Taylor lay and tossed the unconscious man over his shoulder. "I'm gonna tie this guy up and leave him in the bedroom." He chuckled. "It's funny. This is the second time I've knocked him out. Probably not good for his health."

The Helmet Man walked over to the bedroom door and kicked it open. He turned back to face his shocked companions, who kept their distance.

"Better decide now if you're with me or not. Because I'm going for it."

***

"Are you crazy?" Straper asked.

"I want to be of use," Gilda said.

"You are crazy! What are we gonna do? Johnson and Eisenhorn will be back here any minute. We're totally screwed!"

"They're not coming back," Goldberg said, entering the main room.

"What do you mean?" Gilda asked.

"Details are sketchy, but it looks like they were caught on camera. They were in the back of a truck being driven by a known terrorist. Everyone on the news is speculating the two of them are responsible for the attack on the Bunker. A warrant is out for their arrest."

"What?" Gilda cried. She didn't care what happened to Eisenhorn, that insane creep, but Johnson was a different matter. She respected him. He didn't deserve to be hunted down. Even worse, someone had captured them. Was Cloak behind this?

"I'm sorry," Goldberg said. "They haven't talked about any of you on the news yet. If they had, peacekeepers would be knocking on my door right now."

"Great, now we can't contact the president," Gilda said. "And we can't risk going to the police or the military without tipping off Cloak or that mole."

"We should alert the media!" Straper yelled.

"Have you watched the news?" Goldberg scoffed. "The Western Union has a tight grip on all mainstream broadcasts, publications, and websites. They don't like having the occupation criticized or their dirty laundry aired out. And they certainly don't like whistleblowers ..."

"But this is different. Kids are dead. No one can cover up this."

"Straper, someone is trying to kill us!" Gilda yelled. "Whether it's a mole or ... the military itself, we can't reach out to anyone connected with the government."

"That means reporters too," Goldberg jabbed.

"Man, this nightmare will never end ..." Straper groaned.

"Don't worry," Goldberg said. "I'll hide you. But we can't stay here forever. Those terrorists will likely be squeezing Eisenhorn and Johnson for information, which means they'll soon know you came to me for help. We have to act now."

Gilda's eyes lit up. "Are you saying ... ?"

"Yes ... You may be of use. And I don't want to get beaten up by Slate. I'll let you help me fight Cloak."

***

Victoria wept on the bed in the spare room. Her body shook with each sob. All those people were dead because of her arrogance, her belief that she could avenge her father. Goldberg was right. She was useless. It just took her a while to realize it.

After twenty minutes of sobbing into the pillow, she went to take a shower. That was perhaps her best experience of the past few days. The water washed away her cocoon of filth. It took a long time to clean her hair, but the activity kept her from thinking too much about her worthless quest. She had to call Lawrence. The least she could do was make it easier on her brother. He was probably crying his eyes out too.

After putting on a bathrobe, she dialed a number into a hologram transmitter. A floating image of a ringing phone appeared. Her call was answered quickly.

"Hello, who is—?" Lawrence began but stopped when he saw Victoria. Lawrence was several years older than her. He was thin, with a handsome face, and his black hair was combed in an awkward bowl shape. Lawrence now wore a suit, looking so much like her father that she almost thought he had come back from the dead. Lawrence just stood there, his life-sized hologram shimmering. He could only mutter "Victoria ..." before breaking out in a grin.

"I'm not dead," she said, her eyes watering. "Not yet, anyway ..."

"Victoria!" he screamed. "I thought you were gone! Where are you? How did you escape the Bunker? Why is there nothing on the news?"

"Lawrence, calm down," she said, but her brother's grin proved contagious. "I'm fine. Please, let me explain ..."

"Oh, okay ..." He wiped away his tears. "Go on."

"I made it out of the Bunker alive, but I'm in witness protection right now."

"The Western Union is protecting you?"

"Yes, it's possible I was the terrorists' target."

"But why wait so long to call me?"

"Lawrence, you can't tell anyone I'm alive. My life and yours could be in danger if you're not careful."

"Don't worry about me. I'm doing fine. The Helios Tower is perfectly operational, and I'm almost done planning the ceremony. Only a few days till the grand finale."

"Oh, Lawrence. I'm so proud. Remember, no one can find out I'm alive. Wait ... how many people think I'm dead?"

"I only talked to Goldberg. The board members suspect something, but I didn't tell them anything. The Western Union also hasn't spoken to me yet. Victoria, where are you? Let me come join you. I'm sure we can figure this out together."

"Lawrence, someone needs to run the company while I'm gone. It's Father's legacy. We can't let it die along with him."

"No ... I guess not. But at least tell me where you are."

"Sorry, Lawrence. I'm not allowed. Look, I have to go."

"Hey, wait! At least—"

Victoria hung up, Lawrence's hologram vanishing. She closed her eyes.

"Lawrence, I swear ... I'll find out who murdered Father. Just you wait ..."

***

"Slate, are you out here?" Gilda asked.

The Helmet Man stood on the balcony, his hands gripping the rail. Gilda walked out to join him. It was almost evening. The bustling city was calming down now. Goldberg had said they would be leaving the apartment and going to a safer location in half an hour. It felt like the calm before the storm, so Gilda thought now was the best time to talk with Slate.

She took her place next to him. "Enjoying the view?"

"I can't see like you can," Slate said. "Colors are just a memory for me. When I was a kid, all I saw was gray in that lab I lived in. And now that I'm free, now that the world's right in front of me, I can't see anything at all."

"At least you'll never make fun of me for my hair," Gilda said.

Slate chuckled. "Don't worry. There's lots of other things wrong with you."

"Slate, why do you want me to help you fight Cloak?"

Slate stopped chuckling. He let out a sigh. "Being helpless is a familiar feeling for me. The Keymasters controlled every part of my life. Even with my powers, those scientists still had the upper hand. All I could do was be annoying. They took everything from me and gave me back ..." He tapped his silver prison.

Gilda lowered her head. "I still don't ..."

"I'm giving you a chance, a chance to change your destiny, a chance to fight back."

Slate put a hand on her shoulder. Gilda blushed and looked at him. She only saw her eyes in the sharp reflection of his helmet.

"Nobody's gonna decide your fate but you," he said. "I'll make sure of that."

***

They arrived at a small apartment on the edge of the city. The apartment building was gray and covered in graffiti. Several shady individuals lurked about.

"What a dump," Straper said. "But it beats the slum outside the fence, not to mention the desert. At least here I can sleep without worrying about killer robots."

"You might get robbed and stabbed," Gilda said.

"Oh, thanks. I feel much better."

This was where they were going to stay the night. They had driven here in a truck rented by Goldberg, leaving Taylor behind at the apartment. A great debate was had on what to do with him. The Western Union might treat Taylor badly if the authorities found him, and they couldn't take the doctor with them if Gilda planned to fight Cloak. In the end, Goldberg said he would send a man he knew to grab Taylor and set him up in a safe house for now.

They entered their new hideout, a grimy single-room apartment, and saw that the floor was covered in thin mattresses. There were also suitcases filled with clothes and other accessories stacked in the corner.

"You have a lot of friends," Victoria said.

Goldberg winked. "These people are more associates than friends. It helps that investigating is an old pastime of mine."

Slate tore off the scarf he wore around his helmet. "So, what's the plan, Goldberg? Kill everyone in sight until Cloak shows up? Bomb the casino? Steal corpses?"

"You have problems, don't you?"

"Is being too handsome a problem?"

"Wait," Straper said. "I got something to say."

Everyone turned to him.

"Uh ... I've been kind of peer-pressured into following you guys, but Gilda wants to prove something, and so do I."

Gilda narrowed her eyes.

"I'm an asshole," he said. "I picked on Marker just to get popular, and no matter what excuse I give, I'm still responsible. But even though I treated him like crap, the reason I'm alive is because he died to save me, and I'll never be able to thank him for it."

Straper looked around the room at everyone. "So ... if repaying my debt to him means beating up some super-powered criminals, then I'll just have to suck it up."

Gilda punched him on the arm. Straper grabbed his sore limb and moaned.

"What was that for?" he shouted. "That hurt like a—"

"I already knew you were coming with us," she said, smiling. "You just can't help but be the center of attention, can you?"

Slate laughed. "Chick burned you good."

"Yeah, she did," Straper mumbled, but he was smiling too.

Goldberg chuckled. "Okay, kids. How about I explain the plan now?"

Dozens of people crowded inside the terminal, squishing each other as they all fought to be first in line. The ticket collector checked the passengers' identification. Most of these people were Westerners. Only a small handful were from the Middle East. The ticket collector felt his stomach turn as he watched the spoiled fools go to their precious casino. Would this Western dominance ever come to an end? Unlikely ...

A fat man was next in line, dragging another man and three kids behind him. The disgusting tub of lard wore sunglasses and a striped golf shirt.

"Did we make it on time?" the fat man huffed.

"Yes," the ticket collector said. "May I see your ID and tickets?"

"Of course," the fat fool panted, taking out his wallet and five tickets. He handed it to the ticket collector. "I know a casino is no place for kids, but it's the best way to see the pyramids, right? And they got a pool, gym, buffet, you name it."

"Dad, can we hurry up?" a teenage girl said. "The sooner this vacation's over, the better. What's the point in seeing some old pyramids anyway?"

"Your brother seems to be enjoying himself," the fat man said.

"That's because he brought his girlfriend along. They're just going to hang out in the room and make out all day, idiots."

"Who are you calling stupid?" a boy asked, clearly her brother.

"I called you an idiot, not stupid," the girl said. She took out her phone and started texting. "You're an idiot who can't even remember an insult."

"Dad, she called me an idiot. Do something!"

"Sorry about that," the fat man told the ticket collector. "My son brought his girlfriend and her father along with us. My daughter's just a little jealous."

"Dad, stop it!" the daughter whined.

"Have a nice trip," the ticket collector hissed with feigned politeness.

The fat fool and his kids got on the train, followed by a young woman he assumed was the brother's girlfriend and a man who stared daggers at the boy.

The ticket collector sighed. Maybe he should join the United Third after all.

***

Gilda hated acting like a spoiled brat, but she played the part well. They boarded the train with little problem or suspicion. Phase one complete.

Earlier that morning, Victoria had dyed Gilda's hair blonde, since her purple hair had been too recognizable. Victoria had also dyed her own blue-streaked hair a uniform black. The two young women had talked briefly as they did this.

"Do you think this will work?" Gilda asked as Victoria rubbed dye into her hair.

"Your hair is difficult, but we'll tame the beast yet," Victoria said.

"No, I mean this plan of Goldberg's."

"I don't know, but it's well thought out. I don't like how most of it depends on our acting abilities, though. Are you and Straper up for it?"

"I guess … We had classes on espionage and a few on how to act if we got captured by the enemy. Yeah … I think I'll be fine. Don't know about Straper."

Victoria cleared her throat. "So, who is this Henry that Straper talked about earlier?"

"He was the boy you tied me up with."

"Oh …" Victoria blushed. "Sorry about that. What was he like?"

"He was quiet, timid like a deer. I always thought of him as a kid brother. I used to call him Hen." Gilda laughed a little, closing her eyes. "Nobody else ever thought much of him, but he always came through when you needed him to."

"Sounds like my brother. Do you … ?"

"What?"

"Do you blame me ... for what happened?"

Silence blanketed the room for a moment. Then Gilda opened her eyes.

"At first, I wanted to hate you. If it weren't for you, Cloak wouldn't have attacked the Bunker. They followed you, after all." Gilda let out a breath. "But I also blamed that blue-eyed man and his thugs. I blamed Straper for bullying Henry. I blamed the Western Union for making those supersoldiers. I even blamed myself for not being able to help."

"And now what?"

"Now I realize hating you won't help at all. Being angry takes so much work. It's tiring. I don't think I could go on if I keep blaming myself and you."

Gilda stared off into space, remembering Henry's forgetfulness, envying him for that fault. Why couldn't she forget? It'd be so easy then.

"However, in my heart, I know someone is to blame," Gilda said. "Who is responsible? I don't know. But my first guess is someone at that casino."

***

The train was a beautiful feat of engineering. Its narrow, smooth body was painted a brilliant white. It could travel at a maximum of four hundred miles an hour, making the trip from Cairo to the isolated casino in less than thirty minutes.

With a smooth start, the train left the terminal and sped to its destination. It dragged nine railcars, six for the passengers and three for supplies and luggage.

Goldberg, in his golf shirt, sat next to Gilda. She wore a white tank top, dressing sloppily overall. She wasn't wearing any makeup either, an understandable precaution that still irked her. Straper hadn't transformed himself as much, but his pimples were almost gone thanks to some expensive medicine, and he wore a ripped shirt and torn pants. It was the outfit of either a punk or a homeless man.

"Where are the drinks?" he moaned as the train left Cairo behind.

"Josh, you're so silly," Victoria said. She wore a loose yellow dress that made her look even more cheerful than she was acting.

Zubair just looked like Zubair. He didn't really need to dress up like a protective parent. All he had to do was glare at Straper every once in a while, and he would fit the part perfectly. There wasn't much acting involved either.

"Hey, dude …" Straper told Zubair. "It's cool … You don't have to look so mad."

"Welcome to *Ra's Vessel*," a pleasant voice spoke up. A woman in a blue uniform stood at the front of the railcar, smiling with annoying brightness. "My name is Femi, and I will be your tour guide today on *Ra's Vessel*, the most pristine way to view the iconic monuments of ancient Egypt. All luxury, no sand. This train will go by the Pyramids of Giza and the Great Sphinx. We shall also briefly travel parallel to the Nile to see several other famous sites these lands have to offer. Please call me or one of the attendants if you have any questions."

A few minutes later, they passed by the Pyramids of Giza. Straper fogged up the window as he stared keenly outside. Gilda also had a brief look before playing on her phone. The giant stone sphinx passed by their window next. Everyone took pictures with their mobiles. The train turned and ran alongside the Nile for a while. Femi mentioned some interesting tidbits, but everyone tuned her out, too preoccupied with their electronics or drinks.

The train pulled away from the shimmering Nile and went west. They soon entered the desert. Dunes dotted the landscape. Gilda saw a glimmer on the horizon. It took a minute for her to make out a white pyramid. She wasn't all that impressed with it at first, but the closer they got, the more she realized how gigantic the structure was. Everyone was awestruck. Even Zubair seemed unable to pull his gaze away.

"The Pale Pyramid Casino is housed in the world's largest pyramid," Femi told her passengers. "It is fifty stories tall and modeled after the Pyramids of Giza. The polished white surface was also modeled after them, for the ancient pyramids were all originally covered in white limestone that gave them a smooth slope. The Pale Pyramid includes seven floors of gaming area, twenty floors of premium hotel rooms, a theater, an Olympic-size swimming pool, waterslides, a spa, and many other wonderful features. Please be advised there is zero cell reception here, as we are in a dead zone. If you wish to make a call, feel free to use the land-line phones, which are equipped for hologram transmission."

The train went underground. The windows showed nothing but darkness. A few passengers gasped, but Femi said there was nothing to worry about. Decelerating, *Ra's Vessel* came to a halt in a spacious terminal. The doors opened and everyone got off the train, while Femi thanked them all for joining her. Nobody bothered to thank her back.

The group left the terminal and walked down a hallway. It led to a bustling lobby. Red carpets and ornamental Egyptian statues decorated the room. Hieroglyphics were etched into stone walls, almost making the place feel like a tomb. Many smiling employees helped people with their bags. Goldberg and the others, taking in their surroundings, absentmindedly gave their suitcases to some employees.

"Okay, I'm going to check us all in," Goldberg told everyone. "After that, I'm hitting the casino. Why don't you kids go to the movie theater? I heard the documentary on the Korean Invasion is really heartbreaking."

"Dad ..." Gilda whined. "They're not showing that movie right now. We'll probably just see the one about the ex-Marine who hunts down terrorists."

"Fine, but remember, we meet back here at five o'clock. See you later!"

Goldberg walked away. The kids and Zubair went to see a movie.

The theater was nice, but Gilda thought the movie was just awful. A large ex-Marine turned mediocre actor played a gun-wielding maniac who was going after a terrorist leader called Anonymous, an obvious allusion to Incognito and the United Third. When the maniac said, "Time to eat your kitty litter!" and drowned a terrorist in a bucket filled with sand, Gilda decided this was the best time to put the plan in action.

"I gotta pee," she said.

"Planning to use kitty litter?" Straper asked, laughing. That wasn't part of the script, but Gilda didn't have time to punch his arm.

"I also have to pee," Zubair said in an unconvincing voice, but the other moviegoers didn't seem to notice his bad acting. They were too busy watching some on-screen.

Gilda ran out of the theater, followed by Zubair.

"Now that your dad's gone, how about we make out?" Straper asked.

"Don't push your luck," Victoria hissed.

***

Gilda entered a stairwell and went down one level. She took out her phone and turned on the conceal function. The phone vibrated. Any nearby cameras would be unable to see her now. This special function took an image of her body through vibrations, much like a hologram projector did, and sent a signal to the cameras that made them ignore the image.

Making sure no one saw her, Gilda walked into a hallway. The owner of the casino was a man named James Moosvi. Goldberg said there were few actual records of him. He believed James Moosvi was just an alias for the true owners of the world-famous casino, Cloak. Gilda and Zubair's task was to break into Moosvi's office and plant a bug.

A man wearing a suit guarded the office. He seemed to be dozing off. Gilda scrunched up her face, crossed her legs, and screamed. The guard jumped awake.

"Mister, please!" she sniveled. "I have to go!"

"Uh ... Miss ... There's a bathroom up—"

"I need to go now!"

"Okay, uh ... right this way, ma'am ..."

The guard led her to a bathroom on the other side of the floor.

"Oh, thank you!" Gilda cried.

"I'll have to stand guard outside," he said. "This floor has some sensitive areas."

"Thank you!" Gilda yelled again before slamming the door shut.

The guard shook his head. "Geez, girls really can't hold it."

***

The lock was easy to pick. Zubair did it in only ten seconds flat, a new record. He also had a phone that kept him invisible to electric eyes. Gilda had distracted the guard so this break-in could be possible, but her ploy wouldn't last forever.

Zubair opened the door and snuck into the office. The bug itself was a clear liquid kept inside a vial. It was the latest in surveillance technology. One drop of the substance would stick to any solid object. The bug acted as a tracker and could pick up conversation within a thirty-foot radius. The bug had the added benefit of being almost undetectable, for the clear liquid evaporated on impact, leaving behind nanomachines invisible to the naked eye.

Inside the office, Zubair looked around for a decent place to put the bug. The office was filled with books and trophies that seemed more for decoration than vanity. A wooden desk with a tall office chair sat in the center of the room.

Most strange of all, a giant tube rested in the corner. It was made out of a transparent material and had wheels on the bottom that allowed it to be transported with relative ease. It stood vertically and was connected to a large plastic barrel via a rubber tube. What the barrel was filled with was anybody's guess. Zubair needed a second to stare at the alien object. It reminded him of an aquarium, which he doubted it was.

Goldberg had told Zubair to plant the bug under Moosvi's desk. The bodyguard was just about to do that but hesitated. That tube sitting in the corner of the office gave him an odd feeling. Perhaps planting the bug on it would be better. He didn't normally deviate from his tasks, but this time he couldn't help it. Zubair spilled the vial of liquid on the side of the tube. His mission was now complete. All that remained was to get back to the theater, eat some popcorn, and hope the others did their jobs properly.

Just as he was leaving the office, six guards appeared from around the corner and ran down the hall toward him.

They all had their guns drawn.

Zubair growled. He had been caught in the act.

***

Gilda flushed the toilet twice and made moaning sounds. Goldberg had told her to do this for the sake of authenticity, though it seemed kind of pervy to her. Afterward, she washed her hands for effect. Zubair should be finished by now. It was time for her exit.

"I'm done!" she shouted. Opening the door, she expected to see an irritated guard.

Instead, she saw a pair of icy blue eyes trained on her.

Frost grinned. "Hello, English girl."

The idiotic movie ended with the Western Union anthem, its waving flag, and everyone on-screen saluting the audience. Victoria had hated every second of that piece of propaganda, but it wasn't nearly as bad as what she would have to do next.

"So, babe, want to make out somewhere?" Straper asked.

Victoria resisted the urge to shiver. "Sure ... why not?"

They both left the movie theater as the credits began to roll. The duo walked down the hall and went up twenty floors in an elevator.

"Why not make out on this level?" Straper asked.

"Fine ..."

They got out of the elevator and went over to a desk. An overweight guard manned it. He appeared to be looking over some papers. The door to the records room was behind him.

Straper grinned. "Gee, I can't wait for this."

Victoria almost vomited as she closed her eyes and puckered her lips.

They both kissed poorly, and only one of them was enjoying it. The guard noticed this and yelled at the two lovebirds several times, but they ignored him. He was finally forced to get out of his seat and walk over. Again, he yelled at them to stop, but his English was poor, and they didn't seem to care. Having no other choice, the guard grabbed them both by the arms and dragged them away.

"What's the big deal, brah?" Straper yelled.

Victoria did not protest. In fact, she almost wanted to hug the guard.

Goldberg waited down the hall. The two kids had served their purpose. Now it was time to do his part. The big man waddled to the desk. He put his phone next to the door behind the desk. The advanced phone managed to figure out the combination within a few seconds and display it. With his large fingers, Goldberg pressed in the combo on a keypad. The door swung open, and he ducked into the room before anyone noticed.

The records room was filled with filing cabinets. Goldberg huffed. It seemed the financial records of the casino were recorded on paper and not electronically. This would make finding the information a lot harder, but at least he didn't have to hack into a computer.

With haste, he opened a file cabinet and shuffled through its contents. Nothing of value was found in it, so he moved on to the next one. This process continued for several minutes until he found a cabinet that might as well have been a treasure chest. It was filled with recent transactions between the Pale Pyramid Casino and other entities. Goldberg pointed his phone screen at the open drawer. The phone scanned the papers, stored the data, and gave off a green glow that meant it was done. Goldberg knew the guard would be back any minute, so he slunk out of the records room. A sense of accomplishment filled him.

Frantic hands grabbed him by the shirt. He let out a yelp as he was yanked forward. Goldberg was about to defend himself when he recognized that it was Victoria and Straper who were dragging him down the hall.

"What are you kids doing?"

"We've been discovered!" Victoria cried. "We got to get out of here now!"

***

Gilda was face-to-face with Henry's killer. She didn't have time to feel anything but anger and adrenaline. She ran forward and slammed her shoulder into Frost's belly. Frost had blocked the bathroom door with his body, confident she wouldn't be able to topple him.

His cockiness, however, was his downfall. She knocked him backward into the hall. He hissed at Gilda as he managed to regain his balance. He raised his elbow and slammed it into her shoulder blade. She felt a sharp pain.

Gilda punched him in his side with a hook. He hollered and swore, the blow only enraging him further. He made a grab for her.

Not wanting him to get a hold, Gilda ran backward, out of his reach, and kicked him in the chest. He stumbled back, cursing, and pulled out a handgun. He tried aiming it at Gilda, but she ducked down and jabbed him right in the crotch. Frost made a comical face as he bent over, gasping. Using this opportunity, Gilda threw another kick and knocked the gun out of his hand. It landed ten feet down the hall. This was her best chance. She ran for the gun. Frost got his wits together and ran after her.

"You can't win, English girl!"

Gilda skidded to a stop and picked up the gun with her right hand. She spun around and aimed the weapon. Frost slowed to a stop. He spat on the floor and eyed the gun. Frost wore combat boots, baggy pants, and an undershirt. He looked quite different without a colonel's uniform on, but Gilda could never forget him, even without his blue eyes.

"What now, English girl?" Frost asked. "You going to fill me full of lead?"

"I'm not even English!" she yelled. "Why do you keep calling me that?"

"All Westerners are alike. You're all scum. You destroyed my village. You shot my brothers and sisters in front of me. None of you ever bothered to learn what kind of African I was. Why should I bother learning what kind of white devil you are?" Frost squinted. "Almost didn't recognize you. What happened to that hair of yours?"

"I dyed it," she spat.

Frost chuckled. "You spoiled brats and your clown hair ..."

"You killed my friend ..." Gilda's finger began tightening around the trigger. She didn't know what she would do, but something had to give eventually.

"Oh, you mean the stupid boy who talked back to me? Yeah, you were real upset. That face you made even got me worked up for a bit. But that's all it was. Just a face. You may think you're a killer, but you don't have what I have inside me."

"And what's that?"

Frost chucked. "I have nothing inside me, English girl. The West stole my soul. That's why I can't lose, because I have nothing to lose."

The gun flew out of her hand, spinning through the air.

Gilda saw her weapon land in the raised hand of a masked man.

"Keep ... alive ..."

Metal sand crawled on the floor toward her. Gilda didn't notice it, for she was paralyzed with fear by the figure before her. The sand wrapped around her ankles. She lost her footing and hit the floor, slamming her head into the tile. Gilda saw stars as the shifting sand restrained her limbs. Her phone flew out of her pocket and into the other hand of the masked man. His breathing only got more ragged and deeper.

"Use ... phone ... Lure ... Slate ... Others ... die ..."

***

An autonomous forklift unloaded a crate of soft drinks off the train car. It was the last one, and just in time, for *Ra's Vessel* was scheduled to leave the Pale Pyramid in ten minutes. The supervisor had watched these machines unload the supplies for almost an hour, worried they might take too long. Thankfully, his fears were unfounded. Now it was time for his break. He would get the machines to put away these supplies after he had some coffee. Yawning, the supervisor turned off the machines and left his post.

When the coast was clear, Slate ungracefully emerged from the crate. Cans of soda tumbled out. A few of them sprayed their contents all over the floor. Slate got to his feet and tiptoed away from the mess. Goldberg had snuck him into the casino by having him hide in one of the supply crates. It was uncomfortable, but the Helmet Man was too noticeable to ride with the other passengers.

It was only a precaution that Slate was here. If Cloak really was being run by supersoldiers, he was the only one who could take them on. He was supposed to get out of the crate and into an empty one for the journey back if he wasn't needed. The others had only planned to stay for a few hours at the casino, enough time to do their business. Goldberg's cover story for leaving so hastily would be that one of his close relatives had abruptly died, and he and his family had to cut their vacation short. Then they would all head back on the next train and pat themselves on the back.

A phone vibrated in Slate's pocket. He took it out and pressed the screen.

"YOU HAVE A TEXT MESSAGE," the phone read aloud.

"Man, I wish I could read," Slate said. "All right, what is it?"

"MESSAGE BEGINNING. 'HELP, THEY GOT ME. I'M ON THE OBSERVATION FLOOR. COME QUICK.' END OF MESSAGE."

"Aw, crap ... Who sent this?"

"GILDA."

It was clear even to Slate this was a trap, but if Cloak was sending the text, they had to have gotten Gilda's phone somehow, which meant she was captured or worse. The Helmet Man had no choice but to spring the trap.

"And here I thought I'd get the day off ..."

Slate didn't bother with stealth. He ran out of the terminal, sprinted up the hall, and burst into the lobby. Tourists pointed at him and took photos. Slate ignored them and grabbed the nearest employee by the collar.

"Okay, you! Tell me where the observation floor is."

"Sir ... please let—" the employee croaked.

"Do I have to spank you! Where is it?"

"Up–up the elevator ... It's the top floor ... the tip of the pyramid ..."

Slate let go of the man and ran to the elevator. All the guests and employees gave him a wide berth. Security guards ran into the lobby. Their guns were drawn.

"Stop right there!" one guard yelled.

Not wanting to waste time fighting weaklings, Slate shot an electric bolt at the ceiling lights. The yellow bulbs exploded. Shards of glass and sparks rained down. Everyone in the lobby shrieked, including the guards. The guests covered their faces and backed against the stone walls. During this distraction,

Slate pried open the elevator doors with his bare hands and jumped into the shaft. The Helmet Man flew upward. Sparks trailed behind him as he rocketed toward the top of the Pale Pyramid. The phone soon shorted out in his pocket.

"Great, I still had minutes on that thing!"

When Slate reached the top of the elevator shaft, he ripped open the elevator doors and flew out. He landed on the floor and took a fighting stance with his fists up. A few other people were on the observation floor, admiring the sea of dunes far below. They screamed when they saw Slate and ran for the stairs. Only one person stayed behind, a woman in white. She was gazing out through one of the four glass walls. They were so transparent that they might as well have not been there at all.

"I always wondered what our first meeting would be like," she said. "Maybe we'd exchange a few clever lines and banter a little. I'd explain Cloak's master plan, and you'd tell me how we wouldn't succeed and give some pretentious speech justifying all your crimes and indulgences." She gave a small laugh. "Instead, all I want to do is rip that helmet off your head, gouge your eyes out, and crush your skull."

"That's a little morbid," Slate said. "But coming from you, it's kind of hot. Say, what did you do with the purple-haired girl? She's a friend of mine, so I'd be kind of annoyed if you skinned her alive or something."

"Ms. Plato is going to live. But you, on the other hand ..."

With those ominous words, Repulsa attacked.

Repulsa spun around and punched the air. On instinct, the Helmet Man dove to the right. The floor where he had just stood exploded as if an invisible sledgehammer had struck it. Bits of tile flew everywhere.

Pointing his finger, Slate shot a bolt of blue electricity, but Repulsa twirled to the side like a ballroom dancer. The bolt hit the glass wall instead, leaving a scorch mark on its surface. She kicked the air. An unseen force hammered into Slate's chest. It was as if a cannon had fired a bag of cement at him. His recently healed ribs almost broke again. He was knocked off his feet and hit the glass wall behind him. The wall shattered. Slate fell out, plummeting down the side of the twelve-hundred-foot-tall pyramid.

The Helmet Man slid down the smooth slope headfirst. Repulsa jumped out of the window and flew after him. She punched the air. Slate kicked the slope and skidded to the right. The invisible blow missed, creating a crater right where his head had been. He accelerated down the giant pyramid. Repulsa threw more punches. More craters pitted the smooth surface, Slate only sliding faster, now almost halfway down the side of the Pale Pyramid.

Slate then had an epiphany.

"Hey, wait! Can't I fly?"

Another invisible attack nearly turned him to mush. He slammed his foot into the pyramid's surface and launched himself into the air. Slate sent a barrage of lightning at the mystery woman, but she twirled gracefully and avoided the bolts. All they did was scorch the pyramid's flawless white surface. She waved her hand through the air as if backhanding someone. A gust of wind was created. Slate flew upward to avoid the attack. He could feel the air turn beneath him like a mini hurricane. Without a doubt, this woman was dangerous.

Repulsa flew at Slate. Her speed was unimaginable, almost as fast, if not faster than the Helmet Man's maximum. The two of them spun in a tangle of limbs and blows. Slate had electricity coursing through his fists as he threw punch after punch at Repulsa, but she either dodged them or put her hand in front of his attacks and repelled him. They both flew at a forty-five-degree angle toward the ground, neither caring if they crashed.

Ra's Vessel emerged from its tunnel. It was headed back to Cairo to drop off people and pick up fresh customers. Slate pulled away from his enemy and flew above the train. He landed on top of a railcar as the train started to pick up speed. Repulsa landed before him, her hands splayed out and her eyes hawklike.

Slate shot a bolt at her, but she ducked just in time and ran forward. She slammed her fist into his belly, using her powers to really make it hurt. Slate growled. He tried backhanding her. Repulsa ducked. He brought his knee up and made her hop back. Repulsa then levitated over Slate and sent invisible attacks raining down on him. He rolled out of the way, the top of the train getting dented extensively by her unseen strikes.

Repulsa landed far behind him on the end of the railcar with a slight smirk. She didn't even look flushed after all that exertion.

"Geez, lady!" Slate exclaimed. "How often do you go to the gym? I'd be in trouble if I hadn't figured out your powers already."

"Oh? What exactly can I do?"

"You can move matter with your mind using your limbs to channel your power. You can even make yourself fly and send devastating attacks of compressed air my way. Of course, that means you can't manipulate my bolts, since they're made of energy."

"And I thought you were just a pretty face."

"I'm the whole package, baby!"

"Well, I didn't order any package!" Repulsa pointed her palms at Slate. His arms were pinned to his sides, and his legs melded together. He couldn't move.

"Throwing punches is easy," she said. "But this kind of telekinesis requires a lot more concentration on my part. Thankfully, you were stupid enough to stay still for so long ..."

Repulsa curled her fingers. An unnatural force twisted Slate's helmet to the right. It took all his strength to resist her attack. If she kept this up, his neck would snap.

"You shouldn't have stuck your neck out," Repulsa said. "Now I'll have to break it. Goodbye, Slate. Oh, and my code name is Repulsa, though I prefer Naomi. Sorry for not introducing myself earlier when it could have mattered. Now it's just—"

Slate sent a surge of energy into the train through his feet. The charge spread over the surface of the railcar. Repulsa started convulsing and foamed at the mouth. She lost her hold of Slate. He could move his limbs again. His next move was to fly right at her and plow his silver head right into her gut. She threw up her afternoon tea as her eyes bulged out.

"Apology accepted, bitch!"

Both of them flew off the train. They soared through the air, Repulsa barely aware of what was happening. They slammed into a large dune. Sand flew everywhere.

Whether or not either of them realized it, their fight had reached the final stage.

***

Goldberg wheezed as Victoria and Straper led him down the hall. When was the last time he went for a jog? They darted into a janitorial closet, finally finding a place to hide, and were quick to shut the door without slamming it. Guards shouting in Arabic raced by the closet.

"Wa–what's going on?" Goldberg panted. "Did you two get caught?"

"After the guard let us go, we headed back to our rooms like we were supposed to," Victoria said. "Then we heard some other guards yelling to each other. They said they caught a girl and a man trying to break into Moosvi's office."

"All right, we need to get out of here fast."

"How?" Straper asked a little too loud. Victoria and Goldberg shushed him. Straper tried speaking softer. "The only way out of this stupid casino is by train, and it just left."

"There are a few unicopters in an underground hangar," Goldberg said. "They're for emergencies and the private use of Moosvi. We'll have to steal one."

"Swell, we got to break into a secret hangar and steal some unicopters. Sure, no problem. Why not hijack a plane while we're at it?"

"Besides, we can't leave Gilda and Zubair behind," Victoria said.

"Maybe it's time to call Slate," Straper said.

"I already texted him, but it bounced back," Goldberg said. "We'll have to assume he's incapacitated. For now, let's focus on our own safety."

"Crap ... oh, geez ..."

"You agreed to this. You accepted the risks."

"Yeah, but ... didn't think things could go so wrong ..."

"Okay, so where's this hangar?" Victoria snapped.

"On the bottom level of the pyramid," Goldberg replied.

"Sounds like a long way there," she said.

"We have an advantage with these phones. The cameras won't be able to see us, but the guards can. We'll need to get lost in a crowd if we want to avoid detection."

Victoria laughed. "A crowd? Where are we supposed to find one of those?"

"Don't worry. My grandfather was a sheep herder."

***

Slate popped up from beneath the sand. He pulled himself to his feet. The Pale Pyramid was almost a mile away, though it still dominated a good portion of the sky. *Ra's Vessel* could be seen speeding away in the distance toward Cairo.

Slate winced as he tried moving his arm. He hadn't been in a fight like that since before being buried near the Bunker. He had a feeling it wouldn't be the last one either.

The dune shook beneath his feet. The entire hill fell apart. Slate tumbled backward, the sand threatening to engulf him. At the last minute, he managed to launch himself and avoid the avalanche. He floated above the ruined dune, his fist filled with energy.

"Where'd you go, woman?"

A column of sand erupted from the ground like a geyser. Slate flew out of its way, almost getting blown out of the sky. Repulsa emerged from the sand and threw a dozen punches. The sand floating in the air was blown aside as the invisible attacks came at Slate. He flew backward. The devastating strikes missed, except for one that grazed him. It spun him around and nearly dislocated his shoulder. Repulsa kept attacking. She wore a rabid sneer.

Slate flew downward. At least on the ground he could focus his efforts and energy all on fighting, not just trying to stay airborne. He covered his descent with a barrage of electric bolts, but Repulsa raised her arms, creating a wall of sand that shielded her from the attack. He landed on a dune and fired more bolts. Repulsa seemed to be having a harder time dodging. Panting, she moved to the right and lifted some sand into the air to shield her from the electricity, which crystalized the sand on impact. But the wall obscured her vision, so she took it down to properly send more invisible punches at the Helmet Man.

"The injury I gave you seems to be slowing you down!" Slate yelled as he kept shooting lightning at her. He zigzagged backward, evading her attacks. "Give up now, and I might let you go on a date with me. None can resist my chiseled abs."

"Enough!" Her arms twirled. Slate's feet were sucked into the sand. The Helmet Man squirmed, shooting more electricity with pointed fingers, but his aim was terrible due to poor footing. Repulsa didn't even bother to dodge these strikes, which merely hit a nearby dune. She raised her hands and twisted them, walking toward Slate as she did. He sank even farther into the sand.

His silver helmet barely stuck out. He struggled to free himself, but the sand squeezed him so tight that a normal human would have passed out already.

"My anger may be somewhat misplaced, but you are still one of the most infuriating individuals I have ever laid eyes on," Repulsa spat. "Now sink!"

With a wave of her hands, Slate sank below the surface. As she squeezed the sand with her powers, Repulsa could feel his struggling become less and less.

After a minute of pressing, she could feel it stop altogether.

Repulsa lowered her hands, breathing heavily. That man had been something else, but he had died just like any other man. Now all she had to do was tell her employer that she was unable to capture Slate alive. He would be displeased and might even suspect her true intentions, but she was an invaluable asset. Her punishment would be minimal.

Something buzzed.

Repulsa snapped back to attention. Just as she stepped back, a current of energy traveled up her left leg. She cried out as her muscles seized up and the sole of her foot was burned. Unbeknownst to her, she had been standing on the rail that *Ra's Vessel* traveled on, a thin layer of sand concealing it from the naked eye. Slate, while underground, had sent his current through it. She couldn't believe it. Had the Helmet Man set this all up?

The current stopped, but Repulsa was given no chance to recover. Slate launched himself from the sand and slammed his fist into her torso, knocking the wind out of her and breaking a few ribs with sickening cracks. The expression on her face was a mix of shock and gagging. Both of them flew back and crashed onto a stretch of flat sand.

Repulsa gasped and clutched her stomach, trying to stop the fit of coughing. Slate got up on two feet. He clutched his injured arm and hobbled over to her, victorious.

"Don't worry," he said. "I don't kill women. I know ... I'm the sexiest."

Repulsa coughed. "Don't ... you mean ... sexist?"

Slate chuckled. "No, you heard me right."

"I never knew the Gifted came this stupid ..."

"Is that what we call ourselves now? Lady, we ain't gifted. We're cursed."

"Imperialist dog ..." she coughed.

"Hey, I know the Western Union is run by tools, but you guys are a pretty bad bunch, even by my standards. Since when is it okay to murder a bunch of teenagers?"

Repulsa gritted her teeth as she tried to lift herself off the ground. "You ... don't know anything about me ... Where were you while we were tortured ... ? Where were you while we starved ... ? Hiding like a coward ..."

"I got buried six feet underground! How's that my fault?"

"Get used to it ..." she said. "You'll soon be six feet under for good ..."

A cloud of sand floated at Slate. At first, he thought it was just a random gust that picked up some debris, but then metal sand began to cling to him. He didn't notice this until his limbs were completely covered in it. Trying to move, Slate fell to his knees. He sent electricity through the sand. No effect.

"He's mine ..." Repulsa groaned. "Don't touch him ... He's ..."

Repulsa collapsed, passing out from pain and exhaustion.

"No ..." a voice breathed. "Scoundrel ... must pay ..."

The masked man walked over to Slate. Metal sand flowed out of his trench coat. It covered the Helmet Man in thick layers, restraining him.

"That was a cheap move!" Slate shouted. "What's with the mask? Did you get that when you won the ugly competition?"

Out of thin air, another man appeared. Slate was actually surprised. Where did this one come from? The masked man had gotten the jump on him because he was far away, but this new foe had come from nowhere. Then he remembered what Victoria had told him, about the man who killed her father. This was the culprit. This was the Gifted who could teleport. The new arrival knelt next to Slate as the masked man restrained him.

"Time to put you down," Houdini said, holding a gun in his right hand. He shot a dart into Slate's neck. The Helmet Man's struggling slowed. His limbs soon stopped responding to his commands. He could only groan.

"That was enough muscle relaxant to take down a rhino," Houdini said. "I'm surprised you managed to last so long. But like all good things, your luck has come to an end."

The rope dug into Gilda's wrists as she knelt on the office floor. A snarl escaped her. The monster who had murdered over a hundred people was sitting right behind her.

"Not bad fighting, English girl," Frost said, his icy eyes examining her. "You had some training. Where did you learn to take on big men like me?"

Gilda managed to speak without screaming. "I learned to fight from kickboxing classes. My dad signed me up for them when I was a kid. The army also helped. Where did you learn? Oh, right. You can't fight."

"Those are big words for someone who's about to die ..."

"If you want me dead, why haven't you done it yet?"

Frost grabbed a knife from his belt and put it right under her chin. Gilda winced but refrained from showing any concern.

"Houdini wants you alive," Frost said. He put his knife away, smiling. "But I'm not good at following orders, so don't irritate me."

The door to Moosvi's office opened. Houdini strolled inside, followed by the masked man who huffed and puffed. Gilda wasn't afraid of Frost or this Houdini, but that man in the mask was not even remotely sane. When she looked at Sandtrap, a shiver of fear went down her spinal cord, an involuntary reaction to an unhinged being.

"How do you like my office?" Houdini asked, raising his arms. Gilda noticed the hideous black ball he had for an eye. What was that thing? It must be artificial, implanted for some reason or another.

"This little rat's nest is cozy," Gilda said. "You must be James Moosvi."

Houdini smiled. "Moosvi is just a name I took up. Can't call myself Houdini when doing taxes. You must be Gilda Plato, the daughter of the Western Union's top scientist."

"Yeah, my dad's smart, so what?"

"So what? The only reason you are alive is because of him. Sebastian said you would be able to lure Dr. Plato out of his hole. Our Mentor has need of him."

"What did you do to Slate?" she spat.

"Oh, yes, him …" Houdini mused. He turned to look at Slate, who was suspended in a giant tube filled with bluish liquid. It was clear the Helmet Man was still alive, for he occasionally moved, but Gilda couldn't believe he had been captured. She had thought Slate could never be beaten.

"That tube is filled with a liquid insulator used in power plants," Houdini said. "Slate won't be able to conduct a single spark, a useful prison, courtesy of Sebastian."

Gilda felt sick. "Why did you kill everyone at the Bunker?"

Houdini glared at her. "Why not kill them? I had to kill Ms. Zaidi anyway, and those cadets were the children of powerful Westerners. It was a once-in-a-lifetime opportunity. I would have ransomed them off, but I didn't have the time. Even so, Cloak collected bounties from several terrorist cells just for murdering Henry Marker. That boy was the offspring of the US secretary of defense, wasn't he? It's more of a token position these days, what with the Western Union, but it is still a title worth attacking."

Gilda tried to contain her rage, but it managed to leak out. She shivered and breathed more deeply. A few tears rolled down her face.

Ignoring her, Houdini strolled over to Slate's tube. "So, this is our long-lost comrade … I met you only once before, but I could never get you out of my mind. If only you were with us when we were liberated …"

Houdini pressed a few buttons on a control panel. Gurgling, the tank began to drain.

"Boss, is that a good idea?" Frost asked, staring nervously at Slate.

"Do not question me!" Houdini spat. "I am in control."

Slate's helmet was soon exposed. Houdini let go of the control panel. The blue liquid stopped draining.

"Now we can talk," he told Slate. "You don't breathe, but you need air to speak. Of course, I'm not dumb enough to drain your tank completely."

"Did your research, I see," Slate said. "Hey, I remember you! Oh, my dad said you were always running about naked, those buns of yours bouncing in the air!"

Gilda smiled a little. Even Frost had to hold back a chuckle.

"Shut up!" Houdini yelled, slamming his fist on the tube. "I had yet to master my teleportation. But you're not getting out of there. Joke all you want."

"Nah, I'll save my good material," Slate said. "All I want are my questions answered. First off, what happened? We were soldiers of the Western Union, but you turned to a life of crime and evil. Seriously, I wanted to do that!"

"You are evil, Slate," Houdini assured him. "You don't care who you hurt or what you destroy as long as you get what you want. You ruin all you touch, having no conscience or even a sense of loyalty. For you, murder is a daily chore that you enjoy far too greatly."

"Yeah, you bet! But are you saying you're not like that?"

"I have loyalty. You killed one of our own. Where's the loyalty in that?"

"That guy was on a rampage. I was following orders."

"Yet another difference between us. You obey the orders of cowards, men who have never seen war. But we were saved. We rebelled. Our Mentor freed the Gifted from a life of mediocrity and servitude. The Western Union searched for us, trying to find their lost prizes, but they never found us. We were untouchable."

"So, this Mentor made you turn to crime?"

"Our activities had to be financed by some means. It started out with just robberies, stealing from banks and whatnot. But then we moved into assassination and espionage, which not only paid very well but also gave us political connections."

"What happened to the other Keymasters? What happened to my dad?"

"Probably killed by the Mentor," Houdini said. "I remember this 'father' of yours, a hypocritical weakling who thought he could help the Gifted.

But we cannot be salvaged, for we have been consumed by darkness. At least we learned to thrive in it."

"So, what's your goal?"

"Vengeance!"

"You don't know, do you?"

"Silence, you swine!"

"This Mentor of yours is leading you on. You're being bamboozled by a conman who tricked you all into taking up a cause you don't even understand. The Western Union may do a lot of sketchy stuff, but they're definitely better than this bastard you work for. How did you do it? How did you fall so low in so little time?"

Houdini stopped scowling. He began to laugh, his good eye even tearing up. "A little time? You think two decades is a little time?"

"What are you talking about?"

"Slate, you've been missing for twenty years!"

The Helmet Man shook his head. "You're lying."

Houdini shrugged, his laughter subsiding. "It's true. Your hibernation was supposed to last until you were healed. It must have taken you twenty years because of all that radiation inflicted on you during your battle."

"No! It was a few years max!"

Houdini laughed again. "You truly are an idiot, Slate."

Slate didn't respond. He was too busy contemplating this revelation.

"How did Slate get buried near the Bunker?" Gilda asked.

"The Bunker was supposed to be a school for the Gifted," Houdini said. "Most of us were still children at the time. We needed an environment to live in that wasn't some sterile lab. Of course, it was located in the middle of no-where, which was what the Western Union wanted. While being transferred there, the Mentor used the opportunity to free us. I'm guessing Slate's body made it to the Bunker but was buried there by some imbecile who thought he was dead. I can't say for sure, though. It *was* twenty years ago."

"Twenty years ..." Slate mumbled.

Houdini paced around the room. "After it was clear we were gone for good, the Bunker was turned into a safe haven for spoiled brats. To think you were buried there. I can't believe it. Cloak has been eager to get its hands on you."

"Why do you want me?" Slate growled.

"I haven't the faintest idea. The Mentor and Sebastian made it clear that you had to be captured alive. But if I was in charge, you'd be buried again."

"Then why did you kill Ammar Zaidi?" Gilda shouted. "Why are you trying to kill Victoria? What is all this for?"

"Was he talking to you?" Frost yelled. He grabbed her hair and pulled on it. Gilda winced but kept her mouth zipped.

Houdini stopped pacing and took a gun out of his belt. "I don't think I'm going to reveal that to you. It's far too hilarious of a joke to spoil."

The door to the office opened. Two guards came in, dragging Zubair behind them. Houdini stepped in front of Zubair to better examine him.

"Did you really think you could sneak up on us?" Houdini asked. "We knew you were coming. The only reason you fools made it this far was because we needed to capture Slate. It would have been quite messy if we tried to grab him in the city. Luring him out here in the middle of the desert was a brilliant plan."

"It was a stupid plan," Zubair said, raising his head to glare at Houdini. "Who knows what we did while you let us run around your casino?"

"A risk, but we don't have to worry about bugs or other unwanted nuisances. The casino is situated in a dead zone, and we are constantly monitoring all of the Pale Pyramid's landlines. You won't be able to get much information out if you can't even get a signal on those fancy phones of yours. The guests don't much care for it, but I believe isolation is a wonderful rarity in this modern world of ours. And they keep coming back, so on some level, they must agree."

"We will just sneak your secrets out of here," Zubair growled. "Perhaps one of the guests is working for us. Maybe it's hidden on your train. Either way, you failed, arrogant beast."

Houdini scowled, pointing his gun at Zubair's forehead. "Slime like you can't possibly fathom what is going through my mind, what I think."

Zubair stared at the gun, his face stony. "I know what men like you think … You feast when others look for scraps. When the Great Choke devastated the world, scum like you took advantage of the chaos. Instead of helping others, you only helped yourselves. That is the reason the Western Union claims to be here. You are their justification incarnated. Because of people like you, the rest of us are forced to suffer their occupation."

"You think I'm like one of those terrorists or corrupt native leaders?" Houdini asked, the anger just barely hidden beneath his face.

"No … you *are* one of them!" Zubair cried. With great strength, he jerked his right arm forward. The guard tried to keep hold but ended up crashing into Houdini. Both foes fell. Zubair kicked the first guard's head, knocking him unconscious. In a very bad choice of action, the second guard reached for his handgun and now held Zubair's arm with only one hand. Zubair easily tore his arm free and slammed it into the second guard's groin. The guard yelped. Zubair then punched his temple, knocking him out too.

Frost pulled out his own gun, but Gilda got up onto her feet and ran backward, her hands still tied. Although not managing to knock him over, Frost stumbled back and hit the wall. Grunting, he grabbed her by her arm and managed to keep hold of her. Sandtrap didn't interfere, standing still in the corner of the room.

Zubair snatched up a gun off the floor and aimed it at Houdini, who was just getting up.

The bodyguard didn't even hesitate pulling the trigger.

The bullet flew out of his gun, right at Houdini.

Then, like a very good magician, Houdini vanished.

The bullet struck the floor. It did little damage except make a hole in the carpet.

Houdini reappeared behind Zubair. The bodyguard's confusion didn't stop him from throwing a punch at Houdini. Zubair's fist almost made contact, but Houdini vanished into thin air once again. Houdini reappeared to the left of Zubair and kicked him in the side, knocking the bodyguard off balance. Gilda stared, stupefied at this performance. Frost laughed with glee. Sandtrap only huffed and puffed.

Zubair regained his balance and took a fighting stance. "You ... The recording that Victoria found ... It was you. You killed him. You killed Ammar Zaidi!"

He threw another blow at Houdini. Teleporting with a smirk, Houdini avoided the fist. He reappeared to the right of Zubair. But the bodyguard was ready. Zubair kicked Houdini in the leg. Howling, Houdini teleported to the other side of his office, hopping on one foot.

"Your magic won't help," Zubair said. "Dogs like you can't ever be decent fighters. You don't have the patience to learn."

A gunshot sounded through the office. Zubair didn't know what had hit him until he looked down at his bleeding chest.

Frost held a smoking gun and smiled, restraining Gilda with his other arm.

"Stop it!" Gilda shrieked.

Houdini vanished and reappeared in front of the wounded bodyguard. Zubair looked groggy, his defensive stance swaying. The bodyguard tried to throw a punch, but Houdini grabbed his arm with one hand, a cruel grin plastered on his face.

"Your arrogance is astounding," Houdini said. "Do you think you can understand my goal or Cloak's true purpose? Nobody can, except my savior, my Mentor."

He pulled Zubair close to him, staring at him with his one real eye while the black ball bulged even farther out of his skull.

"Teleporting is quite difficult, especially when you're taking objects with you," Houdini explained as though he were giving a lecture. "You have to rip things from their natural environment and enter a new one, pushing out air and other matter to make room for yourself and these foreign objects. However, teleporting only a piece of an object is an even greater feat. Let's say I only wanted to teleport half an apple with me. I would have to literally rip the fruit in half with my mind. Can you imagine?"

"Houdini," Slate warned. "Don't do it."

"Let me demonstrate ..."

Houdini vanished, appearing a few feet away.

He held a severed arm.

"No!" Gilda screamed.

"Houdini!" the Helmet Man bellowed.

Zubair gave an inhuman shriek, holding a bloody stump where his arm used to be attached. Blood poured out of the wound like a waterfall and spilled all over the carpet. The bodyguard stopped his crying and fell to his knees.

"That was the last wonder you will ever see," Houdini told the dying man, dropping the severed arm on the floor. "But I'm merciful, so I won't let you bleed out like a stuck pig."

He pointed his gun at Zubair's head.

"No man is like me ..." Houdini said. "No man is like me!"

With those words, he pulled the trigger.

CHAPTER 24

Guests crowded around the blackjack tables, some drinking beverages while others kept their attention exclusively on their cards. Many people laughed, but just as many moaned about lost money. The pyramid had seven levels devoted entirely to gambling, each one filled to the brim. Several guards scanned the crowd for a large man in a striped golf shirt and two teenagers. Security didn't want to spook the other guests, so the search was done quietly.

With all the noise in the casino, few of the guests noticed when the fire alarm went off. Then the sprinklers turned on for the entire fortieth floor. That got everyone's attention. Guests began to panic and run for the stairs. The guards tried to calm the crowd and continue searching for the suspects, but they were soon dragged away by the human tide.

Goldberg had grabbed some cleaning rags and set them on fire, causing the alarms to go off. Victoria, Straper, and Goldberg now ran with the crowd of guests to cover their escape. While running, Victoria wondered if Zubair had managed to plant the bug. It seemed urgent to confirm. When the crowd came to a halt in front of the congested stairwell, Victoria put her wireless earbuds in and clicked on her phone. She hoped she would be able to listen in.

Miraculously, she could. Voices were talking, but she couldn't make them out. After a bit of fiddling on her phone, she was able to decipher what was being said. A man was yelling madly about how he was saved. Then she heard a voice that she recognized instantly. Slate was alive and well, but he sounded upset.

"No! It was a few years max!"

Victoria listened for several minutes, slowly shifting through the crowd as she did.

Goldberg tapped her shoulder. "There are guards coming. Keep your head low. Wait, are you listening to the bug now? We have to get—"

Victoria shushed him, her eyes widening. Then her mouth dropped open. The gunshot was all too audible. The noise echoed madly in her ears.

"Victoria, what's the matter?" Goldberg asked. "Don't make a scene."

The girl suddenly hugged Goldberg tight, burying her face in his massive frame. She let out a muffled scream and sobs that made her convulse. Luckily, nobody else seemed to notice her sudden distress.

"Victoria ..." Goldberg noticed her earbuds and took one out of her ear. He put it on, now able to hear the cries of Gilda, the curses of Slate, and the laughter of evil men.

"Zubair!" he heard Gilda scream. "You murderers!"

"It is only the beginning!" a man cried. "It's glorious!"

Victoria's sobs only grew louder. Goldberg's shirt became wetter with tears each second.

Listening to the horror, Goldberg felt like crying himself.

***

"Let me give you a history lesson," Houdini told his captive.

Gilda was walking behind the man, being led by Frost, who held the rope restraining her arms. She hadn't uttered a word since they left Houdini's office and headed down to the bottom level of the casino. Her cold need for revenge only grew in her chest as she stared at Houdini. Gilda told herself that she wouldn't hesitate to murder the cretin if she got the chance. Until then, she would only treat him with a hateful gaze.

"The Pale Pyramid was built over seventy years ago," Houdini said. "It was supposed to be the world's greatest casino. All this was back when corporations still ran the world, when the values of the Middle East were almost completely vanquished. Those organizations had so much power, but when the Great Choke came, they proved to be so inept that the people of the world had no choice but to give back the power to the greedy politicians. This led to the Chinese Empire and your precious Western Union."

Houdini walked with his hands behind his back as he led the way to the hangar. Slate followed, still in his tube, the blue liquid covering his helmet again, muffling his roars. His tube was being pushed on its wheels by Sandtrap, who puffed out loud breaths.

"When the Choke swept across the world, many isolated havens such as this one were sought by the wealthy," Houdini said, but Gilda wasn't really listening. "They wanted to wait out the virus in luxury, to slumber in the pyramid."

They came to a large metal door. Houdini walked up to a keypad, pressed in numbers, and stepped back. The door began retracting into the ceiling, groaning as it did.

"But after a few months, things … got out of hand. The world was literally in shambles, civilization on the verge of collapse. These bourgeois cretins had to deal with the fact that there soon might not be a world for them to go back to. Not surprisingly, many of these fools went mad. They killed each other … slowly. I even heard rumors that cannibalism was involved. When the rescuers finally came, there were no survivors. It was literally a blood bath."

The door was finally up all the way. Houdini led the group inside. The hangar was two stories tall, with a concrete floor and metal walls. Six unicopters sat inside the giant space, their single propellers emerging from their bodies.

"Cloak bought the Pale Pyramid at a bargain price," Houdini continued as they walked toward a unicopter starting up. "We even got all the slot machines, blackjack tables, and *Ra's Vessel* with the purchase, though covering up this place's unpleasant history did take quite a bit of hush money. It has served as a decent laundering business. I can't even begin to count how much cash we put through it, let alone made."

They reached the unicopter. Its side door opened and a ramp extended out, touching down on the landing pad with a clank.

"Sadly, our business has been looked into recently," Houdini said, stepping into the unicopter. "The Western Union has become suspicious of our activities, and there is plenty of evidence here to incriminate us. Ammar Zaidi's meddling was the final straw."

Frost pushed Gilda into the aircraft. Sandtrap followed. Slate was loaded in another unicopter. The doors slid shut. The unicopter began to rise.

Sandtrap wheezed. "Repulsa ..."

"She's already left," Houdini said. "Have no fear. Her injuries aren't serious. Let's just hope her defeat teaches her humility."

The ceiling of the hangar opened up. Harsh desert light filled the chamber. The unicopters took off. Gilda looked out the window. She saw they were rising out from the opposite side of the pyramid where *Ra's Vessel* entered the casino. They soon hovered far above the pyramid, its white surface gleaming brightly.

"Support pillars make it so the pyramid doesn't sink into the sand," Houdini said. "Without it, the entire thing would be buried in a matter of minutes."

He took out a black remote. It had a single red button on it.

"What are you doing?" Gilda asked. She could not keep the panic from her voice.

"Laying this tomb to rest ..." he whispered.

Houdini pressed the button.

***

A muffled boom echoed through the Pyramid. The crowd went silent. Goldberg glanced around. Victoria was still crying, but her sobs were now snivels. Nearby, Straper gawked like the rest of the casino guests.

"What the hell was that?" Straper asked way too loudly. Goldberg shot him a look. They were supposed to be hiding from the guards, not attracting attention, although the guards looked just as dazed as everyone else.

A huge chunk of ceiling fell down on an old woman with a sickening splat. Her twisted limbs poked out from beneath the rubble. A young girl screamed.

Now the crowd was in a state of hysteria, yelling and pushing as they all tried to make their way to the stairs. A tall man shoved a woman aside, only for him to trip and be trampled to death. Several women screamed and sobbed as they held their children. The guards also fled to reach the stairs. Some even pulled out their guns and pistol-whipped anyone in their way.

Straper, however, wasn't even headed toward the stairs. He moved for the elevator doors, swimming through the agitated human sea.

"What are you doing?" Goldberg yelled to him over the screams of the crowd. "The elevators aren't working! The fire system shuts them off automatically."

"Just trust me, man!" Straper shouted. He forced his fingers into the crack of the elevator doors and pried them open enough for a person to squeeze through.

"There's a service ladder in the shaft!" he yelled.

A tremor shook the entire pyramid. Three more chunks of ceiling fell on the crowd, killing five people. Goldberg understood now. This was their best shot. Their only shot, really. He grabbed Victoria by the arm and began to move through the frenzy of people. The human mass was so thick that it took almost a minute for them to get to the elevator. Once they did, Straper slipped through the elevator doors and began to climb down the shaft.

"Let's go already!" Straper shouted from the void.

"Victoria, we need to head down," Goldberg told her.

She wiped her tears away and nodded. "Okay ..."

In two minutes, all three of them were climbing down. The shaft had red emergency lights glowing inside, so they weren't in total darkness. Climbing down was easy at first, but the rungs were soon rubbing their palms raw. The sweat also rolled into their eyes, and their biceps were aflame. Straper moaned. Victoria stifled her sobs.

They weren't the only ones to climb down the shaft. A few of the casino's guests had witnessed their escape and decided to follow their lead, despite the danger involved. Their desperation was that great.

A violent tremor shook the pyramid, almost causing the climbers to let go of the ladder, but they managed to hang on through the ordeal.

"Hurry, the hangar is on the bottom level!" Goldberg shouted. He wasn't used to exerting himself so much. Sweat pooled between his many flabs. He couldn't take this. How many more floors until he reached the bottom?

The casino shook again, the most violent tremor yet. The people in the shaft held on to the ladder for dear life, but one man lost his grip and fell to his death. Screaming, he plummeted past Goldberg, slamming into him. Goldberg almost lost his grip too, but a rush of adrenaline came over him and he caught himself.

"We won't make it to the bottom floor!" Straper shouted. "Man, why'd you guys let me talk you into this? My ideas always suck!"

"I hear something!" Victoria yelled. She still had tears in her eyes, but hope glimmered in them too. "Listen!"

Straper and Goldberg strained to hear anything unusual. Then they heard a faint automated voice make an announcement.

"*Ra's Vessel* is arriving ahead of schedule. All passengers wishing to board early may head to the terminal at this time. Thank you for visiting the Pale Pyramid."

"Hey, forget the hangar!" Straper called out. "The terminal's just two floors down."

"I guess we're taking the train ..." Goldberg wheezed.

***

Serpentine cracks began to crisscross the surface of the pyramid. One fracture went halfway up the structure. Another tremor made the casino vibrate, causing even more cracks to appear and old ones to become wider.

"Why is this taking so long?" Houdini growled. They had been hovering in the air for almost ten minutes, but the gargantuan casino refused to cave in. Those charges were supposed to have destroyed the foundation of the Pale Pyramid, make it collapse under its own weight and sink into the desert. Did one of them not go off? Yet another blunder by Frost ...

"You're not just a monster," Gilda told Houdini as she watched the behemoth pyramid break apart. "You're a stupid monster."

Frost smacked her head. Stars filled her vision, her disgust turning into mere confusion.

"Idiot, I need the girl alive and unharmed!" Houdini shouted.

"This is boring," Frost said. "Hey, look!"

Houdini glanced where Frost was looking. He could make out a white train approaching the Pale Pyramid in the distance.

"*Ra's Vessel* shouldn't be coming back here," Houdini hissed.

"What do you want to do, boss?" Frost asked.

"Let the train go into the casino. Then destroy the tunnel entrance. I also want the girl gagged. Her retorts are becoming less amusing and more annoying."

Before Gilda could come to her senses after the blow to the head, Frost tied a rag around her mouth. It tasted a lot like the one Victoria had used on her. Good times.

Ra's Vessel approached the Pale Pyramid and descended into the tunnel. After the train was fully in, the pilot fired a missile, which struck the tunnel entrance. Sand and rock flew everywhere. After the air cleared, Houdini saw the tunnel was now sealed off by debris, trapping the train within the collapsing pyramid.

"We're behind schedule!" Houdini yelled. "Leave behind a few unicopters to kill anyone who might escape, but the rest of us need to leave. We must deliver Slate to the Mentor!"

Goldberg wriggled through the elevator door. Victoria came out next. Straper was already there waiting for them. "Man, I can't believe we made it."

"*Ra's Vessel*!" Goldberg shouted.

The white train had slowed to a stop and opened its doors. Nobody appeared to be on the train yet, meaning it had just arrived. A hefty piece of ceiling came crashing down to the floor, followed by another five smaller chunks. Sharp pieces of concrete flew everywhere. Victoria and Straper shielded their eyes, both of them shrieking girlishly.

"Let's get on it!" Goldberg yelled. "This place could all come down at any time."

To illustrate this point, the casino shook again. More sections of ceiling fell. Floor tiles cracked. Lights flickered on and off. Swarms of people began to flood into the terminal. They stumbled and pushed with only one goal in mind: escape.

"Get on the train!" Goldberg shouted. "Hurry!"

The three of them ran past the white locomotive and got into the first railcar. A herd of people came in right after them. More and more chunks of ceiling fell. There were also more cracks in the floor, flickering lights, and booms even louder than before. Sections of floor caved in, causing many people to trip and be trampled by the mad crowd.

Ra's Vessel was packed with passengers in only two minutes. Even the storage railcars were filled with refugees. The human tide did not end. Hundreds were still in the casino. The doors could only close on them.

"Is the train going to move?" Victoria asked in a distant voice.

With a jolt, *Ra's Vessel* moved forward. Everyone almost fell over from the sudden acceleration, but the crowd stayed standing due to everyone being squeezed close together.

Straper looked out the window and turned white. "Hey ... wait ... what about them?"

The people who hadn't gotten on the train pounded on the sides of the railcars. Many tried to break the windows in hopes of climbing inside. Several desperate people even attempted to hold on to the side of the train, but they all let go when the train entered the tunnel. Victoria whimpered again and covered her mouth. Goldberg wrapped his arm around her and closed his eyes. They knew those people were doomed.

The train began to move so fast that everyone in the railcars screamed. Many soiled themselves. Others threw up. *Ra's Vessel* had accelerated to its maximum speed, over four hundred miles per hour. Then the train hit a barrier.

It flew off its tracks.

Broken pieces of concrete and other debris had been blocking off the tunnel, but the train had gone full speed so it could ram through it. The locomotive crumpled from the impact, shaking everyone in the entire train so hard that bones broke. However, despite the damage, *Ra's Vessel* managed to smash through the wall of rubble, flying off its tracks for just a few seconds, and landed back on the rail with a harsh bang. Screams and vomit were all that came out of the passengers' mouths, but they were the lucky ones.

Goldberg scraped some puke off his beard and checked on Victoria. She was letting loose hoarse shrieks while Straper looked green in the face.

Now that the locomotive was wrecked, the train slowed down. However, because of the frictionless rail, *Ra's Vessel* was gliding at a hundred miles an hour. They would come to a stop halfway to Cairo, far away from the unstable pyramid.

After the passengers calmed down enough, they started to look out the window. The Pale Pyramid had hundreds of cracks covering its surface. Hunks of rubble fell down the sides of the structure and crashed into the sand. Goldberg hated to see such magnificent architecture being demolished like this. Then he remembered the people still inside and shuddered.

The sand around the Pale Pyramid began to swirl like a whirlpool. The groans of bending metal filled everyone's ears. One side of the pyramid caved in.

Everyone on the train screamed as the Pale Pyramid sank into the sand. The train shuddered and shook everyone senseless. The pyramid continued to implode. Now all four sides caved in. The top was completely destroyed. Sand flew into the air, obscuring the destruction of the behemoth.

"Gone …" was all Straper could say as he looked out his window. Victoria buried her head in Goldberg's shirt again, but she didn't cry this time.

The sound of propellers filled the air. Goldberg turned his head and spotted several unicopters heading toward the train.

Their guns were pointed at *Ra's Vessel*.

"Get down!" a random passenger shouted.

Straper was all too happy to follow the advice and hit the deck. Victoria pulled away from Goldberg and did the same, but Goldberg himself kept staring out the window. Something else had caught his eye.

A man had appeared on the roof of the railcar behind them.

He held a rocket launcher.

A rocket flew out of the weapon and hit a unicopter. The aircraft turned into a fiery heap and crashed into a dune. Flame filled the air as more rockets slammed into the sides of the other aircraft. In only a matter of a few violent seconds, all the unicopters had been wiped out.

The passengers on *Ra's Vessel* screamed. These pampered people were not used to such a violent display. Their cries were so loud that nobody heard the hissing. A clear gas filled the compartment. It wasn't noticed until it was too late. Everyone began to move like slugs. Their screams ebbed. Their vision blurred. Goldberg's legs turned to jelly as his giant frame fell to the floor. Victoria went down with him, breaking her fall on his sizable belly.

Straper coughed and began to lose focus. He could tell that almost everyone in the compact railcar had already passed out. The last thing he managed to do before slipping into unconsciousness was see a man open the door to the railcar. He wore a gas mask and held a gun limply in his hand, as if he knew he didn't have to use it. Straper heard the man speak. He didn't recognize the voice at first, but then he remembered.

"I am glad we caught you in time," Barir said. "Incognito did not want you to die in such a way. He has much use for you."

***

"It's time to say goodbye," Houdini said. "Give Klein the girl."

"What about the other one?" Frost asked. "He might escape his tube."

"Repulsa will go along to keep watch over them."

"She couldn't handle him before without broken ribs. Why not go yourself? I can take care of the business in Dubai."

"I trusted you before, and look what happened!"

Frost grinded his teeth but said nothing. He untied Gilda and led her off the unicopter. He handed her over to a British man, presumably Klein. Before leaving, Frost grabbed Gilda by the chin and stared into her eyes.

"Farewell, English girl. I wish I had the chance to teach you a lesson about respecting your elders. Until next time ..."

Gilda spat right in his face. The wet glop hung off his cheek.

Frost wiped it away. "Klein, keep an eye on this one ..."

"Don't worry," Klein said. "I've dealt with kids before. You just need to show them who's boss."

Gilda stomped on Klein's foot and tried to pull away, but he held on to her firmly. Seething, she stopped her struggling.

"That's why I wear steel-toe boots," Klein said.

Gilda slammed her elbow into his crotch.

"Ugh!" Klein cried, but he kept his grip.

"Should have worn a cup too ..." Gilda spat.

Houdini leaned out of the unicopter. "What are you fools doing? Get her on the plane!"

Klein growled and led her away to the private plane a hundred yards away. Gilda considered running away as they approached it, but they were in the middle of the desert. Even if she could somehow escape, she would probably die of thirst.

Gilda was marched up the steps and entered the aircraft. She glanced around the nicely furnished cabin. It had white couches and nine men sitting on them. They wore casual clothes and intense expressions that told her they were professionals.

"Where's Slate?" she asked.

"That's none of your concern," Klein said. He took her to the back of the plane and opened a door leading to a bedroom. A woman was already waiting for her on the bed.

"Fantastic, my bunkmate has arrived," Repulsa said. She wore a loose-fitting blue night gown and slippers. She looked very comfortable and happy for someone who just had her ribs broken by a lunatic in silver headgear.

"Is there anything else you need, ma'am?" Klein asked.

"I'm fine. However, the girl hasn't had anything to eat or drink for quite a while. Get her something with low fat. We don't want her getting chubby."

"I'm not chubby!" Gilda shouted.

"Klein, please be quick. The little one's starting to get cranky."

Gilda blushed. "Shut up!"

Repulsa winked. "It's best not to keep ladies waiting."

Klein's face went red. "Uh ... right away, ma'am ..." He left the room and closed the door, making sure to lock it behind him.

Repulsa gestured to the bathroom. "Why don't you get ready for bed? It's going to be a long flight. We won't be in South Africa until tomorrow morning. You can have the bed, I suppose, or we can share if you're not too shy."

"Shut up!" Gilda screamed. "You monsters aren't going to get away with this."

Repulsa stared at her with a soft smile. Without warning, she threw a pillow right at Gilda, hitting her in the face.

"Let's have a pillow fight," Repulsa said. "Maybe we can watch a movie, or we could just talk if you prefer. Anything to burn the time."

"Fine ..." Gilda said. "Let's talk about Henry, who your friends killed."

"Believe it or not, they're not my friends. Frost is a cruel weakling, Houdini is an arrogant hothead, and Sandtrap ... well ... I'm more of a sympathetic caretaker to him than an actual friend. He's not right in the head. It's sad, really."

"Don't make excuses. You're just as responsible as they are."

"Who is this Henry anyway? Was he an old boyfriend?"

"What? No!"

Repulsa smiled even wider. "You're blushing again ..."

"He was my friend. That's it! Even if I did like him that way, there's more important things to be worrying about, like how you're a child murderer."

Repulsa raised her hands. "Okay, I believe you. But personally, I think your relationship with this Henry could have become a lot more than mere friendship. Yet for some reason you didn't let anything romantic take root. Why was that? Were you scared? Was he not your type? Did you think you weren't good enough for him?"

"Shut up!" Gilda shrieked. She ran right at the woman, but she was stopped in her tracks, restrained by some invisible hold on her body.

"Don't test me," Repulsa said, her smile gone. "Go to the bathroom and shower. You want to wash that dye out of your hair, don't you?"

She relaxed her powers. Gilda stumbled backward, her limbs sore. After regaining her balance, she stared daggers at her captor for several seconds before storming into the bathroom and slamming the door behind her.

Repulsa sighed, smiling again. "Oh, well. I'm sure she'll come to like me yet."

***

Klein rubbed his drooping eyelids, hoping it would make him more alert. He and his men had been lounging about for the entire night on guard duty. Boredom afflicted them all. Worst of all, there wasn't any coffee on board.

Despite all of this, Klein felt a profound sense of satisfaction. He had been working for Houdini for several years, doing the odd job here and there, but never before had he been given such an important task. Messing up now would ruin years of work. Every professional criminal in the world had heard of Cloak, some even claiming to have met one of their elite supersoldiers. Klein, on the other hand, had the privilege of meeting three of them. And soon he would meet his fourth. Hell, he might even meet the Mentor.

Looking around, he studied his men with flared nostrils. They were mostly leaning back on the white couches. One or two of them even appeared to be asleep.

"Wake up!" he yelled. "We're going to land in an hour to deliver the precious cargo."

"Yeah, precious cargo …" one man muttered. Half of the men laughed. They had listened to their captive yelling and cursing throughout the first two hours of the flight.

Klein was about to tell them to shut their holes when an ear-piercing scream came from the cockpit. The men all sat up and reached instinctively for their guns.

Then, as fast as it started, the screaming stopped.

"Get your asses moving!" Klein yelled. He led five of his men to the front of the plane. The rest went to check on the girl and her keeper. One man with Klein took out his gun and kicked open the door to the cockpit. Klein saw inside. The autopilot was engaged and everything looked normal, except for one thing.

"Where's the pilot?" Klein shouted.

"Sir, the others!"

Klein turned around. The blood in his veins turned cold.

The men who had gone to check on the girl were nowhere to be found.

"Stay alert!" he shouted to his five remaining cronies.

"Sir, what's going on?" one man cried.

"Shut up!" Klein told him.

All of them pointed their guns forward and scanned the cabin. However, nothing on Earth could prepare them for the foe they were about to encounter.

A phantom floated out of the floor.

It held a scythe.

The men gaped. One let out a squeak.

The specter glided toward them.

"Kill it! Kill it!" Klein bellowed.

They all fired their guns, but their bullets were useless. The phantom just kept floating toward them, reeling its scythe back.

Klein shrieked as he was cut down.

Gilda woke up on the bathroom floor with a puddle of drool next to her mouth. Had she heard gunshots? It must have been a bad dream. Henry's face still floated in front of her. A horrible cackling echoed in her ear. But the worst part had been the white marble of an eye staring out from the infinite blackness. What a moon that was. She had to remind herself that it was just a dream. There were no such things as killer moon eyes. But there was supposed to be no such thing as telekinetic women either.

Last night, she had locked herself in the bathroom in an effort to stay away from her captor. Her back ached from having slept on the floor. On unsteady legs, she got up and looked at herself in the mirror. She still had the dye in her hair. Her purple hair had been such a defining feature that she didn't recognize the tired and frightened girl staring back at her.

Gilda stripped off her sweaty clothes, put them in the laundry machine, and dragged herself into the small shower. The water was steaming hot, just the way she liked it. While scrubbing her hair, she lost herself in contemplation. Being angry was hard work. But she couldn't give up. Not yet. If she could stay alive for just a bit longer, she could strike when Cloak was at its weakest. She needed to keep the hate boiling. Revenge was still possible. She imagined making Frost hurt again. His screams would sound like—

Then she imagined Zubair being shot through the head. Her bloodlust waned.

After twenty minutes of scalding herself, she turned off the shower and dried off. She wrapped a towel around her torso and went to the bathroom sink. Staring into the mirror, she saw that her purple hair had made a comeback. A smile formed on her face. Familiar was good.

The laundry machine dinged. Her clothes had been washed, dried, and folded. After getting dressed, she felt as if she wanted to put some makeup on, but her stomach growled, making it impossible to think. Food came first, she told herself. Gilda let out a breath and walked out of the bathroom, ready to face her captor again. Perhaps she would try acting a little calmer this time. She should save her rage for when it would be most useful.

But her good behavior was needless, for the bedroom was empty. Gilda looked around. Repulsa was definitely gone. Had the plane landed? No, that couldn't be it. Gilda could see from the oval window that they were still in the air. The woman must have gone to have breakfast in the main cabin. Great, how would she eat a meal with that killer? But her stomach protested with another rumble. It wouldn't take no for an answer. Gilda went to the door that led to the main cabin and pounded on it with her fist.

"Hey, turds! Open up!"

No one answered.

She grabbed the doorknob and turned it, feeling no resistance. That was odd. Any half-decent captor would have locked the door. Maybe it was some kind of trap. She opened the door and peered through the crack.

Nobody was in the cabin.

Not caring if she got in trouble, Gilda stepped out of her room and glanced around. The white couches had nobody sitting on them, and she heard no voices. Maybe they were all in the cockpit, Gilda thought, but that was unlikely, considering at least a dozen people had been on the plane, so where did they go?

Her stomach moaned again. Moaning herself, Gilda went to a cupboard and opened it. A nice juicy pear caught her eye, so she snatched it up. She took a few hearty bites from the fruit and began to properly examine the cabin. Nobody was around. It made no sense. Where could they have gone? They were thousands of feet in the air and flying at hundreds of miles an hour. Could they be planning to kill her? No, it was more likely this was some kind of trick. But what purpose would it serve other than to make her forage for food on her lonesome?

Even after finishing off the pear, her stomach still felt empty. That was no surprise. She had skipped both lunch and dinner yesterday. Gilda went back to the cupboard to get more food, preferably something filling like a protein bar or even—

Gilda stopped walking. A stain on the floor caught her eyes, mesmerizing her. It was all too obvious what it was.

Blood.

Spinning around, she spotted another stain on the carpet, then another on the wall, then one on the couch. It was everywhere! How did she not notice all those little red stains? She started to hyperventilate. The pear she just ate stirred in her gut. Her eyes darted everywhere, searching for some unseen enemy.

Then she caught sight of a shape outside. She spun around to find—

"What ..." Gilda began, but her mind was a complete blank.

A phantom stood on the wing of the plane.

It held a scythe.

Gilda stared out the window, dumbstruck. This was impossible. They were miles up in the sky. Her confusion turned into fear when she noticed something else.

The phantom was staring back at her.

Gilda shivered uncontrollably. She couldn't see its face from here, but she could feel its eyes crawling up her body, examining her. This specter was far beyond human.

The phantom raised its scythe.

It sliced the wing clean off the plane.

The world turned into a blur. Gilda flew off her feet and slammed into the couch, the wind knocked out of her. She grasped her hand around a seatbelt strap and pulled herself into a sitting position. The plane rolled. Gilda barely managed to click her belt in before she found herself upside down. A choked scream gurgled out of her throat. A thousand panicky thoughts ran through her head. Death was right around the corner. She imagined her life ending in a blaze of fire and twisted metal. Those images refused to be pushed out of her mind as she tried to figure out what to do.

Just as a useful idea came to her, the plane rolled again. A can of peas flew out of the cabinet and hit her arm. She screamed. More objects flew out.

All she could do was put her head between her knees, cover the back of her head, and pray for dear life.

***

As the plane plummeted to the ground, the phantom flew lazily behind it. When the plane's spinning fuselage was within reach, the phantom slammed his scythe into its side. The plane suddenly decelerated, as if it had just become weightless.

The phantom grimaced. The girl wasn't going to die.

Not until he was finished with her.

***

The plane slowed down, giving Gilda a nasty case of whiplash. She yelped like a wounded puppy. Her brain rattled inside her skull. Her waistline was bruised thanks to the belt that held her in her seat.

Then all became still.

After a series of moans, Gilda looked around the fuselage. Everything had flown out of the cabinets, food and drink splattered all over the walls. The plane felt as if it was at a forty-five-degree angle, but it seemed stable. Had they crash-landed? No, that couldn't be it. Gilda knew enough about basic physics to know she should have been a gory pancake right now. She looked out the window and saw the plane was still in the air. She did a double-take. This wasn't possible. She didn't hear the sound of engines. How were they flying?

Gilda then made an observation about the ground.

It was getting closer.

A surge of fear jolted through her system. How come she couldn't feel herself falling? Was this all some elaborate experiment set up by Cloak? But what could their motivation possibly be? Whatever the case, she was definitely going down.

Gilda became aware of a strange vibration going through her body. Were the engines still running after all? Then she remembered the specter and shuddered. Gilda had nothing but questions now, all of them unanswered. But at least she was alive. Or at least she thought she was. Being dead would explain a few things, particularly the figure with the scythe.

The plane decelerated even more, almost floating down. Gilda was soon able to make out objects on the ground. Several shabby trees dotted the grassy plain. A large river cut the landscape in half. A flock of birds rested near the side of the bank. She also saw a pack of hyenas lapping up water. It seemed she was over the African savanna. Now the plane was only thirty feet from the ground. The hyenas stared dumbfounded at the floating hunk of metal. Gilda couldn't blame them.

The airplane touched down, though she was unable to feel it. She rubbed her head. The plane then found its weight. A horrible shudder went through it. Gilda gave a girlish squeak, blushing after realizing what she had done. Good thing nobody had been around to hear it. The plane rocked for several seconds before groaning to a stop.

Gilda breathed out. It took all her willpower not to get out of her seat and look around. The plane might move again if she wasn't careful. A normal girl would have been sobbing and whimpering from the incredible ordeal she had just experienced, but Gilda was no normal girl. She had military training and a natural toughness that would make a Marine envious.

It was two minutes before she unbuckled her belt and stood up. Leaving the plane was probably the best course of action. Besides the threat of the plane rolling over or catching fire, Cloak might come looking for her. She had to escape and get as far away from the plane as possible. She looked around the cabin and saw a plastic trash bag on the floor. Gilda filled it with intact cans, other imperishable foods, and six bottles of water. After finding and putting on a sunhat, she was ready to roll.

Getting out of the plane was going to be the dangerous part. The aircraft might decide to roll on her, or she could fall and break something important.

It was best to proceed with caution. She walked over to the emergency exit and opened the thick door. Harsh sunlight hit her eyes, but she got used to it within seconds. Next, she pulled the tab on the side of the door. An inflatable slide came out. Without much enthusiasm, she slid down and landed on the ground.

What next? All she saw around her was a vast brown African savanna and a muddy river. No maps were anywhere to be found in the plane, so the best course of action was to follow the river until she came upon civilization. She was about to vamoose, only to remember how she hadn't been the only one kidnapped.

Slate must still be on the plane. Gilda had seen his unicopter land near the plane when she was boarding it. Most likely Slate was in the airplane's cargo hold, trapped in his tube. Gilda realized rescuing him was now her top priority. Cloak wanted him for some purpose, and she didn't like the idea of letting them have what they wanted. Besides, Slate had saved her life from that drone fighter jet, those Pinocchios, and a gang of murderous mercenaries. She owed him her life three times over. In spite of Slate being perhaps the most obnoxious and insane person she had ever met, she had to save him.

Gilda walked around the sides of the plane and saw that the door leading to the cargo hold was ajar. It looked like someone had pried it open, perhaps the man with the scythe. Gilda was about to investigate when she heard a growl. She froze in place. Her purple hair stood on end. The growls grew deeper. Gilda turned around.

The pack of hyenas had surrounded her. They all foamed at the mouth.

The trash bag filled with provisions slipped from her limp fingers and hit the soil. She resisted the urge to run away. Who could outrun hyenas? She also didn't have a weapon on her, which made her feel like a complete numbskull. All she could do was to try looking as big as possible. Maybe they would go look for an easier meal.

Just as she began to raise her arms and shout, the hyenas yelped and ran away.

Gilda lowered her arms. Had she really been that scary?

A monstrous roar that sounded like a demented pig shook the entire ground. Gilda spun around and spotted the creature that made it.

It was a hippopotamus.

Gilda almost had to laugh. That thing scared the hyenas away? The hippopotamus was large but seemed almost comical standing on the opposite side of the river on its fat legs. It had a dull look in its eyes, barely paying any attention to its surroundings. If this was all the African wild had to throw at her, it wasn't very good.

The hippo began to charge. It roared again.

Now it wasn't funny anymore.

Gilda didn't even bother to look back as her legs moved on their own. She heard the hippo jump into the river behind her. It moved fast for such a large animal. No way could she outrun it. She ran for the plane's cargo hold. It was the only place she could take shelter. With her slim build, she was able to wriggle through the opening and fall inside.

A violent tremor went through the plane as the hippo rammed it. Gilda got to her feet as the hippo slammed its fat body against the aircraft for a second time. She almost lost her balance but managed to put her hand against the wall. The plane was struck again. It rocked in response. Gilda yelped. How long would she be safe here? What could she do now?

Then she saw him.

Slate was still in his tube, somewhat inactive but very much alive. The tube itself, filled with blue fluid, was strapped to the wall. If she could get it open, Slate could save her. But looking at the locked control panel, Gilda didn't see how she could accomplish the feat.

Another tremor went through the plane. Gilda fell on her backside. Her head slammed into a plastic container. Her vision went blurry. Whatever she was going to do, it had to be fast. She shook her head clear and got on her knees. Just as she was getting back up, a nearby box caught her eye. She smiled.

She got the box open and took out a rifle. Shooting the hippo was an idea, but Gilda knew she couldn't aim very well without actually going outside. Not only that, but she ran the risk of angering the beast even more. Then her light bulb went off again. It was risky, but no other option came to mind. Checking to make sure there was ammo inside the rifle, Gilda silently thanked Sergeant Barnes for his lessons, took aim, and fired at the tube.

Bullets slammed into the glass. Cracks spread across its surface. Blue fluid squirted out, leaving a strong chemical smell that made her eyes water. She had been careful not to hit Slate, and from what she could tell, she hadn't.

Roaring, the hippo rammed the plane again. This impact was the strongest one yet. Gilda dropped her rifle and toppled over.

With a loud groan, the plane began to roll.

Boxes and tarps toppled everywhere. Gilda scrambled to grab hold of something. She managed to wrap her fingers around a metal hook attached to the floor. Her entire world shook as the airplane crashed into the river. Brown water began to flood into the cargo hold.

Getting back on her feet, Gilda headed for the opening. The plane was already filled with half a foot of water. She squeezed through the tight gap and tumbled out of the plane, falling into the filthy river water. On reflex, she started swimming. It was tiring work. Her lungs burned from the harsh breaths. She only looked back once to see that the plane was almost completely submerged. Slate was still in there, but she had to worry about herself for now.

She soon crawled onto the riverbank, panting. It took all her strength to stand up. Just how long was this craziness going to last?

The hippo roared again. Gilda felt a rush of adrenaline wipe her fatigue away. The hippo was standing just down the riverbank. Having a closer look, she could now see why the hippo had been behaving so aggressively. Scars covered the animal's back and face. Its right ear had also been torn off. This creature had been targeted by poachers, fighting for its very right to survive for years, a right Gilda had taken for granted up until a few days ago. Its body was tense. Rage filled the eyes of the beast as it stared at her.

It roared again and ran toward Gilda.

But before the hippo could get very far, Slate jumped onto its back.

"Hey, you must be related to Goldberg!"

Slate punched the beast's back, sending electricity into it. The hippo roared. It tried to shake off Slate, but the Helmet Man only persisted in his attacks. Even after having his powers dampened by the water, he was still a formidable foe.

"Now this is a rodeo!" Slate cried. "Giddy up, horsey!"

The hippo roared again. It rolled on its back in an attempt to crush him to death. But Slate was much too quick for that. He jumped into the air, landed on the hippo's exposed belly, and sent a barrage of charged punches into the flabby flesh. The hippo let out such a powerful roar that Gilda had to cover her ears. The hippo convulsed. Bolts of energy filled the air. After a second of this, Slate ceased his assault. The hippo groaned and lay on its side in defeat.

"Wow, I haven't tortured animals like that since I was a teenager!" Slate shouted in his constipated voice. "Brings back fond memories."

Gilda simply stared, agape. She had not expected any of that. Then again, nothing Slate did could be predicted.

"You really are an idiot ..." Gilda said, but she smiled all the same.

***

"Are we even making good time on this thing?" Gilda asked.

Slate shrugged. "Hey, it's better than walking. Move faster!"

The hippo moaned as it trudged along the riverbank. Both of them rode on the fat beast's back, bouncing up and down. Gilda grimaced. Her butt was starting to get sore.

Slate slapped the hippo. "Come on, tubby! Burn that lard!"

Gilda sighed. "So, what's our plan?"

"All right, so we wait until we come across some travelers. Then you act like a frightened girl, crying about your broken nails or something. That's when we rob them blind!"

"I mean about the others. How are we going to find them?"

"Missy, they're dead. If they are still alive, they're in the hands of Cloak and being horribly tortured as we speak."

"You insensitive jackass!"

The hippo gave off another moan.

"Please keep your voice down," Slate said.

"Why? Nobody's around for miles!"

"No, I mean you're upsetting the hippo."

"Is this some kind of joke to you? People are dead! Zubair is—"

Gilda stopped herself. She let loose a shiver.

"We'll give them their comeuppance," Slate said. "Just you wait."

"I don't know ... I'm starting to wonder if I want revenge anymore."

"Then what do you want?" Slate asked.

Gilda glanced across the savanna. She took a deep breath.

"Justice," she told the Helmet Man. "Not just for Henry or Zubair, but for all the people Cloak's hurt and will hurt unless we stop them."

Slate nodded. "Fair enough."

They rode in silence for half a minute before Slate asked Gilda another question.

"Hey, how did our plane crash exactly?"

Gilda got goose bumps just at the mere thought of it. Who was that phantom with the scythe? He clearly wasn't a member of Cloak. Did Slate know who he was?

"Well ..."

"Hold that thought," Slate said. "We've got company."

Gilda squinted and saw a few specks in the distance. The hippo gave off a low, angry rumble and stopped in its tracks. They slid off its back, Gilda almost feeling sorry for it.

"You stay outta trouble," Slate scolded the animal. "Now get going."

The hippo stared at Slate for a second. It then waddled back into the river.

"All right, remember the plan," Slate said. "Rob them blind! Wait, do you hear ... ?"

A familiar voice sounded in the distance. Gilda thought it was her imagination at first, but then she heard it again. Her eyes went wide, and she gave her biggest smile in days.

"It's Dr. Taylor!" she shouted.

Slate cocked his head. "Huh, didn't I kill him?"

"Dr. Taylor!" she screamed.

"Gilda, you're safe!" a megaphone cried.

"We're here!" Gilda cried.

"Aww, man …" Slate said. "Looks like we don't get to rob anyone after all …"

***

"We thought you were dead!" Taylor exclaimed. "How did you escape?"

Gilda smirked. "Let's just say you'll have to sit down for this one."

Taylor had been in one of the trucks, poking his head out the window and yelling through a megaphone. When the convoy stopped, the doctor had run out and gave Gilda a hug, chuckling. He appeared frazzled but otherwise unchanged.

"Hey, where's my hug?" Slate asked.

Taylor ran up and kicked him right between the legs.

"Oh!" Slate croaked, hunching over.

"That's for knocking me out!" Taylor snapped. "Twice!"

Slate lifted his head and growled. "Why, you little …"

Half a dozen trucks rolled to a stop near them. Gilda glanced at them and wondered who was driving them, but then she saw a sight that made her smile yet again.

"Straper! Johnson! You're okay!"

"Gilda, looking good for a dead chick!" Straper yelled.

Johnson and Straper had emerged from the back of a truck, smiling and waving. General Eisenhorn also got out with a smirk plastered on his face. Goldberg and Victoria appeared as well, but they seemed less joyful than everyone else. Gilda had a good idea why.

"Thank goodness you're alive," Johnson said, giving her a quick hug. She didn't like hugs in general but decided not to protest.

Straper grinned. "Time for my hug."

"In your dreams," Gilda scoffed. "How did you find us?"

"Zubair planted the bug on one of you," Johnson said. "If it weren't for him, we wouldn't have found you. Anyway, we were headed to your crash site when we spotted you."

General Eisenhorn was the first to greet the Helmet Man. "Chrome dome, did you manage to kill any of them cretins?"

Slate chuckled. "No, but I did beat up a woman."

Eisenhorn nodded. "That's exactly what I would have done."

Slate turned to Victoria as she approached. She had removed the dye from her hair, her blue streaks noticeable again.

"Hey, spoiled brat!" Slate yelled. "Nice to see you again."

With no warning, Victoria wrapped her arms around him, shoved her head into his vest, and began to cry. The Helmet Man froze. Everyone went quiet.

"Slate, please ..." she sobbed. "I ..."

Then the strangest thing happened.

Slate hugged back. He didn't really know how to do it, but he managed to get his arms around her. Everyone looked a little puzzled, to say the least.

"Yeah, I know ..." Slate said. "Zubair ..."

"Please ..." she said. She calmed her voice down but still cried.

"Don't worry ... I'll kill Houdini myself."

Goldberg walked over and put a hand on Victoria's shoulder. His eyes were also red. Victoria pulled away from Slate and wiped the tears from her face.

"I'm so sorry," Goldberg said. "I dragged you all into this. All those people ... Zubair ... Just because I wanted to solve a foolish mystery ... play detective ... I'm a fat joke ..."

"It's not your fault," Slate said. "I made you take everyone."

"We didn't do too hot either," Johnson admitted. "The general and I were abducted right before we could make contact with the president."

"I was abducted as well," Taylor said. "I was tied up in Goldberg's bedroom when they grabbed me. Goldberg's friend wasn't able to pick me up. They just made him send you a fake text message saying I was stashed away in a safe house."

"All three of you were kidnapped?" Gilda asked. "By who?"

"I hate to disrupt such a tender reunion," someone said. "But we have much to discuss."

Barir walked up to them. His attire was a simple white outfit. He also had on a warm smile, but it did little to hide his impatience.

"Great, it's you again ..." Slate said.

"You made a rather rude exit the last time we met," Barir said. "But I suppose I was just as wrong for withholding information."

"Like the fact you're terrorists?" Gilda spat.

"The Western Union is the one doing the terrorizing. We are merely reacting to their presence in our lands. You would shoot a robber if he tried to break into your house."

"Spare me the ethics lecture," Slate said. "What do you want?"

"Our leader, Incognito, wishes to give you a proposal."

"I'm not ready for marriage. Is he rich and handsome?"

Barir ignored the quip. "He wishes for you to join him."

"Forget it. I ain't interested in fighting the Western Union."

"No, you misunderstand us. We do not want you to fight them. That is my privilege."

Taking a few steps closer, Barir's polite smile vanished.

"Helmet Man, Incognito wants you to fight Cloak."

Slate, Gilda, and the rest of the group all sat in the back of a large truck that drove through the savanna. Barir sat toward the front, facing his guests. Africa, meanwhile, rested near the back doors. He was not as cheerful as when they had first met him.

Slate shrugged. "What? What did I do?"

Africa's eyes narrowed.

Slate snapped his fingers, chuckling. "Oh, yeah. Sorry about electrocuting you and pushing you out of a moving truck. Relax, I took only a little pleasure in doing it."

"Shut up ..."

"Let us not fight," Barir said. "We are all friends here."

"Friends?" Eisenhorn scoffed. "In your dreams, terrorist."

"You do not think us allies? Half of your friends would have died in the Pale Pyramid if we had not been there."

"That was before you gassed us?" Goldberg asked. "Wow, thanks, buddy."

"Plus, you kidnapped General Eisenhorn and me right when we were about to get help from the president," Johnson said. "Zubair might still be alive if you hadn't intervened."

"You Westerners would have just covered up your crimes," Barir said. "For years, your government has ignored Cloak's existence. It could not bear to stare its sin in the face like a man and instead tried to hide its shame like a dog."

"Quit making excuses for acting like a sneak," Slate said. "Why are you interested in Cloak anyway?"

"They are monsters," Africa said. "They have killed hundreds of thousands."

"Whoa ... that's a lot," Straper said.

"Many of the victims are innocent civilians and fellow countrymen," Barir said. "You may think us monsters, but the United Third has always tried to limit itself to military targets. In fact, Cloak has killed almost double the number of civilians we have. And let us not forget these supersoldiers are creations of the Western Union. It is only right we hunt them."

"I get it now," Johnson said. "You defeat Cloak and string them up. Then you point the finger at the Western Union, all to get support for your cause."

"Even if we wished to do that, it would be difficult to prove the Western Union created them. Incognito simply has great motivation to destroy Cloak and kill its members, especially the Gifted. You also have the same goal, Victoria Zaidi."

Victoria jumped in her seat. "Me ... ?"

"Your father was killed by Cloak."

"How do you know that?"

Barir smiled. "I did not know for sure until just now, but we believe Cloak is plotting to hurt you some other way."

"How? They've already—"

Then it dawned on her. A black dread spread throughout her heart.

"They're going to kill Lawrence ..." she whispered.

"Yes, but that is not all. We believe they are planning to destroy the Helios Tower, killing everyone inside it, including your brother."

Victoria's face went blank.

"What!" Goldberg shouted. "Why would they do that?"

"The same reason they killed Ammar Zaidi. Someone hired them to do it. We have reason to believe that Cloak is planning an arms deal. In exchange for killing Ammar Zaidi and destroying the Helios Tower, Cloak would receive a weapon of mass destruction."

"How do you know that?" Johnson asked.

"Incognito told me."

"What is this weapon of mass destruction that Cloak wants?" Taylor asked.

"I have no idea, but if Cloak wants it, that is reason enough to worry."

"Who hired Cloak?" Gilda asked. "Whoever did is responsible for everything."

"I can answer that," Goldberg said, raising his chin a little. "Our trip to the Pale Pyramid wasn't for nothing. I managed to scan and decipher sensitive transcripts of Cloak's transactions when I was in the records room."

He took out his phone and began to text rapidly. "Recently, the Pale Pyramid sent funds covertly to a group that goes by the name of Caravan Works. These funds were meant to cover expenses, but they don't go into detail as to what those expenses were."

"Caravan Works is an arms-producing company that emerged a year ago," Barir said. "I have heard of them. It is rumored they sell weapons to extremist groups and terrorist organizations under the guise of a legitimate corporation. The United Third had never dealt with Caravan Works before, so I do not know much else."

"All right, I'm confused!" Slate yelled.

"Just read the accounts yourself," Goldberg snapped.

"I can't read!"

"Dude, don't you know braille?" Straper asked.

"No, who's she?"

"Shut up!" Victoria snapped. "I need to figure out what to do. My brother and thousands of people are about to be blown up by Cloak."

"Why don't we just call the cops?" Straper asked.

Johnson sighed. "Straper, please don't—wait … you may actually be right."

"I am?" Straper asked.

"He is?" everyone else asked.

"Yes," Johnson said. "General, could we still contact the president?"

Eisenhorn groaned. "Nah … the system locks you out after you access it so the enemy can't use it if you get captured. We blew our one shot."

Johnson stroked his chin. "Then we'll have to give an anonymous call to the peacekeepers and tell them to beef up security at the Helios Tower. Even if there is a mole in the Western Union, it won't matter, since peacekeepers have to respond to a terrorist threat."

"Okay, but there are several problems with that," Taylor said. "One, they might not take us seriously. Bomb threats are always being made, after all."

"We have Goldberg's files," Johnson said. "That can back up our claims."

"Perhaps ... but they might take time to decipher and verify. Two, Cloak would probably find a way to destroy the tower anyway. I mean, they are supersoldiers. Third, even if Cloak decides not to do it, Houdini and his henchmen will likely escape with their weapon. Fourth, the mole could block our call and perhaps even track us down if we send a warning. Finally, I believe Barir is not inclined to let us warn the Western Union."

"You are correct," Barir said. "We do not want the Western Union getting involved, but we do not want Cloak succeeding either."

He turned to Slate. "And that is where you come in."

"Me?" Slate asked. "You're acting like I've already agreed to join you."

"I have a strong belief that you will. Why do you think we helped you out in the desert? Incognito knows how invaluable your abilities are and how eager you are to battle this foe."

"What exactly do I have to do, go door to door and sell Girl Scout cookies?"

"No, you will be a diversion."

The Helmet Man chuckled. "Sounds like you're trying to sneak into an R-rated movie."

"We need you to prevent the attack on the Helios Tower. Meanwhile, a separate team can stop the arms deal and capture Cloak's second-in-command."

"So, if I agree to help you, Houdini and his cronies will come after me?" Slate asked.

"Yes, that is the idea."

"Okay, sounds good to me!"

"What!" Eisenhorn shouted. "I knew you couldn't be trusted."

"Quiet, you old coot! You don't understand the young people."

"I'm sitting here listening to all this nonsense, and the only reason I haven't spoken up yet is because I'm doing Johnson a favor!"

"You mean you're afraid of being slapped silly by him again."

"Shut your hole!"

"Sir, that's enough," Johnson said.

"Why won't you take my side?" Eisenhorn yelled.

"No, sir. You're right. Just give me a chance, please."

General Eisenhorn grumbled but nodded.

Johnson nodded back. He turned to the Helmet Man. "Slate, I know you don't have much loyalty to the Western Union, but you can't join these men, and you can't involve my cadets any more than you already have. Let's alert the authorities. They can deal with Cloak."

"Houdini will get away if I do that," Slate said. "I'm the only one who can fight the Gifted. Anybody else who tries to stop them will only be throwing their lives away."

"Hey, I don't think it's a good idea to join them either," Straper said. "They gassed us, brah. You can't trust terrorists for a second."

"Be reasonable, Slate," Taylor said. "The Western Union might not be a sure-fire alternative, but it's the best we got. Taking matters into your own hands isn't the answer. Have you forgotten what happened at the Pale Pyramid?"

"Hell no! But now I know what to expect. Fighting Houdini should be a lot easier now."

"I have to agree with these guys," Goldberg said. "Don't get me wrong. I want Cloak to pay for what happened, but you got really beat up by those other supersoldiers."

"Hey, I'm all better! I don't even have a limp anymore. I could even take tap-dancing lessons if I was lame enough."

Goldberg slapped his head. "Idiot! We all barely survived that encounter. Don't expect that to happen again. I learned my lesson. You should too. We're just outgunned."

"What, are you saying I can't take them on?"

"Slate, I want justice," Victoria said. "But I think we should call the Western Union, even if we run the risk of the mole blocking our call and finding out where we are."

"Come on! I thought you were on my side."

"That was before my brother's life was at stake."

"He is a man!" Africa shouted. "Be quiet and let him decide for himself."

"What about you, Gilda?" Slate asked. "I haven't heard your whining yet, and I know how much you love to do that."

"Shut up." She sighed. "I don't know …"

"It's simple. Should I join up with the lesser of two evils, or should I let the Western Union muck things up?"

Gilda sighed again. What should she do? She had the unquestionable desire to fight Cloak, to make them answer for what they did to Henry and Zubair. But she knew that Slate might not be able to take these guys on, not to mention how helpless she had been at the casino. She remembered what Taylor had told her at Goldberg's apartment about her not being useful. Now that she had the taste of defeat, those words rang far truer in her head than before.

But something else rang within her, some compulsion that told her it wasn't over, that she still had lots to do. The world needed Cloak to be defeated.

In her heart, she knew she had to try.

"Why not do both?" she asked.

Slate gave a harsh laugh. "Oh, there's a third option?"

"We could see what the Western Union does with Cloak from a distance. If Houdini's determined to blow up the Helios Tower, he'll try to fight any peacekeepers who get in the way."

"I get it … We wait for Houdini to fight the Western Union. If the peacekeepers get whooped, I'll step in and clean up their mess, and Houdini will be preoccupied with them to boot, making my job easier. Pretty smart."

"Are you suggesting we use our comrades as decoys?" Eisenhorn growled. "Have you two no shame? Oh, they're definitely gonna prune you both!"

"I don't like it either," Johnson said. "The idea of Slate flying around when the Western Union shows up is troublesome enough, but this? I may not be a soldier of the Western Union anymore, but I'm still a patriot. Thousands of lives will be at stake."

"But how many more will die if we don't stop Houdini once and for all?" Gilda asked. "I've seen what the Gifted can do, and you've seen what Slate can do. Besides, even if the peacekeepers don't believe us or can't handle it, at least he'll be there to stop the attack."

"If you alert the Westerners of the attack, you'll risk ruining the element of surprise and put all our lives at risk," Africa warned. "Cloak might also decide to postpone its attack or arms deal. We'll miss our chance, and they'll get to live for another day."

"This is also meant to be a test for Slate," Barir said. "Incognito wants to see how well he does with fighting Cloak. Throwing the Western Union into the mix will only skew the results."

"Screw your test," Gilda snapped. "We need to stop Cloak."

"You seem so ready to put lives on the line," Johnson told her. "Putting Slate in the middle of this situation could mean a lot of collateral damage."

Gilda almost snapped again but took a breath. "I know this is a big risk, but we can't let Cloak keep killing people. I know what the Gifted can do. Slate's our best bet."

"You don't have faith that the Western Union can stop them?"

"To be frank, I'm starting to lose faith in the Union altogether."

Johnson wanted to rebut but shook his head instead.

"Hold on a second …" Taylor said. "When is Cloak planning to attack the Helios Tower exactly? Forming a counter strategy might be easier if we knew the time frame."

"The opening ceremony for the Helios Tower will be tomorrow at noon," Victoria said. "Almost every wealthy individual in the Middle East will be there, not to mention several Western Union officials and military leaders."

"Johnson, I change my mind," Eisenhorn said. "Let's follow the girl's plan."

"Sir, I can't let this happen," Johnson said.

"Shut up, Johnson! I've had it with running away. And I'll be damned if we rely on peacekeepers to save the day."

"Sir …"

"Johnson, as your superior, I order you to let Slate fight. He's a moron, but he's a moron that can throw a punch. I say we sic him on those goons."

"What do you think, Johnson?" Taylor asked. "I'm personally stumped."

Johnson deflated and rubbed the side of his head. His entire body seemed to melt. It took a full minute of thinking before he made up his mind.

"I'm tired of running. Ever since the attack on the Bunker, I haven't been able to sleep without seeing the cadets' faces."

Taylor lowered his head. "Me too."

"This won't stand anymore. It won't. We're going to get every soldier in Dubai, drag them all to the Helios Tower, and bring those monsters to justice." He turned to Gilda. "And we'll have Slate waiting just in case."

"And who's to say we'll let you warn the Western Union?" Africa spat.

Slate made a fist that sparked. "That would be me ..."

Africa scowled and tried to stand up from his seat, but Barir raised his hand. Africa flared his nostrils and forced himself to relax.

"We're not going to let all those deaths go unanswered," Johnson went on. "Too many have suffered already, and I can't keep trying to pass this fight off to someone else anymore. It's time we stood our ground."

"No more ..." Goldberg growled.

"They're not touching my brother," Victoria spat.

"Time to bring the fight to them," Taylor said.

"Does anyone care what I have to say?" Straper asked.

"Enough is enough," Gilda said.

"You Westerners are amusing," Barir said, smiling softly. "I will have to get Incognito's approval of this plan before anything happens, but I am warming to it, even if it means warning the peacekeepers. Your enthusiasm is that contagious."

"Does this mean we're working with the United Third?" Victoria asked.

"For now," Johnson said. "We may have Slate, but we don't have the resources to get to Dubai on our own." He stared at Barir. "While I'm indebted to you for saving my cadets, just remember that we're not your soldiers.

We won't tolerate any action against the Western Union or civilians, and I can't guarantee kind treatment if the peacekeepers catch you."

"How blunt of you," Barir said. He rose from his seat. "We are almost at a small airport. From there, we will fly to Arabia and drive to Dubai where the Helios Tower is."

"Yeah, then we're gonna blow it up!" Slate yelled.

"We're supposed to save it, imbecile," Victoria said, smiling.

"I guess things are just getting interesting!" Eisenhorn cackled.

Nobody knew how right the general was.

"Have you taken all your pills?" Barir asked.

Gilda nodded. She had swallowed three in the past six hours. Taylor had examined the pills beforehand, saying they were okay to swallow, but he had also given her a glance. The pills were apparently for radiation poisoning. Gilda had no idea why she needed them, but Barir had insisted. Then she figured it out.

"It's about the scythe guy, right?" she asked.

Barir didn't answer. Gilda huffed and crossed her arms. She had told the others about her encounter. Slate, Eisenhorn, Straper, and Goldberg had only laughed, but the rest, especially Barir, did not find her tale amusing.

"Okay, why doesn't Slate need these pills?" Gilda asked, but she didn't expect an answer. To her surprise, she actually got one.

"Slate should be able to heal on his own," Barir said. "He has unnatural abilities."

"What about me? Do I have to worry about anything?"

"You will have stomach troubles in a couple of days and possibly be a bit weak in the knees, but you should be fine."

Gilda sighed. The idea of being radioactive was unpleasant. And if she was, she doubted she would get superpowers like Slate.

Gilda sat in the passenger seat of a small brown truck driven by Barir, driving down a highway that cut across the desert. She wore a green combat uniform with the sleeves rolled up. Everyone else wore similar outfits, except for Slate, who sported his trademark black attire.

Eisenhorn and Johnson, meanwhile, sat silently in the back with Gilda. Johnson didn't like the idea of letting Gilda and Straper go on this mission, but not only would it be difficult to prevent them from coming along, but he also had to admit that Gilda and Straper were actually pretty good at this sort of thing. It seemed the cadets had become soldiers.

Africa drove a truck ahead of them that carried Slate and Victoria. A third truck followed in the rear, containing Goldberg, Straper, Taylor, and one of Barir's men. A fourth truck took the lead, full of United Third terrorists. Their destination was Dubai.

"Are you sure they got the tip?" Johnson asked.

"You made the call yourself," Barir said. "You also emailed Goldberg's files and your own personal account of what has happened since the Bunker attack. If the peacekeepers refuse to believe that, I am not sure what else could convince them."

"At the very least, it will put them on high alert."

"I must admit, I am surprised Incognito approved your plan. We could very well be driving into a trap because of our warning."

"I wouldn't expect a United Third member to have faith in the Western Union. But I do. Even though I don't agree with all the methods, I still have faith in our cause."

"You mean trying to bring peace to the world?"

"Yes, I have faith we will do that one day."

Barir gave a withered smile. "You know what is funny? I once had faith in that too."

"Nobody cares!" Eisenhorn squawked. "Go back to driving, smooth talker!"

Johnson wished he could brush off Barir's remark as easily. Instead, he stared out the window as the arid landscape sped by.

***

"Time to explain the plan," Barir had told them half a day ago. They had been flying on a rusty old plane. Everyone except Slate was munching on bread and dried meat while they sat in moldy passenger seats and listened.

"We have already informed the Western Union of the impending attack," Barir said. "Whether or not they believe us is up to them, but we expect at least a modest response from the peacekeepers. All of us will wait a safe distance from the Helios Tower until Cloak reveals itself. We will then determine if Slate should intervene or not. I expect he will have to."

"Wait, how is Cloak gonna blow up the tower?" Straper asked. "Are they gonna fire a missile at it or something?"

"No, but Ms. Zaidi knows how to destroy the tower, do you not?"

Victoria nodded. "Destroying the support columns with a bomb is the best way to ensure the tower collapses."

"Yes, should the need arise, I shall have the dubious pleasure of disabling the bomb. Slate will be there to give me some breathing room and fight the Gifted if they show themselves. The peacekeepers may try to assist Slate, but they may also try to shoot him."

"Then I'll shoot them right back!" Slate yelled.

"No, you will not!" Eisenhorn barked. "Don't make me smack you, boy."

"What, so I can't even kill defensively? You're giving me no leeway here!"

"Slate ..." Gilda said, giving him a stern yet pleading look.

Slate threw up his hands. "Fine, take all the fun outta life!"

"As I was saying ..." Barir said. "I will be defusing the bomb. I need three volunteers to help me with this task."

Barir glanced at Goldberg.

"What, me?" Goldberg asked as he swallowed some bread.

"I need a guide who knows the layout of the Helios Tower."

"I've only been there twice."

"Why not me?" Victoria asked. "I have superior knowledge of the Helios Tower, or don't you like the idea of a young lady telling you where to go?"

"Frankly, I do not like the idea of Mr. Goldberg telling me where to go," Barir said.

"Hey!" Goldberg yelled.

"Besides, I need you to evacuate the Helios Tower should Slate start fighting the Gifted. Africa will be your bodyguard, so you have nothing to worry about. Meanwhile, Goldberg and another two volunteers will assist me."

"I'll go," Gilda said.

"That is considerate, but I shall need stronger individuals to help me move the bomb if we are forced to do so."

"It doesn't sound like we're really volunteering," Taylor said.

"You and Straper will come and help me," Barir told Taylor, ignoring his comment. "The rest of you will stay near the entrance to the Helios Tower, where you will help direct peacekeepers and warn away civilians."

"You mean I'm a traffic cop!" Gilda burst out. "But I'm at least two times stronger than Straper, and you're taking him instead?"

"She's right," Straper whined. "Take her instead for the suicide mission. I'm all for affirmative action."

"Is this all because she's a woman?" Victoria scoffed. "I don't exactly find the thought of going into battle appealing myself, but she should have her chance."

Slate chuckled. "What did you expect from a Middle Eastern terrorist?"

"He has a point," Goldberg said, wiping off his thick fingers.

"I believe women should stay away from the battlefield," Barir said. "They simply are not physically strong enough. It is best they tend to the wounded and other such tasks."

"At least that's one thing the terrorists got right," Eisenhorn grumbled.

"Your jobs are what they are," Barir said. "That is the plan. Questions?"

There were none.

"Good, then get some rest. We shall be in Arabia in a few hours."

As the meeting ended, Straper got out of his seat and went over to Gilda.

"Sorry, Gilda. That really sucks. If it makes you feel better, I think you should have been the one to go on the suicide mission."

Gilda sighed. "Gee, thanks ..."

***

The lamb was tender and juicy. Houdini took another bite and closed his one eye, savoring the taste. He sat in a comfortable leather chair. A bowl of lamb stew rested before him on a small table. He had thought the plane ride would be awful, but the stew was sublime and everything was proceeding on schedule. Slate and the Plato girl were captured, Victoria Zaidi and her swine friends were dead, and the prototype would soon be in Cloak's grasp.

A bit of stew splattered on his gray suit. Houdini wiped it off nonchalantly with a napkin. Under normal circumstances, he would have been spitting fire right now, but his mood was oddly calm. Never before had he experienced such peace. Was this all because he had killed all those people? No, he had killed many before, and their deaths never made him this content. It must be because Cloak's plans were now in the final stages of unfolding.

Houdini had no idea what the ultimate design of his master was, only a vague idea, a deep yearning. He knew Cloak would impose its will on the world. They would destroy the Western Union and all the vermin who had tortured them. Only then could they find meaning to their pain. That was their destiny. That was the will of the Mentor.

Houdini's reflection was interrupted when Frost opened the door.

"We'll be landing in an hour, boss," Frost said.

"Good, anything else?" Houdini asked, taking another bite of lamb.

"Yeah, a call for you."

"It must be Sebastian. Congratulations, I suspect. Leave me. I shall take the call as humbly as I can."

"Got it, boss," Frost said, trying not to roll his icy eyes as he left.

Chewing his lamb, Houdini took a remote control out of his pocket and pressed the red button. He wondered if he could get seconds as the hologram materialized before him.

"Houdini, is there anything to report?" Sebastian asked. He was wearing his usual blue suit, round sunglasses, and trademark slimy grin.

"I'll arrive at Dubai in an hour," Houdini said. "I have attended to all matters. Ammar Zaidi's brat is dead, Slate and the girl are heading to you, and there is no more evidence of the Pale Pyramid's laundering activities. All that's left is to destroy the Helios Tower and get the prototype from our contact."

"You seem sure of yourself."

"Because I am." Houdini chuckled, taking another bite of lamb stew.

Sebastian sighed, still grinning. "It's too bad. I always knew you were simpleminded, but I honestly thought you knew Slate had escaped."

Houdini almost choked on his lamb. "What!" He jumped up, knocking over the table. His bowl shattered on the floor. What was left of the stew soaked into the carpet.

"Also, your unicopters were destroyed at the Pale Pyramid, and a train full of passengers escaped, alive and intact. Now James Moosvi is wanted for questioning by the Western Union."

"But ... but ... No! My pilots sent confirmation!"

"Verbal confirmation?"

Houdini tried to answer but now found himself choking on outrage.

"Seems the enemy is more sophisticated than you gave them credit for," Sebastian said. "My, this is a rather ... public fiasco. There's even a story that just aired on the news. Lucky for you that Moosvi isn't your real name, or your situation could be a whole lot worse."

"This is impossible! Repulsa was on the plane, along with Klein and a dozen other mercenaries. Slate was also trapped in that tube you gave me. If anything went wrong, it's because the prison failed. You are responsible!"

"Excuses, excuses, excuses ... Unfortunately, Repulsa is missing. I must assume she is dead. As to how the plane crashed ..."

"Who is behind this?" Houdini cried. The veins in his head bulged out, as did the black ball in his empty eye socket.

"That's not really important. Our schedule is what matters. All the other Gifted are busy establishing a partnership with the Chinese Empire, so it's just you, me, and Sandtrap."

Houdini was breathing rapidly. He grabbed his chair for support.

"Call your contact," Sebastian said. "Have him find out if anyone has reported a bomb threat against the Helios Tower. If so, have him delegitimize it accordingly. We make no changes to our plans beyond that. Oh ... and I still want Slate alive."

Sebastian snickered. "Goodbye, Houdini. Do well and I might not slit your throat."

The hologram turned off.

Houdini turned around and left his cabin. Frost was standing near the door, wearing a smirk. He had overheard the conversation.

"Did you enjoy the lamb?" Frost asked.

Houdini took out his pistol and smashed it into Frost's temple. Frost cried out and fell to his knees. He covered his bleeding head with his hands.

A scream came from the front of the plane. A quivering flight attendant stood there, about to burst into tears.

Houdini turned toward her. Before she could flee, he vanished and reappeared in front of her. His fist stuck out of her back. The flight attendant wore an expression of simple shock as she realized an arm was now going through her chest.

Houdini pulled out his arm, making a sucking sound. The flight attendant collapsed. Blood covered his appendage. His one eye stared at the gaping hole in her chest. Blood spurted from her mouth. Her body shook a little. It took all of his effort not to spit on her. Instead, he gave her the gift of mercy. He unloaded his gun into her head, screaming as he did, not stopping until he had fired every single bullet.

The body stopped twitching, as did Houdini's screams. He turned to Frost, who stared at him in awe and horror, gingerly touching his wounded head.

"Let this be a lesson to you ..." Houdini said. "Do not mock me!"

Victoria looked out the window as they drove through the desert. Sitting in the passenger seat had its perks, especially since she didn't have to be next to Slate in the back. But she soon regretted that decision. She would rather have him make crude jokes and talk in his silly voice than have to sit here in silence. Her mind kept coming back to Zubair's horrific death and what might happen to her brother, what additional horror she might have to endure.

Then she saw it.

"Look," she said. "It's magnificent, isn't it?"

Miles away, a long, vertical sliver could be seen poking out of the horizon.

Africa squinted at it as he drove. "What is it?"

"The Helios Tower," Victoria said.

Africa's eyes went wide. "That cannot be. We still have over an hour until we enter Dubai. I heard the tower was tall, but not *this* tall."

"It was built upon the old foundation of the Burj Khalifa, the world's former tallest building. But the Helios Tower is almost twice that height, over five thousand feet."

"Wow, that is tall!" Slate exclaimed. "No wonder someone wants to blow it up."

"If the tower is destroyed, it will ruin my father's company, and killing all our investors at the opening ceremony would doubly seal that fate. Caravan Works makes weapons. They might want to get rid of Zaidi Industries in order to eliminate the competition."

"Relax," Slate said. "I'll deal with those guys after I finish with Houdini. Geez, my revenge list is getting long ..."

"Why do you need to build such a high tower?" Africa asked.

"It's space-based solar power," Victoria said. "The Helios Tower is designed to receive microwaves from our satellite array. The array itself gathers the microwaves from the sun. The top fifty levels of the tower are primarily devoted to converting the microwaves into electrical energy and transferring that energy to the outside world. Our first test run is scheduled in two weeks, but construction is officially complete today."

"How much energy is that thing supposed to make?"

"Enough to power the entire Arabian Peninsula," Victoria said with pride.

"Impressive, but that power will just go to the safe zones, not to the villages or towns that need the most help, the ones that still don't even have clean water or medicine."

Victoria's smile turned to a frown. "It's a step in the right direction. We're rebuilding the Middle East from scratch after thugs like you tore it down."

"All you are doing is strengthening the grip of imperialism."

"This is my father's legacy! How dare you claim—"

"Hey, no need for arguing," Slate said. "Africa, where's that cheerful mood I saw when we first met you?"

"Thrown out of a moving truck."

"You just can't get over that, can you? Man, I didn't realize there was so much tension in here. What we need is some fresh air!"

Slate leaned over to the window on his right and punched it. The glass shattered. Victoria yelped. Sand blew inside the vehicle. Africa and Victoria started coughing.

"What are you doing?" Africa yelled.

Slate shrugged. "I don't respond well to conflict."

***

The light was harsh and blinding, but Houdini wouldn't have to be in the sun for long. He climbed out of the plane and stepped onto the tarmac, glancing around with a scowl. Where was that driver? He needed to be at the Helios Tower in ten minutes. Too bad he could only teleport within his field of vision, or he wouldn't have to rely on fools.

His phone vibrated in his pocket. That could only be one person.

Houdini picked it up. "What is it this time?" he snapped.

"I recently intercepted a call," the contact said. "A good thing I'm on the job, or else you might be wearing handcuffs right now."

"Stop flattering yourself. What are you talking about?"

"A call was made yesterday to the Western Union embassy in Dubai. The caller warned of an attack on the Helios Tower."

"Curses! We'll have to hold off on the plan until the peacekeepers lower their guard."

"Relax, they were only there a few minutes. Do you know how many bomb threats that tower gets daily? The peacekeepers won't take it seriously unless they got legitimate cause. The caller did send some documents, but I managed to garble them before the peacekeepers had a chance to verify or properly read through them. I also smoothed things over with the local embassy. We're fine. Just wait until I call you back."

"Don't give me orders. You better be right about this."

"I am right. And guess what else? A surveillance drone just spotted a small convoy of trucks headed for Dubai. A man with a silver helmet was inside one."

"What? You should have told me that first. Go deal with them!"

"Didn't you want this Helmet Man alive? And shouldn't Cloak handle him? After all, you and your colleagues have powers to match his."

"I don't expect you to kill Slate. You're too incompetent for that. All you can do is slow them down so I have enough time to set up the bomb."

"I don't appreciate the way I'm being—"

"Don't call me again!" Houdini hung up the phone and threw it on the tarmac, breaking it into a dozen pieces.

"Do you have your phone?" Houdini growled at his lackey.

"Yeah," Frost said. He had a growth patch on his temple where Houdini had hit him. It was no surprise that Frost looked almost as unhappy as his boss.

"At least you did that right. As soon as you get the call, plant the bomb."

"What about you?" Frost asked, clenching his teeth.

"That's none of your business. Now get out of my sight!"

Frost squinted his icy eyes and growled. He then walked away. Houdini watched him go. Perhaps it was time to kill Frost. Not only did he keep failing him, but now he was making a habit of defying him. Houdini had mainly hired Frost because of his ruthlessness and lack of scruples. But those assets could only carry him so far. Yes, Frost would need to die soon, and his death would not be pleasant.

"Houdini ..." a voice huffed.

An involuntary chill went up Houdini's spine. He turned to see Sandtrap standing right behind him. The brown mask stared down at him. Houdini moistened his dry lips. How had Sandtrap been able to sneak up on him like that?

"Repulsa ..." the masked man breathed. "When ... ?"

Houdini had not told him that Repulsa was missing and thought dead. He lacked competent men and needed Sandtrap to be at his best. More importantly, Houdini didn't want to see Sandtrap angry. He was the only one Houdini had ever truly feared besides the Mentor. Insanity dwelt beneath that mask, something even Houdini's raw anger couldn't match.

"She's just fine," Houdini said, smiling as confidently as he could. "Slate did hurt her when he escaped, but he will suffer a fate worse than death. You'll see to that, won't you?"

Sandtrap's trench coat fluttered in the wind. The scars on his bald head were redder than ever. His breaths became murderous howls.

"Slate ..." he huffed. "Scoundrel ..." he puffed. "Scoundrel ..."

***

"Hey, I see some vehicles behind us," Victoria said, checking her mirror.

"Yeah, the two other trucks," Slate scoffed. "Thanks for the news bulletin."

"Imbecile, these are new vehicles, half a kilometer behind Goldberg's truck."

"We were bound to come across others," Africa said. "The city is not too far away. Even with the barrier around the safe zone, there is still going to be some traffic."

"You don't understand. Most travelers coming to Dubai usually do so by air or sea. We're only coming by land because I have a special permit. There was no other way to bring these weapons into the city, not to mention Slate. Are you sure these vehicles are friendly?"

"Do not worry. They may be the first cars we have seen in about an hour, but that does not mean we have to get suspicious."

"Those aren't cars," Slate said. "We got some hogs on our tail."

"Huh? What about pigs?"

Victoria sighed. "He's talking about motorcycles."

Africa went alert.

"What's wrong?" Victoria asked.

Africa snatched up a handheld radio from the cup holder. "Barir, we got a problem."

"What?" Barir asked from the other end.

"Drones ..."

***

"We have a situation," Barir said over the radio. "Drones."

Ahmad tensed up. "What do I do?"

"Tell your passengers to prepare."

Ahmad turned to his passengers in the back. "Hey, get your guns out!"

"What's going on?" Goldberg asked, sitting in the back with Straper.

"Drones are coming!" Ahmad shouted. He was a stout man with a short beard and thick glasses who had joined the United Third over seven years ago. Ahmad had known the risks of this mission, but he didn't think they would be in hot water so soon.

"Do as he says," said Taylor, who was in the passenger seat.

"Relax, dude," Straper said. "Dying is the last thing on my list."

"You have a list?" Ahmad asked.

"It's a joke," Taylor said.

"Bad time for jokes!"

"Since when did you become a critic, brah?" Straper asked as he leaned over the back seat to grab two rifles. He handed one to Goldberg.

"Hey, I don't know how to fire a gun!" Goldberg yelled.

"Don't worry," Straper said. "I've done it loads of times at the Bunker. Just flip the safety forward, aim, and shoot. Careful. It has a kick."

"What are we even firing at?" Goldberg asked.

"Look out the back window," Taylor said.

Goldberg and Straper turned around to look at the desert road behind them. Cracks crisscrossed the concrete, which explained all the bumps. But what they were really interested in were the four sand-colored motorcycles gaining on them. They had no riders and drove low to the ground. These bikes had no handlebars or seats, which gave them a very streamlined design. Along with a rearview camera, each motorcycle had a single lens mounted on its front that zoomed in on its new targets.

Each drone was also equipped with two machine guns.

"Ah, nuts ..." Goldberg moaned.

"Don't you mean nuts and bolts?" Straper jested.

"I'm going to beat you ..."

The motorcycles opened fire.

"Duck!" Taylor screamed.

Goldberg and Straper didn't need to be told twice. They covered their heads and ducked as low as they could. Bullets slammed into the back of the speeding truck, shattering the rear window. Ahmad was unable to get down in time. Three bullets went through his chest. After a brief gasp and shudder, he was dead at the wheel. The gunfire from the drones ended, leaving a ringing in everyone else's ears.

Taylor hopped to Ahmad's seat and opened the door.

"Apologies, sir ..."

Taylor shoved the corpse out of the vehicle and took the wheel. The body hit the pavement hard. By the time anyone noticed, it was already a spot in their rearview mirror.

"Oh, my god!" Goldberg cried.

"Way to respect the dead!" Straper yelled.

"Shoot back!" Taylor yelled, too full of adrenaline to care. He turned the wheel sharply to the right, driving the truck off the road. One of the motorcycle drones broke out of formation to follow them. Straper and Goldberg popped out from hiding and fired their weapons, but the drone swerved to the right, evading the attack.

It fired at them again.

"Seriously, brah!" Straper yelled.

***

"Slate, hurry up!" Victoria screamed. She heard the gunfire from behind her and saw that Taylor's truck had driven off the road.

"Fine ..." Slate sighed. He poked his right arm out of the window he had broken. "Hey, Africa! Drive off-road so I can get a good shot at them robots. Barir's stupid truck is in the way."

"I got a better idea," Africa said. He yelled into the radio in Arabic. Barir's truck went off the road without delay, revealing three motorcycles close behind.

"Victoria, take the wheel!" Africa ordered.

"I don't know how to drive!" she yelled. "Zubair did that for me."

"Then now is a good time to learn."

***

As Barir drove off the road, Gilda watched Slate from her window. Johnson and Eisenhorn did the same. The Helmet Man fired seven lightning bolts from his truck. Most of them just struck the concrete, leaving scorch marks on the asphalt, but one motorcycle was hit dead-on. It wobbled a little before falling on its side and skidding to a stop.

The other drones avoided the bolts and swerved around their fallen comrade. They fired their guns. Bullets hit the bumper of Slate's truck. Africa got their vehicle out of the line of fire, avoiding any serious damage. Slate kept firing electricity at his foes, but the drones learned fast, now driving in a zigzag pattern so they could evade his bolts. Gilda saw Africa lean out of his truck. What was he doing?

Then she spotted the bazooka in his hands.

Africa aimed the big green tube at the drones and fired.

Smoke trailed behind the projectile as it flew at its target. The two motorcycles were not quick enough to evade the rocket. It exploded between them. Flames and shrapnel knocked the two bikes on their sides. They each gave a few mechanical coughs before dying.

"Yeah, take that, you scrap heaps!" Eisenhorn yelled. "That'll teach you to replace hardworking soldiers on the battlefield."

***

Taylor had driven the truck some ways off the road now, but the motorcycle was still hot on their trail. Goldberg and Straper kept firing out the back window. The drone had no trouble avoiding their bullets.

"Try aiming!" Taylor yelled. "Didn't Sergeant Barnes teach you that?"

"Yeah, but there's so much going on!" Straper yelled.

"Shut out all the noise!"

"How do I do that?" Straper shrieked.

"Pretend that Slate's talking!" Goldberg yelled.

"Hey, good idea!"

"Just do it!" Taylor shouted. The drone fired at the truck again, but they managed to duck in time. They might not be so lucky again.

The drone stopped firing. Straper poked his head out and aimed. His eyes followed the swerving pattern of the motorcycle.

Straper stopped breathing. He fired.

The bullet slammed into the drone's front wheel. The motorcycle flipped over and spun through the air. It smashed into a dune, finished.

Straper laughed. "Yeah, that's what I call shooting!"

"Good hit!" Taylor exclaimed.

"Nice one, kid!" Goldberg yelled, patting Straper on the back.

"Oh, no ..." Taylor groaned.

"Great, what now?" Straper asked.

"I don't think this is quite over yet. We got a walker up ahead."

***

Africa sat back in his seat, grinning. Victoria was still driving the truck. She had a strained look on her face, but she wasn't doing bad for her first time.

Africa laughed. "I love using that thing. Those drones were blown away!"

"Um ... Africa," Victoria said. "We got a problem."

"What?" he asked.

"Something's blocking the road ahead of us."

"Do you know what it is?" Africa asked Slate.

"Yeah, I can sense it ..." Slate groaned. "It's a fricking walker."

Africa's face went blank. "Are you sure?"

"Kind of hard to mistake it for anything else."

Africa grew cold. "Then we do not stand a chance ..."

The mecha fired a shell at them.

A whistling resonated through the air. The shell hit the lead truck, annihilating the vehicle and all the terrorists in it. Africa, who had resumed driving, barely had time to swerve around the flaming remains.

The second shell struck the road. The explosion was earth-shattering, literally. Chunks of road flew and hit the side of Africa's truck. One of them smashed through the window, sending shards of glass at Victoria. She shielded herself from the debris with her arms.

Africa swerved again, driving off the road. Another shell hit nearby. A cloud of sand flew up. Victoria's ears rang from the blast.

"Slate, do something!" she screamed.

"Is it too much to say please?" Slate asked.

"Please save us, you idiot!"

"Guess this is the only way to teach you manners." Slate opened the passenger door and jumped out. Blue streaks of energy trailed behind him as he flew.

The enemy walker stood far ahead of their truck. All walkers were humanoid in shape, headless and about fifteen feet in height. They had boxy bodies with big metal gorilla arms. Each one of their arms had a three-clawed pincer for grasping objects, but the right arm was for shooting heavy artillery and the left for firing bullets. Their legs were stubby and thick. They could walk over rough terrain, drive on paved roads, and jump surprisingly high.

This particular walker was a drone with sand-colored armor plates. Most walkers had human pilots, especially in combat scenarios, but using drone walkers for protecting safe zones was considered the new norm, unfortunately for Slate.

Slate sent a bolt at the walker and hit it dead-on, but it didn't even phase the mecha. Instead, the walker aimed its cannon at him. A shell shot out. Slate flew to the right. The shell exploded near where he had just been, sending sand flying about. Slate pointed his finger at the walker and sent more bolts at the mechanical foe. No damage was taken, but it decided to change tactics.

The metal bolts that had kept the walker's feet attached to the ground retracted. Its wheels touched down on the pavement, and the walker began to move forward. It was an odd sight, a giant metal gorilla skating down a desert highway.

But there was nothing comical about this scene. The machine crouched down and picked up speed. The walker could only use its cannon arm when it wasn't moving, so it would have to resort to tracker bullets. It fired them at Slate.

"I hate robots!" Slate yelled as he flew. "Why can't we be Amish?"

But Slate had dealt with tracker bullets before. He made a sharp turn. The bullets flew right past him. They had to make a large U-turn before they could come at him again.

The walker did not sit idly by. It fired more tracker bullets to its right. Slate noticed this and flew low to the ground, toward the incoming fire. The second barrage of tracker bullets flew over him and started to circle back for another attack. Slate was now flying toward the walker. He came so fast that the mecha didn't have time to move aside. The Helmet Man flew between its legs. The walker swung its gorilla arms at Slate and kept on doing so as the tracker bullets slammed into its body.

"Use regular bullets next time, jackass!" Slate jeered.

The Helmet Man's plan had worked. Tracker bullets were not only poor at turning around but also at avoiding obstacles. They could even circle back and kill the very person who had fired them. That was why it was against military law to use them in safe zones, and now that Slate had them figured out, they posed no real threat to him.

But they still could do damage to the walker. Most of the bullets only hit its armor, making unsightly marks. However, one managed to hit a vital component for the functioning of the walker's left arm. Now it was useless and limp, though the walker still had its right arm, along with its cannon.

The walker slowed to a stop and bolted its feet to the ground. It aimed its cannon arm and fired another shell. But it hadn't aimed at Slate. The walker had learned that wasting its ammo on the Helmet Man was unproductive.

It would focus on its secondary targets.

"Shit!" Slate yelled. "It's gonna turn them to paste."

The three trucks had gotten back on the highway, since the terrain was becoming too hazardous to drive off-road anymore. Turned out it was even more hazardous on the road. Barir braked as the shell exploded in the truck's path but crashed into the crater the shell left behind anyway. Gilda and Barir were cushioned by airbags. Johnson and Eisenhorn only had flimsy seatbelts that broke as they slammed into the front seats and gritted their teeth.

"Get out!" Barir shouted.

Gilda was the first to gather her wits and swing her door open. Johnson grabbed Eisenhorn's arm, but the general didn't need that much motivation.

Slate fired more bolts. Most of them hit the walker, but they had no effect on the metal monstrosity. The walker was made to operate in the harsh desert environment and often encountered electrical storms. This was no worse.

The walker fired its cannon and hit the crashed truck.

Gilda was the farthest away. Nevertheless, she almost fell over when the shell exploded, feeling the heat on her back. Eisenhorn and Johnson toppled, only able to shield their heads from the debris. Barir managed not to fall, but a piece of smoking metal hit his shoulder. All that was left of the truck was its fiery skeleton.

Taylor and Africa kept their trucks on the road, for the terrain was still too treacherous. However, despite the time constraint, the two trucks decided to turn around, driving away from Dubai and the walker. That didn't stop the walker from aiming its cannon at them. Gilda felt lightheaded. What could they do? How could they possibly beat that thing?

Then she remembered. She had been training to be a walker pilot for years and knew that the standard walker had a serious weak spot.

"Slate!" Gilda yelled. She hoped he could hear her.

The Helmet Man did, but he was busy trying to distract the walker by firing bolts at its feet. It did little to bother the mecha.

"Slate, attack its ankles!" Gilda shouted.

"Huh, what for?" Slate yelled.

"The walker needs to bolt its feet down so the cannon's recoil won't topple it! But if you damage its ankles, the bolts won't be able to retract. It'll be stuck!"

Slate gave her a thumbs-up. "Good advice! About time someone else contributed."

Taylor swerved his truck. A shell exploded to his right, almost destroying him and his passengers. The walker aimed again. It would use a shrapnel shell this time. This kind of ammo would do some damage, even if it didn't get a direct hit.

But Slate had flown down and landed right beneath the walker. The Helmet Man sprinted over to the mecha's feet and punched the metal, blue sparks flying about, until it looked completely malformed. This assault didn't go unnoticed. The walker stopped aiming and swung its massive arm at him. Slate rolled out of the way in time. The mecha punched concrete instead. Slate jumped onto the walker's back. He punched the body repeatedly, making dents and scorch marks. The walker sent electricity through its outer armor, a method of getting enemies off it, but the electricity didn't deter Slate and perhaps even made him stronger.

With a jerk, the walker attempted to lift its bolted foot from the concrete, but its ankle had been so badly damaged that the bolts wouldn't retract. Slate focused his punches around the walker's right arm joint. The arm shuddered and went dead. Now the walker was immobile. The mecha tried to attack but only succeeded in moving its free leg forward a little.

Slate jumped off its back and punched the air in victory. "Yeah, I wish I drank fluids so I could piss on you!"

"Get in the truck!" Victoria spat. Africa had pulled up next to Slate.

Slate did as he was told, mumbling about the lack of gratitude. As he sat, he suddenly twisted his head to the side.

"What now?" Victoria asked.

"Unicopters," Slate said. "Better get the hell outta Dodge."

Africa floored it.

***

Taylor looked over his shoulder. Western Union unicopters were closing in from behind. He knew they wouldn't be able to outrun them.

"Crap, they must have been patrolling the desert," Straper said. "Hey, aren't we gonna pick up the others? They're right up ahead."

"We can't stop," Taylor said. "Our only chance is if the unicopters decide to pick them up instead of go after us."

"Whoa, we can't just leave them! What if they get tortured?"

"We don't have much of a choice," Goldberg said. "But they'll be all right. Peacekeepers will go easy on Westerners."

"But Barir isn't a Westerner. And what if the peacekeepers work for Cloak?"

Goldberg lowered his eyes. Taylor's lips tightened. They didn't have a good reply to either of those points.

***

"Hey, slow down!" Eisenhorn shouted at the speeding truck.

Taylor's truck didn't slow. It even accelerated. It barreled past Gilda and the others, who were left next to the smoldering wreck that had been their ride. Eisenhorn gave the passing vehicle a rude gesture and kicked some sand into the air. Gilda sighed and crossed her arms.

Barir grew tense. "If the peacekeepers capture us, tell them I'm your driver."

"In your dreams, terrorist," Eisenhorn said. "No way I'm gonna lie to my fellow soldiers to protect the likes of you."

"Sir, we could be—" Johnson said, but he was cut off by the sound of air being chopped. A unicopter hovered above them while the second unicopter went after the other two trucks.

"STAY WHERE YOU ARE," the unicopter said. "DO NOT ATTEMPT TO RUN, OR YOU SHALL BE FIRED UPON."

Eisenhorn laughed. "About time them cowardly peacekeepers showed up."

"WE ARE LANDING," the unicopter boomed. "DO NOT MOVE."

Sand flew up as unicopter blades chopped the air, forcing Gilda and the others to cover their faces. She didn't know what to do except regret not being in one of the other trucks. Barir wished the same thing for himself, not because of his need to defeat Cloak but because he didn't want to end up in a Western Union prison.

The unicopter unfolded its legs but kept its propeller out. Four peacekeepers in sky-blue uniforms jumped out of the aircraft and pointed their machine guns at their captives.

"Don't move!" one soldier shouted.

"Glad to see the professionals have arrived!" the general yelled.

"Hands on your heads!" the soldier ordered.

The captives complied. Another soldier took out a tablet computer from his jacket. He walked over to Eisenhorn, taking baby steps like he was approaching a wild animal.

"Put your hand on the tablet," the soldier said.

Eisenhorn chuckled. "These nitwits can't even recognize a superior officer? All right, I shouldn't be indulging bad memory, but I'm in too good a mood to refuse."

Keeping a hand on his head, Eisenhorn put his other one on the tablet until it beeped. The peacekeeper examined the screen and saw the general's file photo appear.

Beneath it read, "SHOOT ON SIGHT."

"Impressed yet?" Eisenhorn asked. "I can tell by your expression."

CHAPTER 32

Dubai was right in front of them now, skyscrapers towering ahead, the Helios Tower standing the highest. The tower was light blue, cylindrical, and ludicrously imposing.

"Excellent," Victoria said. "Now there's no excuse for getting lost."

"Up ahead," Africa warned.

A wire fence surrounded the city. But unlike Cairo, there was no slum around Dubai, just barren desert. Six armed peacekeepers blocked the entrance. A concrete barrier rose up behind the soldiers, ensuring no trucks could drive through.

"Slate, clear the way!" Victoria yelled.

Slate moaned. "I just got in the truck …"

The peacekeeper began shooting at them.

"Okay, no need to sell it so hard!" Slate yelled, opening the door and flying out of the truck. He could see Taylor's vehicle coming up from behind, and the pursuing unicopter was almost there. Not only that, but he had promised not to kill any Western Union soldiers.

"Is it too late to join the bad guys?" Slate had to ask himself.

Bolts of lightning flew from his hand, striking in front of the peacekeepers. Bits of concrete hit them in the face. They reeled back and stopped shooting.

Slate landed near the peacekeepers. One soldier got his wits about him and aimed his gun, but Slate kicked it out of his hands before his opponent could fire. He gave the soldier a quick punch to the face, knocking him out.

Two other soldiers fired at him. Slate ducked and shot electricity at them. They flew backward, but the other three peacekeepers now shot at him as well. In an astonishing feat, Slate flew over their heads. He landed behind two peacekeepers, grabbed their heads, and bashed them together. Both men collapsed.

The final man stood frozen, gaping like a suffocating fish. Slate knocked the peacekeeper's machine gun aside with a casual backhand and head-butted him. The peacekeeper went unconscious and fell at the feet of the Helmet Man.

Slate pointed his finger at the two peacekeepers he had shocked and zapped them both again. They convulsed and went into a coughing fit.

"This is ridiculous," Slate said. "I can't just start sparing people all the time. Everyone might start thinking I'm a hero!"

***

Over three hundred investors sat inside the Helios Tower's ballroom, waiting to see the unveiling of the revolutionary power plant. Most of them were from Western Union member nations, but there were also some Middle Eastern investors. A majority wore tuxes and sparkling dresses, while the military guests wore green uniforms for regular army, sky-blue for peacekeeping, gray for air force, and dark blue for navy and marines.

The ballroom itself was the size of a cathedral. It took up the center of the Helios Tower, the ceiling ten stories high. The round tables were covered with silverware and folded napkins. Guests sat around these tables and talked. A fountain rested in the middle of the ballroom, spouting dark metal sand instead of water. Magnets in the fountain caused the sand to take on elaborate shapes, such as a life-sized camel or a pyramid, shifting its form every minute or so. There was a stage at the front of the room. Resting on it was a large object covered by a sheet. The guests wondered what was underneath, but the host interrupted their gossip.

"May I have your attention?" Lawrence Zaidi asked.

Everyone turned to see him. Lawrence was a very handsome young man, his hair now combed to the side instead of its usual bowl shape. His suit was black and worn with a blue tie, worth more than most used cars. But the strangest thing about Lawrence now was his confidence. Most of the guests who knew Lawrence had always considered him awkward and isolated.

Now they could only shrug. Perhaps the death of his father had forced him to come into his own.

"Good evening, my esteemed guests," Lawrence said. "It's no secret that businesspeople aren't as powerful as they once were. After the Great Choke, corporations took the blame for the fallout. Now the Western Union calls the shots with us at their beck and call."

The military guests thinned their lips at that statement.

"But what the smartest of us know is they need us as much as we need them. Otherwise, we all might as well be communists!"

Many of the guests laughed.

"It's time to remind the world why corporations such as Zaidi Industries are still needed," Lawrence continued. "We are going to have several major reveals today. The Helios Tower is by far the grandest of these, but we also have a new walker model, a special report on growth patches, and improvements on drone technology that shall revolutionize the world of robotics."

A round of applause erupted. Some tipsy guests even stood up.

"Please enjoy the meal, which will be served shortly. Our presentation will begin in one hour. And thank you all again for your attendance."

A minute later, Lawrence was heading down a hallway on his own. The echoes of the guests and their empty talk followed after him, but he paid the noise no heed. The board members hadn't cared for his sudden departure. Then again, he was the boss. They could wait. He was just adjusting his tie when someone spun him around.

Lawrence Zaidi was now face-to-face with the barrel of a gun.

"Time to conduct some business," Frost told him.

***

The two trucks bolted down the road, the unicopter hot on their tail along with seven peacekeeper trucks. Slate stood on top of the first truck, firing bolts at their pursuers.

"Would it kill you not to swerve?" Slate yelled as he almost lost his balance. The unicopter fired dozens of bullets. They barely missed.

"Probably!" Africa yelled. "Just fly away and fight them!"

"And leave you weaklings unprotected?" Slate scoffed.

They were now driving through the city and had begun to enter a construction area a mile wide, the Helios Tower in the center, so few civilians were around to get in the way. Zaidi Industries had finished building its tower but still had to complete the surrounding buildings, making the area look like a bombed-out neighborhood from World War II.

Most of the construction workers ran away when they heard the unicopter fire its gun. The trucks sped forward, followed by the peacekeeper vehicles and the unicopter, as the street grew narrower. Slate fired a shot of lightning at the lead truck, which caused its battery to short out. The vehicle died, blocking the road for the other six trucks.

Now only the unicopter was left. It was very impressive how low it flew, weaving between incomplete buildings. It couldn't fire tracker bullets in a safe zone, but one of the men leaned out and fired a net launcher. Africa swerved again. Most of the nets hit the ground. One net did strike the roof of the truck, but Slate rolled out of the way in time. Meanwhile, another peacekeeper in the unicopter readied an ultrasonic cannon.

"Thanks for the free ammo, morons!" Slate yelled. He tore the net off the roof of the truck and threw it. The net got tangled in the unicopter's rotor. The unicopter dropped suddenly, and the peacekeeper with the ultrasonic cannon fell backward, causing him to miss. The pilot nearly crashed into a half-finished building. The unicopter disappeared from sight, having to cease the chase to make an emergency landing.

"Wow!" Straper shouted from the other truck. "That was boss!"

Goldberg shook his head. "Fantastic, I really am a terrorist now."

***

The unicopter flew far above Dubai. Colorful skyscrapers shined in the desert sunlight, but Gilda barely glanced at them. She sat with her hands cuffed behind her back, as did her other three companions. They were all unharmed except the general, who had a black eye and a bloody lip. Eisenhorn had been struck several times, for obvious reasons.

"Those punches felt like chocolate kisses ..." Eisenhorn slurred.

"Quiet!" one peacekeeper warned. He was Sergeant Hobbes, the leader of this squad. Despite what the scanner had said, he did not shoot these four people on sight. After all, one of them was just a kid. He had discovered the two American adults were the survivors from the Bunker attack that had been spotted in Cairo. Now it seemed a cadet had survived as well. Maybe they could shed light on what had happened at the Bunker, yet another reason to keep them alive. He had been unable to identify the Arab man. Was he really just their chauffer? Doubtful.

"Sergeant, please listen," Johnson said. "Terrorists are about to attack the Helios Tower. We warned the embassy earlier—"

"I don't care," Hobbes said. "You should have turned yourselves in. People would have thought you were innocent. But now ..."

"We couldn't turn ourselves in," Gilda said. "We're being hunted."

"Yeah, by who?"

"Cloak."

A few peacekeepers laughed. Gilda swore to herself.

"You're spouting an old myth," Hobbes said. "Government-made super-soldiers that control the criminal underworld ... That's the gist of it, right?"

"It's true, damn it!" Eisenhorn yelled. "Those terrorists are planning to kill thousands, and you lazy peacekeepers are just diddling around!"

"Do you need another shiner, old man?" one peacekeeper yelled.

"That's enough!" Hobbes shouted. He turned back to Johnson. "We've sent a few trucks to the Helios Tower already. Nothing suspicious was reported."

"You have to believe us!" Gilda yelled. "Cloak's going to—"

"Sorry, girl. I know you've been through a lot, but—"

"Sergeant, you remind me of myself," Eisenhorn said.

Hobbes turned to him. "Oh, how so?"

"I was so sure I knew everything. But then I saw war. I saw good men get their legs blown off and cruel men get away. I saw innocents get shot and mothers cry over their dead sons. I saw those Union bureaucrats forget about the fallen and sweep aside the veterans who sacrificed it all. After the war, I knew nothing."

Eisenhorn turned to Johnson and gave him a half smile. "But then this pencil-neck kid decided to take care of me, even when my ex-wife of all people wouldn't. Johnson even quit the service so he could help me run the Bunker. Despite my best intentions, I grew a little attached to the cadets that walked my halls. I enjoyed my early retirement ... somewhat."

Johnson glanced at his feet, wearing a half smile as well.

Eisenhorn looked Hobbes right in the eye. "Then a bunch of thugs came and shot my kids. I watched as they walked through my halls and laughed at our misery. These animals killed a young woman's father. They even blew up a casino full of civilians."

"Is he talking about the Pale Pyramid?" one soldier asked.

"It's all over the news," another said.

"Quiet!" Hobbes spat. He was too engrossed by Eisenhorn's words.

"Now these same cretins are planning to blow up a tower and get their hands on a weapon of mass destruction," Eisenhorn said. "And all you can do is arrest a sick old man, a girl cadet, a loyal friend, and their butler. Have you no shame?"

Barir didn't care for being called a butler, but he kept his mouth shut.

Hobbes frowned. The story had a hint of truth. Of course, he wasn't sold on the supersoldiers. He wasn't even sold that these fugitives were being framed.

What did make him think twice was what he heard from the cockpit.

"Emergency!" a voice yelled over the radio. "Terrorists have driven into the construction site surrounding the Helios Tower. Requesting immediate backup. Peacekeepers, riot control, combat troops, walker squad ... Everyone, just come!"

The peacekeepers muttered among themselves. It was then Hobbes decided what to do.

"Pilot, turn this heap around!" Hobbes yelled. "We're headed to the Helios Tower!"

***

Victoria used her ID card to open the wire gates. The two trucks entered the private parking lot behind the Helios Tower. They soon unloaded from their vehicles. Straper, Victoria, Taylor, and Goldberg had pistols. Africa, meanwhile, had a black machine gun and a grenade belt slung over his shoulder. Being this close to the tower made everyone realize how tall it really was. Straper strained his neck just to see the top.

Goldberg scanned the area. "Where are the peacekeepers? They should have my documents, so why aren't there any protecting the Helios Tower?"

"It must be the mole," Victoria said. "Fantastic, all we did when we sent that message was let Cloak know we were coming."

"No time to speculate," Africa said. "We need to split into two groups. Barir is no longer with us, so that leaves no one to defuse the bomb. All we can do is find it and tell the peacekeepers where it is. Let us hope they can disarm it in time."

"What about the people in the building?" Victoria asked. "They need to be evacuated."

"Get to your brother or someone else in charge," Africa said. "But Cloak might be lurking nearby. That is where Slate comes in, so contact me if you see any hostiles."

Victoria's pocket buzzed. She took out her phone to check it.

"Teenagers," Slate scoffed. "Always texting."

"Shut it," Victoria said. She looked at her phone and gasped. "It's Lawrence!" She was quick to pick it up.

"Hello?"

"Your brother has a very nice phone, Ms. Zaidi."

Victoria's heart stopped.

"Do you know where he got it?" the voice asked. "I am in need of a new one."

"You ..."

"You led all the peacekeepers here," Houdini said. "I assume it's a trap to catch me with my hand in the cookie jar. But I'm not afraid. Let them see."

"Where are you?" Victoria seethed.

"I'm in your dead father's office. I wonder why he put it on such a low level, but I do admire the glass floor. You're able to look down on all the worms this way. Better hurry, Ms. Zaidi. The bomb could go off any minute ..."

The phone hung up. Crying out, Victoria smashed it on the ground.

"Whoa, that was a new phone!" Straper exclaimed.

"Houdini has my brother!" she yelled.

"Where?" Slate asked.

"In my father's office. I'll lead you there."

"I am coming too," Africa said. "The rest of you get security to start sweeping the building. Find that bomb. Let us put an end to Cloak's evil."

Victoria knew her way around the Helios Tower reasonably well, but even she made several wrong turns, getting lost in the labyrinth of service hallways. She hoped the other group wasn't having this much trouble navigating the lower floors.

"Take your time," Slate said. "It's not as if the building's about to blow up."

"Hush up," Victoria said. "Houdini wouldn't blow himself up. He's too selfish."

"Maybe he wants to lure us into the tower before it blows," Africa said.

"No," Slate said. "Houdini wants me alive, or at least to see me suffer in person."

"Is that why he sent drones after us?"

"All right, good point, but we don't have much choice."

"And my father's office is the best place to initiate an evacuation of the Helios Tower," Victoria said. "No matter what, we have to go up there."

They came across a door with a stairwell sign on it.

"Let's go up here," Victoria said. "This is the best way to—"

Vents hissed above their heads. The hallway was soon filled with white gas. Africa and Victoria coughed. Their eyes teared up.

Slate didn't seem to be that affected, though his skin was a bit itchy.

"Wimps! I can't believe you're letting a little tear gas get to you."

Six men in gas masks appeared at the opposite end of the hall, holding automatic weapons with suppressors. They opened fire.

"Move it!" Slate yelled. "Start cooking them buns!" He grabbed Africa and Victoria by the scruffs of their necks as they continued coughing. Bullets whizzed by, but they missed their mark. The Helmet Man turned and gave a swift kick to the door. It gave in, revealing a stairwell. Slate shoved Africa and Victoria through the doorway.

"I'll catch up!" Slate yelled. "Get to safety or something!"

Africa and Victoria took a few breaths of clean air from the stairwell. Victoria coughed a little more before speaking. "Slate, come with us! We need you."

"And let these guys shoot us in the back? No way! You need to go and save your cousin while I fight these morons."

"It's my brother!"

"Whatever, sheesh!"

Africa coughed. "Let us go! We have wasted enough time."

"Good luck, Slate," Victoria said with a small smile before she and Africa ran up the stairs, making their way to the late Ammar Zaidi's office.

Slate gave them a quick salute. He then sped down the hall.

The bullets continued to fly. Slate fired a few bolts. The gunmen took cover around the corner. When the bolts stopped flying, they came back out and continued shooting.

Then they ceased fire, seeing no sign of the Helmet Man.

"Us three will sweep the hall," one merc said. "The rest of you cover us. Remember, this guy is dangerous. Houdini said we should try to capture him alive, but don't hesitate to shoot."

Three men crouched down and moved forward. The air was thick with tear gas, so seeing was difficult. Despite that, they were thorough in their sweep. No sign of their enemy could be seen anywhere. After half a minute of searching, they were stumped.

"Damn, he got away ..." the leader of the three said. "Well, now that the cat's out of the bag, some men need to go guard the bomb until showtime gets close. Let's head—"

A bolt of lightning came from above. The leader convulsed before dropping. Another man yelped and looked up. He was also shocked to death. The third man managed to fire a few bullets at the ceiling before Slate fell. The Helmet Man had been bracing himself against the two walls of the hall. It was too bad the mercs didn't think to look up. Slate landed on his feet and knocked the gun out of the third man's hands. He gave the merc a good gut punch. The mercenary doubled over as Slate grabbed and hid behind him.

"Wait, no!" was all the beaten mercenary could say before his other comrades fired from down the hall. Bullets hit his head, killing him instantly, but his bulletproof vest offered Slate considerable protection. It wouldn't last for long, so Slate sprinted forward, still using the enemy corpse as a human shield.

"Keep firing!" one shooter screamed.

The hall split into two at the end. Mercenaries were shooting around the corners, two on the left and one on the right. It was easy for Slate to decide what side to take on first as he reached the end of the hall. Just as the mercenaries turned their guns on his exposed sides, he threw the corpse to his left. The two mercs were caught off guard and fell backward.

Slate grabbed the gun barrel of the man to the right. A merc on the left was about to shoot him, regaining his focus, but Slate swung around, ripping the gun away from the man on the right. With a crack, the Helmet Man hit the merc on the left with the butt of the gun, knocking him out. Now the other merc on the left was getting up as well, but Slate shot him with a bolt. It stopped the man's heart, and he collapsed.

In a dumb move, the merc on the right came at Slate with a hunting knife. Without much effort, Slate elbowed him in the throat. The merc made a choking noise. Slate punched him in the arm. The merc dropped the knife, still trying to catch his breath. Slate used the opening to grab his throat and slam him against the wall.

"All right, you ass! Tell me where the bomb is, or you'll be crapping teeth out!"

"You ain't gonna live for long, freak ..." the merc sneered. "I hear my pals coming now ... They're gonna fill you full of holes ..."

The door down the left hallway smashed open. Slate could sense a bunch of men with guns over there, but they didn't run forward, instead taking cover.

"No, wait!" the merc screamed. "I'm still here!"

Slate chuckled. "Looks like you're outta luck."

"Idiot, do something! You're in the same boat as me."

"Yeah, you'd think that ..."

A mercenary on the other side of the door pulled a pin from a grenade. Like a hot potato, the merc tossed it at the Helmet Man.

Chuckling, Slate threw his screaming captive at the grenade.

***

Goldberg had taken the lead, Taylor and Straper running close behind.

"Do you know where you're going?" Straper asked again.

"Yes, it takes a while, so shut up!" Goldberg snapped.

"I see a security guard!" Taylor yelled.

A guard in a suit was patrolling the halls, a muscular thirtysomething man who looked dull but was somehow even duller than that.

"Hey, party guests need to stay in the designated areas," he told them.

"Do we look like party guests?" Goldberg barked, out of breath as he stopped in front of the guard. Taylor and Straper also stopped, but they weren't panting like Goldberg.

The guard squinted. "Not really. May I see your invitations?"

"We don't have invitations," Goldberg said. "Don't you recognize me? I'm Goldberg, Ammar Zaidi's chief accountant."

Goldberg didn't expect to be recognized, but the guard nodded. "Oh, yeah. I know you. Do you need directions?"

"No! There's a bomb near the foundations of the tower. You and the rest of the guards need to evacuate and sweep the building."

The guard made a farting noise with his mouth. "It's just another bomb threat. We get five of them a week. I'm not going to evacuate an entire building while this company's biggest event of the decade is going on just because you said so. I'd get fired for sure. Besides, peacekeepers were just down here. I doubt they missed anything."

"Dude, it couldn't hurt to look again," Straper said.

"But it'll waste my time," the guard scoffed.

"You're a waste of time!" Goldberg yelled. "Get this building cleared, or I'll make sure you won't even be able to get a job at a falafel stand!"

The guard sighed. "All right, I guess we can look at the support pillars."

In a slow shuffle, he led them through the halls and down a stairwell. They were hoping he would move a little quicker, but the guard didn't seem to be all that worried.

"We're here," the guard said in a tired voice. He took out his key card and put it in a door. "This is the lowest level of the tower where the main support pillars are located. It's the best place to do damage if you're going to do it."

He jerked open the door and gestured inside. "See, nothing here but a ..."

A humming black box sat in the middle of the room.

"... bomb."

***

Africa took Victoria up to the floor below Ammar Zaidi's office. He didn't want to take on any of the Gifted without Slate, but he also had to face the possibility that Slate might not be coming back. Africa tightened his grip on his gun. He had been aiming it at the stairwell door in case any mercenaries were pursuing them. But no one came.

Victoria squeezed the butt of her pistol until her knuckles turned white. "We can't wait for Slate. My brother could be killed at any moment."

"Listen, girl. Those men wanted to separate us from Slate. That is why they used tear gas. Cloak knew it would not bother him. It is an obvious trap."

"Then what do you propose we do?"

"VICTORIA, CAN YOU HEAR ME?" a voice boomed on the intercom.

"It's Lawrence," Victoria almost screamed, but she kept her voice down.

"SECURITY SHOT A MAN CALLING HIMSELF HOUDINI, BUT IT'S NOT SAFE. GET TO THE OFFICE NOW."

Lawrence kept repeating this message over the intercom. Victoria squeezed her pistol tighter and tighter with every recitation.

"We got to go up!" she yelled. "I don't think he's being forced to say anything. He doesn't sound all that scared."

"Keep your voice down," Africa said. "You are right. He does not. And we cannot wait here forever with a bomb under our feet."

"So, we're going?"

"Yes, but slowly …"

Both of them went up the stairwell again and made it to the floor of Ammar Zaidi's office. Neither of them spotted a soul, but Africa didn't drop his guard. He pointed his machine gun forward. Victoria tailed him, holding her pistol.

They came upon an imposing wooden door. The door still had Ammar Zaidi's name on it despite his passing. Africa nodded to Victoria. She nodded back. With a quick jerk of his hand, Africa turned the knob and swung open the door.

The large office was painted a brilliant white. A black desk sat on the far side of the room. Other furniture included leather chairs and couches, which seemed almost too nice to sit on. Photos hung on the walls. All of them depicted Ammar Zaidi with various celebrities. But any other feature of the room was ignored when one glanced at the glass floor. It was a crystal-clear one-way mirror that looked ten stories down at the ballroom. All the guests were busy eating their meals as they waited for the presentation to begin. But Victoria didn't notice any of these details, for she could not take her eyes off the man who killed her father.

Houdini stood in the middle of the room, relaxed and calm. He didn't seem all that interested in the two arrivals but smiled when they came in.

Africa took no time considering his options. He fired.

Houdini vanished. None of the bullets hit their mark. The one-eyed man appeared next to them and grabbed Africa's machine gun. Before Africa could react, Houdini disappeared again, taking the gun with him. Reappearing, Houdini now stood in front of the duo.

He aimed the gun at Africa and pulled the trigger.

It was over in a brutal second. Africa was shot over a dozen times. His corpse fell to the floor with a dull thud.

Victoria screamed. With massive eyes, she brought out her pistol and pointed it at her enemy. Her gun flew out of her hand. Sandtrap walked out from the corner of the room and caught the pistol with a raised hand like someone would a softball. Victoria tried to run away, but Sandtrap pointed his free arm at her. A geyser of silver sand erupted from his sleeve. The sand latched on to Victoria, covering her torso and limbs. She gasped and fell to the floor. The sand tightened around her until it was almost impossible to breathe.

"Don't kill her yet," Houdini said, dropping the stolen gun on the floor next to Africa's corpse. "We still have to keep her hostage in case Slate manages to defeat my men."

Sandtrap walked over to Victoria, deep huffs emitting from the grill of his mask. He wrapped a large arm around Victoria and lifted her off the floor until she was on her knees. The sand loosened a bit. She took in a harsh breath.

Houdini put his hands behind his back, chuckling. "Unlike your father, you're not afraid to get your hands dirty. Good! He was a coward and a fool, but you are only a fool."

"My father was not a coward!" she cried, hot tears streaming out. "The only coward here is you."

A flash of anger went over Houdini's face, but he suppressed it. "I am somewhat retired from field work, but every now and then I must handle things myself. Your father knew how to hide. I'll give him that. When I found him on his yacht, he had locked himself in his cabin and surrounded himself with guards. If that's not cowardly, I don't know what is."

"Monster! You killed my father. You killed Zubair. You killed all those people at the Bunker and the Pale Pyramid. Now you have my brother! Where is he?"

"Safe," Houdini said, scratching his beard. "Out of curiosity, how much do you truly know about our plans?"

"Cloak made a deal with Caravan Works. They're giving you cretins a weapon of mass destruction for destroying the Helios Tower and killing my father. But then I found out about your sick plans, so you had to hunt me down."

Houdini clapped, raising an eyebrow over his real eye. "Very impressive. I'm surprised you fools could figure out so much, but still so little ..."

"Stop mocking me!"

"You may come in!" Houdini yelled. A second later, he burst out laughing, leaning back and clasping his hands.

"Shut up!" Victoria screamed, but this only made Houdini laugh louder. Sandtrap cocked his head, confused.

A figure stepped into the room. Victoria turned to see who it was. Her rage evaporated. A sense of relief draped over her. A small smile even escaped her before the seeds of doubt took root. Then all that relief left her as she comprehended what she was looking at.

It wasn't possible ... It couldn't be ...

But it was inescapable.

"I guess it's over ..." the contact said.

"Almost," Houdini said, his laughter subsiding. "Slate's all that's left."

The contact leaned toward her with a soft smile.

All Victoria could murmur was "Why ... ?"

"Because Zaidi Industries needs to be destroyed," Lawrence told his sister.

Nobody had expected Slate to chuck a live person. The mercenary collided with the grenade in midair and landed near the open door where the other mercs had taken cover.

There was no time to run. The grenade went off. Shrapnel tore flesh apart. Slate's former captive was the first to die, the explosion ripping him to pieces. About half of the other mercenaries were killed or mortally wounded. The rest tumbled back.

Only one man had gotten back up when the Helmet Man arrived. Slate shot him down with a bolt before the merc could even raise his weapon. All the remaining mercenaries still able to fight got on their feet and aimed their guns, but the room was filled with so much smoke and tear gas that it was hard to make out anything. Slate didn't rely on sight, so the smoke was his ally. He shot a bolt at another man. The mercenaries now had a general idea where Slate was and fired at him, but he ducked and shocked two more men, killing them.

Slate pounced forward and slammed into another mercenary. The Helmet Man ripped the gas mask of the merc, who began to choke and tear up. Despite his missing mask, the merc tried to shoot. Instead, because he was blinded, he hit two of his own comrades, who shot back at him in return. All three were killed in the brief firefight.

The remaining mercenaries had lost sight of Slate. One man got his neck snapped. Another got a lightning bolt between the eyes. The mercenaries were shooting everywhere. Some of them managed to scream, but most died silently.

After a man was punched in the stomach and shocked to death, only one merc was left. He was large, with bulging muscles and a foul attitude. But he was also out of bullets. Slate ran up from behind, planning to zap the sole survivor in the back.

The merc, however, pulled out a machete and swung it. The blade almost sliced Slate's head off, but he ducked, and it harmlessly hit his helmet. The merc swung overhand. Slate hopped backward. Snarling, the merc swung again, but his machete only struck the wall.

Now it was the Helmet Man's turn. Slate threw a barrage of punches at the man's stomach. The big guy curled up. Slate gave him an uppercut. For good measure, electricity spurted out of his fist. After this finishing blow, the merc went down.

Slate cracked his knuckles. "You're only warming me up, Houdini …"

***

"Don't just stand there!" Goldberg yelled.

The security guard tore his eyes away from the bomb. "Uh … right. We need to start evacuating everyone and call the bomb squad."

"The sooner the better," Taylor said.

"I can't get my radio to work down here. Got to run up!"

The guard hustled away, leaving the three of them alone with the bomb.

Taylor glanced at the device. "I think I should examine it …"

"What, no way!" Straper shouted. "You might set it off or something."

"I was a field doctor once. I was trained on explosives. It's best that I take a look at it. That bomb could go off at any minute."

"Just be careful," Goldberg said. "We'll scram if there's nothing we can do."

Taylor nodded and moved to the bomb. The room was barren with a concrete floor and had eight pillars that were crucial for supporting the tower. The bomb itself was encased in a black box that had been bolted to the floor.

Taylor knelt beside the device. He touched the surface of the bomb and felt around its contours. "I can't feel or see any sensors, so I think it's safe to take the cover off."

Goldberg and Straper gulped but didn't say anything.

Taylor's hands were steady as he took off the cover. It wasn't even screwed on, but when the guts of the bomb were revealed, he saw why. Wires of all colors and strange canisters of all sizes had been assembled together in some elaborate configuration.

"This is beyond my expertise," Taylor said. "I only learned how to deactivate simple explosives. All I can tell is that it's going to go off in at least half an hour, judging by the fluid in these canisters. I don't even think a professional bomb expert could defuse it in that time frame. No wonder the bomb is so poorly guarded."

"Wait, doesn't that thing have a remote?" Straper asked.

"This isn't a television!" Goldberg snapped.

"No, I mean does Houdini have a detonator?"

"I don't see a receiver or antenna on the bomb," Taylor said. "And the guard said reception was poor down here."

"Why don't we just move it, then?" Straper asked. "Barir told me it was a short-range bomb that's meant to be really hot and have a small destructive radius. We could get it out of the tower and let it explode somewhere else. Houdini can't blow it up at will, so why not?"

"Because it's bolted to the floor," Goldberg said. "And it's probably wired to explode if we try to move it."

"Yes, it's too risky," Taylor said. "We must wait for help."

"Dude, the building won't be evacuated in time," Straper said. "And the bomb squad will be too late to help. We got to do something."

"No, not yet. We could kill thousands. We need to wait for the bomb squad."

"What if nobody shows up in time?" Goldberg asked.

"Then we'll have to roll the dice."

***

Lawrence sat on the edge of his father's desk with folded hands and a small grin. Meanwhile, Houdini smiled down on the girl who had caused him so much trouble. Her misery was like nectar to him, sweet and filling. Sandtrap still restrained

Victoria, but it was unnecessary. All the fight had left her the moment the truth was revealed.

"Why?" she asked again. A small tear rolled out of her eye.

"I'm in a good mood, so I'll indulge your whimpers," Houdini said. "Months ago, Cloak approached your father, Ammar Zaidi, and we asked him to build a prototype weapon for us, since Zaidi Industries was one of the few entities that could fulfill our request. However, despite our promises of compensation, Mr. Zaidi stupidly refused."

Houdini chuckled and walked toward Victoria. "We decided to kill your father and get someone to take his place. Our best candidate was his son, Lawrence. From what we had figured, Ammar would have left the company to his only son in his will. If we could control Lawrence, we'd have the perfect replacement. We assumed the boy, unlike his father, was weak-willed enough to succumb to our manipulations, so I was assigned to personally 'convince' him to assist us. But then something surprising happened ..."

The one-eyed man gestured to Lawrence. "He was willing! He even asked us for a favor. In exchange for murdering his father and destroying the Helios Tower, he would make us our weapon. Naturally, I agreed. It's much better to have a loyal dog than one on a leash."

Victoria let out a small sob, her face twitching.

"We created Caravan Works, a dummy corporation, in order to funnel money to Zaidi Industries. This way, Cloak could cover the expenses of making the prototype, preventing anyone from taking notice. Not even the scientists who built the thing had any idea what was really at work. Our layers of insulation were that great. Then it was a simple matter of killing your father. It wasn't hard. All I did was pop in and spray him with nerve gas. Stupid fool sucked it all up!" Houdini laughed so hard that his black eye looked like it was about to pop out of its socket. Lawrence's smile grew. Sandtrap kept quiet.

Houdini calmed down some, sighing. "Then you came along ... Not only had your father made you heir to his empire, against our predictions, but you had begun to snoop around, so it was with great ease that I asked your brother if we could kill you."

Houdini knelt next to Victoria. He put his mouth right by her ear.

"Can you guess what he said?"

"Please ..." Victoria whimpered.

"Not only did he say yes—he helped! When your brother called you, we traced your cellphone to the Bunker. Most of the Western Union's drones were created by Zaidi Industries, so he was able to hack into them with administrative codes. He also made it so you would all be shot on sight right before you came here to Dubai. It's a miracle you aren't dead already."

Houdini stood up. "Of course, the only factor I did not predict was Slate ..."

"Scoundrel ..." the masked man breathed.

"Shut your trap!" Houdini yelled. Lawrence chuckled at the unintentional wordplay.

Shattered and alone, Victoria asked again, "Why ... ?"

"Stupid cow, I just told you!" Houdini barked.

"I think she wants an explanation from me," Lawrence said. He got off the desk's edge and walked over to her. "Oh, dear sister. How can I make you understand?" His smile disappeared. "I don't. I never expected you to understand. That's why I didn't tell you about my pain, and that's why I don't love you. You only ever cared about being Daddy's little girl, thinking I was weak and worthless. All you ever felt for me was pity."

The gates of shock broke. Victoria began to sob. The pain kept building inside her and flowing out in a cascade of emotion.

"Silence ..." Sandtrap commanded. The metal sand tightened around her throat, ceasing her cries, but the tears continued to roll.

Houdini laughed. "Good job taking the initiative. Just don't kill her yet."

"Where was I?" Lawrence asked, sighing. "Your crying distracted me. Even made me a little sad. Guess I still have empathy ..."

"That will go away in time," Houdini assured. "I remember how annoying that was, but you'll find that your wrath slowly erodes it away."

"Good to know," Lawrence said. "Oh, right. I was telling my life story. Well, it began when my mother died, my *real* mother. So, if it makes you feel better, I'm only your half brother. Father never wanted you to know. Yes, Father … My mother was his girlfriend before he met *her* … My real mother was a native who was killed in a Western Union airstrike. With no known relatives, I was taken in by my rich father, almost like a fairy tale."

Lawrence looked to his sister. "But then my worthless father showed me his true colors. When you were born, he immediately took you under his wing. You were his legitimate daughter, while I was just a mistake. He took you on business trips, taught you how to do everything, and left me at home with … *her* … that Western harlot … that creature …"

Houdini licked his lips as he listened.

"Do you know what she did to me?" Lawrence asked. "Physical … It was torture … He knew … I'm sure he knew … She was a filthy … That horrid …"

Lawrence smiled, the corners of his lips twitching. "That's when I decided to push her down the stairs. *She* didn't know what happened until *she* was three steps down. That was some years ago, but I still remember the look *she* gave me, like the one you're giving me now."

Victoria didn't react to this additional revelation. She just kept crying.

"Then I was safe … but alone. You were spoiled, happy, and loved. You even got the company. What did I have? Not you, not my father, not my real mother, not even *her* anymore. All I had was hate. I still have it. But now Father is dead, and soon his legacy will die as well. I will destroy this tower and take down the Western Union's corporate puppet with it. Zaidi Industries will be no more. The earth will be salted. Will it make me feel better? No … of course not. But someone's got to pay … someone …"

Houdini sighed. "Yes … a sad story, like ours. Sandtrap was burned and disfigured by a landmine. I got my eye ripped out by the Western Union, replaced with this hideous ball. We were just tools to them, born to kill. Now the stupid sheep think they can judge us after they mutilated and dehumanized us. Slime! They can't condemn us. They can't stop us. Our suffering has made us strong, cunning, hard, and vengeful. Only a fool would ever think that they could fight this rage! Only a fool would face us! Only a fool—"

"Hey, the fool's standing right here!" a constipated voice yelled.

The doors smashed open. Two corpses flew through and landed at the feet of Houdini. Smoke came off the bodies. They smelt of ozone. Houdini recognized the corpses as his men. He stared with one wide eye at the dead mercs. He then looked back up at his enemy.

The Helmet Man chuckled. "Knock, knock."

The Helmet Man hardly seemed concerned with his surroundings as he walked through the doorway. He turned to Lawrence Zaidi. The young man gulped.

Slate pointed an accusing finger at the boy. "I should have known you were behind all this, Lawrence of Arabia ..."

"Are you trying to be funny?" Lawrence asked, standing a bit taller. "It wasn't very clever. Goldberg makes that stupid joke all the time."

"Wow, you're an even bigger brat than your sister!"

"Slate ..." Sandtrap seethed.

"Hey, aren't you supposed to be terrorizing teenagers at a summer camp?"

"You arrived," Houdini said, grinding his teeth. "You are annoyance incarnate ... Don't move, or we'll squeeze the Zaidi girl till she pops."

Slate turned his head toward Victoria. "Don't worry, Princess. I'll get you outta here."

But Victoria simply kept on crying. What could he possibly do now?

"Lie down so we can restrain you," Houdini ordered Slate. "You can't beat two of the Gifted, and we have a hostage."

"You act as if I have a rational mind!" Slate cried, giggling and waving his hands.

"Then we'll just kill you. The Mentor wanted you alive, but even my loyalty has limits."

Slate crossed his arms. "Man, you have one stupid boss."

"Silence! The Mentor shall not be mocked."

"I wasn't talking to you. I was talking to Sandtrap."

Sandtrap raised his head. His breathing deepened.

"Your boss doesn't respect you," Slate told the masked man. "Hell, I don't think he respects anyone other than that Mentor of his. Seriously, why work for Cloak? You don't seem to take joy out of killing like Houdini does."

"Quit your lying!" Houdini yelled. "Sandtrap, do not listen to him."

"Houdini doesn't even have the respect to tell you the truth. I know you care about that chick, Repulsa. She seemed like a real catch. But you're not in love with her or anything. I think you just like her because she treats you like a human being, just like how my dad treated me. She doesn't make you kill. She doesn't use you. Unlike Houdini ..."

"Be quiet, or I'll kill the girl!"

"Guess what else? Houdini's afraid of you. He's afraid of what you'll do when you figure out that he killed Repulsa."

Sandtrap stopped breathing. He turned to Houdini.

"This man is a liar!" Houdini told Sandtrap. "He knows he can't fight us both, so he's turning us against each other."

"You people are supposed to be professionals!" Lawrence yelled. "Kill him already!"

"Liar ..." Sandtrap hissed at Slate. He commanded the metal sand to contract. Victoria whimpered as the life began to squeeze out of her.

"Don't kill her," Slate said. "If you do that, you'll be just like me."

Sandtrap let go. Victoria fell to the floor, the sand now loose and falling off her. She curled up in a fetal position and began to cough.

"What are you doing?" Houdini bellowed. "You let her go!"

"What ... ?" Sandtrap breathed. Absolute hatred rang in his voice.

Slate laughed. "Yeah, you guessed it already. I killed Repulsa. Me. Not your idiot boss. I got out of my tube, murdered everyone on board that plane, and crashed it. Houdini knew she was probably dead but didn't even have the decency to tell you."

"That's a lie!" Houdini shouted.

"Look how your boss is panicking. He knew you'd go crazy, so he treated you like a five-year-old and lied to your face."

Sandtrap's breathing grew more rapid and deep.

"Yeah, killing her wasn't that hard, especially since I broke her ribs earlier. She begged me to stop, but I totally didn't. Then I gave her corpse to the crocodiles."

"Shut up!" Houdini screeched.

Slate chuckled and rubbed his hands together. "Yep, they ate her up, all right, but not before I had a taste."

Sandtrap shook like a cement mixer.

The Helmet Man shrugged. "What? What did I do?"

No more. Sandtrap couldn't stand it. A scream erupted from his mask. He raised his arms. Houdini was about to yell again when almost every piece of furniture floated up in the air, including a variety of other objects. The items accelerated toward Slate. A couch slammed into Houdini, who fell on the floor and lost consciousness. Lawrence was hit on the shoulder by a chair, causing him to cry out and fall too. Since Victoria was already lying down, all the objects flew right over her as she kept on coughing and crying. Rolling out of the way, Slate managed to avoid being hit. The items crashed into the wooden door instead and knocked it off its hinges.

As Slate got to his feet, he fired a few lightning bolts at his masked opponent. Sandtrap created a small shield out of the metal sand and blocked the electricity.

Counterattacking, Sandtrap pointed his hand at Slate. Small knives flew out of his sleeve. Most of the knives hit the wall as Slate ran to the right, but one ricocheted off his helmet and another grazed his left arm, causing it to bleed. Slate sprinted along the wall and kept firing bolts with one hand. In need of a much larger shield, Sandtrap summoned the desk. It floated in front of him and blocked all the bolts, which left scorch marks across its surface.

"You can control metal within a certain range!" Slate yelled as he kept running and firing bolts. "Interesting powers. Must be great for party tricks! But my helmet isn't affected by magnets, and magnetic powers are only useful when you have metal to work with. My ammo, on the other hand, never runs out. I paid the electric bill!"

"Fool!" Sandtrap screamed. The masked man made the table fly forward. Slate leaped over the desk as it slammed into the wall and broke into several pieces.

It was time to get up and close. Slate ran right at the masked man and threw a punch. Sandtrap moved to the side, avoiding the electrified blow. A steel whip shaped like a scorpion tail and covered in blades flew out of Sandtrap's sleeve.

Slate threw a roundhouse kick. Stepping back, Sandtrap flicked his whip. Slate ducked, the whip sailing over, and threw more punches. Sandtrap dodged these blows too and started swinging the whip. The Helmet Man moved to the side, out of the whip's range.

Slate, however, was now standing on top of metal sand. Sandtrap raised his free hand. The sand wrapped around Slate's legs. Losing his balance, Slate couldn't avoid a chair that struck him in the back. More sand came out of Sandtrap's sleeve, covering Slate's torso and arms. Still standing but restrained, Slate could only shout insults and squirm as Sandtrap twirled the whip in his hand. The masked man would take his time finishing his opponent off.

Slate grunted, struggling against the sand. "You know ... metal conducts electricity ..."

Sandtrap didn't reply, only walking toward Slate.

Slate laughed. "Look down, dumbass!"

Electricity went through the sand and into Sandtrap, who began to convulse. The sand went slack. Slate sprinted forward. He slammed his silver helmet into Sandtrap's torso. Sandtrap toppled over and fell on his back, coughing.

"Guess you were too stupid to live!" Slate yelled. He jumped into the air. Electricity gathered in his fist. Using gravity to help him out, he drove his fist into his enemy's gut. Arcs of energy went all over Sandtrap's body as he shrieked. The glass floor shattered around Sandtrap. Slate hopped away just in time as the section of floor gave away. The masked man fell into the ballroom, a ten-story fall.

***

A minute earlier, everyone in the ballroom had looked up, wondering what the commotion was about. One of Zaidi Industries' executives went onstage to assure everyone that it was just an unscheduled renovation. Meanwhile, a security team headed upstairs to see what was actually going on in the late Ammar Zaidi's office.

That was when Sandtrap smashed through the glass ceiling. A few women yelped as Sandtrap crashed on top of a dining table, which collapsed from the impact. The couple sitting at the table screamed and ran away. Soon, all the other guests were also screaming and fleeing the ballroom. The security guards stopped heading upstairs in favor of crowd control.

"Please, leave in an orderly fashion!" a guard yelled.

Meanwhile, up above in Ammar Zaidi's office, the Helmet Man landed near the broken desk. After dusting himself off, he turned to where Houdini lay.

"Your turn, douchebag ..."

Slate fired a bolt.

Houdini vanished, the bolt hitting the floor instead. Slate swore. It seemed Houdini had regained consciousness. Houdini reappeared next to Africa's body. He snatched up the machine gun, some extra magazines, and the grenade belt. Slate fired another bolt, but Houdini teleported again, appearing beside him. Seething, Houdini raised his weapon and fired.

In order to avoid the point-blank bullets, Slate dove down the hole Sandtrap had fallen through. The Helmet Man was now flying around in the ballroom. Some of the guests saw Slate and pointed, but most were too busy fleeing to notice him.

"What, nobody's even gonna take a picture?" Slate cried. "Great, how the hell am I supposed to get famous?"

Bullets whizzed past him. Houdini had teleported into the crowd and had resumed firing at Slate, screaming. Slate dodged the gunfire and made rude gestures. Houdini's bullets soon ran out. He cursed and reloaded.

Peacekeepers stormed the ballroom, pointing their guns and scanning the room. Before they could tell Houdini to surrender, the one-eyed man vanished. The soldiers blinked several times, but then they saw Slate in the air and began shooting at him.

A bullet ricocheted off Slate's helmet. It was time to go. Slate accelerated toward the ballroom floor and pulled up right before crashing. He flew low and aimed for the window that let light into the ballroom. At maximum speed, Slate smashed through it. He was now outside. A crowd of people screamed below him, shielding their eyes from the falling glass.

"Oops!" Slate yelled. "Don't try catching those snowflakes with your tongue, folks!"

"Surprise!" Houdini spat, appearing above Slate in midair.

Slate groaned. "Should have dealt with you first ..."

Houdini fired his weapon.

***

A dozen peacekeeper trucks pulled up before the main doors of the Helios Tower. They were there in response to the terrorists. One terrorist was apparently wearing a silver helmet, of all things. A few unicopters landed nearby, one of which held Gilda and the others.

"Looks like there really is trouble," Sergeant Hobbes said. "Jackson, you watch these four prisoners while the rest of us assist the other squads. All right, move out!"

Hobbes and his men jumped out before the prisoners could protest.

"This blows," Gilda complained. "We get to do nothing."

Johnson shrugged. "At least they came here."

Hobbes and his men pushed through the crowd. It took them a minute to reach the ballroom. A few dozen peacekeepers were already there, bewildered and disorganized. Hobbes went over to the nearest one for information.

"What's the situation?" Hobbes asked.

"Well ... ah ... a guard told us there's a bomb in the tower," the peacekeeper said. "Then a man fell from the office above and—"

Hobbes sensed movement and turned on instinct. A masked man was getting back on his feet, huffing and wheezing.

"That—that's impossible!" a soldier yelled. "He fell ten stories!"

"Put your hands up!" Hobbes yelled, raising his weapon. The other peacekeepers raised their weapons as well.

Sandtrap turned toward them.

"Fools ..." he huffed.

Hobbes scowled. "Hands up, or we will shoot!"

"Fools ..." he puffed.

"Fire!"

"Fools!"

The men fired. But none of the bullets hit their mark. All of them were deflected around Sandtrap. Then, lifting his arm, Sandtrap commanded all the silverware around him to float up into the air.

Hobbes felt his stomach turn inside out.

"What the ... ?"

The silverware flew forward. Most of the peacekeepers and Hobbes managed to duck, but two men were stabbed to death by the flying utensils. While the peacekeepers were distracted, Sandtrap began to approach the magnetic fountain.

"Keep firing!" Hobbes yelled.

The peacekeepers got up and fired their weapons, but the bullets were deflected by the masked man's power. Sandtrap reached the fountain, staring at the shifting sands that now took the shape of a cactus. He put his hand into the black sand. It started crawling up his arm.

Hobbes stopped firing, his eyes now wide.

"Pull back! Pull back now!"

But it was too late. The sand consumed them.

Jackson watched the front entrance of the Helios Tower. He was told to guard the prisoners while Hobbes and the others stormed the tower. But he was hearing a lot of gunshots coming from the building, and now a crowd of frightened people was running out too. Several other peacekeepers directed the crowd to move away from the tower. Jackson shook his head. Peacekeeping was supposed to be an easy job.

Barir, meanwhile, had managed to pick his handcuffs' lock. He slipped out of them and snuck up behind the peacekeeper. Jackson didn't notice him before it was too late. Barir wrapped his arm around the soldier's throat and tightened it. He didn't let go until Jackson passed out.

"What are you doing?" Johnson yelled.

"I cannot be taken prisoner," Barir said. "Now turn around. I must free you."

Screams echoed from the tower. They were followed by gunshots.

"Looks like Cloak showed up," Gilda said.

Johnson turned around. Eisenhorn and Gilda did the same. Barir soon freed them all.

Gilda rubbed her wrists. "Do you think Slate's fighting right now?"

"That clown better be," Eisenhorn growled. "Otherwise, my boot's going—"

"What the hell is that?" a peacekeeper shouted.

A blob of black sand over twenty feet tall smashed through the front entrance. Two shapeless limbs hung off its sides, almost giving it a humanoid appearance. A brown mask poked out of the sand, but other faces were also there. One of them belonged to Sergeant Hobbes, whose corpse was now a part of the monstrosity that had emerged from the tower.

Not waiting for orders, the peacekeepers shot at it. The sand and corpses took the damage, but the masked man went unharmed. Sandtrap, inside the blob, made its right limb swipe at three peacekeepers, breaking the necks of two. The other was consumed by the sand, his screams cut off as it forced its way down his throat.

The blob's other arm wrapped around the nearest peacekeeper truck. It picked up the vehicle and threw it at the unicopter Gilda and the others sat in.

"Run away!" Johnson screamed.

All four of them jumped out of the unicopter, even managing to kick out the unconscious Jackson. The truck slammed into the aircraft. Broken metal flew everywhere. Eisenhorn and Johnson fell to the ground. The unconscious peacekeeper landed next to them, while Barir was hit on the head by a hunk of metal and knocked out.

"We got to lead that monster away," Johnson said. "There are too many people."

"Johnson, go hijack a truck!" Eisenhorn ordered. "Get something with four-wheel drive!"

"Now's not the time to be picky. Come on!"

They left the two unconscious men there. Johnson noticed that Gilda wasn't around but assumed she had gone somewhere safe.

Gilda had indeed run away, not knowing what else to do. A deep urge within her had beckoned her to go back and fight. And yet another urge told her to flee. It was an urge that was primal and logical, basic and humiliating. Gilda knew she had only managed to get this far on pure luck and Slate's strength. Now she was alone, without anyone else to help her carry the burden, weak as a newborn. All she could do was flee the scene and pray more peacekeepers arrived in time to help Johnson and Eisenhorn.

Then something grabbed her attention. As she was running past a broken window, she couldn't help but notice a towering metal figure on the stage inside the abandoned ballroom. What was it? Gilda didn't know why she had gone through the broken window, but she was glad she had. Bullet casings and bloody silverware littered the ballroom floor. For Gilda, the scene brought back images of Henry's corpse and those of the other cadets. Only adrenaline and the prize ahead kept her from turning back.

When Gilda finally got on the stage, she saw that a sheet had been covering the object but had fallen off in the chaos. It took a moment for her to comprehend what she was staring at.

Standing in front of her was a walker unlike anything she had seen before. It had thin arms instead of the gorilla-like ones most mecha had, the walker having a slender build overall. Another notable difference was that this walker's hands each had five fingers rather than the usual three. The digits looked sharp enough to carve a turkey.

To top it all off, the walker was magenta. Although Gilda had gasped at the reveal, she snorted at the paint job. This wasn't supposed to be a sports car. Zaidi Industries must want to market this piece of equipment for buyers besides the military, meaning this walker either had serious flaws or was too expensive to mass produce.

But Gilda had to admit the bold color suited her. She had always wanted to become a walker pilot, training on the simulator for hours on end. It never occurred to her that she would be able to pilot a real one so soon.

Without a second thought, she climbed into the cockpit.

The inside was just like the simulator. There were sleeves for her arms and legs, which allowed the user to control the walker's limbs. She slid her limbs in, grasping the triggers and pressing the pedals. The cockpit closed. A holographic password screen appeared. Gilda panicked. How was she supposed to know the password? Then she saw a sticky note on the control panel. A bunch of numbers were written on it. She smirked. Talk about bad security. She said the numbers out loud, and the screen changed into a view of the outside world.

"Hello!" a disembodied voice said. Gilda jumped in her seat. "I'm Tim, your autopilot. You are now operating Magenta. Pretty cool, right? A bold color for a bold machine. This custom walker was created by Zaidi Industries and features a vast array of—"

"Be quiet!" Gilda snapped. Most walkers came with an autopilot, but they were simple programs that didn't have personality like this one, perhaps for good reason.

"Don't you want a tutorial before we begin?" Tim asked, almost sounding hurt.

"No, I don't! Now hush up." Gilda moved her leg forward, which made the walker take a step. Magenta was quiet when it walked, but she didn't have time to awe at the marvels of this machine. All Gilda did was check the screen to see if the walker had ammo.

It did.

"Sorry, Victoria ..." Gilda muttered. "But I have to give this a field test."

***

Johnson and Eisenhorn jumped into a peacekeeper truck, which still had keys in it. Meanwhile, the giant blob picked up another truck and threw it at the fleeing crowd. Two people were killed and five injured.

Johnson honked the horn. Sandtrap took notice of them. The blob shifted toward the truck, about forty feet away. Johnson put the truck in drive and slammed his foot on the gas.

But it didn't move forward.

"Johnson, did you leave the parking brake on?" Eisenhorn barked.

The truck began to move toward Sandtrap.

"It's pulling us backward!" Johnson yelled.

The blob slunk toward Johnson and Eisenhorn. Smoke came out of the truck's engine, the wheels screeching in vain against the monster's magnetic pull.

"I knew we should've sprung for the four-wheel drive!" Eisenhorn cried.

But then the blob stopped in its tracks as a barrage of bullets hit its back. Sandtrap screamed. The masked man lost his invisible hold on the vehicle. Their truck sped forward, heading away from the blob.

"What happened?" Eisenhorn asked. "Who shot the blob?"

Something metallic smashed through the entrance to the Helios Tower. It was a walker, but it was definitely not a standard one, what with its long, slim limbs and odd color. Despite the odd arrival, Johnson and Eisenhorn found themselves both breathing out a sigh.

"It worked!" Gilda yelled from inside the mecha. "Wait till I show—"

The blog turned toward her and raised its limbs. Gilda cursed. The bullets must not have done enough damage. She decided to give the fiend another dose of lead.

Before she could, however, the walker began to move backward on its wheels. She was thrown forward. The walker must have been going over fifty miles per hour.

"What's happening?" she demanded.

"I'm sorry!" the autopilot called Tim told her. "That's my fault. I detected a strong magnetic field coming from that target. We have to keep back, or else we could be in serious trouble. Also, you just fired rubber bullets. This walker is only equipped with nonlethal weapons and one shell for demonstrating purposes. Magenta isn't ready for a real battle."

The blob chased after the walker. Magenta went down a dirt road in reverse, away from the Helios Tower and into the surrounding construction zone. The blob moved fast. It glided forward as if on an ice rink. Gilda saw her pursuer and aimed the walker's gun again.

"Do we have any useful weapons?" she asked.

"You do have one shell for your cannon," Tim said. "But it's made out of metal, so I suggest not using that. Try the nets."

"Guess that'll do!" She fired her cannon. Nets came out. They hit the sand blob dead-on, one of them striking Sandtrap's mask. The blob slowed but kept coming after her. It snatched up a parked car and threw it at her walker. She made Magenta go right. The car crashed down right where her mecha had just been.

"Sorry, you're out of nets," Tim said. "We are approaching a dangerous factory zone. I suggest we change course."

The blob threw another car. Gilda moved the walker to the left as she kept speeding backward, dodging the falling vehicle.

"No!" she told Tim. "Keep going. I think I have a plan."

***

Taylor, Straper, and Goldberg had already waited ten minutes. Worse still, they heard gunshots upstairs. They couldn't sit still anymore.

"Don't think the peacekeepers are coming," Straper said.

"It's settled, then," Taylor said. "We'll move the bomb."

The doctor crouched down and took out a pocketknife. He began to examine the bottom of the bomb. It took a minute before he gave the thumbs-up.

"Good to move?" Straper asked.

Taylor wiped his forehead. "It is now. The bomb was rigged to explode if you tried to move it, but I managed to take care of it."

"Holy shit! Give us some warning next time, brah!"

"Whatever, let's get on with it!" Goldberg yelled, holding a crowbar that he had found in a utility closet. He wiggled it under the bomb and pushed down.

"Easy ..." Taylor said, watching the fluids in the bomb. "Straper, go help him."

Straper went over and helped Goldberg push down on the crowbar. After a minute of pushing, the bolts securing the bomb to the floor broke.

Taylor sighed. "At least it didn't blow up."

"Dude, don't jinx it!" Straper yelled.

"Let's get this rotten thing out of here," Goldberg said. All three of them lifted the black box up. They shuffled out of the room and managed to make it to a service elevator.

"Okay, where to now?" Straper asked.

"To the surface," Taylor said. "We got to find a place to dump this bomb."

***

Victoria finally found the willpower to stand up. She wobbled and swayed, but she managed. The room was trashed, the furniture broken and a huge hole in the glass floor. Victoria didn't care about that. Only one thing was on her mind now.

Lawrence moaned and got to his feet. His lips were curled as if he wanted to snarl.

"What … What is this?" he spewed. "Nothing is going right … Nothing at all!" He turned to his sister. "It's you … All of it! Father liked you best. You were his. Now you're ruining my dream!"

"Lawrence, I'm sorry," Victoria cried. "Please, I want to help."

"Help?" Lawrence laughed. He took out a small pistol from his pocket.

Victoria took a step back. She almost fainted right then and there.

"Nothing can help me now!" he screamed, raising his gun.

Victoria screamed and covered her face.

"You're a decade too late, Victoria! A decade too late!"

Gilda rolled her walker into the factory zone. The blob was right behind her. It pointed a limb at a stack of girders. The stack toppled over, the girders crashing down on the concrete. One even hit her walker on the shoulder. A shudder went through the mecha and up Gilda's back. She scowled at her clumsy driving.

"Weapon error!" Tim cried. "Sorry, but your gun broke. All you have is the cannon with one shot. Again, my apologies."

"One is all I need," Gilda said. "But I can't find the feet-bolt release on the console."

"You don't need bolts. Magenta is designed so the force of the recoil goes downward instead of backward. You'll be able to fire your shell without falling over."

A gray factory loomed ahead. Smoke billowed from its stacks.

"Tim, what's in there?" Gilda asked.

"I detect high temperatures, so I assume molten metal."

"Excellent," Gilda said. The walker headed in that direction. Sandtrap followed. She was soon inside the factory. The workers had already evacuated after hearing about the terrorist attack on the Helios Tower. Steam rose from large vats. Gilda eyed them carefully.

"They have molten metal in them, right?"

"That's what I sense," Tim told her. "Just what are you planning?"

Gilda spun Magenta around. She now drove in reverse so her walker could properly face the approaching monstrosity. The blob picked up a forklift, preparing to throw it at her. But Gilda fired her cannon. The shell slammed into a vat and exploded on impact. A wave of molten metal, a brilliant bright orange, spilled out of the shattered container. Sandtrap shrieked as the molten metal covered the blob. It melted the forklift and metal sand while instantly burning all the corpses embedded in it. Smoke and fumes obscured the final result.

Gilda drove the walker out of the factory, which was now on fire.

"Very clever," Tim said. "But you could have died doing that."

"An occupational hazard," Gilda replied.

"I bet you steal your lines."

"I don't have time to be creative."

After getting a safe distance from the burning factory, Gilda saw a peacekeeper truck stop in front of her. Johnson and Eisenhorn jumped out.

"Gilda, is that you?" Johnson shouted. "Did you burn down the factory? What were you thinking? People could have gotten hurt!"

"But I took care of that monster," Gilda said over the walker's loudspeaker.

"See, Johnson?" Eisenhorn said. "This is why women shouldn't drive."

A whistling noise made Gilda forget about her conversation. She floored the pedal, the walker rolling back. Johnson and Eisenhorn also heard the shell and took cover. It exploded in a bright burst of flame where Gilda had been. Chunks of rock flew everywhere. She heard some of them bounce off her walker's armor.

"Another walker is attacking!" Tim shouted. "Behind you!"

Gilda spun around. A standard walker had appeared. It fired its machine gun. She moved to the left, the bullets missing her. She then made Magenta drive toward the attacking walker. Since she couldn't leave Johnson and Eisenhorn alone, and because her walker had no more ammo, close combat was the only option. The attacking walker tried to throw a punch, but she had Magenta block the attack with its forearm.

"Surprise, English girl!" a voice boomed from the other walker.

"Frost!" Gilda spat.

"I couldn't resist another meeting!" Frost yelled. "I stole this walker in hopes of getting past those idiot peacekeepers, but it looks like I get to teach you that lesson I promised!"

Frost pulled his walker away from Magenta and raised his cannon, preparing to blow her away. Gilda made her mecha kick Frost's cannon arm. With the cannon's aim skewed, the shell struck the ground nearby, exploding. Frost and his walker reeled back, for he had forgotten to bolt the mecha's feet down, the fail-safe having been overridden. While Frost was distracted, Magenta jumped up in the air. Gilda couldn't believe how high it went. It had leaped right over a fifteen-foot-tall walker with room to spare.

Magenta landed behind Frost and tried kicking his walker's stubby legs out from under it. This didn't cause the walker to fall, but Frost lost his balance and futilely attempted to counterattack with a swinging cannon arm. Gilda blocked this and punched the enemy walker's shoulder joint. Sparks flew. The arm's circuits were severed. Before Frost could strike again, Gilda had Magenta kick her foe square in the chest. His walker fell on its back with a loud crash. Frost cursed and pointed his cannon arm at her, but Magenta stepped on the walker's shoulder, causing that limb to go dead as well.

Victorious, Magenta grabbed the front cockpit door of Frost's walker and tore it off. Frost was now exposed, staring slack-jawed at his enemy from inside his cockpit. Hastily, he tore out his arm from a sleeve and took out a handgun. He fired at Magenta. The bullets bounced off the walker, leaving only tiny dings that could easily be buffed out. Magenta tore Frost out of his walker and dropped him on the ground.

"You psychopath," Gilda snarled. "Just how many people have you killed?"

"Hey now, English girl ..." Frost said, lying on his back. "Don't do anything you'll regret later ..."

"Regret? You mean like kill you?"

"You can't! It is not in your nature. You can't capture me either. You are a fugitive. Just let me go. I'll stop working for Houdini. I promise!"

"No more killing?"

"I won't! I swear! Just let me live."

"You killed Henry. He never did anything to you."

"The English boy was a mistake! Heat of the moment. Let me go. Please!"

Gilda clenched her teeth. Hearing Frost beg only made her loathe him even more. She raised her walker's foot and slammed it down.

Frost screamed a scream unlike any other.

Gilda had stomped on his leg with her walker. Judging from the twisted shape of the limb, it must have been very painful.

"You crippled me! I'll kill you! I'll kill you, English girl!"

"You're right," Gilda said. "I'm not like you. I'm not a cold-blooded killer. But I can't let you go. You've done too much evil."

"Filthy Western shrew! I shall gut your loved ones like fish! I'll tear your nails out one by one! English girl! English girl!"

Gilda drove her walker away from the scene. Magenta fired a flare in the air. A peacekeeper Jeep spotted it and began driving toward the scene. Gilda kept her lips tight as she lowered her head briefly. Then she looked back up. Her victory yielded no other reaction, at least none that was visible to the naked eye.

Tim broke the silence. "I have learned something important today."

"Yeah, what's that?" Gilda asked.

"Don't get on your bad side!"

***

Johnson and Eisenhorn had ducked behind their truck when the shell exploded. Far off, Gilda was fighting the walker. Now the dust was settling. Everything was quiet.

Johnson poked his head up. "Sir, we got to get moving."

"You're gonna let her take on that maniac alone?" Eisenhorn cried. "I ain't about to let a teenage girl fight my battles!"

"I don't think we have any other options. We can't—"

"Johnson ..." Eisenhorn said, raising a quivering finger. "Johnson!"

The general was pointing at the burning factory.

"That–that–" Johnson stammered. "That's not ..."

Sandtrap swayed as he walked. His mask was scorched by the flames. Most of his trench coat had burned away. But he was alive and mobile. At the last second, he had created a cocoon out of metal sand to protect himself from the molten metal. He had almost burned to death in the process, yet there he was, huffing and puffing.

Johnson saw the masked man's tattered coat was barely hanging off his frame, his bare chest now exposed. Scars and burns, some new and many old, covered his body. When Johnson looked at Sandtrap's arms, he saw they were made of silver sand, shifting and turning. The masked man's legs were also constructed out of sand.

"He has no limbs ..." Johnson whispered.

Eisenhorn could only stare.

Sandtrap was now walking toward them. The tortured creature raised a hand. Shards of scrap metal flew to his arms, covering them until they became thick and formidable.

Then the masked man attacked.

***

Houdini appeared on the ground and shot at the Helmet Man. Slate shot a flew bolts in retaliation, but Houdini teleported away. Slate now flew above the construction zone. Not a soul was in sight. He knew Gilda and the others wouldn't like it if civilians got involved, so fighting here was the best option.

Houdini reappeared on top of an unfinished building and fired his machine gun. The bullets barely missed. Slate fired more bolts at Houdini, but he once again disappeared.

"Quit living up to your name!" Slate yelled. This was getting tiresome. He couldn't fight at his fullest while flying. If he was going to defeat Houdini, it would be on the ground.

After surveying the area, Slate landed between two incomplete buildings. Dirt roads and piles of building material were everywhere. He stood his ground, waiting for Houdini. Nothing seemed to move until Slate heard a voice.

"What wolf sides with the sheep?"

Slate twisted to his right and shot a bolt, but it just hit a brick wall.

"You should have joined the pack!" Houdini yelled from behind.

Slate spun around and fired a bolt. Once again, Houdini had teleported away.

"Always hated hide-and-seek!" Slate yelled.

Houdini appeared behind Slate. "Then let's play tag!"

Slate swung around and threw a punch, but Houdini had already vanished, leaving behind a present for the Helmet Man.

A live grenade.

"Shit!" Slate flew straight up in the air. The grenade blew up less than a second later, but the shrapnel failed to hit him. While Slate was busy escaping, Houdini had teleported inside the fifth floor of a nearby building and fired at him. One bullet grazed Slate's arm, but he dropped down and avoided the others.

Slate landed near an incomplete brick wall. He kept his fists raised, trying to figure out his foe's position. The one-eyed man appeared next to Slate. Instead of shooting at him, Houdini made a grab for his silver helmet. Slate ducked. Houdini's hand smacked the brick wall instead. Slate threw a futile punch, and Houdini disappeared once again, taking a chunk of brick wall he had been touching with him.

"You tried to touch my helmet so you could rip my head off, just like what you did to Zubair's arm!" Slate yelled. "Very smart. I can shock anyone who touches me, except when they touch my helmet. It's too good an insulator, my Archie's heel!"

"It's Achilles' heel, fool!" Houdini spat, shooting at Slate from behind a nearby dumpster. Slate shot back. The dumpster shielded Houdini, but he teleported anyway on reflex.

"But you also got a heel," Slate told him. "That stupid billiard ball of an eye!"

Houdini appeared near Slate and fired, but the Helmet Man dodged the bullets. Slate raised his right hand, creating a bright flash. Houdini cried out as he was momentarily blinded. He was quick to vanish.

"You need to see where you're gonna appear!" Slate yelled. "That shiner must help you not to teleport into walls and stuff. But what if you can't see? My guess is you'll be screwed!"

But Houdini managed to teleport next to Slate and drop another grenade. His black eye had not been affected by the flash of light, one of its special features. Slate barely had time to dash the other way before the grenade exploded. Shrapnel struck his right calf. He cursed and fell. Houdini appeared right over him and emptied his machine gun. Slate rolled away, the bullets only hitting the ground. He fired a few lightning bolts, and Houdini teleported away.

"Guess I dropped the ball on that one," Slate grunted.

The one-eyed man reappeared inside a half-finished building, safely away from Slate. Houdini swore. He was out of bullets and had only three grenades left. He was also exhausted and filthy, his gray suit covered in dirt. But he still panted with rage, his mouth a horrible scowl. He threw his gun on the floor. This was becoming hopeless. But he couldn't retreat—not that he wanted to—since he could only teleport short distances. There was only one option left for Houdini. He scanned the barren room. His human eye spotted a wooden pole on the floor, presumably a broom handle. Yes, that could work ... but he had to be precise.

Slate didn't like this. Houdini had been gone for a while. Had he run away? Slate didn't think so. He kept his fists charged.

"Come on, you fricking cyclops ... I just need an opening, just one—"

Houdini appeared behind him. Slate froze. He tried to speak, but his body shuddered in response. His arms had trouble moving. Shock overcame him.

A wooden pole was now going right through his abdomen.

"You're right," Houdini told him. "I can't touch you. That's why I had to get creative. Good thing wood is such a poor conductor."

Houdini twisted the pole. Slate shuddered again. Blood dripped down the wood. The Helmet Man tried to pull away, but all he managed to do was make himself bleed more. Houdini found the whole thing hilarious, the ichor dribbling down and coating his hands.

"I hope your fake father really is dead!" Houdini shouted. "He'll be able to see what a failure his so-called son is when I send you to the afterlife!"

Slate then sent all his energy into Houdini. The one-eyed man convulsed, his beard smoking and black eye bulging. While it was true that wood didn't conduct electricity well, blood sure could, which was why Slate had made himself bleed.

"Houdini!" Slate bellowed. He spun around. Houdini lost his grip on the pole. Slate slammed his fist into Houdini's face, breaking his nose and knocking loose almost all his teeth. Houdini flew backward almost ten feet and landed on his side. He was still alive despite the assault. He grimaced and reached for his grenades. But then he noticed something.

One of his grenades no longer had a pin in it.

Slate held the pin in his left hand, chuckling as he bled.

Houdini gasped. "Sla—!"

The grenade exploded. A smoke cloud consumed Houdini and blew Slate backward. The Helmet Man fell on his back, the pole sticking out of him snapping in two. Debris rained on him, but Slate didn't care as he continued to bleed.

After the smoke cleared away some, a black orb stained with blood rolled out of the smoldering remains. It came to a stop at Slate's feet.

Houdini had performed his last trick.

Slate groaned. "Guess he dropped the ball that time …"

CHAPTER 38

Sandtrap made the metal shards on his arms fly at his opponents. Johnson and Eisenhorn jumped behind the truck. The shards struck the vehicle, sticking out of it like darts.

"Johnson, you got a gun?" Eisenhorn asked.

"No, but there's a piece of wood near your foot!" Johnson yelled. He noticed Eisenhorn was very lucid right now, just like when the Bunker was being attacked. Did the stress of war actually bring something back in him?

But Johnson didn't have time to ponder the question. With a wave of Sandtrap's arm, the truck began moving sideways, almost running over Johnson and Eisenhorn. They rolled out of the way in time, managing not to get turned into pancakes.

Sandtrap smashed his metal arm where Johnson's head had been. Johnson scuttled back as another blow came down. A third one followed that almost took his arm off.

Eisenhorn ran from behind and slugged Sandtrap in the back of the head with his piece of wood. Wheezing and roaring, the masked man turned and swung a metal arm. Eisenhorn blocked the blow with the wood, but it broke in half and he tumbled over. Sandtrap reeled back his metal arm to finish off the general.

Several bullets hit Sandtrap in the shoulder and chest. The masked man froze. Blood trickled down his scarred torso. He collapsed as a peacekeeper truck pulled up.

"Like them plastic bullets?" Straper asked from the back of the truck, holding a rifle. "Try deflecting those, creep!"

Goldberg, who was driving, honked the horn. "Hurry up! We got a bomb in the back."

No obvious questions were asked. Eisenhorn and Johnson hopped in the rear. Taylor and Straper were already waiting for them there, along with a black box.

"That's the bomb?" Johnson exclaimed.

"We were about to ditch it when we saw you," Straper told him.

"Let's get it out," Taylor said. "The fluids have begun to heat up."

A dozen metal shards slammed into the truck. One even smashed through a window. Sandtrap huffed and puffed as he rose from the ground.

"He's still alive!" Eisenhorn yelled.

"Shit, I'm outta plastic bullets!" Straper cried.

Goldberg cursed and hit the gas. The truck sped forward, away from the masked man. They had gotten about a hundred feet when their truck was forced to a stop.

"He's using his power!" Johnson yelled. "Floor it!"

Goldberg pressed down on the gas until his toes went purple. Sandtrap stood far behind them, bleeding but alive. He kept his arm raised as he willed the truck to come to him. The wheels spun futilely. The engine squealed.

"The bomb's fluids are bubbling!" Taylor warned.

Johnson noticed the bomb had slammed against the back doors, trying to push its way out of the truck. That was when it hit him, a way to solve two problems at once.

"Push the bomb out!" Johnson yelled.

"Are you crazy?" Goldberg cried. "Don't drop a bomb on the ground!"

"Nobody asked you, fat boy!" Eisenhorn spat.

Johnson and Taylor got behind the bomb and pushed. Straper opened the rear doors and Eisenhorn pulled the bomb his way. Just as they opened the doors, however, the bomb flew right out of the truck of its own accord. It sailed through the air toward the masked man.

Before Sandtrap realized his mistake, the bomb detonated in midair.

They managed to shut the truck's doors, and it jolted forward just as the bomb went off. A bright flash erupted. A wave of fire knocked Sandtrap back.

The windows of the truck blew in. Everyone in the car ducked their heads. While the bomb didn't do widespread damage, the center of the explosion was hot enough to melt steel. Eisenhorn grimaced. Johnson felt like he was about to burst into flames. Everyone else screamed for dear life.

After half a minute, the explosion died down. Goldberg stopped the truck. They all looked around, dazed but okay. Johnson opened the rear doors. Lots of smoke filled the air, not just from the bomb but also the burning factory. Johnson coughed a little.

"I think I see a crater!" Johnson yelled. "It's huge! It's—"

A piece of metal flew out of the smoke and impaled Johnson in the chest.

"Johnson!" Eisenhorn cried.

Only a gasp escaped Johnson's mouth as he fell out of the truck.

Screaming, General Eisenhorn grabbed a shotgun resting next to him. He jumped out the backdoor and dashed into the smoke.

"Sir, wait!" Taylor called from behind, but the general ignored him.

Sandtrap emerged from the smoke, mask-less and staggering. The bomb had blown him back, only scorching his chest and breaking his mask.

But before Sandtrap could attack, Eisenhorn pumped his shotgun and fired. Sandtrap stumbled back, the shell hitting his shoulder.

But he kept on walking.

Eisenhorn screamed even louder and fired again. Sandtrap continued his approach, despite taking another shell. The general fired a third time, getting the same results. Eisenhorn tried to shoot again, only to realize he was out of ammo.

Sandtrap stumbled to a stop just three feet away. Eisenhorn's rage vanished. He couldn't help but stare at the disfigured face. Very old scars and burns covered Sandtrap's hairless face and head, his nose and ears almost completely gone. He had no jaw, only neck skin that hung like a rooster's wattle. He also had a plastic hole that he spoke and ate from. Wet wheezes escaped the hole, along with a gurgling sound.

But his most chilling feature was his eyes. They were filled with pure malice as they stared down at the general. However, there was something else in them.

Eisenhorn didn't know if it was sadness or dementedness, but he knew that look all too well.

"Who ... Who did that to you?"

Sandtrap took a breath in. His eyes twitched.

"Scoundrels ... All of them ... scoundrels ..."

Sandtrap turned around and began to walk away.

"See ... Repulsa ... Repulsa ... see ... me ..."

He stumbled as he approached the burning factory. Entering it, he kept saying the same name over and over again.

"Repulsa ... Repulsa ..."

Sandtrap disappeared into the inferno.

He never came out.

Eisenhorn stared for a moment.

Then he remembered.

"Johnson ..."

He ran as fast as he could to the truck. Taylor was examining Johnson, while Goldberg and Straper watched from the sidelines, pale and silent. The general reached the scene and fell to his knees beside Johnson.

"Taylor, fix him now!" he yelled.

The doctor closed his eyes. "General ..."

"No!" Eisenhorn spat. "Johnson, quit faking!"

"Sir ..."

"Johnson! You can hit me as much as you like. Just don't die. I don't care if you ain't my blood. You're my son. You don't deserve this. My son doesn't deserve this!"

"I'm so sorry, General ..."

"Johnson ..." Eisenhorn whispered, tears crawling down his face.

Goldberg, Straper, and Taylor could only stand there as the old man cried.

***

"We're almost there," Lawrence told his sister.

Victoria could barely suppress her whimpering as the elevator neared the top of the Helios Tower. As they began to decelerate, Victoria let out another sob.

"Stop that!" Lawrence hissed. He shoved the pistol into her neck, making her yelp.

The elevator opened. A rush of wind hit them. They proceeded to walk out onto the highest manmade point in the world that one could stand on. A new fear now engulfed Victoria. She shivered as she saw just how high they were. All the buildings surrounding them looked like anthills by comparison. The Persian Gulf stretched out to her right, while the desert could be seen in the distance to the southeast. A unicopter drone flew nearby, circling the tower.

"Here we are," Lawrence said. "Walk to the edge of the platform."

"Brother ... please don't do this ..."

Lawrence fired his gun into the air. "I said walk!"

Victoria stifled a scream and took a few steps forward. The platform was only twenty feet in diameter, with no guardrail to speak of. An antenna came out of the center of the platform, going up another fifty feet. The antenna was meant to unfold into a massive dish that could catch the microwaves beamed down from the satellite array. The tower would be able to generate enough power to meet the energy needs of a dozen cities. But Victoria couldn't take pride in it. Not now. Not after what she had learned.

Lawrence closed his eyes and took a breath in. "I thought I might survive. But no ... I guess not. I could escape after shooting you, but then I wondered, what would be the point? Cloak would probably kill me as soon as they got what they wanted. I don't even know what they'll use the prototype for. They might try to sell it. Maybe mass-produce it ..."

He walked over and leaned against the antenna, his face lifeless. "No point ... There's no point anymore ... All that had driven me for so long was getting revenge against *her* and that neglectful father of ours. I'm so close to destroying his dream ... but now I don't feel better or even angrier. I just feel empty."

Lawrence turned to his sister and smiled. "Is this what being a killer feels like?"

A lightning bolt struck near his foot. Lawrence stumbled to the side, panicking.

"What was that?" he shouted.

The Helmet Man flew down, swerving. He landed on his feet but fell on his stomach after trying to take a step.

After the initial surprise, Lawrence began to laugh.

"Slate!" Victoria cried.

"Stay back ..." Slate growled. He had managed to cauterize his wounds with a chunk of metal he heated up with electricity, though blood still oozed from where Houdini had teleported the pole inside him. It had taken all of his energy to fly to the Helios Tower, but he had a strong feeling that Victoria was in danger and chose to go back anyway. He had flown high to avoid detection by the peacekeepers, and because of it, he was able to sense Victoria on the roof with her brother. But after firing that last bolt, Slate had difficulty summoning even a little energy.

"So, this is what being a hero gets you?" Lawrence asked, laughing. "I'm glad I'm not one! I'd rather be empty than look that pathetic."

"I'm no hero ..." Slate mumbled. He put a hand on the platform and pushed himself back up. "And you're no villain ... Just a twisted little fart with bad parents ..."

"This tower is about to blow up," Lawrence spat. "You fools have failed."

"Those 'fools' already moved the bomb ... I also killed your partner in crime ... Give up ... I'm too cool to lose ... and you're too dumb to win ..."

Lawrence's face transformed into a distorted expression of anger. "No! That's not right! This filthy thing has to fall!"

He aimed his gun at Victoria, who screamed. The unicopter drone was nearby now, its blades chopping the air.

"Your sister ... has done nothing but worry ... about her pathetic brother ..." Slate said. "Ignorance isn't a crime ... Half of the world would be in jail if it was ... She didn't know ... You can't blame her for what your parents did ..."

Lawrence smiled. "Well ... perhaps she does deserve a stay of execution." He swung his gun toward Slate. "Fine, I'll just kill—"

Victoria tackled him. Lawrence wasn't prepared for her to act so rashly. Twisting, he tried to get free from her grip, but she held onto him for dear life.

"Let go, you stupid girl!" her brother shouted.

But she held on, crying. Lawrence and Victoria struggled over the gun. They had begun to move dangerously close to the edge of the platform. Slate stumbled forward. He had to stop them before they fell off the edge.

Then the unicopter drone started shooting at Slate. Lawrence had summoned it to assist him, having foreseen a possible interruption. Slate was almost hit, but he fired a wild bolt, which struck the drone's blades. The drone stopped firing and decreased in altitude as it spurted smoke. Slate limped to where the siblings fought and grabbed Lawrence by the scruff. He pulled the boy away from his sister, but Lawrence pulled back, and Slate, critically injured, lost his balance.

They both tripped and fell off the platform.

Victoria screamed and ran forward. She grabbed the closest limb she could find. Her arms felt like they were about to pop out, but she held on tight, summoning the same strength a mother would when rescuing her child from beneath a car. Slate grabbed back with the little strength he had left. Lawrence, meanwhile, held onto Slate's ankle as he dangled five thousand feet above the Earth. The drone was below them now, struggling to stay airborne.

Lawrence laughed. He aimed the gun in his free hand at his sister. "Looks like we're all going to die up here!"

"No ..." Slate growled. "*You're* just gonna die down there ..."

The Helmet Man sent what little electricity he could manage into Lawrence's arm. The boy cried out as he convulsed and let go of Slate's ankle. Lawrence began his fall off the tallest building in the world.

But he never reached the ground. He only managed to scream as he fell right into the drone's propeller.

Victoria squeezed her eyes closed, missing the bright flash of red.

The propeller made a grinding sound. The drone swerved in midair and slammed into the Helios Tower. A giant cloud of flame, glass, and wreckage resulted. The platform tilted. Victoria began to slide off the edge of the platform.

"Let go of me!" Slate shouted.

But Victoria would not let go. She couldn't. She couldn't even open her eyes. All she could do was let out a little shriek as she slid off the platform.

Victoria fell with her savior, but she didn't yell or scream. This was a silent fall, the images of the past week flashing by. The Bunker. The Sahara. Cairo. The Pale Pyramid. The savanna. Dubai. Victoria saw it all. It all seemed to happen at once. It all seemed—

Victoria opened her eyes. Something was happening …

They were no longer falling.

Victoria twisted her head, not sure if she had died or not. Slate lied beside her, bleeding and muttering. She saw the Helios Tower disappearing behind her. Smoke rose from the hole now in its side. They were flying away from the skyscraper. But how?

"Good thing Tim gave me a crash course on how to pilot this crazy thing!" Gilda yelled through her loudspeaker. "Wish I'd known how to do it earlier, but at least you're safe now!"

"This isn't anything close to safe!" Tim scolded.

Metal wings that looked like those of a dragonfly extended from the walker, glowing a bluish hue. Victoria only then realized that one of her father's last wonders had come to save her. Zaidi Industries had created a walker unlike any other, and not just because it didn't need bolts on its feet or could jump really high.

Magenta was the first walker capable of flight.

Gilda sighed. "Let's get the hell out of here …"

The walker cradled Slate and Victoria in its arms as it soared through the sky.

What was the next step?

It was obvious that Slate was injured. Gilda decided she needed to get him to a doctor as fast as possible. Taylor came to mind. But where was he?

"Gilda, are you there?" a voice crackled on the radio.

She answered it immediately. "Straper, is that you?"

"Yeah, the general said you'd be in a walker. Are you okay?"

"I'm fine, but Slate's injured. Is Taylor with you?"

After a few minutes of following haphazard directions, Gilda flew down toward the burning factory and landed near a truck. Taylor, Straper, and Goldberg ran forward, gaping at the flying walker. Eisenhorn was not with them. He was still mourning his dead comrade.

"Is that our new walker?" Goldberg asked. "How did she get it?"

Straper shrugged. "Hey, it suits her."

Magenta rested Slate and Victoria on the ground and powered down its engines. The cockpit opened. Gilda climbed out.

"Gilda, what is this?" Taylor shouted. "Where'd you get a flying walker?"

"Slate's hurt," she told the doctor. "You need to do something."

Taylor glanced at the Helmet Man and decided to save his questions for later. He ran up to Slate and knelt beside him. It only took him a moment to make a diagnosis.

"He needs to get to a hospital," Taylor said. "Straper, call—"

"Don't even think about it," a voice interrupted.

Barir had been knocked out for five minutes after Sandtrap threw the truck. After waking up with a splitting headache, he managed to track them here. His motives, however, were not completely pure, for he was holding a gun on them.

"What is the meaning of this?" Goldberg asked. "I thought we were allies!"

"I apologize," Barir said. "Incognito wants his prize. I cannot disappoint my elder, and I do not want Africa to have died in vain. Taylor, you and the boy put Slate in the truck."

"You can't treat us like this!" Gilda yelled. "What about—"

Barir cocked his gun. "Do not make me repeat myself."

Gilda stared at him icily. If only she were still in Magenta ...

Straper and Taylor picked up Slate together and carried him to the truck.

"Slate!" Victoria cried. She got on her feet.

"Do not follow him," Barir warned.

Goldberg ran over to Victoria and grabbed her by the shoulders. "Are you okay? Did something happen to Lawrence?"

Victoria burst into tears and hugged him. "Lawrence ... he did it ... He was the mole ..."

"No," Goldberg said. "No ... That's not possible ..."

After Taylor and Straper put Slate in the truck, Barir coerced Straper and Gilda into the vehicle as well, leaving Taylor standing outside in a dazed state. Goldberg hugged Victoria as she kept crying. Neither of them noticed Barir climbing into Magenta.

Barir closed the cockpit. A holographic password screen popped up.

Smiling, he noticed the sticky note on the control panel.

***

A blonde woman in a blue uniform stepped into the holding room. The walls were painted white. A couch and a couple of metal chairs were situated in a circular formation. The woman briefly eyed the four detainees before speaking.

"Greetings," she told them. "My name is Camilla Ryder. I am a special operative of the Western Union. Although I am technically a member of the military, I have no official rank, so please simply refer to me as Ms. Ryder."

General Eisenhorn sat on the couch, covering his face with his hands. Victoria sat next to him. She leaned against Goldberg, who had wrapped his large arm around her. Taylor merely remained quiet with his hands folded. All of them looked lost and empty. None of them really cared what this Camilla Ryder had to say.

"General Randolph Eisenhorn," Ryder said. "You are not facing criminal charges at this time. However, you shall remain in protective custody."

"Fantastic …" Eisenhorn scoffed. "No trial, then … Just going to shoot me while I'm looking the other way. Always figured I'd die like that."

"On the contrary. The president has asked me to ensure your safety. The Secret Service has even taken charge of your security. You seem to have a powerful friend."

"Nice to know I still got friends, I suppose …"

"You shall be transported to the USS *Liberation*," Ryder said. Two Secret Service agents came into the room wearing suits, sunglasses, and wooden expressions.

Eisenhorn sighed. "At least I get to retire now."

"That is unlikely in the immediate future," Ryder said. "You still have many uses to the Western Union, though you shall have several months of recuperation."

"No rest for the wicked. Johnson's funeral—"

"Is being held on the USS *Liberation*. Now please …"

General Eisenhorn got out of his seat and turned to Victoria. "Don't worry. You'll get over it. Just don't stop loving your brother. It'll only make it worse."

With those parting words, General Eisenhorn and the two agents left the room.

Ryder turned to Taylor. "You have no family, correct?"

Taylor looked at her. "No, I only had my job and my cadets. Now I have nothing. Not quite sure what to do with myself …"

"The military is always in need of good medical personnel, Dr. Taylor. I am sure we can find a place for you to settle."

"What about Plato and Straper? Will the Western—?"

"We will retrieve them. That I can assure you."

Taylor only gave a weak nod. He was escorted out of the room by another set of men in suits and sunglasses.

Ryder turned to her two remaining guests. "Mr. Goldberg, please leave the room so I may talk with Ms. Zaidi alone."

"We told you people everything already," Goldberg seethed. "I won't leave her alone. She's been through enough."

"No, it's okay ..." Victoria said. "I know what this is about."

"Are you sure?" Goldberg asked.

"Yes, it's fine."

Goldberg got off the couch. He stole another look at his dead friend's daughter before leaving the room and closing the door.

Camilla Ryder sat down in a metal chair. She wore a dark blue navy uniform that didn't have a rank on it. She was also very attractive with her blue eyes, pinned-back blonde hair, and a very fit physique. But there was something off about her. Her face was expressionless, almost non-blinking. Little to no life was in her eyes. Not only that, but her voice was a constant drone. Victoria would have been more concerned about Ryder's abnormal behavior if her thoughts hadn't been in a thousand other places.

"Ms. Zaidi, do you know what we want from you?" Ryder asked.

Victoria gave a small nod. "Yes ... you want to ... prune me ..."

Pruning was a controversial procedure, but it was still used by the Western Union, which had a monopoly on the technology. The procedure literally involved erasing someone's memory, whether it was a certain name or a week's worth of events. One could even completely wipe the memory of a subject, but that was only done in extreme circumstances.

"Yes," Ryder said. "Goldberg too. Zaidi Industries is essential to the Western Union's ongoing occupation of Africa and the Middle East. We need you, Ms. Zaidi, especially after the events of yesterday, but you and Goldberg know far too much sensitive information."

"Like how you people created supersoldiers who now run the world's most dangerous criminal organization," Victoria said, wanting to get angry but not able to do so.

"Correct."

"Will I forget about Slate and Cloak and … him?"

"You will forget the events of the past two weeks and all details regarding Cloak. Our cover story is that you received a concussion during the terrorist attack on the Helios Tower. Your bodyguard, Zubair, and your brother were both casualties."

Ryder folded her hands in front of her, examining Victoria with a robotic gaze. "So, what are your thoughts on the matter, Ms. Zaidi?"

Victoria closed her eyes and breathed in.

"I want to forget."

***

One day later, Victoria found herself lying in a plastic tube. A cheerful technician in a lab coat adjusted the machine's settings. Ryder stood next to him, silent.

"All right, we've just given you a sedative," the technician said. "Do you know how pruning works? Well, first off, you'll be shown some pictures of the terrorists and the events of the past several days. This machine will sense which neural connections are activating in your hippocampus. Then we inject nanomachines into your head that will destroy these connections, effectively erasing your memory."

"I'm ready," Victoria said. "Will it hurt?"

"No, you shouldn't feel a thing."

The holographic screen above her began to flash images. She saw the Bunker, Johnson, Gilda, Taylor, Straper, Barir, the Pale Pyramid, Houdini, Sandtrap, and many others things. Then she saw her brother with a gun and almost cried.

But the most images she saw were of Slate, who flew around and shot electricity, fought off all foes, and had that constipated voice that made her angry and happy at the same time. Victoria teared up. Was she going to forget all that?

"Ms. Ryder, what's going to happen to Slate?" she asked.

"He cannot be ignored," Ryder said from outside the tube. "He has joined forces with Incognito, the most dangerous man alive. We must act."

Victoria felt a needle go into her neck. She started to black out.

"Have no fear," Ryder told her in a vacant tone. "He will soon be in our custody."

Before Victoria could say anything, she slipped away.

***

"I am sorry for the rough treatment, but I had to act fast," Barir told his prisoners. "Slate could not fall into the hands of the Western Union."

Gilda and Straper sat across from Barir, watching him like rattlesnakes. Days ago, Barir had used Magenta to pick up the truck that they and Slate had been in and flown away. Reinforcement peacekeepers and walkers had begun to pursue Barir at this point, but he managed to reach the Persian Gulf and rendezvous with a stealth submarine hired by Incognito. Thanks to good planning, they had eluded the authorities. Gilda and Straper, however, were far from happy with their captivity in this submerged vessel.

"Let us go already," Gilda snapped. "There's no point in keeping us around."

"You will not be allowed to leave just yet," Barir said. "I must give a proposal to the two of you first. If you refuse, we will gladly let you go."

"We're not going to join the United Third," Gilda said.

"Then why did you work with us before?"

"Extraordinary circumstances," Straper said. "We had to stop a fricking terrorist attack. We're not about to help you perform one."

"Listen, Incognito has contacted me. He wants you two to join him in his war against Cloak, not the Western Union."

Gilda snorted. "I thought you said girls couldn't fight?"

"I was wrong. You piloted that machine like a true warrior. Lacking a man's body, you use a metal one instead. And your young male friend is an expert marksman. We would be foolish not to solicit your talents, or his."

"Wait, I thought you only wanted Slate," Straper said.

"Slate has already accepted our offer."

"What? That can't be right! Slate doesn't want to fight the Western Union."

"Correct," Barir said. "But he does want to fight Cloak."

"Then I'll join too," Gilda said.

"Yeah, we're not—" Straper stopped midsentence and shot a glance at her. "You're serious? But you're a cadet!"

"The Western Union won't try to stop Cloak," Gilda told him. "You've seen the news. They're already covering it up. Slate's being blamed for everything. Incognito is the only one who cares. I'm not going to help him hurt innocent people, but Cloak is far from innocent. Houdini was just the beginning. There are other Gifted."

"Marker is avenged! Let's quit while we're ahead."

"Straper, I'll be pruned if I turn myself in. I won't forget. I can't."

"Oh, forgot about the pruning ... Wait, no! It's still not worth it!"

"You're just going to leave Slate?" Gilda asked. "Incognito could turn him against the Western Union if we're not there to help him."

"What's to stop Incognito from doing the same to you? Didn't you swear an oath? Didn't you want to be a walker pilot? You're throwing your life away, Gilda!"

"I'll be wasting it if I don't help Slate."

Straper stared into her eyes, hoping he could convince her or at least intimidate her. But Gilda wouldn't budge, and the more he looked at her, the more he felt his own conviction waver.

"Are you ... Are you really going to do this?" Straper asked.

"Yes," Gilda said. "I have to. Not just for Henry either."

Straper lowered his head and nodded. "Fine ... then I'm going with you."

"You don't have to do anything. This is my decision. I don't need protection."

"Hey, I can't leave you alone with a bunch of terrorists. It's not like I'm leaving much behind. Besides, Johnson died ... All my friends ... All those cadets died at the Bunker. They deserve better than to have their deaths covered up."

Gilda leaned in. "Are you sure, Straper? We might not come back from this."

"Hey, I'm sick of being a chicken. We're in this together, Gilda. For Henry."

Gilda nodded. "Yeah, for Henry ... and everyone else."

Barir clapped his hands. "Splendid. You convinced yourselves. And here I thought my job would be a challenge."

Gilda turned to Barir. "Yeah, but you and Incognito hear this. We won't hurt the innocent, and we won't fight our own people. The moment you try to make Slate or us harm civilians or turn us against the Western Union is the moment we'll kill Incognito."

Barir smiled. "I doubt you could do that, but I promise we will not make you fight the Western Union. Cloak will be your only adversary."

Gilda nodded. "Then I accept."

"Me too," Straper said.

Gilda smiled. "You know, I had already assumed you were going to join too."

"Wow, glad my sacrifice is so appreciated!"

Both of them began to laugh.

***

Barir and Gilda reached Slate's room. Barir unlocked the door and held it open for her.

"Do not make Slate strain himself," he said. "He is still recovering."

Gilda nodded and stepped inside. Barir closed the door. The room was small and spartan, with only a bed in the corner. Slate was sprawled on it, his chest bare and his stomach bandaged, the silver helmet on his head as shiny as ever.

"Hey, Slate ..." Gilda said. "You doing okay?"

"Yeah, not the first time I had a huge hole in my torso!" Slate yelled in his constipated voice. "At least I didn't go into a healing coma like last time."

"The United Third's doctors did a good job patching you up."

"Meh, the quacks did all right. How about you? Heard you had a little tummy ache."

"Yeah, threw up twice. Must be that radiation kicking in from when we were rescued by that scythe guy. No worries. I'm getting over it."

"So, what are you planning to do after puking your guts out?"

"I'll be helping you fight Cloak. Straper too."

Slate laughed. "Good. I need some sidekicks."

Gilda smiled, but it went away as she remembered something. "Slate, I heard from Barir ... about Victoria ..."

"Yeah, her brother was working with Houdini."

"Awful ... Cloak really is poison. They have to be stopped."

"Definitely, but I wonder ..."

"Wonder what?"

"Us supersoldiers ... We had it pretty rough. Getting liquid metal poured on your head ain't no picnic, you know, especially if you're just a kid. Houdini and the others, they were saved by their mysterious leader, this Mentor guy."

"They weren't saved, Slate. You know that."

"I know, but what if I had been with them? What if the Mentor came to me right after I got my helmet? I can't help but think I'd be working for Cloak. I mean, who wouldn't grab that olive branch when you're living that hell? If it weren't for my dad ..."

"But you did have a dad. You had a dad who loved you. You're talking in hypotheticals. Yeah, maybe you'd be working for Cloak under different circumstances. But you're not. You know the value of love, of companionship, of protecting others. You're our friend, Slate. And believe it or not, you're our hero too."

"Thanks, kid. Guess I'm just venting. Who knows? Maybe I can also find my dad while fighting Cloak. He must still be alive. If not, I'll find out what happened to him and the other Keymasters twenty years ago."

"I'll make sure to help." Gilda paused. "But ... is that all you want?"

"No, I got to do something else."

"What else is there?"

Slate turned to her, his helmet reflecting her face back.

"I'm gonna kill that Mentor ..."

***

"There's nothing here," Incognito spat. "No Sebastian ... No weapon ... Just disease-ridden seagulls and pollution ..."

Incognito stood on the deck of a cargo ship anchored near Alexandria. The arms deal was supposed to have taken place here yesterday, but no one had shown up. Sebastian had likely changed the exchange point at the last minute.

"Woman, what do you have to say for yourself?" Incognito asked. He wore a white, oval-shaped mask with eyeholes. It was covered in black Arabic calligraphy, twisting and interweaving. His long gray hair was braided into a ponytail. He also wore black gloves and a white suit with golden buttons.

In his right hand was a scythe.

"I honestly don't know," Repulsa said, wearing a white blouse and jeans. "Houdini said this was the meeting place, but it seems he was kept in the dark as well."

"Foolish wench. That was our only chance to capture Sebastian and uncover the Mentor's plans. But while we are on the subject of failures, may I ask again why you tried to kill Slate when I told you to bring him to me alive? You better have a good excuse. If it weren't for the transmitter the buffoons planted, I might not have been able to find your plane."

"He irritated me."

"You irritate *me*, and I'm managing to restrain myself from cutting your fingertips off."

"Then you must have excellent self-control," Repulsa said, smiling.

Incognito ignored the comment and began to pace methodically, using his scythe as a walking stick. "I have just heard from Barir that Houdini and Sandtrap perished. Tell me, does this affect your feminine emotions significantly?"

"No," she said, but the smile left her face. "How did they perish?"

"Houdini was blown to pieces, and your masked friend committed self-immolation, a most ineffective way to kill oneself."

Repulsa closed her eyes. She had expected this, but it was no less painful.

"What happens now?"

"You cannot go back to Cloak," Incognito said, staring out at the sea with cold black eyes. "They think you perished in that plane crash. It would only raise suspicion if you returned to them now. Your days as a double agent are over. But have no fear. There are still many ways in which to obey me, Repulsa."

"Please, call me Naomi."

***

The yacht was filled with dozens of businesspeople wearing arresting clothes, gold watches, and excessive jewelry and drinking Champagne. They stared at the Helios Tower, watching the grand reveal from the sea at night.

"This is it," Goldberg said. "Too bad your father and brother couldn't see this."

"Don't forget Zubair," Victoria said. "And I'm sure they can."

Goldberg grinned. "I didn't know you believed in the afterlife."

"Guess there's hope for me yet." Victoria gasped. "Look, it's starting!"

The Helios Tower's top unfolded like a metallic flower blooming. It finished unfolding in about a minute. The silver bowl glinted in the moonlight.

"Silver ..." Victoria said.

"What?" Goldberg asked.

"Oh, nothing. Just a silly daydream."

"The Helios Tower is now absorbing the microwaves being beamed from the satellite array," an announcer said. All the lights in Dubai flickered briefly. Everyone cheered. The tower was generating power for the whole city and soon would be for the entire Arabian Peninsula.

"You did an amazing thing today," Goldberg told her.

"Yes," Victoria said. "Another step forward ..."

EPILOGUE

At the bottom of Africa, off the coast of Cape Town, a cargo ship was anchored. Frost breathed in the sea air and looked at the coastal city. The surrounding mountains made Cape Town look like it was in a stone bowl. The moon illuminated their peaks as though it were daytime. A marvelous sight that Frost doubted could be compared to any Western city, but these foreigners had tainted the continent with their materialism and arrogance. This place had become a shade of its former self. Frost spat over the side of the boat and turned to his employer.

"I suppose I should thank you for helping me escape jail," Frost said. "I'd be getting electrocuted for information right now if it weren't for you."

"Whatever are you talking about?" Sebastian asked with an oily smile. "You died of shock on the way to the hospital. The records confirm it, as does your corpse."

"Clone, I assume?"

"Very expensive. How ever will you repay Cloak?"

"For starters, take a look at this," Frost said, holding up a briefcase. "The Zaidi boy gave it to me as you instructed. I was smart enough to hide it before getting caught."

"I hope you didn't mind going behind Houdini's back," Sebastian said. "After our plane crashed, I realized there may be a mole in our lower echelons. That's why I had to take such drastic measures."

"But you trust me?"

"Your background indicates that you work for the highest bidder. I had no doubt you would obey me, since I have plenty of money to spare."

Cloak's second-in-command wore his usual blue suit and round sunglasses. His right hand grasped a white cane. A yellow dog sat next to him, panting happily.

Frost noticed these eccentricities with a mild smirk. "You blind or something?"

"Yes, a necessary restraint. May I have the prototype now?"

Frost nodded and hobbled over to him on a crutch. That English girl had shattered his leg, but he could afford all the medical treatment needed to fix it once he had his payday. Then he would hunt her down and take his sweet time ending her.

Just as he reached Sebastian, the dog growled and bared its teeth. Frost almost fell over in surprise. He suppressed a growl of his own and handed over the briefcase to his boss.

"A lot of trouble for something so small," Frost said.

Sebastian opened the case, his grin growing even wider. A transparent orb rested inside. A gray blob was suspended within. Sebastian caressed the orb, savoring its smooth surface. He then closed the case and turned to Frost.

"It seems all our losses were worth it in the end," Sebastian said. "Well, almost worth it. If only we had Slate, the Mentor could ..."

"What about the money?" Frost asked. "I was promised cash."

Sebastian pointed at a nearby crate with his cane. On it sat another briefcase.

Frost laughed and hobbled over to the briefcase. He wasted no time opening it.

But he found no money inside. A Pinocchio pounced out and latched onto his face, wrapping its legs around his skull. Frost screamed and fell on his back. He tried to rip the machine off, but it refused to let go, practically glued on. Barbs came out and sank into his skin. He screamed at the top of his lungs as blood spurted from his wounds.

"Madman! You cannot kill me!"

Sebastian grinned. "There can be no loose ends. We are finished with this desolate region. Cloak now sets its sights on the Far East. Any usefulness you ever had just ran out."

"English foo—!" was all Frost said before the Pinocchio exploded.

Blood splattered all over Sebastian. He wiped the gore off his face with a smile and licked his fingers one by one. The dog let out a growl.

"Go on ..." Sebastian urged. "Devour his flesh ..."

The dog pounced on the headless corpse and began to feast. Sebastian kept licking the blood off himself, unable to stop his laughter as the moon shined down upon him.